PRAISE FOR
CONDUCT IN QUESTION

"Martin whips up a highly original plot spicing it with some psychological horror. All the characters are subtly woven into the threads of the story."—Norm Goldman, Editor, BookPleasures.com

"[an] intricately woven web of greed, power and insanity. I was caught up from page one."—Roxanne Sailors Taplett, Editor, *Simple Things*

PRAISE FOR
FINAL PARADOX: THE SECOND IN THE OSGOODE TRILOGY

"Ms Martin is a talented author with great ability to spin a tale."—Debra Gaynor, readerviews.com

"*Final Paradox* is an intriguing story that resonates in the mind after the last page is read."—Mary Ann Smyth, bookloons.com/ reviews

"Characters are introduced subtly in an original plotline spiced up with a bit of psychological horror."—Brenda Snodgrass, thecompulsivereader.com

A TRIAL OF ONE

A TRIAL OF ONE

THE THIRD
IN THE OSGOODE TRILOGY

The gathering of the ravens presages a disturbance of the natural order.

A Novel

Mary E. Martin

iUniverse, Inc.
New York Lincoln Shanghai

A TRIAL OF ONE
THE THIRD IN THE OSGOODE TRILOGY

iUniverse books may be ordered through booksellers or by contacting:

iUniverse
2021 Pine Lake Road, Suite 100
Lincoln, NE 68512
www.iuniverse.com
1-800-Authors (1-800-288-4677)

Because of the dynamic nature of the Internet, any Web addresses or links contained in this book may have changed since publication and may no longer be valid.

This is a work of fiction. All of the characters, names, incidents, organizations, and dialogue in this novel are either the products of the author's imagination or are used fictitiously.

ISBN: 978-0-595-44571-4 (pbk)
ISBN: 978-0-595-68831-9 (cloth)
ISBN: 978-0-595-88897-9 (ebk)

Printed in the United States of America

To my family, David, Stephen, Timothy and Susan and to my Muse who is always beside me.

CHAPTER 1

▼

Officially, Harry Jenkins' elderly client, Norma Dinnick, had committed no crime. While she embroidered tales of murderous revenge in a singsong voice, her doctors rubbed their jaws to hide their smirks. Such a sweetly smiling woman could not have committed the cruel and devious acts she so vividly described. Their diagnosis was psychotic dementia with a touch of Alzheimer's thrown in. Court documents, stamped with a gold seal, declared her mentally incompetent. After all, psychiatrists were not so easily fooled.

Once appointed as her legal guardian, Harry found her accommodations in the most luxurious mental hospital possible. Their deal was unspoken—a nice, permanent home with refined residents, not a jail. For him, Norma remained a fascinating conundrum, and after all, lawyers only wanted to know so much.

His next task? Locate the missing shares in Elixicorp Enterprises hidden by her deceased husband, Arthur. Their value? Thirty million dollars or so. Only *she*, Norma insisted, had any right to them, but Harry knew that some had died trying to wrest them from her. He envisioned a line of brutal successors lurking in the shadows, waiting for him to falter. Those shares had to be somewhere. As he drove off to see her today, he determined to find out as much as he could.

In declaring Norma incompetent, the court, in its wisdom, required Harry to consult with her on decisions, if possible. But fortunately, he was not bound by her instructions. Today, he might jog her memory for clues to the missing shares, although her recollections ran from the unreliable to the fantastical.

Gravel crunched beneath his tires as the road to the Mercer Mental Hospital narrowed and mounted steeply between jagged rocks. A small green sign, with white lettering, marked the entrance. Getting out of the car, Harry took off his jacket. The sun bore down, and the heat hit hard. The breeze sang softly through the grasses and caressed his face. In the field below, a group of patients gazed skyward, while an attendant pointed at black ravens circling against the brilliant sky. A nature outing, Harry supposed, but Norma would not be among them. Unless she could command a group, she would have no part of it.

Suddenly, one bird broke from the military precision of the flock and swooped down upon a patient who, clutching his head, ran in circles. As the attendant warded off the attacker, the inmate cringed beneath a tree. Harry turned away and collected his briefcase.

He had heard many versions of Norma's story of the Elixicorp shares. Some hung together—for the most part. Others were so absurdly confused that they strained the credulity of the most gullible soul. As best as Harry could determine, her husband, Arthur, had been part of a consortium to raise money in the nineteen sixties for the development of a wonder drug to forestall memory loss. Ironic that everyone seemed to have forgotten just where those shares might be! Now, all the partners—George Pappas with his underworld connections, Arthur, Archie Brinks, and David Parrish were dead. So, who *was* entitled to the money?

Walking up the path, lined with tall maples, he saw the white clapboard buildings with their green awnings and wide verandas. Norma sat near the screen door of the main entrance. She wore a pretty, floral dress, neatly cinched in at the waist, giving her a decidedly girlish appearance. Easy to spot her in the midst of all the hospital gowns. A piano rendition of *My Blue Heaven* floated out on the summer air. Only her foot tapped to the music. Harry had a vision of a single flower sprouting in a dry, stubbly field.

Bending awkwardly to kiss her cheek, he saw the glint in her eye, which said, *This is a huge joke. We both know I don't belong in this nuthouse.*

"Have you found the missing shares yet, Harry?" Norma demanded.

"Not yet. I need more information."

"I've told you everything I know. And you *still* haven't found the bank accounts?"

"I need the bank transit numbers."

She peered at him sternly. "Arthur would have dealt with only the *most* reputable financial institutions."

"Even so, that narrows the field only slightly, to dozens of banks with innumerable branches."

"You're not afraid of a little work, are you? Do I have to hire a private detective?"

Harry shifted in his seat. Norma was not above bullying in order to mislead him for her own murky purposes. But if she had any more information, why send him on a pointless and costly venture? *No doubt, it would be fun to scour Europe for the money,* he thought, as visions of medieval towns flashed before him. But he would have to account for every penny on a court audit of his expenses.

Harry jumped when a birdlike hand pinched his knee. Glancing sideways, he saw the beady eyes of a tiny, wizened woman boring into him. *Surrounded,* he thought.

"Donald, what have you done with my money?" Her bright red nails dug into his kneecap. "You always were a deceitful child," she gasped, and then spat out, "You've spent it on that hussy, haven't you?"

Norma muttered in disgust, "Stupid woman! Doesn't even know her own son. See what I mean, Harry? Lunatics everywhere!"

A nurse hurried down the veranda. "Mrs. Burke! That is not your son, Donald." Swiftly, she removed the offending hand from Harry's knee. "So sorry, sir." She smiled apologetically. "I'm sure you understand."

She held Mrs. Burke's hand firmly until she lapsed into reverie. Harry rubbed his knee.

Norma was halfway down the steps. "Take me for a walk, please. We can talk privately in the garden."

Carrying her cane, Harry rushed to catch up with her as she hobbled through the trellised gardens. In the glaring sun, the bees hummed among the blood red roses drooping in the heat. At last, he steered her toward a bench in the shade.

Norma pointed to the residents standing motionless in the field below. Old faces squinted upward in the sun, transfixed by the circling crows. "Look at those fools. They're waiting."

"For what?"

"Something to happen." She shrugged. "They're mad, you know." She plunked herself down on the bench and continued, "I do not belong in this insane asylum."

Harry raised his hand to quiet her. "You know, Norma, I can't get you out of here."

Despite her prior confessions of murder, Norma was fond of changing her tune.

"Harry, I would never harm Archie or David. I loved them dearly." Glancing downward, she spoke in darker tones. "Granted, George was another matter."

Patiently, Norma explained away all the suspicious deaths to which she had confessed. "I was caught up in a terrible nightmare!"

He shook his head solemnly. "No. You got out of a real corner last time. Besides, admitting the confessions were false lands you right back here."

Norma sat in obstinate silence. At last, she said quietly, "If you can't get me out, then you'd better find the money, Harry."

She was right, of course. As her legal guardian, he was sworn to locate all her assets and prepare an inventory. Even suspected ill-gotten gains had to be listed. Although George Pappas and Archie Brinks were dead, Harry was chilled by the prospect of an endless chain of ruthless pretenders.

As if reading his mind, Norma shifted the brim of her hat against the sun and said, "Really, Harry!" Her glance was withering. "You know everyone is dead. They never had any right to that money. It was Arthur's and mine."

"They didn't think so!"

Norma, her jaw rigid, jerked away.

A fine time for her to become difficult, he thought. "Any more information will make my job a lot easier and less expensive," he said.

Norma's lower lip trembled. After a few sniffles, she spoke angrily. "I know you, Harry Jenkins! You think Arthur bilked a bunch of rich old biddies with some crazy scheme for a wonder drug."

"I *never* said that. But George and Archie certainly had a fraudulent scheme. Who's behind them?"

"You're right!" she said primly. "Those two jailbirds were at the very center of the whole scheme. We knew nothing of it."

"So where did all this money come from?"

"There was only a tiny bit to begin with, and it was just our share," she insisted. "Arthur was a genius at investing!"

"All right, Norma. I'll try to find the accounts with what I've got. You said I should start with the banks in London. But when I find the money, we have to establish your right to ownership in court."

"I *told* you it belonged to Arthur and me."

"That's not good enough. We need a court declaration stating you're the lawful owner."

Norma was aghast. "That's useless! Those people laugh at court orders. Just scraps of paper."

"What people?" he demanded. "Just a minute ago you said they were all dead!"

Her eyes glassed over. "So I did. Well then …" She began to fidget.

"What aren't you telling me? Who's behind Pappas and Archie Brinks?"

Norma gazed at him. In the beating sun, Harry loosened his tie.

"All I know is they're a *very* dangerous, rapacious bunch, who won't give a damn about any court orders!"

Norma's expression chilled him. "Like who?" he asked more quietly.

She touched his hand. "Be *very* careful, Harry! They're always watching and working together!"

"Where *are* they?" Harry pushed back his matted hair and swallowed hard.

"Mrs. Dinnick? There you are!" The nurse who had rescued him earlier was now marching around the rose bushes. "You're due for your medication."

Immediately, the intelligence in Norma's eyes faded.

The nurse held out her hand. "Come with me, dear. It's time for your injection."

Harry knew Norma's *mad act* was coming. "Don't, Norma!" His desperation mounted swiftly. "Who are these people?"

But the transformation was swift. Her face slackened, and her body slumped against his. The nurse helped her up, and Norma limped and swayed up the path after her. There was nothing he could do. Norma had raised the curtain just an inch, only enough for him to glimpse her shadowy world, where no one else could enter.

He stared at the huge roses looming grotesquely over him. In the lengthening shadows, the patients at the foot of the garden had grown to sinister proportions. *And* the damned crows were still circling! It seemed unnatural.

Alone, Harry climbed up the pathway. Norma would be lying down in a cool, dark room to receive her injection. Smiling docility would soon erase her shrewd intelligence along with any chance for further information. He knew he was on his own.

CHAPTER 2

▼

Dr. Robert Hawke sank into his bath at the King Edward Hotel. Although briefly amused by the pulsating jets of water, he soon turned them off to concentrate on the problems at hand.

Mildly annoyed, he called out, "Ronnie!" His voice rebounded within the confines of the huge tub. Gently swirling the mountains of suds about, he waited. No answer. *Where can that woman be?*

"Mrs. Deal?" he called, in a more formal tone.

The door opened, and a dark-haired woman looked in.

"What took you so long?" the doctor asked peevishly. "I waited, and then I had to run the bath myself."

"Surely you want privacy, Robert." Veronica Deal said from around the half-open door. She was a mature and highly capable personal assistant who anticipated the needs and catered to the whims of her employer. However, running baths for the able-bodied hardly seemed appropriate. Entering the bathroom, she studied herself in the mirror.

Hawke sat up straighter in the tub. Veronica averted her eyes.

"I was waiting for your report. Have you got a lead on Norma Dinnick?"

Veronica tensed. Her employer could become enraged, like a caged panther at the smell of blood. "Not too much, yet. But Garth is—"

"You're leaving this important matter to your brother, Garth?"

"He was at her apartment building this morning. It's vacant and there's a "for sale" sign on the lawn."

As Hawke sank further into the tub, his flaccid jowls bobbed above the soapsuds. She avoided his penetrating blue eyes. She knew her attraction, which, although definitely not sexual, was completely ridiculous. The man was physically repulsive, yet even naked in his bath, power radiated from him. Some force— it was not love or desire—drew her inexorably to his very core. His scientific work was supremely important. Hope for a cure for Alzheimer's disease rested upon his clinical trials. Sometimes, she felt like a deer frozen in the headlights.

Hawke swirled the washcloth in the water above his chest and spoke mildly. "Perhaps Garth should start looking for her in nursing homes."

"He already has, Robert."

"Good! Then, while you're at it, you might call the real estate office and find out if a lawyer is handling the sale."

"Already done."

Hawke blew a handful of suds in the air. "Ah, very good, Mrs. Deal. And who might he be?"

"Harold Jenkins. He's on the listing agreement as her legal guardian."

"Aha! Excellent. Full marks!" He smiled up at her. "Hand me the soap, will you?"

Veronica grimaced. "Where is it?"

"Somewhere in the tub, near my foot."

Pulling up her sleeve, she dove her hand into the water. "Actually, Garth is very good at tracking people down."

Hawke smiled slyly. "Loyalty is a fine trait, my dear. Your brother needs all the encouragement he can get." Paddling his fingers on the surface of the water, he continued, "By the way, Ronnie, was there any trouble at the Dinnick house?"

She handed him the soap. "Certainly not! I've discussed the job thoroughly with him."

"Good, my dear." His face darkened. "You know, Ronnie, I tolerate Garth's limited abilities simply for your sake. I know what a burden he must be."

"Thank you, Robert," she said quietly.

Soaping his arms and chest, the doctor spoke irritably. "Norma Dinnick is the obstacle." Then his bow like mouth pursed and tightened into a hard, straight line. "That wretched miscreant! She stands in the way of money desperately needed for medical research." Angrily, he kicked at the soap, making the water slosh over the edge of the tub.

"I know, Robert." Veronica spoke soothingly. "Stealing the money from Mr. Pappas proves she has no conscience or moral fiber whatsoever."

In disgust, the doctor slapped the washcloth on the water. "Just think, Ronnie! If we'd had that money from the start, millions of minds would have been saved. At the very least, Alzhe-

imer's would be just another chronic, controllable condition."
He struggled to stand. Swiftly, Veronica turned away.

"Get me my robe!" he demanded.

She held the thick, white robe out to him. She glimpsed his albino skin, covered with masses of freckles and red hair. Unable to bear such exposure, she closed her eyes.

He fumed, "By God! We'll track that Dinnick woman down. That fraud will regret she ever crossed my path."

Veronica hurriedly turned her back as he tossed on the robe. Her employer's moods pitched from frenzied summits of success onto jagged rocks of despair. She was weary of trying to steer him clear of the precipice.

Tying the robe around himself, he waved dismissively at her. "I shall dress now, Mrs. Deal."

Veronica nodded. "I'll prepare your notes for the meeting with Dr. Tasker."

"When is he coming?" Hawke patted his face in the mirror.

"At two o'clock." Veronica hurried from the room.

Robert entered the dressing room overlooking the portico of the hotel's main entrance. Glancing out the window, he wrinkled his nose. *Toronto! Godforsaken provincial backwater*, he fussed. Engrossed in choosing his wardrobe, he decided upon his purple, velvet suit and cream shirt and tie. After viewing his attire from every angle in the triptych of mirrors, he went into the bedroom. Mrs. Deal was nowhere to be seen. *That Norma Dinnick*, he thought, *is a truly wicked soul!*

In the lobby of the King Edward, Dr. Brian Tasker straightened his tie and smoothed the strands of hair across his forehead. The gleaming brass doors of the elevator reflected his smiling face and the banks of flowers behind him on the hall tables. Years of hard work in administration at the Queen Mary Hospital had brought him to this meeting with Dr. Hawke. He, the chief administrator, was about to bring revolutionary research to the hospital. Rumors of a Nobel Prize for Hawke's work had been whispered. With a cure for Alzheimer's on the horizon, huge sums of money were at stake. Tasker wanted in.

The elevator took him to the penthouse suite. When he knocked, a handsome woman in her early forties answered the door.

"Dr. Tasker? I'm Veronica Deal, Dr. Hawke's assistant. Please do come in."

With her warm welcome, Tasker relaxed. Maybe some day, he could have his own personal assistant.

Mrs. Deal led him across the expanse of oak flooring and oriental rugs.

"Coffee, Dr. Tasker?" she asked, motioning him toward the chesterfield. Tasker nodded. "Dr. Hawke will be with us once he's finished a few calls." Pouring coffee from a silver carafe, she then handed him a cup, as he sat perched on the edge of the chesterfield. When she joined him, he could not prevent his eyes from lingering on her black-stockinged legs.

Mrs. Deal always set the stage for Dr. Hawke's entrance. "Alzheimer's is such a pernicious disease, isn't it Dr. Tasker?"

"Pardon?" He recovered and sat up a little straighter. "Oh, yes indeed."

"Considerable progress has been made at the Hawke Institute." She leaned closer toward him. Eyes widening with excitement, she continued confidentially, "As we speak, new ground is being broken."

"Really? There's more than the initial reports?"

Mrs. Deal glanced over her shoulder. "Perhaps I'm letting the cat out of the bag, but...." She smiled conspiratorially. "They've had some very exciting results just in the last few days."

"What sort of results?"

"I'm just in administration, Dr. Tasker, so I don't really know." She hesitated, and then continued. "Something to do with reversal of the effects of the disease. Even patients who have been afflicted for years …"

Tasker was breathless. "Regeneration?"

The door flew open. Dr. Robert Hawke entered and rushed to greet the chief of administration. He held out his hand. "How good of you to come, Dr. Tasker."

Brian rose swiftly and shook the pudgy hand. "It's a very special venture. The Queen Mary Hospital is delighted to be part of it. Are there new developments?"

Robert's eyebrows rose in surprise. "My assistant has been filling you in?"

Veronica nodded sheepishly.

In hushed tones, Hawke said, "It's all very new and confidential, Dr. Tasker. I trust I may rely upon your discretion?"

"Of course," breathed Tasker.

"We are on the threshold of great things." Hawke beamed.

"More test results?"

"Indeed! The two of us shall have lunch next week, and I will show you the latest reports." Hawke relaxed into an armchair and smoothed his pant leg. "Well then, let's get down to business."

Tasker took out his notebook.

"I have a proposal for you, sir."

"Yes?" Tasker took up his pen.

"The Hawke Institute wishes to conduct its clinical trials at your prestigious institution. For that privilege, we are prepared to fund a new wing for the hospital." Hawke put his finger to his lips and stared at the ceiling. "I was thinking such a marvelous new facility might be called the Hawke-Tasker Geriatric Center for Research."

Tasker was stunned. He had always dreamed of a permanent monument.

"What do you say?" He patted Tasker's knee affectionately and then jumped up to pace. "Naturally, we have a few small requirements. The Hawke Institute must have complete control over the operation of the trials and the assessment and presentation of the results."

Delighted, Tasker was still mulling over the proposed name. He smiled up at Dr. Hawke, poised above him. "Of course, several bodies must approve the conduct of the trials," he said quietly.

Hawke stared down on him. His lips were rigidly pursed.

Tasker averted his eyes and continued with a short laugh. "Mostly bureaucratic details, which I'm sure, can be worked out."

Robert Hawke relaxed. He clapped Tasker on the shoulder. "I have every confidence that a man of your leadership abilities will take care of them." He resumed his seat. "Do you foresee any obstacles on the board?"

Brian fidgeted with his pen. The faces of Dr. Philip Glasser and his sidekick, Dr. Michael O'Hearn, rose before him. "Not that can't be overcome," he said at last.

Hawke stared at him for a moment. "Good!" he said.

Veronica Deal raised the silver carafe. "Some coffee, Dr. Tasker?"

Tasker shook his head. He was well aware that important medical research could be stalled. If the right people were not supportive, a worthy project might never see the light of day. A political battle lay ahead.

"If you encounter any problems with the board, please let me know." Hawke stared out the window, and then said quietly, "My staff would want the opportunity to deal effectively with any objections."

"Certainly, sir. I'm sure everything is open to discussion."

"When is the next board meeting?"

"On Thursday at two."

"Good. I'd like to invite the board, all the geriatric physicians, and any other staff you think appropriate to the St. Stephen's Club for a drinks and a buffet on Thursday evening. Could you let Mrs. Deal know how many will come?"

"Certainly." Tasker nodded at Veronica. "My secretary will be in touch no later than four tomorrow, if that suits?"

Veronica smiled in agreement.

Quiet settled over the room. The meeting was over. Tasker was ushered to the door. Not until he entered the downstairs lobby, did he give serious thought to handling the opposition that would undoubtedly form on the board.

CHAPTER 3

▼

Be very careful, Harry! They're always watching and working together! Was it Norma's paranoid prattle or a warning of utmost seriousness? Whichever, it haunted Harry. With his dress shirt matted to his back, he drove out of the Mercer parking lot and down the steep gravel road.

A vision of George Pappas loomed before him. That vicious hoodlum had an organization of unknown proportions behind him. His death did not erase the sense of menace now engulfing Harry.

Arthur's hiding the shares had exposed Norma and himself to great danger. Peter Saunderson, Harry's roommate from law school, was George Pappas' lawyer. On the payroll, Peter had spent his career unsuccessfully hunting down the shares. Harry would always be haunted by the specter of Peter's dead white face as he saluted him, and then jumped from a bridge to his death. Poor Peter knew his chances—*I'm a dead man anyway. Pappas will execute me in an excruciatingly gruesome fashion. Probably castrate me first. So you see, this really is the easiest.*

The afternoon sun dropped behind the hills, and shadows raced across the sunlit farmland below. As Harry wound down the road and through the darkened woods, he suddenly felt chilled.

Back into the light, he could see across the shrinking expanse of farmland in the valley to the industrial complexes near the airport. In the hazy distance, the towers of the downtown core clogged the skyline. Sprawling along Lake Ontario, Toronto no longer had any real beginning or end, he thought.

Suddenly, he smiled. Off to London in a few days! Maybe Natasha would come with him, even on short notice. Both of them needed time away together—she from her real estate brokerage and he from his law practice. Surely, she'd appreciate such romantic spontaneity. Longing swept over him as he visualized the curve of her shoulder and imagined the touch of her hand. When Laura, his ex-wife had left him, he had felt like a patient fresh from the surgical knife. But then Natasha had appeared like a soft summer breeze, soothing yet tantalizing him, at the ragged edges of his life. Although she wanted time for love to grow, Harry could not entirely extinguish his craving for certainty.

Of course, other people were far more expeditious when it came to love and sex. His deceased partner, Richard Crawford, the unrepentant womanizer, was never troubled by the niceties of emotional entanglements with women. In an apoplectic fit of lust for his client, Marjorie Deighton, the old man had dropped dead at his feet little more than a year ago. Harry never forgot his last few words. *If you have not experienced the passion, the thrall, you have not lived!* By nature, Harry sought order, not chaos, in his life.

Several days ago, Natasha and he had gone through Norma's six-plex to list it for sale. Starting in the basement, which was crowded with shovels, garden hoses, and stacks of newspapers, they had progressed upward in the gray light to the third floor. As the heat pressed in, summer storms rumbled in the distance.

Despite his yearning, moments of intimacy seemed fragmented and distant. On the stairs, he reached out to steal a kiss. But at every turn, she seemed to float away, more fantasy than reality. In the third floor apartment, under the steep eaves, her cell phone rang, and she moved away to answer. He stared out the window as he heard her low intimate laugh. *Who the hell is it?* he wondered.

He followed her into the next room. "A buyer, already?" he asked with a laugh.

She smiled briefly and then said, "Just my friend Sheila, Harry."

"Sorry, I didn't mean to …"

She snapped her cell phone shut.

"Natasha?" He followed her from the apartment to the top of the stairs. "Please." He touched her arm. She turned around. "It's just that …" He shrugged helplessly. "Sometimes you seem so far away."

She smiled slowly and said, "I'm right here, Harry." She kissed his lips lightly. "But I do have a business to run and people to see."

"Of course you do. I know *that.…* "

She squeezed his hand and then started down the stairs. When she stopped on the landing, the slanting sun caught her features. *Sphinx-like,* he thought. On the stairs, he felt alone and stranded. And yet, he was helplessly drawn by the mysteries within her. He rushed after her.

Now, as he clutched the steering wheel, he remained puzzled at her coolness, which left him adrift in frustration. Resolving to invite her to London as soon as they spoke, he followed the ramp into the downtown.

At last, he pulled up the circular drive to Norma's place. The leaves of the maples in the front yard hung down lifelessly in the early June humidity. The "for sale" sign from the real estate company had been hammered into the lawn near the street. Natasha had been right on the job.

Norma's building, a solid, red brick six-plex in the Georgian style, stood empty. Darkened, dirty windows reflected the harsh sunlight and created a sense of impenetrable gloom within. Squinting upwards at a dormer window, Harry saw that a tree branch had cracked several panes of glass.

The lock was stiff, but at last, the door swung open. To his right was Norma's apartment. Inside, the air was cool and tomblike. On the kitchen counter was her jumble of keys for the other suites. He could check the building in less than ten minutes. He trod up the staircase to the apartment directly above hers.

When her madness had descended months ago, she began to creep upstairs to confront whatever visions or ghostly spirits beckoned her. Once he found her in the back bedroom in a white wicker chair, disoriented and shivering. Now, that chair was the only remaining stick of furniture in the building.

He opened the door and gazed into the living room, suffused with pale light. Beside the massive fireplace sat the white wicker chair. He struggled to comprehend. Who could have moved it from the back bedroom? Beneath the chair was a small sack of something. He pocketed the keys and walked behind the chair to tip it forward.

Jumping back, he swore. *Jesus! A cat?* Expecting it to spring and hiss, he poked it gently with his foot. Nothing. Carefully, he lifted the chair away. It was indeed a dark, honey-colored, very dead cat. Shifting the body on to one side, he lurched back when he saw its eyes bulging from their sockets. The head lolled at a strange angle atop the still body.

Good God! Who would strangle a cat?

Harry hurried from the room, down the stairs, and out into the sunlight. To his knowledge, only Natasha had been in the house. He *knew* she would immediately report anything untoward.

In the car, he tried to steady himself. *Who to call? The police or the Humane Society?* He dialed and got the animal control office. They would remove the cat and file a report. After several moments, he called Natasha.

Hearing his voice, she asked, "Harry? Are you all right?"

"Natasha? When were you at Norma's last?"

"Yesterday afternoon, around three. Why?"

"Did you go upstairs?"

"No, I just made sure the sign was up and got rid of some newspapers on the porch. What's wrong?"

He took a deep breath. "I just found a dead cat in the upstairs apartment."

"How awful!"

"Yes. Especially since it'd been strangled."

There was a long pause before Natasha spoke. "My God, Harry! Who would do such a thing?"

Harry shook his head. "I don't know. I'm going to look for signs of entry." Sighing deeply, he glanced up at the house. "I'll call you back later." It was scarcely the moment for a romantic invitation.

Slowly, he walked around the house. At the back, he found a window had been pried open just a crack. Back in the car, he called the police to find little enthusiasm for investigation. Thank Heavens, the Animal Control office had agreed to remove the cat. He filed a report with the insurers and left for his office.

Alone in the office, Harry's secretary, Miss Giveny, spoke authoritatively into the phone. "For the last time, Mr. Deal, I cannot give out Mrs. Dinnick's phone number!" Hanging up, she glared at the tiny blue birds floating across her computer screen. "People are getting ruder by the day!" she muttered.

Gladys, a tiny woman, felt increasingly lost in the world of modern-day law practice. According to her, the firm had slipped badly since Harry had taken over when Mr. Crawford had died. Lawyers used to take charge, but nowadays, they were too busy with investments and looking after mental incompetents to bother with the bread-and-butter clients.

Norma Dinnick was nothing but trouble. She had kept Mr. Crawford at her beck and call right up until his death. Now, Garth Deal was pestering her for information about her, which she could not give out.

Restlessness coursed through Gladys. Recalling herself as a young secretary at Crane and Crawford, her eyes grew blank. Just nineteen, she had fallen passionately in love with Mr. Crawford. No man had ever looked at her that way. She had shivered when he appraised every inch of her with his cool eyes. Convinced of his secret love for her, she was certain he would divorce Mrs. Crawford and marry her. Then she could leave mother and her sister, Merle, behind.

Gladys smiled faintly at her memories. Alone in her bed at night, she would practice her declarations of love for Mr. Crawford. But next morning, in his presence, her voice would desert her. She decided to write him a letter. When he read it, *surely* he would come to her. But Gladys was not then sufficiently experienced in life or love to imagine what he might actually do. Of course, he would embrace her passionately and shower her with kisses. That was in all the novels. But then, her imaginings swooned into suitably vague paroxysms of bliss.

The corners of her mouth tugged downward, and she tried to banish her recollections. She jumped when Harry stuck his head in her doorway.

"Miss Giveny, could you please bring in the Dinnick real estate file?"

File and steno pad clutched to her breast, Miss Giveny marched down the corridor to Harry's office. Wistfully, she imagined her old boss, the elegant Richard Crawford, behind the desk. Entering the office, she handed Harry the file and took a seat.

Good grief, he thought. *The poor woman looks even more shrunken than yesterday.* He spoke breezily. "Just a few things to tidy up, Miss Giveny. What's been going on here?"

"Mrs. Crawford called from London. She wants to see you to settle all outstanding matters on Mr. Crawford's estate."

Harry frowned. "It's a big estate. Have we got an interim report ready?"

"Yes."

"Well then, set up an appointment for her when she's back."

With deep furrows darting across her brow, Miss Giveny snapped open her steno pad. *It's now or never,* she thought.

"We have to talk."

Harry knew that grating voice presaged a litany of complaint.

"Yes, Miss Giveny?" In hopes of deflecting an assault, he strove for a light tone and regarded her as attentively as possible. Until she had her say, attempts at dictation would be futile. Intent on masking his annoyance, he disregarded a faint rustling behind him.

The afternoon sun had dipped between the westerly office towers. Through pulled drapes, its rays illuminated the room in a soft, gold haze. He did not notice the slight sway of the curtains behind him.

"Everything's in a muddle around here," she grimaced.

"Could you be a bit more specific?" Obviously, this was not a simple matter of running out of paper clips. "What's wrong?"

Harry knew any change caused her pain. For years, she had stood at the helm with his esteemed partner, whose sterling qualities she constantly praised. For her, law practice still meant endless will preparation and real estate closings. But that musty old office, where afternoon tea was served in china cups, had disappeared years ago. Law practice *did* include attending to investments and substitute decision making for incompetent clients.

"You're hardly ever here! That Norma Dinnick is taking all your time, what with investment meetings and the mental institution. Besides, you leave me to deal with the *worst* people. A Garth Deal has been calling about Mrs. Dinnick."

Harry was cautious. "Who's he?" He glanced over his shoulder. *Is that a scratching sound*, he wondered?

"I don't know, but he's an uncouth boor. He's been demanding I give him her address and phone number."

"And you didn't, I trust?" he asked carefully.

"Of course not!" Any suggestion of impropriety angered Gladys. "He said a Dr. Robert Hawke wanted to speak with her."

Harry frowned. The name meant nothing to him.

"Then Dr. Hawke, himself, called. He wants you to phone him at the King Edward Hotel." She handed him the message slip.

Harry reached for the phone.

"That woman is taking up far too much of your time," Miss Giveny declared. "What about all the other clients?" Her tone was ominous. "They'll leave you, Harry."

"Any other problems, Miss Giveny?" He spoke with considered formality. "You'll have time to catch up on everybody when I'm away."

"You're going away?" Miss Giveny was aghast.

Suddenly, his patience evaporated. "Yes, to London." He peered crossly over the tops of his reading glasses. "England."

"But why?"

"I have to track down some investments for Norma." Impatiently, he turned back to the window. For an instant, he thought the curtain swayed. "If you can't manage on your own, say so."

The corners of Miss Giveny's mouth tugged sharply downward. Rising with considerable dignity, she said, "I'll certainly *manage,* but you might have given me more warning!" She was gone, closing the door behind her.

Moments later, the telephone rang.

"Robert Hawke on line three." Miss Giveny said coolly over the intercom. Harry picked the phone up.

"Mr. Jenkins?" The voice was little more than a whisper. "This is Doctor Robert Hawke speaking. I'm in Toronto for only a short time." The soft and sibilant words hung in the air for a moment. "You don't know me, but I would like an appointment with you."

"You need some particular legal advice?" Harry ignored a faint rustle behind him.

A low chuckle rose almost to a giggle. "Yes, Mr. Jenkins, in a manner of speaking. It's about Mrs. Norma Dinnick. I understand she regards you most highly."

"You know her well?" Harry probed for the connection. Again, he was barely conscious of the swaying curtain.

"Oh, indeed," the caller said merrily. "Her husband and I were old chums."

"At medical school?"

"Mr. Jenkins, surely you know Arthur Dinnick was a professor of law?"

"Yes, of course." Harry added hastily. Indeed, Harry was well aware of the fact, having been one of his students. Hawke's knowledge gave him a glimmer of legitimacy.

"Could you come to my suite at the King Edward tomorrow for lunch? You see, Mr. Jenkins, I am bound to a wheelchair."

Harry checked his agenda. "Around noon?" he asked.

"Excellent. I shall look forward to our little meeting. Good day, sir."

The line went dead. Harry stared at the receiver. *An odd undercurrent to the conversation*, he thought. Seeking distraction, he began tidying up various tiresome details on his desk.

Reaching for the Henderson file, his hand stopped midway. What in hell was that on the file cover? He pulled it closer. Miss Giveny must have spilled some whiteout on it. He began to scrape at the grayish-white substance splattered over the cover. This was not whiteout. Jesus! It was bird excrement!

Shit! Some of the stuff had flaked onto the sleeve of his new suit. Annoyed, he brushed at the fabric and stabbed the intercom button. "Miss Giveny. Could you come in now?"

He heard a rustling sound. More flakes were on his pant leg. Jumping up, he continued to brush and sweep at his suit.

Pulling the curtain aside for more light, he flew back. Black wings swooped up to the ceiling and beat down upon him. Blindly, he covered his head in swift and frantic motions.

Miss Giveny flung open the door. Her shriek joined the cawing of a huge black crow, which was now flapping and circling about the ceiling. At last, the bird settled in silence on the desk.

"Oh, my God!" Harry struggled for air. "How on earth?" Panting, he stared at the beady-eyed bird, which had now hopped to the back of his chair.

Miss Giveny edged backward to the door.

Harry shifted away from his chair. "Call maintenance. They can get it out."

Wordlessly, they gaped at the creature as its wings began spreading to grotesque dimensions.

"How did it get in? It's been behind the drapes all the time." Harry choked.

"You must have left the window open," Miss Giveny gasped as she broke away and fled to her office. Harry followed and slammed the door behind him. At the deserted reception desk, he called maintenance. Two wildlife removals in one day!

CHAPTER 4

▼

Harry cursed as images of black, beating wings pursued him down to the lobby of his office building. Spinning through the revolving doors, he strode onto the broad plaza surrounded by bank towers. He checked his watch. Just enough time to visit Dad at the nursing home.

At six o'clock, long black shadows divided Bay Street, flanked by office towers, posted like silent sentries along his path. Harry chose the sunlit side on his three-block walk to the parking garage. Only a few beautiful old buildings with polished brass and inlaid tiles remained, nestled among the cold, vast structures of concrete and glass.

Suddenly, he stopped in front of one of the few shops fronting the street. Jefferies and Son Ltd. was the oldest and finest haberdashery in the city. The mellow glow of the shop windows seduced Harry inward. Bolts of wool fabric, in the subtlest shades of gray and blue, were displayed on a mahogany table. Yards of suits, important looking even on their hangers, lined the far wall.

Dad's suits were made of scratchy wool, worn thin at the cuffs and shiny at the knees. Harry imagined his thin-lipped disapproval at the sight of the finery before him. For Dad, unnecessary expenditure of money was immoral. For Harry, his refusal was a bitter denial of life and small pleasure.

"Good afternoon, sir. May I be of assistance? Perhaps you are looking for something to complement your suit?"

Harry felt favorably appraised. "I was really just browsing …" He hesitated. "Actually, I could do with another suit."

"Certainly, sir. Our tailor is expert at custom-made."

Within moments, Harry stood before a three-panel mirror. The salesman hung up his jacket, and the tailor set about measuring. Bolts of material were held out for his inspection. His hand lingered over the dark blue fabric with the finest gray stripe.

The salesman's mustache twitched with pleasure as he unfurled a yard and let it drape against Harry. Instantly knowing it was right, Harry ordered the suit.

As if in a dream, he examined exquisitely matched shirts and ties. Creams, blues, and soft yellows and burgundy. Dad would have never understood his sensuous pleasure, as his fingers caressed one incredibly soft sleeve after another. Visions of Natasha expressing delight floated before him. Smiling, he ordered the whole display. His father's determined thrift seemed a sad and bitter denial of life. Harry glanced at his watch as the man rang up the order. Now, he really would have to hurry.

Last fall, Harry had placed his father at the Foxcroft Nursing Home, set in a densely wooded area in the middle of the city.

Prepared for protest, he had wheeled Stanley up the ramp. Clutching his tartan blanket tightly, the old man stared vacantly out over the pond caught in the golden sunlight. Stanley's pale, pink head lolled dangerously to one side. Harry caught his shoulder and looked into his eyes. Of course, there was intelligence and recognition. Dad looked back at him with interest. Or did he? Harry turned to see gray squirrels bouncing about on the back lawn. Stanley's eyes followed their chase, first up a tree, then along a branch. His shoulders sinking, Harry almost wished for an argument to have *some* communication.

Thank God, by some miracle, they had started talking last year while it was still possible. But for years, Harry's life with Dad was mired in silent misunderstanding. When his sister Anna, nearly catatonic with polio, had taken her last breath inside that iron lung, Dad died too. Harry was only eight then. Dad slipped ever downward and was closed off to him until last year. Suddenly released from a coma after a fall, his father began to talk. The first thing he asked for was forgiveness for all the lost years between them. They had made a start. *But you could never really forgive until the wounds were healed.*

Today, he spotted his father outside in the courtyard. How extraordinary to hear his voice so loud and clear.

"May I please have a glass of water?"

Two nurses on break chatted at a nearby table.

"Please! I would like a glass of water?" Insistent but still polite. Such clarity for a man who rarely spoke! The women continued to talk as if he existed in an unreachable dimension.

His father's voice became piteous. "I'm very thirsty. I need water."

"Jesus!" Harry strode down the steps. Turning on the nurses, he said, "Can't you hear Mr. Jenkins? He's asking plainly as can be for water." How right his father was in his complaints of nursing homes!

The nurses gaped at him, open-mouthed. "But we gave him one ten minutes ago. See! The glass is still there."

Harry saw a small but empty glass set on a table beside his father. He was incredulous. "Hasn't it occurred to you he might like some more? It's the simplest of requests."

Anger rose in him. *Christ! Is everyone deaf, dumb, and blind?* Then a wave of sadness swept over him. *No one gives a damn.* At last, one of the women slouched off resentfully for more water. Harry almost laughed at the enormity of the logic. Such a request was evidence, not of thirst, but mental derangement. Undoubtedly, in their minds, compliance would only encourage endless demands. The nurse returned with a large pitcher of water. The ice cubes clanked, and the water sloshed as she set it on the table.

Harry's tone was formal. "Thank you, madam," he said, pouring a glass and holding it to his father's lips.

Staring at the nurse, Stanley drank noisily, and then looked up at his son with something resembling warm affection. Taking his hand, Harry cleared his throat to speak.

With neither warning nor reason, Stanley's eyes narrowed with burning fury as though accusing Harry of unspeakable crimes.

"What is it, Dad?" Harry asked gently.

Stanley growled, "You goddamned fucker!" He lurched back in his chair. "Your kind always thinks you'll get away with it!"

Spittle sprayed on Harry's sleeve. "Always cheating and shitting people. Shitting and cheating everyone." He grasped his cane and raised it.

Harry took his father's arm as gently as he could. "Dad, please!" he whispered hoarsely. "It's me, Harry, your son. What's wrong?" Carefully, he pried the gnarled fingers from the stick.

His father had suddenly grown insanely paranoid before. Harry wondered why some lessons in his life had to be repeated time and again. But at last, he was learning that the need for love never ended.

For several moments, he tried calm reason and soothing tones, until at last, Stanley slumped back in his chair and began to weep. Tears flowed unabated down his cheeks as if he were a small boy again. When his sniffles subsided, he looked at Harry with rheumy eyes.

"It's you, son," he whispered. "Thank you for coming."

Harry sighed in relief. Just like Norma, his father tripped into shadows of madness and back again to the light.

Harry pulled up a chair and held his father's hand. "It's nice in the garden at sunset, isn't it, Dad?"

"You could die of thirst here, though," said Stanley with a wry grin. "These damned jail guards!" He glared back at the nurses who, ignoring him, had returned to their conversation.

Harry took a moment to examine his father's arms and hands. The skin was so thin, it was almost translucent. He made a mental note of the few bruises, which were often caused by the carelessness of the staff. Such compassionate keepers naturally disavowed any knowledge of them.

With Alzheimer's, no one *really* knew the cause of the short-circuiting. Harry took the glass and touched his father's wrist. "Dad? I'm going to be away for a little while." Since communication could fizzle out without warning, he came to the point quickly. "I'm going to London."

"England?" his father whispered.

"Yes, on business. For a week or so."

"Laura, too?" his father mouthed.

Sadness clouded Harry's eyes. Dad had forgotten about the divorce *and* Natasha. He shook his head. "It's for a client. A lot of money is involved."

Stanley nodded approvingly, or so Harry thought. Then his head began to sink toward his chest. His eyelids drooped.

Harry stood up. "When I'm back, we'll go out for real drinks."

When Harry tried gently to rouse him, Stanley smiled vacantly. Like a submerged sea creature, the madness of the disease could resurface at any moment. He kissed his father's brow and hurried up the steps from the courtyard.

Outside, on the gravel drive, he glanced at his watch. It was only a quarter to eight, and he was not yet ready to face his empty house. He drove past a duck pond surrounded by mansions on a hill to the entrance of the park. The stone gates led him to the cobbled street lined with tiny cottages, once inhabited by the servants for the nearby mansions. To his left were the garages of the city transit company. Five sets of metal doors, at least three storeys high, faced a field of stubble. A distant smoke stack poked upward from the buildings, silhouetted against the burnt orange sun. Two red and yellow streetcars were marooned on a track. A steel gray Jeep with outsize tires idled nearby.

At the lights, Harry turned west onto St. Clair Avenue into the now blood red sun. Squinting, he saw several passengers from a streetcar step onto the deserted street.

Huge headlights stared into his rear window. Annoyed, Harry tapped on the brake. The vehicle dropped back and flashed its high beams. Harry moved into the curb lane, and the vehicle swerved in behind him, touching his bumper.

"For Christ sake!" He shot back into the passing lane.

Roaring, the truck raced along his passenger side.

It was the Jeep at the rail yards! Massive tires grazed the side of his car. Harry grew cold. Black tinted windows hid the driver. The Jeep had lain in wait for him.

Fear seized his gut as he barreled through the intersection, swerving left on a yellow light. Effortlessly, the Jeep chased after him, clanking his rear bumper on the turn. Rattling down the steep cobblestone hill, Harry raced on.

The Jeep crowded him all the way, right into the dark of a railway underpass. Lights glared in his mirror. The driver gave three long blasts on his horn.

Who was it? He could see only the black windshield, not into the cab. Where to turn for help? If he stopped, the Jeep would stop. Shooting past rows of deserted gas stations, he searched for his cell phone. Never a cop when you needed one.

The menacing black form loomed in his mirror, then shot out from behind to graze his side and then kiss his front bumper. Harry slammed on the brakes, pitching hard against the steering wheel.

Suddenly, the Jeep blasted its horn twice and careened onto a side street. Harry glimpsed a dark, hulking figure at the wheel. Gone.

Although he was shaking, he pulled over and parked carefully. Taking deep, noisy draughts of air, he finally calmed himself. His shirt was soaked. He did not even know the license plate, but he could give a pretty good description of the vehicle.

Without further thought, he called Natasha. The line was busy, but at least she was home. In ten minutes, he could be at her condo overlooking the lake.

"May I come up?" he asked Natasha on the phone at the concierge's desk. She sounded hesitant and distracted.

"Yes, but I have a friend over, Harry."

Harry's face burned. Stupid to assume he could just walk in on her. "Oh, sorry, Natasha. I didn't mean to.… I just thought, since I was passing by.…" Jesus, he was sounding like a school kid. He drummed his fingers on the marble counter top and averted his eyes from the increasing scrutiny of the concierge.

"Come up. It's just an old friend of mine, Sheila."

Sheila? A girlfriend? Harry grinned in relief. Natasha's voice was warm in his ear. "Please. Come up and have a glass of wine with us."

"Oh, no, I shouldn't interrupt."

"Harry, I insist."

He sighed in relief. "Maybe just for a moment." Anything to blot out the goddamned Jeep. Anything to forget his empty house. A chance to see Natasha, if only for a moment. "All right. And thanks."

In the elevator, he thought of his first visit to her apartment, also on short notice, and their first lovemaking.

When he knocked, he heard muffled voices behind the door and then she answered, drawing him inward with her smile. Her dark hair, shining in the light, fell free to her shoulders. Always enveloped by her intimacy, he reached out to kiss her, but she stepped back and squeezed his hand. Her smile tightened with some remote and unrecognizable tension.

"Come in, Harry. I want you to meet my friend."

He had known Natasha for over a year and had never met any of her friends. He welcomed the chance to learn more of the woman he loved.

Seated demurely on the chesterfield, Sheila rose to greet him. She looked younger in her summery dress and, despite her mass of red hair, more waif-like and unassuming than he had expected. By contrast, Natasha radiated vibrancy and life, as if she carried the energy for both of them. An interesting combination. Had he expected them to mirror each other? He was surprised that he had any preconceptions at all.

Pleasantries were exchanged. Natasha poured the wine and gave Harry a glass. She returned to her seat by Sheila on the chesterfield. Harry glanced about and then sat in an armchair.

"Sheila and I go back to high school days," Natasha began. "You remember last summer when I was away, Harry? Sheila was my traveling companion."

Harry nodded agreeably and sipped his wine, but could think of no reply.

"Sheila does the appraisal work at our office."

"Really?" said Harry. "What training do you need to become an appraiser, Sheila?"

"Oh, there are courses you take for what seems like years." Sheila began. "That way, you can get accredited while still holding down a job."

"Have you worked together long?"

"Oh, ages!" Sheila laughed and then glanced at Natasha. "Or at least it seems that way, doesn't it, Natty?"

Natty? A pet name? Ridiculous! Suddenly, Harry wished the tiresome woman gone. Why was he compelled to cross-examine her?

After the Jeep, he had only wanted Natasha's comfort and concern. "Here's a funny story for you," he began. "You know those monster Jeeps? People drive them like they own the road." The two women nodded in unison. "Tonight, I was going west along St. Clair, and one pulled up behind me. I tapped my brakes to get him off my tail."

Concern crossed Natasha's face.

Caught up in his story, Harry smacked his hands together. "He pulled up beside me and scraped the side of my car."

"On purpose?" Sheila asked, wide-eyed.

Harry ignored her.

Natasha set down her glass. "Harry, are you hurt?"

He was pleased at her concern.

"Didn't you get his license plate?" Sheila chimed in. "Or call the police?"

Harry shook his head in annoyance. Was she questioning his competence? What was the point in calling the police when the Jeep was long gone? His first thought had been Natasha.

Natasha frowned. "What about your car, Harry?"

"It's okay. No dents, just a few nasty paint scrapes." He searched her eyes for … what? Love, communication, intimacy?

"What about the insurance company?" Sheila persisted.

Harry stared at her.

Natasha nodded to Sheila. "Pour Harry some wine, will you, darling?"

Sheila rose to get the bottle.

His head was spinning just slightly. "No, please. I really must go," he said.

Sheila retreated to sit beside Natasha.

"Are you all right to drive, Harry?" Natasha asked.

No 'darling' for me, he thought distractedly. Frustrated, he rose. "Of course, I'm fine. But I must be off."

Natasha followed him to the hallway. He turned to take her in his arms, but she held his hand. He wanted to kiss her good night. She stood to one side and Harry could see Sheila's shadow on the wall, just over her shoulder. He touched her cheek. She gave him a brief kiss and said, "Call me, Harry. Soon."

Any chance for intimacy was gone. She held open the door for him and, as he turned to say good-bye, the two women waved together and closed the door. He hurried to catch the elevator. Grumbling, he reminded himself they had agreed to give each other time and space to let it happen, to let their love grow, but it was damned frustrating. Of course, she was entitled to have her friends, but….

When Harry had left, Natasha began washing the wine glasses. Sheila sat at the kitchen counter.

"So *that's* Harry Jenkins, is it?"

"Yes." Natasha busied herself with the coffee pot.

"Well, I don't mind so much, darling, if that's the competition." Sheila gave a short laugh.

For Natasha, the situation was becoming intolerable. A part of her came silently screaming to the surface. *Caught between the two people I love!* Sheila was demanding she choose between them. Of course, she didn't deserve to be kept in limbo, but Natasha did not know herself what she wanted. Sheila hid her hurt behind joking, sarcastic comments, but her sniping was stretching the limits of Natasha's sympathy.

Natasha was suddenly suffused with recollection. *Why her, my mother, at this moment,* she wondered?

She remembered herself at thirteen. From behind the door to the cellar, she had heard her mother and Aunt Mila talking in the kitchen. Mother had a job at the factory on the line, but for two years, she had taken bookkeeping courses at night.

Once I get into the front office, her mother used to say eagerly, *life will be better.*

But that day her mother spoke angrily at first. "What do you expect me to do, Mila? My boss, Mr. Blackstone, has got a gun to my head."

"And he wants you to sleep with him?"

"Yes!" Natasha could hear the tears in her mother's voice. "He said if I didn't, he wouldn't let me off the line and up to bookkeeping."

"What are you going to do?"

The chairs in the kitchen screeched backward on the linoleum floor. There was such a long pause, Natasha thought they had left, but then Mother had said, "What do you think? I'm not going to be trapped for the rest of my life."

"But, honey! You can't let...."

"Nothing needs to be done. I've got the job already."

"You didn't!"

"Of course, I did."

"Oh, Renee! You poor kid!"

After a long silence, her mother said softly, "Once we'd done it, his eyes looked so sad and ashamed, like being him just wore him down."

Mila was aghast. "You felt *sorry* for him?"

"No, not really. But I can see how loneliness can make you crazy." Afterwards, we talked a bit, sitting on the bed in the motel. He was living all alone there because his wife had run off with the kids."

Natasha sighed as she served the coffee. *When you see people that way*, she thought, *what can you do? One person needs this, another that. Is there no middle ground for me?*

Returning to the chesterfield, Sheila said, "You're going to have to make up your mind, Natasha."

"Please! Let's not get into that tonight," Natasha said wearily as she sank back into the cushions.

Sheila spoke confidently. "In the real world, you *do* have to make choices, honey."

Natasha closed her eyes and thought, *Why can't she understand that I love both of them?*

CHAPTER 5

▼

At noon the next day, Harry entered the King Edward Hotel. Yesterday's conversation with Robert Hawke had grown in his mind from merely odd to downright sinister. At least four lives had been lost in the battle for the Elixicorp shares—Norma's millions. The prospect of meeting the successor to the brutally rapacious George Pappas set him on edge. Hawke didn't sound vicious, just creepy. Despite his concerns, Harry's curiosity mounted.

At the desk, he asked for Dr. Hawke. Within moments, he spotted a woman striding briskly toward him.

"Mr. Jenkins?" Smiling warmly, she held out her hand. "I'm Veronica Deal. It's a pleasure to meet you."

Hawke's emissary, thought Harry. *But isn't that the same name as the man who upset Miss Giveny? Maybe a husband and wife team?*

When Mrs. Deal shook his hand, he relaxed slightly in her warm and open expression.

Glancing about, he asked, "Will Dr. Hawke join us?"

"I'll bring him down shortly." She looked up at the bank of elevators. "He'll be only slightly detained. He'll meet with you in the Victoria Café."

The main restaurant? *Strange choice*, Harry thought, *for a highly confidential meeting.*

The maitre d' whisked them inward to the dining room. Harry was seated at a banquette in the far corner under high windows, covered with lace curtains. Mrs. Deal disappeared. Five waiters, in their immaculate vests, stood in a semicircle about the servery.

"Something from the bar, sir?" Harry hesitated. The steward continued, "Your host is momentarily delayed." Dubious about what lay ahead, Harry ordered mineral water.

His eyes were drawn upward. The thirty-foot high ceilings of elaborately sculpted alabaster dwarfed him. But tables, spread with white linen, and urns of sunflowers dotted the room, suggesting warm and pleasant afternoons in the garden of a country inn. Harry glanced at his watch. Already twelve-thirty, and he was the only customer in the vast dining room. Very odd for a busy midweek lunch hour. Now, the emptiness of the cavernous room chilled him.

Mrs. Deal appeared at the entranceway pushing a pale, pudgy man in a wheelchair. Harry put down his napkin and stood up.

The sunlight caught the soft folds of Dr. Hawke's upturned face. Although his smile was sweet and shy, intense curiosity enlivened his bright blue eyes. In a soft and sibilant voice, he said, "How very good of you to join me, Mr. Jenkins. It is, indeed, time we met."

Murmuring the usual pleasantries, Harry assisted the maitre d' in making room for the wheelchair at the table. Mrs. Deal disappeared again.

"Will you join me in a glass of wine, Mr. Jenkins?" Hawke asked, delicately dabbing his lips with his napkin. The steward appeared at Harry's side.

"Certainly." Harry handed him the wine list. Over Hawke's shoulder, he could see the maitre d' turning customers away.

"This is a very popular restaurant, Dr. Hawke. Odd. They seem to be turning business away."

"Please call me Robert, Harry." Hawke smiled merrily, then his face darkened. "The restaurant does not have its customary luncheon crowd because I reserved all the tables."

Surprised, Harry carefully set down his glass. "Really, Dr. Hawke? Why would you do that?"

A waiter delivered the breadbasket. Hawke's pudgy hand shot out and hovered over it. Daintily, he took a roll and replied, "I want to have the utmost privacy for our discussions, sir."

Harry waited until the steward poured the wine. "You have my fullest attention. What sort of legal matter requires such precautions?"

Hawke leaned across the table. "Are your parents alive, Harry?"

Harry blinked in surprise. "My father is. My mother died some years ago."

"Is your father well?"

"Yes and no."

A smile crept over Dr. Hawke's face. When he tapped his forefinger to his lips, Harry noticed for the first time that each finger of his left hand was decorated with a ring.

"Are you referring to his mental health, Harry?" he asked quietly.

"Physically, he is fairly sound, but some days, he's not particularly alert." Harry watched as the doctor nibbled on a piece of roll. "Why do you ask?"

"His connections to this world seem frayed?"

Harry was intrigued with the image. "Something like that, I guess," he said, sipping his wine.

"How long has your father suffered this difficulty?"

"Almost two years." Harry answered as he began to study the menu.

Hawke looked at him expectantly.

"And yes. As your analogy suggests, on and off," Harry continued.

"I like to think it is similar to my disease."

"Which is?"

"Multiple sclerosis. Some days are better than others." His smile was charming. "Today, I'm in the chair, but on others, I can walk fairly well."

Harry's mind drifted off. His father seemed to disappear into a dark well, only to resurface at the most surprising moments. Usually, he was quiescent. But some times, a violent personality would leap out from his father's gentle being with the random force of a spinning wheel detached from its center. Then, he would curse and strike the nurses as they tried to wash or shave him. If such a creature inhabited his father, Harry knew it was in every person. But how helpless he felt in the face of such madness!

If nothing else, Harry knew he must bear witness. *This is my father. I cherish his mind, his memory, his being.* It was a small enough act for a son but, given their years of silence, how much did he actually know of him? Surely by now, he must have *really* forgiven Dad.

"Thinking of your father?" Hawke asked quietly as he poured more wine. Harry nodded absently. "Likely, at times you do not recognize him? Does he suffer from psychotic episodes?"

Harry nodded again and lifted his wine glass.

"When the circuitry is severely damaged, nightmarish devils escape." Hawke stared at him over the top of his glass. "Unfortunately, the beast is within all of us. Civilized behavior is a most tenuous membrane." His eyes sparkled with challenge. "What do you think about the kind and gentle soul, then?"

Harry spoke thoughtfully. "I think it must still exist, somewhere, if it can return."

"Precisely, Mr. Jenkins!" said Hawke, with the energy of a religious zealot. "It is my fervent hope that we can repair the damage that permits these demons to escape." He slapped the table with the palm of his hand. "They have no place in our civilized world."

Harry wondered about the direction of the conversation. Interesting enough, but perhaps facile. He said, "Dr. Hawke, you didn't arrange this luncheon to discuss my father. Is there some legal matter I can help you with?"

Although Hawke appeared disappointed, he quickly brightened. "Sometimes, I become too enthused." He shrugged amiably. "But it is my passion. Shall we order lunch?"

Harry nodded. They ordered, and waiters came and went.

"I understand you represent Norma Dinnick," Hawke said.

"I'm her court appointed legal guardian," Harry answered carefully.

Robert nodded enthusiastically. "Good. Then I am speaking to the proper person."

Harry waited and said nothing.

"There is some money missing, sir." Hawke's eyebrows rose unpleasantly. "A great deal of money."

Harry remained still and silent.

Motioning for the waiter, Hawke ordered, "Draw the screen around this table at once."

Swiftly, two men shifted a silk brocade screen around the dining table. After several moments of the doctor's hectoring, a suitable degree of privacy was achieved.

"That money was intended to fund research on Alzheimer's. It is desperately needed."

"What does Mrs. Dinnick have to do with it?" Of course, Harry knew it was the same money Norma was after.

Hawke clenched his fist. "Mrs. Dinnick knows where that money is! If the Hawke Institute is to establish its clinical trials at the Queen Mary Hospital, then we must have it." In a more conciliatory tone, he concluded, "Millions of people need this drug, Harry."

Harry reviewed his obligations. As her legal guardian, standing in her shoes, his job was to act solely on her behalf. Obviously, the ownership of the money remained in dispute, but it could be a stalemate. No party could have a legitimate claim to proceeds of fraud.

"Dr. Hawke," he began slowly, "If, in fact, Norma Dinnick knows the location of these funds—and I am not saying she does—she claims them for herself. Any other position would be strenuously resisted."

Hawke's lips began to tremble in rage. "Sir, the funds were raised by a conglomerate charged with the responsibility of using them for medical research. Mrs. Dinnick selfishly stands in the way of desperately needed scientific work. Surely, she can be reasoned with?"

"Dr. Hawke, any dispute as to ownership *must* be determined in court."

The doctor's eyes narrowed in appraisal. At last, he smiled. "Spoken like a true advocate, Mr. Jenkins." He patted Harry's hand. "I must take the proper measure of you as an opponent and a man."

Harry shrugged and picked up his salad fork. He sought to learn as much as he could. "What can you tell me about these trials?" he asked mildly.

The corners of Hawke's mouth began to twitch. The waiters with the lunch appeared from behind the screen. Hawke motioned for silence until they were gone. Harry cut into his club salad. Hawke tore another roll, then stirred his soup reflectively.

"It's truly wonderful," Hawke breathed. "For the first time, we hope to reverse the effects of Alzheimer's. The mildly addled will become reliably lucid. The violent will become calm and stable."

Harry was intrigued with the claim. From his father's state, he knew, all too well, the ravages of the disease. Yet, to his knowledge, understanding of the cause and the process of the disease remained in its infancy. To forestall and mitigate its effects was the goal, not to reverse damage already done.

"How can you repair what has apparently already been destroyed, Dr. Hawke?"

A slow and patient smile crept over the doctor's face. He covered Harry's hand with his. "I do admire your energy and reserve. Rather like dealing with a panther in captivity." Hawke removed his hand and returned to his meal.

Harry took a moment to consider the repetition of the gesture and comment. A direct question was always deflected. And what about the personal commentary?

Harry set down his knife and fork. "You still haven't answered *my* question, Dr. Hawke. Are you really claiming your research supports the hope for a cure?"

"Black tangles in the brain," muttered Hawke.

"Pardon?"

"The cruel ravages look like black tangles of neurons in the brain."

"And?"

"They must be undone, and new pathways constructed."

"Your drug can do this?"

"I'm *so* pleased, Harry, at your interest in our project. Because it's difficult to imagine such a miracle from reams of data, could you come to our little party for the medical profession?" Hawke looked beseechingly at Harry. "It's at the St. George's Club this evening, say, about seven. You'll meet one of the participants in the trials, and you can ask him any questions you like." Hawke leaned over and squeezed Harry's hand again. "The results to date are most promising."

Once released, Harry quickly withdrew his hand and busied himself with his salad. "Haven't you obtained funding from any of the usual sources?" he asked.

The doctor smiled sadly and shook his head. "Oh, yes, we do have the usual funding. But it is never enough. You know how niggardly governments can be with research money in both our countries."

His tone suddenly became fierce. "George Pappas raised the money to save minds! Mrs. Dinnick is preventing very important research from going forward."

Hawke's knee was touching his. Harry was unnerved by the advances. He must be mistaken, but no, the pressure was becoming intense. Quickly, he shifted on the banquette.

"You will talk to her, Mr. Jenkins?" His eyebrows arched again. "If she understands what hangs in the balance, perhaps she will change her mind."

"Some days, I can discuss matters with her. And some, I can't."

"On the good days, Mr. Jenkins, I am sure you can be most persuasive. You have a magnetic spirit, sir. I have no doubt that your energy can be absolutely overwhelming."

Harry's discomfort grew rapidly. "Dr. Hawke, I'll speak with Mrs. Dinnick, but I won't promise anything."

The doctor waved his hand impatiently. "I only ask that you present our case and advise me personally whether you have been successful." Hawke brushed a crumb from his lips. "I look forward with great eagerness to seeing you again. Not just for our little business at hand. I am attracted by your vitality, Mr. Jenkins."

In the coolness of the room, Harry felt his color rise.

"Listen, Dr. Hawke, I'm not certain what your intent is here."

In silent mirth, the doctor rolled from one side of his chair to the other. After considerable effort at control, he said, "Not only have you a keen intellect, you are also most perceptive." He patted Harry's hand. "I will embarrass you no further, my friend."

Harry breathed in silent relief. Unable to think of any words, he simply nodded curtly.

The waiter appeared, and they ordered coffee. Harry gazed out the window.

"You do not suffer from color-blindness, Harry?"

Harry frowned. Hawke's conversational sallies were becoming tiresome. "No, Dr. Hawke, I do not," he answered stiffly.

Hawke spoke softly and lyrically. "Then, you enjoy the full spectrum of color?" Harry nodded impatiently. "Can you imagine red without green, or yellow without a lovely blue to enhance it?"

"Dr. Hawke...." Harry shifted uncomfortably on the banquette.

"Imagine, my friend, becoming at least partially color-blind. You can see the cardinal's red feathers, but the leaves of the trees have become an abysmal gray. The ocean is blue, but the sun is a dull disc. Cruel reminders of the riot of color once enjoyed." Hawke paused thoughtfully.

Harry was almost seduced by the imagery, but he said impatiently, "Where is this leading, Dr. Hawke?" He made a show of checking his watch. Not another picture of the cruel effects of Alzheimer's, he hoped.

Tracing the heavy design of one of his rings, Hawke continued. "I like to think, sir, that being struck color-blind, or being deprived of any other sense or ability, is not so different from becoming mad. When insanity descends—as with color-blindness—one day, the world looks quite normal. The next, it has lost its usual vibrancy, because all the contrasts and beauty are gone. *And* unless you are entirely mad, you will be tortured by the faint remembrance that both greens and reds exist—blues and yellows, too. With the dimming of *this* world, the eye turns inward to be confronted by those nightmarish devils of which we have spoken. Imagine, Harry, the horror of traveling back and forth between lucidity and madness. *Always* the divided soul!

Hawke peered intently at Harry, but then lowered his eyes and played with a sugar cube. "It is so *very* sad, Harry, to be deprived of any dimensions in this riot of life, when you lust for the full array of vibrant color." Again, the doctor's knee pressed his. "For some, the hunger is always there, longing to be satisfied."

Harry had no idea what to say. Deep within, he struggled with a growing distaste for the pudgy man, whose intense blue eyes subjected him to keen scrutiny. But he knew better than to antagonize him. The man exhibited such a strange intellect and heightened sensibility, completely unlike the thug Pappas, who killed on a whim.

At last he spoke, "Dr. Hawke, I certainly sympathize with such a plight, but I fail to see how this relates to the matter of my client."

Hawke's eyes twinkled. "Surely it's obvious, Harry. Norma Dinnick must realize she could well benefit from such a drug. In her lucid moments, she will enjoy the full array of color, but as her madness descends, like gathering clouds, she will experience the blotting out first of reds, then of greens." Robert Hawke shrugged. "Who knows? She might even be considered as a candidate in our trials."

The man, thought Harry, *is charming, but odd, even creepy.* But intent on remaining noncommittal, he only smiled and said, "You have an interesting flair for images, Doctor."

Hawke leaned closer. "If we were to cooperate in finding the money, Harry, then we could fight it out in court. Why waste time, energy, and money in the duplication of effort to reach the same goal? We would submit all issues to court, just like gentlemen. You have my word."

Harry groped for some way to end the meeting. "I'll do as I said. I'll present your case to Mrs. Dinnick and report back. That is, when she is able to discuss matters."

"Thank you, Harry. I rely on your word as a gentleman."

When the two men had shaken hands, Mrs. Deal appeared from behind the screen.

Wheeling himself from the table, Hawke said, "Do say you'll come to our little party at the St. George's Club." His eyes narrowed. "I *know* you'll be most impressed."

Harry nodded curtly. "All right. I'll see you there."

Hawke turned to Mrs. Deal, "Now my dear, please wheel me upstairs. I'm afraid our little luncheon has wearied me somewhat."

Mrs. Deal took her charge across the floor of the still empty restaurant. At the door, the retinue of waiters stood back to make way. The doctor's pink head lolled to one side as they said good-bye to the maitre d'.

Harry collected his notebook and headed back for the office. Walking up Yonge Street in the intense heat, he felt chilled. Hawke and Pappas could not be more different. Still, greed and determination united them. However, Norma was just as determined, and she and Arthur had been crafty enough to outsmart them all. But he had not heard a more eloquent description of the slide from lucidity to madness.

In the suite, Mrs. Deal asked, "Was the meeting a success?"

Hawke stood up and pushed the wheelchair into the corner. He gazed out the window. "Quite successful, Ronnie. Our friend Mr. Jenkins is a worthy opponent—intelligent and perceptive. We must be on our toes with him at all times. But he has agreed to present our case to the Dinnick woman."

Hawke turned back into the room. Chuckling, he said, "I behaved shamefully, Ronnie."

"Meaning?"

"I led him to think I was interested in him sexually."

"Why?"

Robert pursed his lips and appeared thoughtful. "Because, my dear, it is his weakest point."

Mrs. Deal sighed but made no comment. She knew her employer had his own agenda, which would never be revealed until the moment of his own choosing. "Would you like some coffee, Robert?"

"Thank you, my dear. We must have clear heads to best this gentleman. He is a most worthy candidate."

"Candidate for what?" Mrs. Deal asked, handing him his cup.

Hawke pursed his lips in childlike delight. "My trial of one. In time, the world will learn of my *real* contribution to medical science."

CHAPTER 6

▼

That night, Gladys climbed down wearily from the bus. It swerved sharply from the curb, enveloping her in black clouds of exhaust. She regarded Mortimer Avenue balefully.

Dwarf maples lined her wide street of bungalows. Leaves hung limply in the evening humidity. Couples did not stroll on her street: there was no particular place to go. Children did not play on her street: the traffic was too heavy. Tonight, people stayed inside their boxy houses with the world blotted out by the whir of air conditioners. Gladys wished desperately for an air conditioner, but her sister, Merle, would not hear of it.

"Do you want to make me really sick?" Merle would whine as she fanned herself with a cheap, lacquered fan purchased from Woolworth's last summer. "I got to think of my arthritis." When Merle said that, it sounded like *Arthur Itis*.

Gladys sighed as she unlocked the door.

"That you, Gladdie?" Merle always called out.

"Yes, Merle," Gladys said, almost crying at the heat in the house.

Merle was at the kitchen table in her pink nightie. Everyone knew something was wrong with her, but no one could say what. Gladys knew whatever it was could never be cured, and she just had to look after her for the rest of her life, which would likely be longer than hers.

Gladys eyed her dinner: a slice of ham, some tomato, and one wilted lettuce leaf wrapped around a pickle. *Merle's notion of culinary art*, she thought as she sat down heavily.

"What's in the case, Gladdie?"

"Work from the office."

Merle looked slyly at her sister. "Who's the new love? You haven't brought work home since Mr. Crawford died." Merle teased and then rolled her eyes. "When you were trying to make a big impression."

Gladys had to squelch Merle's stupid ideas fast. "You don't know a thing about working in an office. Sometimes you have to bring work home." She poked at the food. Fortunately, Merle just grinned foolishly and began cleaning up.

When Merle turned on the television, Gladys struggled to open the dining room window for a breeze. Her sister had seized upon her weakest point, Richard Crawford. And now his widow wanted to wind up the estate, meaning that money would have to be paid out. She would do the calculations. Harry never appreciated everything she did for the firm. She set the files on the table.

Later, when Merle was snoring lightly in front of the flickering TV screen, Gladys wandered out to the back stoop. Sitting in the rocker, she smoothed her skirt and stared at the boarded-up bungalow across the laneway—a vision of dirty browns and grays.

Memories of those first few months at the firm always filled her mind with vibrant color. Just a young woman, she had fallen passionately in love with Richard Crawford. One afternoon, when Mr. Crawford was meeting with Marjorie Deighton in the library, she had put the love letter on his desk. She had written it time and time again, until she was satisfied. A thousand times, she started up to retrieve it, but did not.

An hour later, when she returned from the washroom, she saw the library door was open an inch. The woman must have left. A frisson of terror shot through her as she realized Mr. Crawford would be in his office, reading her letter. Intending to tidy up the books and files for him, she flung the door open.

Stunned, she stopped. Her eyes blinked their incomprehension. Curvaceous silk-stockinged legs rose above the settee. Mr. Crawford's white shirt was rumpled and undone. He bent between the legs, which now began encircling his waist. The woman's blond hair spilled down the back of the settee as she softly laughed, "Richard, darling! Come to me."

Miss Giveny's gasp was almost a shriek. Only nineteen, she did not understand such things, nor did she wish to. Mr. Crawford seemed paralyzed at first. In shock, his hardened eyes locked with hers. With scarcely contained fury, his eyes turned cold with contempt.

Gladys backed out of the room. *Such contempt!* How could she have thought Mr. Crawford loved her? Slamming the door, she raced to his office and snatched the unopened letter from his desk. In the washroom, with tears burning her cheeks, she shredded the letter into tiny pieces and flushed them down the toilet.

Gladys had quaked with the dread of banishment. If only she would be permitted to see him each day at work, that would be enough. But no reference was ever made to her indiscretion and so, she remained in his employ for the next thirty-five years. She still firmly believed Mr. Crawford had to be protected from women, especially his wife.

The back door creaked on its hinges.

"Hi, Gladdie. You're not mad at me, are you?" Merle pressed her nose against the screen and smiled sweetly. "Want some lemonade, Gladdie?"

Gladys stifled a sob. Her fate was to look after Merle. "No, thank you." She tried to smile. "Don't forget to brush your teeth and wash before you go to bed."

CHAPTER 7

▼

Richard Crawford's widow, Dorothy, entered the front hall and set her luggage down. In the oppressive heat, dust floated upward in the fading beams of light. During her visit to friends in England after his death, the house had stood empty. Everything was exactly as she had left it.

If they had had children, even only one, perhaps now she would not be so alone. *With children,* she thought, *you could see along the dark tunnel to the future, like a silver thread of life down the years.* Richard had not been opposed to having children. It just never happened. Once, so long ago, she was thought she was pregnant. She imagined new life wiggling within her. *My little tadpole,* she smiled clasping her hand over her belly. But then, in a torrent of red, it was simply gone.

Then later, without words between them, Richard and she began to sleep in separate beds and then in separate rooms. Of course, with his odd hours, it was for the best. *Who was that child,* she wondered? *Would it be here with me now?*

After removing her Chanel suit jacket, she steadied herself against the hall table. In the dining room, the buffet and hutch looked like dark, monstrous forms crowded into corners, waiting. Turning back to the hall, she caught her breath. Richard's suit jacket still hung on the coat tree. Was he somewhere in the house? She shook her head as if to clear an apparition. With a tiny sob, she held his collar to her cheek, her face powder clinging to one spot.

Bits of the funeral were coming back. Mostly women packed the home for the visitation. Dry-eyed beside the open coffin, she had been amazed at the number of women engaged in public displays of grief.

"Harry? Who are these women?" she whispered in his ear.

Harry patted her hand and replied smoothly, "Clients, Dorothy."

"But why are they all so upset?"

"You should be very proud. Richard was a wonderful solicitor. He advised so many women, after the death of their husbands. They were very loyal to him."

Dorothy was no fool. She knew of Richard's affairs, but how many had there been?

At the funeral home, a small, round-faced woman peered up at her. Through pursed lips, she said, "Mrs. Crawford? We'll all miss Richard, terribly. Did he go quietly in his sleep?"

Tensing, Dorothy drew herself inward. "No. He died at the office."

"I'm Norma Dinnick, dear. Richard was such a fine man." When she squeezed her hand, Dorothy winced.

Another woman approached the casket. *Buxom and well dressed*, Dorothy thought. As Richard lay cold in the casket, the woman touched her fingers to her lips and then gently touched his. Dorothy was dumbfounded by the sorrow passing in her eyes.

"Harry! Who is that woman?" she hissed.

Harry turned around. "Her? Marjorie Deighton. Why?"

"She just kissed Richard!"

"What?"

"With her fingers, I mean."

"Oh, well, then...." Fortunately, Marjorie had disappeared in the crowd. "Her whole family has been clients of the firm for years."

In the darkening front hall, Dorothy hung his jacket in the closet and shut the door firmly. The silk lampshades in the living room were limp with humidity, just like herself. Nearing seventy, she felt herself shrinking, and her energy ebbing. Richard's mantle clock had stopped at two. She set the hands to eight o'clock and wound the key. The harsh ticking filled the room, just like his hectoring voice.

Noticing the mail on the floor, Dorothy stooped wearily to retrieve it. One envelope was covered with large, spindly handwriting. She knew it was from her friend, Clarissa, who would not write so soon unless there were trouble. Dorothy sank into the hall chair and slit open the envelope.

Dear Dorothy,

My sister Grace died suddenly, just after you left. Gone. She was planting begonias in the garden, when she collapsed from a massive stroke. Best

*she didn't suffer. I had to tell you as soon as I could. Hope your trip home
was good. Write soon,*

Love,

Clarissa.

Dorothy sat motionless. The letter slipped from her fingers
and floated to the floor. *Poor Clarissa*, she thought. *Poor Grace.*
One never knew when it might happen. She tried to imagine
being in a garden and then not. But where would she be? Closing her eyes, Dorothy hoped to be elsewhere when she opened
them. But no! The minute her lids flew open the damned stifling house was still there, and so was she.

Rising with determination, she pulled at the buttons on the
cuffs of her silk blouse and shoved up the sleeves. "I am leaving
this house," she whispered.

Slowly, her energy began seeping back. She pulled open the
dining room curtains and struggled with the window. She
threw open the back kitchen door in hopes of getting a cross
draft. But there was no cool air outside. She opened the front
door wide. The hot night closed in.

*Why is he still here? I have to get away, while I still have time for
a life.* She sank onto the staircase and decided to call Harry Jenkins in the morning and tell him to sell the house. Once she had
made that decision, restlessness coursed through her.

In the kitchen, she made tea and toast and ate looking out
over the garden. Vines and weeds had run riot over the patio.
Eager tendrils pushed up between the flagstones and wrapped
around the leg of an iron chair. Their lushness revolted her.

Even without Richard, life went on. At first, she had almost hoped that without him, she would wither and die.

She decided to clear out Richard's attic office. With little notion of what to keep, she pitched most of his papers into the wastebasket but set a few aside for Harry to look at. Only once did her eyes mist over, when she looked at a few photographs of the two of them standing stiffly apart. The state of their marriage was recorded in the distance between them.

She dragged a lamp into the back of the closet and sank to her knees before several boxes. Opening the first one, she saw a number of small, bound notebooks. Overcome by the mustiness, she dragged the box out into the room.

She expected to find old office agendas. Instead, they were personal diaries. She sank onto the small chesterfield near the window.

Entries sprang from the page and drew her in.

> *February 4. Visited dear Q around dinnertime. I am most concerned about her. I like to think that she will come to her senses soon and realize the danger she may be facing. But she is infuriatingly determined. After we had sherry and sandwiches, she told me to leave. I felt quite ill, but I suppose it may be the tension arising from these conversations about her husband.*

Dorothy stared out the window. She had never heard Richard complain about feeling ill. And what about this husband? She read on.

> *February 14. Brought flowers for Q, hoping to put her in a better mood. However, she still insists that neither she nor her hus-*

band has done anything wrong. Got away just in time to see M D who was, by way of contrast, in a very jolly mood and happy to see me. Then home to Dorothy. The ever dutiful but exhausted husband. PS: the pains didn't start until about 2 in the morning.

Dorothy's intake of breath was sharp. *Typical of Richard,* she thought. Running off to see his women and then too tired for her. But he was the kind of man women could not resist. He never said anything about pain to her.

The diaries became repetitious, and she flipped past several pages. The entry for March 21 caught her eye.

March 21. I've been feeling so sick for the past week. Stomach cramps and even vomiting some blood. The doctor can't seem to find anything wrong, despite the battery of tests. I wonder if someone is trying to poison me. Surely not Dorothy?

Dorothy sat rigidly for several moments. *He* was accusing *her* of attempted murder? The page blurred before her eyes.

Staring down into the shadows of the garden, she saw nothing. She struggled to control her mounting fury. Carefully, she shut the window and pulled the drapes. In the absolutely still room, she slowly took deep breaths. *He must have been utterly mad!* When she had calmed herself, she pulled back the curtains and opened the window. The cursed world was still there.

She settled on the chair and read one more passage.

March 30th. Was at Q's this evening. She cooked my dinner, and then we talked. I think she may be softening in her views *about her husband's actions. It is hard to criticize him, particu-larly now he is dead. The stomach pains are growing quite severe. I really must get some better medication from the doctor.*

On the day before his death, he had eaten at *Q's* house. Dorothy flipped back to the February 4 note. Richard had eaten there that night and become sick. Quickly, she checked the dates she had skipped in late February and early March. Numerous visits to the mysterious *Q's* house were followed by bouts of stomach problems. Instead of accusing his wife, the fool should have put it together. But who on earth was *Q*?

Dorothy frowned in deep concentration. If Harry would let her go through Richard's old files, surely, she could locate *Q*. Quentin, Quance, Queen? How many clients starting with the initial *Q* could there be? She felt the tiniest pinprick of life and challenge within, but then it subsided, and her shoulders slumped. She knew nothing of his work, his law practice. How could she, *only* the dutiful wife, never included in his world, ever unravel such a problem? She heard his snort of disgust and imagined his turning away at such silly notions. After a moment, she rifled through more pages until Richard's cutting scrawl blurred before her eyes. She could not let go of the puzzle! What if it were the initial for the first name? She could think of no woman's first name starting with *Q*.

Richard's hectoring voice grew fainter in her mind. She pulled herself up from the chesterfield. Strange and furious excitement rose within her. A puzzle. A mystery. At last, a challenge! To find Richard's murderer, she would have to enlist Harry's help. She was suffused with an energy she had not felt in years. Hoping for some clues, she dragged more boxes from the back of the closet. A battered tin container caught her eye. Popping the latch, she withdrew the contents and spread them on the desk.

My Darling Dickie,

I received your letter, which must suffice until you return and I can feel your loving touch once more. I think only of our long walks and chats. You cannot imagine how much I miss seeing you at the house. I know you must be away with Dorothy [she is very elegant and loyal]. You must know how lucky you are [you devil] to have two women in love with you. When you get back from your trip, do come to see Suzannah and me.

All my love,

MD.

A mortal cry came from her breast. She clasped her hand to her mouth and then sank to the chesterfield. Once her tears abated, Dorothy checked the date. April 25—their wedding anniversary. The bastard had been corresponding with another woman while they were in Paris on their anniversary! She tossed the letter down and kicked the metal box. Her anger nearly blotted out all her curiosity. But who was this Suzannah?

Dorothy stiffened, as she read the next letter from years back. MD was no brief fling. The bastard had been with this woman for most of their marriage. How many had there been?

Darling!

Suzannah is so beautiful. She grows so quickly. You must come and visit our daughter as soon as you can!

With all my love ... waiting for you,

MD.

A strange and furious beast raged within Dorothy. Tears of rage stung her eyes. Blinded, she jumped up, tipping the chair backward to crash on the floor.

"Daughter?" she shrieked, clutching her head as if she would go mad.

"Not a daughter!" She scurried in ever tightening circles about the room.

She flung open the dormer window. "Dear God! Take me from this!" She tore at her blouse, making the buttons scatter on the floor.

The June night sky was hazy with starlight. The heavy, choking air made a cruel mockery of her pleas. Her rasping breath filled the room, and then she slammed the window shut.

Silhouetted in dim light, her tiny form teetered at the top of the stairs. From her heaving chest came the deep keening of a mortally wounded creature. "What child did you give to her and not to me?" she screamed in the silent house.

She sank to the stairs and, biting hard into her hands, she slid downwards chattering, "A daughter. A child. To her, not to me."

Shrieking from the upstairs landing, she sought anything to grab. Her hands scrabbled along the planter filled with pots of dead foliage. At last, she grasped one and, holding it high, she screamed, "I hate you Richard, with all my heart!" And then she pitched it down the staircase. "All I ever wanted from you was a child, a baby!"

She looked downward. Shards of pottery, dry earth, and rotted tendrils were spewed across the tiled floor below. She sank in grief at the foot of the stairs.

"Why, Richard? Why? I wanted your child with all my heart!"

She looked at her hands, covered in blood, and dragged her fingers down her face. "I am *so* alone." With dirt smeared on her cheeks, she wept loudly, until only dry, racking sobs could be heard.

In the night, she awoke to the sound of a baby's cry. Dazed, she felt her way along the hallway and into the other bedroom. She sank onto a straight-backed chair by the dresser and waited. She heard nothing. No baby, after all. She went into the bathroom and took the sleeping pills from the medicine chest. *It must have been a dream*, she thought.

Sinking to the toilet, she stared at the tiny black-and-white patterned tiles on the floor until they began to shift, then spin before her eyes. The golden-haired child must be haunting her. Richard's child. Not hers. She took just two pills and prayed her restlessness would subside. She left the bathroom.

Her wraithlike figure, in its long white gown, wavered at the top of the stairs. When she heard the baby's fussing from somewhere in the house, a strange, heaving sensation seized her breast. She cried out and raced down the steps, through the dining room, and into the kitchen. Snatching up a carving knife, she hurried to the front hall and flung open the closet door. Her eyes gleamed in the dark as she arranged Richard's overcoat on the rack. Fury seized her, and she tore time and again at the black cashmere with the knife.

Each thrust was direct to his heart. *Goddamn you for murdering me!*

Each yank of the knife through the cloth was a joyous frenzy. *Bastard! You left me without a child. Where is that golden-haired girl?*

Dorothy reveled in the sound of the knife ripping through soft fabric. Furious tears sprang from her eyes as she cut and tore. At last she was spent and sank to the chair. The coat hung in tatters. She would not permit his commanding presence to inhabit her.

At last, she rose and went outside to the patio. The first rays of sun had turned the night sky to an angry red. She surveyed the rank, tuberous growth that nearly choked off the tiny garden. With shears in hand, she attacked one stem and then another. Dry rot had set in and the vines and tendrils could not be sliced through. As she labored, the heavy shears twisted in her hands, making her cry out. She sank to the garden bench and examined her raw hands. *Too bad. The blades must be dull,* she thought. Tears of frustration made trails down her soft cheeks. *I want to wither up too. I cannot stand the pain of this fury.*

Dorothy sat in the garden watching the light creep over the rockery. *If I cannot die, then I must find a way to live. But how?*

As the cool morning air crept around her ankles, she tried to form a plan to retain her sanity. Although she could never forgive Richard, his death presented her with a mystery. If only to save herself, she would find Q and congratulate her. Harry could help. In the morning, she would show Harry the letters. At last, she went inside. She folded up Richard's coat and tossed it on the floor at the back of the closet. Upstairs, she fell exhausted onto her bed and into a deep and dreamless sleep.

CHAPTER 8

▼

After rush hour, Harry stood on the subway platform, headed for Dr. Hawke's reception at the St. George's Club. The yellow-tiled walls shone in the stark light of the nearly empty station. Trains from both directions rumbled in the tunnels. A faint breeze swirled and lifted up newspapers and candy bar wrappers. From a stairwell, an older stocky man entered the far platform with a small boy by the hand.

Grandfather and grandson, Harry thought smiling wearily. In play, the man stooped down to let the child pull his red, peaked cap from his head. Laughing, the little boy put it on and marched about the platform.

Harry moved closer to the yellow safety line. *To have a son!* Laura and he had produced no child after twenty years of marriage. Suddenly, nothing was right between them, and his life was torn apart in an instant. He watched the grandfather scoop up the giggling child in his arms to quiet him. *To link myself to the future with a child!*

Trains from both directions burst into the station. The screech of metal wheels on tracks deafened him. With brakes screaming, the trains shot past. Through the windows of the passing trains, Harry could see the little boy grinning and pulling the cap down over his ears.

Second chances, Harry reflected, *are the sweetest. Grandchildren give a chance to do it right.* Slumping into a seat on the train, he closed his eyes. He had barely known his father's touch. Now, Dad's hands and wrists were curled inward, lying uselessly in his lap.

Harry tried to piece the chain together. Dad had grown up downtown in the Depression. Only once or twice had he ever spoken of his own father, Thomas.

His right arm was severed in an accident at the factory, so I left school to sell insurance door to door. When the Depression came, no one had any money, so I got into teaching. That was all Harry knew. Such a slender thread seemed destined to end with him.

Gazing down at his own soft hands, he sighed. He had no tales of hard times and *real* sacrifice. Then he saw Hawke's soft, effeminate hands flutter before him, and he shivered at the recollection of them resting on his. The doors of the train heaved open. Harry rose quickly and got off.

Moments later, he was at street level next to the St. George's Club, a massive pile of red brick and stone constructed in the Romanesque style. Harry entered the shadows of the main floor. Rays of sunlight filtered from the stained glass windows at the top of the broad staircase. Caught in the play of light and shadow, Harry saw the heads and shoulders of the guests clustered in groups throughout the foyer. Music from another era floated inward from the string quartet on the stone terrace.

Without success, he sought his host. Then, deciding he could use a drink, he strolled out to the garden and past clusters of dark-suited doctors, all of whom seemed to patronize the same tailor. Edging his way to the bar, he caught snatches of conversation.

"Hawke? A *very* secretive guy. He's got research facilities somewhere in the hills outside San Diego that nobody's ever seen."

"Somebody said there's a mega-lawsuit in the works from some of his former patients."

Harry paused in hopes of hearing more, but the two doctors strolled toward the flower beds.

"Is he going to fund the new geriatric wing?" asked a man fiddling with his swizzle stick.

"I think so, but there's a *very* big price tag," said a woman from underneath a broad brimmed floral hat.

Drink in hand, Harry wandered about the main floor. In the dining room, the waiters were setting out covered serving dishes on the buffet. Suddenly realizing he was hungry, he popped an hors d'oeuvre from a passing tray into his mouth and stood back to observe the crowd.

Nearby, Dr. Michael O'Hearn scanned the room for his superior, Dr. Philip Glasser, and the good doctor, Robert Hawke. Glowering into his drink, he thought the club reeked of wealth and privilege. Money was everywhere, but always with strings attached.

At the age of thirty-four, he was already the assistant director of research in the geriatric department at the Queen Mary.

Uncompromising in his standards, he considered himself direct and forthright. Others conceded his brilliance but feared he was a loose canon.

He had left his opinion of Hawke's research on Philip Glasser's desk. Now, he wanted to discuss it with him before presenting it to the hospital board in the morning. No one had studied the file and proposals more carefully than he. In his view, the initial trials were not only improperly constituted, but also dubious in their preliminary conclusions. Hawke Pharmaceuticals needed the imprimatur of the Queen Mary Hospital, which was world renowned in geriatric research. Michael was not entirely devoid of political sense. Just give Hawke carte-blanche with his trials, and his own research into Parkinson's would be funded. With a sexy name for the drug, sales would rise off the charts. Better than Viagra.

Philip Glasser, the Chief of Research, sauntered through the door.

"Phil?" Michael grabbed his arm and drew him to a corner. "Did you get my report? I left it on your desk."

"Yes, I did, Michael. Fine work, but…." Glasser bent slightly closer. "You might want to be a bit more diplomatic."

"Diplomatic? But the quality of research is poor. Are we supposed to applaud everything our benefactor does? What about …"

"Have you seen our host?" Glasser broke in.

"No."

Philip nodded. "Tasker's headed this way. We'll talk later, Michael."

With a wide grin, Brian Tasker approached. "Philip!" He grasped his elbow and briefly nodded at Michael. "Come join me at the bar. There are some people you must meet."

Michael trailed after them. The string quartet broke into a rendition of *Summertime*.

By the time Michael caught up, colleagues had surrounded the two men. *Much back patting accompanied by conspiratorial chuckles*, he thought.

Michael raised his voice. "Has everyone studied the initial trials?" Silence fell over the group. Grudgingly, the wall of shoulders turned.

Carefully, Tasker took a sip of his drink and then said, "Yes, I'm sure we've all considered them carefully, Michael. This is a great opportunity. Hawke's institute has an excellent record of funding cutting-edge research." With a slight smirk, he continued, "Research much like yours, I might add, Michael."

Michael cleared his throat and steamed ahead. "I've studied the research thoroughly, Dr. Tasker, and I cannot find any evidence that the drug should proceed to further clinical trials."

Silence greeted Michael's words. Even the quartet paused. The sun dipped beneath the back garden wall, and shadows deepened along the veranda.

"So you've said before." Brian coughed gently. "Nevertheless, the board met this afternoon."

"What?" Michael backed away. "I was told the meeting was postponed."

Tasker's shrug was elaborate.

Glasser tugged at Michael's sleeve.

Snatching his arm away, Michael moved into the circle. Tasker coughed nervously.

"I was asked to present my report to the board tomorrow morning, and now you're telling me it's already decided?"

"There was a lengthy meeting this afternoon, at which the board gave the matter *very* serious consideration," Tasker said smoothly.

"They didn't have my views! I considered the research carefully, sir, and in my opinion, it does not meet the minimum standard."

Tasker grew pale. His eyes flitted about the circle. After a moment, he tossed his head back and laughed. "Ah yes, gentlemen. Who does not remember the certainty of youth?"

Voices rose jovially, and someone patted Michael on the back. "Son, many fine minds have considered the research, and…."

"But, somebody called me to say the meeting was postponed."

Tasker shrugged again. "I've no idea how that happened. Scheduling foul-ups do occur. We'll certainly file your report."

Grasping Michael's arm, Glasser whispered, "Not now, Michael!"

"So the board just went ahead without my report," Michael concluded.

"The board voted to proceed with the trials," Tasker said softly. Then his face brightened. "I believe our host is arriving! Do excuse me, gentlemen."

The group broke off and began drifting out to the main entrance.

"Philip?" Michael followed him. "Did you know about this?"

His superior spun around. "No! Not until it was too late." Angrily, he strode off to the foyer.

Harry watched the white limousine slide underneath the grand portico. A somber man with sunglasses emerged from the passenger side. Muscles bulged everywhere beneath his black suit. He slowly circled the car once, and then motioned the driver to open the rear passenger door. Harry moved closer through the hushed gathering. Michael O'Hearn crowded in.

A woman with dark hair curling sensuously around her collar emerged from the limousine. *Mrs. Deal always makes the entrance*, thought Harry. Shaking her hand, Tasker grinned foolishly.

Next, a highly polished leather boot appeared, topped by a white pant leg. A small man with glasses and a white fedora slid from the back seat. The sun glinted on his glasses as he looked upward to the porch. Harry was surprised at the doctor's smooth movements. Not tied to a wheelchair today.

"Dr. Hawke, sir," Tasker murmured as he held out his hand.

Hawke pulled on his white kid gloves and then shook Tasker's hand.

"Dr. Tasker. You have met my *personal* assistant, Mrs. Deal?" Hawke breathed as he took her arm.

"Yes, of course! What a pleasure to meet again, Mrs. Deal." Brian shook her hand.

"I have brought a guest, Dr. Tasker, for the edification of this gathering." Hawke stepped back.

Slowly, an elderly, stooped gentleman stuck his head out and blinked in the light. Mrs. Deal rushed to help.

"No ... no, Mrs. Deal." Hawke touched her arm. "Let Professor Jefferson manage on his own. He will receive the injection soon enough."

"Certainly, Dr. Hawke," Veronica smiled as she backed away.

The old man squinted in the light. His face seemed unaccountably scruffy, as if he had not shaved for several days.

Harry thought of his father's *badge of dignity*. Insisting on independence, he refused all attempts to shave him. He would do it himself!

"Gentlemen," said Hawke grandly, "may I present Professor Andrew Jefferson? I am extremely proud of him. He is one of our first patients in our trials conducted in San Diego."

Unsteadily, the professor leaned on Veronica Deal's arm. His glassy eyes tried to focus on his surroundings. His voice fluttered in the night air. "So glad ... I thought the bricks ... when he made his first ... she read stories to me as a child, you see, and then we watched the moon landing." He smiled vaguely at the gathering.

Michael smirked. *Word salad*, he thought. *At first, the speech sounds rational, but soon nothing makes sense. Just a wilted green salad of a rotting mind!*

"Gentlemen," Hawke began softly, "tonight, you will witness the effects of our new drug Emerituus. At this time, our patient is weak and disoriented. Within twenty minutes of the administration of the drug, his former vigor will be restored."

The old man's steps were stiff and jerky. In an instant, his benign gaze turned to blazing, irrational hatred.

"Fuck off!" The old man struck out at the chauffeur, who was assisting him from behind.

Parkinson's gait, Michael observed. *Alzheimer's aggression*. Despite years of research, no one could explain or prevent the escape of the wild beast from the Alzheimer's patient, especially in the advanced stages. Symptoms could be ameliorated but only for a time.

When Jefferson's knees buckled, Hawke and Veronica Deal rushed to support him.

Harry shook his head. *Just like Dad*, he thought. Drugs hobbled the march toward death, but nothing defeated the inexorable pull of such diseases.

After Jefferson recovered, Robert Hawke placed his hand on Tasker's arm. His upturned lips quivered as he said, "I am so *very* pleased with the decision of the board today. Your support and cooperation will not be forgotten, Brian."

Brian grinned and, skipping up the remaining steps, opened the door for the doctor.

The interior lights of the rooms glowed, and the aroma of hot food wafted out to them.

Harry saw Jefferson awkwardly lowered to a chair on a dais only to gaze vacantly outward over the heads of the guests. So much like Norma when she tripped into madness! Hawke bent to whisper something in his patient's ear. The chandelier swayed slightly as an underground train departed the station. The guests began to form a line to greet the professor.

Jefferson's gaze fell upon Dr. Philip Glasser. "Good evening, sir. How good of you to come," he said politely.

Dr. Glasser offered his hand. "Good evening, sir. I am Dr. Glasser."

"Good evening. How good of you to come." Jefferson's eyes drifted over the doctor's shoulder.

By now, the line behind Glasser had grown. Swiftly, he withdrew to allow others to meet the guest.

"Good evening, sir. How good of you to come." The old man smiled vacantly as he greeted each person in an identical fashion.

Dr. Michael O'Hearn mounted the dais and presented himself.

"Good evening, sir. So good of…."

"Professor Jefferson. How long have you been taking Emerituus?"

Panic flashed in the old man's eyes. "The roses in the garden … running, you see. Always running."

Michael shook his head and withdrew. *Continuous repetition of a few polite phrases, interspersed with total nonsense.*

Microphone in hand, Dr. Hawke ascended the dais. "Ladies and gentlemen!" His voice, an eerie whisper, wafted throughout the room. "Today, a truly marvelous meeting of minds has occurred. I am absolutely delighted to announce the culmination of many months of hard work. The Hawke Institute and the Queen Mary Hospital have joined forces to embark on a program to effect nothing short of a miracle—t hanks to the efforts of Dr. Brian Tasker and the members of the hospital board." When Hawke pointed in his direction, Tasker gave an embarrassed shrug. "We are indeed privileged to conduct our trials of the drug Emerituus at your esteemed institution."

Hawke waited until the murmuring died down.

"Dr. Jefferson is a patient in the preliminary trials for Emerituus. Ten milligrams of this drug is administered by subcutaneous injection on a daily basis. Unfortunately, although we have found substantial improvement in both cognitive and motor functions, the results are not uniformly reliable. We believe it is a matter of adjusting dosages. Tonight, when we inject our patient, I believe you will see its most beneficial effects."

Mrs. Deal helped the old man with his coat, carefully folding it on a chair. When his shirtsleeve was rolled up, he fixed his eyes heavenward as if struck by a revelation. Hawke took a needle and syringe from a case and drew a clear liquid from a vial. With a flourish, he held up the needle and then swabbed Jefferson's arm.

"Tonight," Hawke intoned, "you will witness the transformation of a debilitated man in his eightieth year to a vigorous one still in his prime."

Lights illuminated the doctor and his patient. Glasses were set down, and waiters disappeared to darkened corners of the room. The professor's gaze was beatific. The doctor injected his patient and guided him back to his seat.

"Professor Jefferson," Hawke continued, "has exhibited all the usual signs of Parkinson's disease and Alzheimer's. Stiff, jerky gait. Slow and garbled speech followed by irrational outbursts of anger."

Hawke continued to regale his audience with anecdotes, facts, and figures. Within five minutes, Jefferson's eyes began to roam about the room, making eye contact in a friendly and interested fashion.

With his back to his patient, the doctor said, "We expect the drug to take effect within ten minutes. I would be happy to answer any questions in the meantime."

The professor cleared his throat. He checked his watch and then stretched his legs without any cramped motions. His eyes grew lively and intelligent. The subway, deep underground, rumbled and turned like an awakened beast.

The doctor continued in his whispery, amplified voice, "Sometimes, we get lost in reams of dry statistics and results. But tonight, you will witness, firsthand, the effects of this drug in our initial research. However, much work lies ahead. In conjunction with the Queen Mary and...."

Jefferson began to rise and tugged on the doctor's sleeve.

Hawke turned to his patient, whose face was wreathed with smiles.

"Ah, Professor Jefferson, are you ready?" beamed Hawke. "Please, come to the podium."

Head held high, the professor walked smartly toward the microphone.

Hawke's voice was a stage whisper. "As you can see, ladies and gentlemen, Emerituus has taken effect. This should last for approximately twelve hours."

The old man assumed his post behind the podium. "Good evening, sirs. How good of you to come."

The room was silent except for a snicker or two from the back. At first, Jefferson appeared to falter. His eyes darted about. Veronica Deal smiled her encouragement. Dr. Hawke beamed fondly at him. Nervous coughs flitted about the darkened room.

The old man blinked in the spot light. "Ladies and gentlemen, I am Professor Andrew Jefferson. I am eighty years of age." After a pause, his voice grew in strength. "During my career, I taught philosophy and medical ethics at Stanford University. Four years ago, I was diagnosed with Alzheimer's." His lower lip trembled. "For one who prized intellectual pursuit, the diagnosis was cruel beyond all imagining."

Jefferson's eyes glistened in recollection. "Then, another devastating blow! Within months, my hands began to shake, and I could not write. The diagnosis was Parkinson's. The abilities I cherished most were snatched from me by the cruelest of fates."

By now, Harry had worked his way close to the dais. He frowned to see tremors course through Jefferson's body as he grasped the podium.

Righting himself, the professor continued, "Relegated to the scrap heap, I was incarcerated in a nursing home. The means of escape was the ability to key in a five-digit numerical code. No one with Alzheimer's could do that."

The old man's shoulders slumped. His voice choked. "Dr. Robert Hawke rescued me from the dense, black fog of my mind. By entering the initial trials of Emerituus, my life was transformed." Looking out over the crowd, his knees suddenly buckled, and he began to sink. Mrs. Deal rushed forward, but Hawke waved her back. Jefferson regained his strength and appeared to straighten.

Lips twisted in scorn, Michael raised his hand. "Professor Jefferson? Could you describe for us the effects of this drug?"

Recovered, Jefferson gave a small smile. "I would be delighted, sir," he said faintly. Grasping the podium, he looked outward upon his audience. His voice rose in strength.

"For one as stricken as I, it is like the sun coming through the blackest of clouds. It is like coming to sit by the fire on the coldest day of the year." Tears brimmed in the old man's eyes. "Like hearing one line of poetry containing the wisdom of a lifetime, or listening to music that stirs the soul to its most fabulous depths."

The room was filled with a reverential silence. Distant tremors of the trains below could be felt.

"That, sir, is the effect of Emerituus," the professor whispered into the microphone.

Hawke bent into the light. "Ladies and gentlemen, Professor Jefferson will only be able to take one or two more questions."

Jefferson reached for the microphone. "When I was referred to Dr. Hawke, my entire being was rescued. Before Emerituus, I tripped and stumbled from tenuous lucidity to utter madness, where uncontrollable forces swept over me. Those forces buffeted me without mercy, and I stood helpless before them. My memory narrowed to a slit, leaving me with only glimpses of a far shore where I had lived my life in peace and harmony. I *had* to return to that safe harbor of remembrance and sanity. Only Dr. Hawke was able to help me on my voyage."

Several people began clapping slowly at the back of the room. Soon the rest of the gathering took up the applause.

Harry did not move. How could a man, apparently suffering severe mental deterioration, paint such vibrant images? The professor's words had stirred him to the beginning of hope for his father. Excited murmurs rose in a room once filled with skepticism.

Hawke resumed the podium. "Gentlemen, I trust you share my enthusiasm and commitment to forge ahead with further testing of Emerituus. You have seen firsthand the results of our initial research. Much hard work lies ahead. But, in conjunction with the Queen Mary, we hope that we will find answers to many questions. We do not know precisely how the drug works, but we are determined to find out. We *do* know that it does work wonders."

Michael's hand shot up at the back of the room. "Dr. Hawke? Could you describe for us exactly how you intend to select candidates for these trials?"

Hawke smiled warmly as he focused intently on the young doctor. "An excellent question, to be sure. Of course, we will adhere to the usual standards of selection. Sufferers of this disease will first be divided into categories determined by the progression and severity of the disease. Then, on the basis of random selection, we will choose an equivalent number from each class or group to enter the trials. One group of each will receive the drug, and the other, a placebo."

The gathering of doctors nodded. Michael raised his hand again. "Given Professor Jefferson's performance here tonight, can you speculate upon the effectiveness of the drug on a long term basis?"

Hawke shook his head sagely. "A bright young man, indeed." He smiled at his audience. "That is precisely one of the most important questions we must answer."

Professor Jefferson had been casting an intelligent eye over the crowd. Suddenly, he began to slump to one side and mutter. Mrs. Deal rushed to his aid with a glass of water.

With a raised hand, Hawke silenced the group. "Gentlemen, as you can see, we have wearied Andrew Jefferson. Out of concern for him, we really must conclude." At Mrs. Deal's request, two men assisted the professor from the dais. Hawke hurried behind him.

When they entered a small anteroom, Jefferson sank into a chair.

Veronica asked. "How did you think it went, Robert?"

He patted her arm. "Like a charm, my dear. Jefferson was excellent."

"What about those questions?"

Hawke shrugged. "Entirely typical, Mrs. Deal." Then he smiled. "But I can tell you one thing. Only the brightest and the best will actually get Emerituus. I have no intention of wasting such a drug on the substandard."

Lost in thought, Harry entered the cavernous depths of the subway station.

Not a cure, but do I dare hope for some remission of my father's disease? He saw him slumped in a wheelchair, vacantly gazing outward. Only a squirrel hopping on a branch seemed to engage his interest on most days. On bad days, he raged within himself and struck out at his dreary fate.

Harry realized that, for years, he had been marching along a sunlit corridor, oblivious to what lay at the end. *Other people* grew old, fell ill, and died—peacefully or horribly—suddenly or after excruciatingly long waits. Protectively he had held that knowledge outside himself and never considered his own fate. But recently, when he went to see Norma or many other mad, frail and sick clients, he would hold his breath in their dark, dank rooms. Glancing outside their windows, he would long for the moment when he could stride with purpose into the outside world filled with reds, greens, yellows, and blues and overflowing with laughing, singing, and shouting voices.

CHAPTER 9

▼

In the morning, Harry studied the brilliant sky from his office window. A phalanx of glistening office buildings allowed him to view just a sliver of the lake, where already, he could see heat rising.

He sipped his coffee. Andrew Jefferson had certainly stolen the show last night. Perhaps Hawke was on to something that would rid the world of the pernicious diseases of the elderly. But what on earth would Norma be like without her unfathomable eccentricities? He could scarcely imagine his father restored to normality, whatever that might be.

Dad had been kicked out of too many retirement homes and was a constant worry when he insisted on living alone at the house. Guiltily, Harry thought about how much easier it was once his father could no longer offer resistance. He turned to his desk and glanced at his daybook.

What? Miss Giveny had penciled in a ten o'clock appointment with Richard Crawford's widow, Dorothy. He grabbed the phone.

"Miss Giveny? I didn't know Mrs. Crawford was coming in this morning."

"Remember, I said she wants to settle *all* matters." said his secretary flatly.

"What *matters?*"

"I don't know, Mr. Jenkins. She never said."

"We're up to date on all the loan payments to her?"

"Yes."

"Good," he said, trying to recall the terms of his agreement to buy out Richard's interest in the firm. "Is there an early buyout clause?"

"Yes. And your balance as of last week was seventy-five thousand, four hundred and ten dollars."

Harry was relieved. Although Miss Giveny tried his patience daily, she did think ahead. If necessary, he could simply pay off the loan for Richard's remaining share of the business. Wives of deceased partners could sometimes cause havoc.

"Thank you, Miss Giveny," he said quietly. "Please bring in the accounting."

Within moments the business file was on his desk. Harry sat back and breathed more easily. Weary of their skirmishes, he proffered an olive branch to his secretary. "Thank you. You handled that well," he said warmly.

She shrugged.

"You know, Miss Giveny, I have to attend to different needs of clients. Law practice is changing. It's not just property conveyancing and wills."

"I realize that," she said.

More was necessary. "I trust you. I know you'll look after everything when I'm in London tracking down Mrs. Dinnick's investments."

"I know you have to make a proper inventory. But you need to pay more attention to the bread-and-butter clients. Mr. Crawford always said...."

Harry cut her off with a wave of the hand. "That's why I have you, Miss Giveny." He tried a smile. Her frown relaxed slightly. "You're extremely capable, you know."

She pursed her lips to fight off the tiniest of smiles.

"When I'm away, I'll call in every day or so. Don't worry."

Miss Giveny did not seem convinced.

Tired of protracted conciliation, he sighed. "Don't worry. It'll work out all right."

She rose to leave. "By the way, Natasha Boretsky called first thing."

"Really?" Harry grinned. "I'll call her back now." He stood in an effort to encourage her departure and then closed the door softly behind her.

They had not spoken since the night that woman, Sheila, was there.

"Hi," he said when she answered. He felt each muscle relax. He desperately craved her intimacy. It was far more than just attraction. He had a gut need for something deep within her that eluded him. The word *enigmatic* floated into his mind.

"Harry!" Her voice was warm in his ear. "Are you free tonight?"

Always free for Natasha. "Yes, of course."

"Could you come for dinner, darling? Around seven?"

"Indeed!" He grinned. *Darling!*

"Wonderful …" Her voice was soft with promise.

When they hung up, fantasy began to dance in his head.

The intercom buzzed. "Mrs. Crawford is here. Says she knows she's early and not to rush."

"Tell her I'll be right out." His heart went out to Dorothy. She was an elegant woman who had borne the burdens of marriage to a constant philanderer with dignity and grace. His own partnership with the man had been fraught with endless turf wars that had nearly worn him out. Buttoning his jacket, he strode with energy into the reception room. Anticipation of an evening with Natasha always made for a great day.

Dorothy Crawford looked like a faded flower shrinking in the light. He rushed to take her hand. "Dorothy! Wonderful to see you," he said warmly. "Please come in. We'll have coffee and a chat."

He guided her down the hall to the library. Seated in a leather chair, Dorothy crossed her legs. *Still shapely*, thought Harry.

Smiling tentatively, she opened her purse. "I went through some of Richard's papers," She handed him a manila envelope tied with a red string. "I need to find out if Richard had any clients with the initial *Q*. I thought you might help."

Carefully, Harry spread the papers on the table. "*Q*? Well, there wouldn't be too many of them, I guess." He looked up at her. "What are you concerned about?"

She made a tiny shrill sound, almost like a laugh and then said, "Someone murdered Richard."

"Pardon?" Harry's mouth hung open.

"Likely an angry husband or jilted lover." Her fingers turned white as she clutched her purse.

Harry's hand froze over the papers. He did not know what reply to make.

"Don't worry, Harry." She smiled bravely at him. "I've always known about Richard and his ladies."

How could you have borne it, he wondered? His own wife, as far as he knew, had taken only one lover. Jealousy stabbed hard, and his cheeks burned in the air-conditioned cool of his office. He had only buried the fury. "I'm sorry, Dorothy," he managed to say. "I know these things are *very* difficult."

"Just read, Harry," she said faintly.

His partner's writing was a cutting, aggressive scrawl. Immediately, he realized it had nothing to do with the law. *What possessed the man to commit such lascivious thoughts to paper?*

Harry closed his eyes at the memory of Richard's last moments of life. The old man had swayed dangerously before his desk, consumed with fantasy and lust for his client, Marjorie Deighton. His last words were, *Have you ever experienced the thrall, Harry? If you have not, then you have not lived.* Then he had simply dropped dead at his feet. Harry tried his best to sympathize with his partner, a man consumed by his passions. Was it death by thralldom?

Harry opened the first letter, presumably the most damning, and began to read.

Darling Dickie,

You must visit me as soon as you can. I live to hear your voice. Alone at night, I torture myself with your imagined touch and kiss. Such sweet pain it is!

You must see our beautiful, golden-haired daughter, Suzannah. How quickly she grows. But the pain of pretending she is not ours is more than I can sometimes bear.

With every bit of my love,

Marjorie.

Harry groaned. *Jesus!* Why would anyone keep such incriminating evidence at home for his long-suffering wife to find? Evidence of an affair was one thing—paternity, quite another.

Dorothy gave a delicate cough. "Harry, tell me about this Marjorie, please. And," she said with dignity, "Suzannah."

Harry was hopeless at dissembling. He spoke slowly and carefully to ensure he made no slips. "Several generations of Marjorie Deighton's family were clients of this firm. Richard acted, not only for her, but for her parents and several brothers and sisters. Marjorie died shortly after Richard."

Dorothy's eyebrow rose. "Where is the child now?"

"Suzannah Deighton left the country shortly after her mother's death. I haven't heard from her since."

"Is there any way to contact her?"

"Not that I know of." Harry patted her hand. "Suzannah was in her late thirties and extricating herself from a difficult relationship with a man." He smiled weakly and then asked, "Why do you think Richard was murdered?"

"Read the next letter and the diary entries in March."
The letter was addressed to *Q.*

> *Please let's not argue. Your husband is gone. I must see you and have you close to my heart. Please reconsider as we must have clear consciences.*

Crawford's signature was scrawled across the bottom: *Your loving boy, Dickie.*

Harry almost laughed out loud. Dickie certainly was a busy boy. But he must have been completely mad to leave such fulsome declarations of passion. Harry had thought Richard's love for Marjorie Deighton was deep and genuine, not a just a fling. But here he was writing to someone named *Q.* A tiny sliver of pity cut through him for a man with such compulsions. But poor Dorothy!

Her voice intruded upon his bleak whirl of thoughts. "Look at the diary, Harry."

Richard's intense nausea and pain were recorded on numerous pages. They did seem inextricably linked to visits with the mysterious *Q.* He sought clues, a description of the house, personal characteristic, but could find nothing to indicate the woman's identity.

Dorothy waited patiently until he finished.

At last he said, "Obviously, he was concerned someone could be poisoning him. But as far as I know, Dorothy, he died of a stroke, right here in the office."

"If he were being poisoned in small doses over a long period of time, that could have brought on the stroke," she insisted.

Although he had never heard of such a thing, Harry paused to consider her theory. At last he said, "You think this *Q* person is the killer, and you want to look at all the *Q* files."

"Yes," she said.

Harry did want to help. "Ordinarily, I wouldn't reveal client files, Dorothy."

Her expression knotted into stubbornness.

"But, under the circumstances…."

"Thank you, Harry."

He buzzed Miss Giveny. "Would you please check our records for files beginning with the letter *Q* opened in the last two years?" Within five minutes, his secretary brought in a printout.

"I don't think we'll learn anything. Just routine matters. Richard did an incorporation of a building contracting business for Mr. Quentin. A Mrs. Quance wanted a will. And Mr. and Mrs. Quill bought a house." Her disappointment pained him, and he hastened to add, "If you like, we can look through the preceding years."

"Thank you, Harry. Let me know if you find anything at all."

After he collected the papers for her, they stood at the door.

She searched his face. "Do you think I have enough to go to the police?"

"And say what?" he asked carefully.

Her eyes grew panicky. "Haven't you listened, Harry? That Richard's murderer must be caught!"

Dorothy had almost nothing to go on except Richard's expressed concerns. But she looked so frail and insubstantial that he felt compelled to help. He reached for her elbow to guide her. "I suppose you could talk to them," he began. He visualized the police officers hiding smirks behind patient smiles.

Suddenly, she stopped in the corridor. "Harry, could you come with me?"

"Take a day or two to think it over, Dorothy. Then, if you decide to go ahead, call me."

She smiled bravely up at him. "I *am* sorry, Harry. I shouldn't have troubled you."

He took her hand. "Call me in a day or two."

Stepping onto the elevator, she gave a small, distracted wave.

A sad lady, indeed, he thought. So many women, dominated by their husbands throughout marriage, were completely unprepared to live alone after the death. But Dorothy seemed ready to try.

At street level, Dorothy blinked in the hot sun. Suddenly enervated, she nearly lost her balance. As if floating adrift, she began to walk with no destination in mind.

Harry didn't take me seriously. But I have to find his killer to congratulate her!

The darkness of the Arcade, with its narrow passages of shops, beckoned her. Cool shadows spread before her as she struggled with the brass door. At last she was inside.

As if emerging from fog, people appeared dwarfed by the vaulted ceilings, patterned with inlaid tiles. In the distance, she saw the Tea Room, Richard's favorite spot for late afternoon assignations. Very occasionally Richard and she had eaten lunch there. Somewhat revived by the cool air, she stepped along the passages lined with tiny shops selling linen, jewelry, and books.

At the far end of the broadest lane, she saw the old clock with its huge Roman numerals. It was only eleven. Once or twice, she had arranged to meet him under the clock. Arriving early, she had seen him leave the Tea Room with a lady on his arm. His farewell consisted of a courtly bow and the tipping of his hat. If she asked about the woman, he would invariably say, *a most distraught widow, Dorothy.*

Barrenness embraced her like a chill hand. Richard's women were bigger than she, more feminine, buxom, and *fertile.* And somehow, they were jollier. Likely, they all had scads of children. And, she wondered, how many were his? A little cry caught in her throat as she looked down at the bones and veins of her hands. Almost weeping, she stumbled toward the Tea Room.

The bastard got what he deserved. Why should I care?

Thank God, the Tea Room was open. She stood unsteadily at the doorway, blinking in the rose light of the room filled with tables of snowy white cloths. Although the sense of his presence nearly choked her, she sat at a table. Voices and laughter drifted from the kitchen. Suddenly, the door flew open, and a young man entered with a silver tray.

"Madam?"

"I'll have a pot of tea, please." She arranged her purse and jacket on the next chair. "And do you have any scones?"

"Certainly," the boy bowed and turned to leave.

"Does Armand still work here?" she asked.

"Yes ma'am. He's in the kitchen. Shall I ask him to come out?"

"Yes, please. Tell him Mrs. Dorothy Crawford is here to see him." In the boy's absence, she fiddled with her reading glasses and visualized Richard at a table, charming his ladies. Armand was not long in coming.

"My dear Mrs. Crawford!" A tall, willowy man of at least seventy years pulled up a chair beside her. "It is many months since I have had the pleasure …?" Armand's voice trailed off in a question.

Dorothy laid her hand on his sleeve. "I need your help, Armand."

Armand looked slightly alarmed. "How may I assist you, Mrs. Crawford?"

"Don't worry, Armand." She patted his arm. "It's about Richard and I *do* know about all his ladies."

A blush rose from Armand's collar to the roots of his white hair. "So tragic, his passing." He lowered his eyes respectfully. "He was a fine gentleman, and I do not believe he could help himself, Mrs. Crawford. What can I do for you?"

"Armand, if you could think back to last March."

Armand frowned in recollection.

"I'm sure most of Mr. Crawford's meetings were … congenial?"

Armand nodded.

"Was there ever an unpleasant or argumentative meeting, especially in March?"

The waiter stroked his chin thoughtfully. "Yes. There was one meeting, although I do not know if it was in March or February."

"Yes?"

Armand gestured over his shoulder. "He sat with a woman at the large table next to the window. I knew at once it was not a … how shall I say this?" He cleared his throat. "It seemed to be a business meeting rather than a personal one. It was not friendly."

"What did she look like?"

"She was a small woman." Armand seemed embarrassed. "Not quite of the same class as his usual clientele, although she was well dressed."

"Were they arguing?"

The waiter shook his head. "Not until they were joined by another guest."

"Really? Who?"

"I do not know, but he was a very tall man with collar-length white hair. I remember this because he became very angry with your husband. Suddenly, he stood up and knocked over the table with all the tea and cakes on it." Armand shook his head sadly and sighed. "Such a mess on the carpet!" He paused when the boy came in with the tea and scones, and then continued, "His eyes were red, just like a rat! Your husband seemed very small next to such a violent man."

"What were they arguing about?"

"I do not know, but Mr. Crawford was extremely upset. When the tall man left with the lady, Mr. Crawford ordered a glass of milk."

"Milk?"

"Yes. He said his stomach was causing him pain. Then he called me over and offered to pay for the damage." Armand shrugged and held out his hands, "I said there was no damage to speak of and not to give it another thought."

"Was he in great pain, Armand?"

"I cannot say, Mrs. Crawford, but he did sit for at least half an hour, sipping his milk."

"Thank you, Armand. You have been most helpful."

The elderly waiter stood. "My dear Mrs. Crawford, your husband was a fine gentleman, always most polite. I am glad to have been of some service to you." Bowing, he disappeared through the kitchen door.

Dorothy poured her tea. She *knew* it! An angry husband had murdered Richard. A highly suitable fate!

CHAPTER 10

▼

Bathed in soft lamplight, Natasha stood before the mirror of her dresser. Slowly, she undid the buttons of her silk blouse. With a shrug, she let it drift to the floor. Pressing her thighs tightly against the dresser, she leaned into the mirror for a closer view of her face. Although men found her attractive, they often seemed blinded to her reality. Some were slightly in awe of her. It was her manner, of course.

She undid her brassiere, revealing her dark nipples, which grew taut in the cool air. Harry was the first man in years to reach her with his touch. His smell and the texture of every inch of his body were emblazoned on her memory and incorporated into her every cell. And, she knew the rhythm of each and every breath of his being. Strange how he had opened her eyes inward to see her life, herself, and him!

Her breasts fell free as she hunted in a drawer to choose a lace brassiere. Could she trust him enough to reveal herself? He had not liked Sheila but was unaware of his own jealousy. In time, she hoped he would understand and accept.

Tonight should be light and fun. What did she fancy? From the drawer, she took a black lace bra. Its wispiness displayed the swell and curve of her breast to perfection. In her closet, she found a starched, white shirt with fulsome French cuffs. Buttoning only the last three buttons, she tucked the shirt into her jeans. She turned in the mirror to examine the effect. Harry would be unconsciously aroused by the contrasting masculine and feminine touches.

For Natasha, only love and desire mattered. Gender was incidental, because a good man or woman could stir her. The nature of her spirit floated free, but she knew few people could accept that. She was weary of Sheila's demands that she choose. It forced her to build walls within herself where none should be.

My body has always betrayed me, she suddenly thought. She smoothed her shirt, her hand lingering protectively over her left breast. She remembered most of all the smell of the grass as boys—three of them—had shoved her to the ground between the flower beds in the park. She could not breathe when one sat on her stomach and another held her ankles hard against the stones. Groping, squeezing hands seized her breasts, then tore her blouse. She turned her head to see the third boy—no more than fourteen—with sweaty, pimply skin, seated on a rock. She tried to wrench away when she saw him yank and pull on his frighteningly huge penis. But then, seeing the frantic loneliness in his eyes, she gazed at him sorrowfully. She knew she could endure whatever compulsion had seized him, if she had to.

And then there was shouting from a distance. The boys ran off, and a man stood over her. He turned away and waited as she struggled to arrange her clothing. Then he gently helped her up. In silence, he took her hand and led her to a drinking fountain where he knelt at her feet and did his best to wipe away the mud and speckles of blood on her knees with a rag. Tears burned her cheeks as she looked down on his bald head, bobbing as he worked. When he said he would call the police, she ran off as fast as she could. Only later did she regret not thanking him for his kindness. *No one must ever know*, she thought.

Home at last, she sank to her bed. *Why did this happen?* Her breasts were bruised and tender. She wasn't doing anything bad. She didn't want boys to bother her. But her breasts, her body at thirteen, betrayed the reflective girl inside, who began to hide in loose and bulky clothing.

Natasha glanced once more in the mirror. Such remembrances had only begun to surface in the last year, since she had met Harry. Of course, they had been buried deep within, but now they dared to come forth in the safety of his presence. Recollection tumbled out as she hurried to the kitchen to marinate the steaks. For a while, she had taken to wearing boys clothing, although it had not seemed to matter. Men still whistled and tried to follow her down the street.

One night, when she was a third-year university student, she and some friends had gone to a bar where she met Amelie, sitting alone at the far end of the counter. Amelie's blond hair was cut short, and her green eyes kept wandering in her direction. They began to talk. Suddenly, Natasha was aware of something different, the missing piece within her. That night, she went home with Amelie. Her room—she was a student of philosophy—had only a ceiling light harshly illuminating a narrow cot, a desk, and straight-back chair. A wintry draft blew in at their ankles from a window that would not close tightly. They lit candles and turned out the light. With their tall shadows flickering on the wall, they drank cheap wine and talked. Amelie seemed to listen with an intensity she had never known and to understand her. The blankets were thin and scratchy, and still, they grew warm beneath them. That night, Natasha found the other person within her who craved the gentle softness and the love she had been missing. At one moment, it was the same, and yet so different, in a parallel world.

Although Natasha had not thought of Amelie for years, now she was suffused with the poignancy of her memory. With piercing immediacy, she could hear her voice and feel her touch. Strange how the past always stood right there, silent and unseen, but ready to enter the present at any time.

Shaking her head, she opened the fridge and got out carrots, red and green peppers, and onions. She marinated the steaks, made a salad, and then set a bottle of Shiraz on the counter.

Now, thoughts of Harry roamed free in her mind, blotting out all recollection. Even after a year, the attraction was elemental. As a rule, men were caught up in their own pleasure and oblivious to hers, but Harry was different. She had no words for her sense of finding her own self within him, and she wondered if she brought the same feeling to him. In their lovemaking, he would study her face searching for guidance and expressions of pleasure, just like Amelie. But still, he might well be threatened by her nature. Searching for the salad dressing in the fridge, she worried that Harry could not really see her on the far side of his fantasies. With Sheila, lovemaking was of an entirely different quality or kind. Afraid of losing her, Sheila had grown demanding and possessive. Perhaps familiarity had dulled their responses. Claustrophobia was setting in.

Harry left plenty of time to get through the downtown traffic to Natasha's on Lakeshore Road, just past the Exhibition grounds. Mesmerized by the red taillights stretching ahead, Harry let his fantasies roam. Hearing Natasha's soft voice, he imagined stroking her smooth, cool thighs and caressing her breasts. Slamming on the brakes, he veered, just missing the car in front. He took a deep breath and loosened his collar.

The road curved past the tall, stone gates of the Exhibition Grounds, festooned with fierce gargoyles. In childhood memory, he saw the lights of the spinning Ferris wheel against the summer's night sky and the garishly painted clown faces on the midway of the fair. The eager, demanding cries of hawkers floated from a distance on the air of recollection.

How easy to recapture moments of his eight-year-old self. That child was always there, just as the young man in law school and the newly married man still lived within him. He could feel his mother's hand on his arm as he begged for one more ride and could smell the starchiness of his father's shirt when he carried him home on his shoulder. Daily events, innumerable choices of each hour and day, each month and year, seemed like eddies on the surface of a river breaking over rocks. But the swift, unseen current below never varied in its fundamental direction. If only he had faith in the sureness of that force, perhaps he could trust to the future and a lifetime with Natasha. Once past the park grounds, he saw the sun, low on the horizon, glistening on the lake. He put on his sunglasses.

Brakes squealed. A horn blared. From behind, two huge headlights bore straight down on him. He swung to the inside lane, but the vehicle clipped his rear bumper. Swerving, he just missed the curb. Jesus! It was the huge Jeep from the other night. Flashing its lights, it roared past. Harry pulled off onto a ramp and dialed 911.

"I've just been run off the road," he said.

"Do you need a fire truck, ambulance, or police car?" came the reply.

"Police."

"Where are you, sir?"

"Off Lakeshore Road Park on a closed off ramp."

"Is the other vehicle there?"

"No, of course not."

"Are you injured, sir?"

"No," he said quietly.

"Then you should file a report with the Accident Reporting Center and notify your insurers."

"Yes, of course," he mumbled and hung up.

Undoubtedly, it was the same Jeep. Norma's warning rang in his ears. Only her business could make him such a target. Hawke had been more than plain. He wanted the money for medical research, or so he said. But legitimate businessmen, much less medical doctors, did not run people off roads. Backing his car up the ramp, he turned again onto Lakeshore Road. Thank God he didn't have far to go.

Natasha finished setting the table. She drew back the curtains to display the ever-changing sky above the lake. The telephone rang. Hoping Harry was downstairs, she hurried to answer it.

"Hello?"

"You haven't called me for two days." The voice was small and wounded.

"I've been busy, Sheila," said Natasha patiently, but drawing protectively inward.

"Shouldn't we be planning our trip to Stratford?"

"There's plenty of time for that." Natasha began lighting the candles on the table.

"So, I got the tickets for the play yesterday."

"Wonderful!" Natasha winced as the match burnt her finger.

"We're staying overnight, aren't we?" The voice was querulous.

"Sure," she said uncertainly. Once Sheila had been a comfort, a buffer against brutish male egos. Now, if not constantly reassured, she became whiny.

"You're not going to disappoint me again, are you?"

Natasha closed her eyes. She felt her throat dry. Sheila brought out her domineering nature. "No, of course not. Listen, I've got to go. I'm expecting dinner guests any moment." If she did not cut her off, she would be on the phone for hours.

"Well," Sheila grew huffy. "Sorry to intrude! Is it Harry?"

"No," she lied, unable to bear further inquisition from one she had loved for so long. "Listen, darling!" Natasha rushed in with warmth. "We are going to have the *best* time in Stratford. I'll book a bed and breakfast for us."

"All right," said Sheila petulantly. "Have a good time tonight with *whoever* it is."

"I will, and I'll call you tomorrow with all the arrangements." Of course, she was being unfair, but she couldn't help it.

Harry knocked. Wordlessly, Natasha drew him in at the door. She kissed him with such hunger that he teetered against the wall. She undid the first few buttons of his shirt and traced his collarbone with her finger. He sank at her touch.

"I've missed you," she said, taking him into the living room. She sat him down on the chesterfield. The evening sun on the lake shone so brilliantly, he squinted.

"Scotch?" She held up the decanter. *Questions always disappear when Harry's here*, she thought.

Sliding back into the pillows, he nodded and smiled. She leaned over him and handed him his drink.

So lovely, he thought as he took his first sip. Her white shirt was open to show her breasts resting in a black lace brassiere. When she sat beside him, he rested his hand on her thigh.

Momentarily, Natasha considered postponing dinner. She loved his touch. She took his hand and kissed it, placing it on her breast.

Gently, he caressed her nipple. She kissed him once more.

"Shall we?" He nodded in the direction of her bedroom.

"After dinner, Harry," she smiled.

In her thrall, he watched her cook the steaks and toss the salad. Dinner was a quiet affair with a faint air of urgency. Their conversation was shaped by soft and occasional murmurs. He could not take his eyes from her.

When they were done, she took him by the hand into her bedroom. *How easy to love this man*, she thought. Entranced by the intensity of his gaze, she drew him onto the bed.

Slowly, they undressed each other and lay beneath the covers. Harry reveled in the smooth coolness of her skin, and she clung to the warmth and texture of his. There was no need to rush tonight.

His concentration was shattered by the telephone. She touched her fingers to his lips and shook her head.

A strident voice filled the room. "Natasha? Are you there? Pick up, will you?"

Natasha groaned and reached for the volume control on the answering machine. Harry rolled onto his back.

"Just wanted to tell you not to book the *Poodle and Partridge*. I hear it's not so good."

Harry rubbed his eyes. *Fine time for interruptions*, he cursed. Sounded like that friend of hers.

"Sorry, Harry. It's just Sheila."

Stroking her hair, he said, "It's okay. Damned telephones. The more means of communication the less meaning."

He moved above her, and she drew him close. But their lovemaking was rushed. She was distracted. He was determined. Finally, they lay side by side, exhausted.

He rested his hand on her thigh. "Sorry, Natasha."

"Don't be silly!" she laughed softly. "Next time when I seduce you, I'll disconnect the phone and bar the doors." Gently, she traced his lips with her finger "Really, it's silly to have such an old-fashioned answering machine."

"Actually, I was a bit preoccupied myself," he sighed. The image of the Jeep had roared back into his imagination. "I was followed again tonight."

Concerned, Natasha raised herself onto her elbow. "Who on earth is following you?"

"I'm not sure. Remember, I told you about the Jeep tailgating me the other night? Well, the same one clipped my car tonight."

"Why would anyone be after you, Harry?"

He pulled a pillow behind him and sat up. "It's very complicated. It's to do with some money I'm trying to locate for a client."

She laid her head on his chest.

"I have to go to London at the end of the week." He tipped her chin up toward him and looked into her eyes. "Would you come with me? I know it's short notice."

She frowned and then gently kissed his forehead. "I would *love* to Harry, but I can't right now." Once again, Natasha felt torn. Like a magnet between poles, she was frozen by indecision. At the one end, stood Harry and at the other, Sheila. Until now, it had not been hard to balance life with Sheila, only because there was no Harry. "How long will you be gone?" she asked.

"Maybe a week." He sighed and shifted onto his side. He traced the line of her neck and arm. "Probably just as well." He kissed her nipples playfully. "I'd never get any work done, because I'd be in bed with you all day."

She held her finger to his lips. He saw her eyes grow distant as she rose from the bed. More than anything, he wanted her warm and close beside him, but he had been too slow. He should have asked her earlier to go to London. Now the invitation sounded like an afterthought.

Drawing her robe around her, she asked, "Shall we have coffee and dessert?" She wanted to go to London with this man, but she could not work it out. First there was business and then, of course, Sheila.

"Sure." He slid into his pants and shirt and followed her into the kitchen. "Natasha?"

"Yes?" She began making the coffee.

"I'm sorry. I should have asked you sooner."

She shook her head and smiled sadly. "It's not that at all, Harry. I couldn't have gone anyway." She wound her arms about him and they kissed. Then, moving away, she said, "I've got an important closing coming up next week." She paused. "And then, there's Sheila...."

"What about Sheila?"

"I promised to go to Stratford with her. You heard her on the phone." The roar of the coffee grinder filled the room.

"Doesn't a trip to London beat Stratford?" he asked. "You can go to Stratford almost anytime."

She poured water into the coffee pot, and then turned to him. "It's not that simple, Harry," she said, smiling sadly.

"But surely, Sheila would understand...."

Briefly, Natasha closed her eyes. "Well ... I could speak with her...."

Harry frowned but said nothing.

After she had put the fruit into bowls, they sat with their coffee and dessert in silence, in front of the television. Twenty minutes later, standing in her foyer, they kissed. Going down in the elevator, Harry knew he was missing something.

Natasha sat in front of the television but did not turn it on. *He doesn't see it yet*, she thought. Suddenly, she got up and began loading the plates and glasses into the dishwasher. Years ago, Sheila had rescued her from the despair of her brother, Joseph's, death. Back then, life had been without pleasure—lifeless, in fact. With Sheila came hope for a new start. Natasha poured a glass of wine and settled in the living room. She hated the thought. She *owed* Sheila. Was obligation the only tie remaining? What was the choice? Between male or female, as Sheila would have it? Or was it more fundamental, between different kinds of people?

CHAPTER 11

▼

The next morning, Harry set out to deliver Hawke's proposal to Norma. In the car, his thoughts quickly returned to Natasha and the evening before. Her mystery marooned him in frustration. Once or twice before, he had asked about her friends, but he had been thwarted by a distant edge within her. *This far and no further,* she seemed to say. Now, he had met one of them.

His mood turned grumpy at thoughts of Sheila, the one favored with the intimate touch of old friendship *and* the one who had interrupted their lovemaking. Testily, he continued his inquisition. Any talk of men seemed to belong to the distant past. In his worst moments, Harry envisioned a line of them, for, after all, who would not desire the lovely Natasha? He blushed to acknowledge the flames of jealousy within himself. But if he sought to possess her, he would be stranded with her phantom.

Today, Rattlesnake Point lay under sullen, gray clouds. After he parked, a sharp rap came at his window. A man with a blackened eye and swollen lip leered in. Cautiously, he lowered the window an inch.

"Hey, mister!" Harry recoiled, but then the face grew friendly. "You got a cigarette?" The man stretched his fingers through the open window and waggled them under his nose.

One of the inmates, Harry supposed. Nodding curtly, he got out and handed him his cigarettes.

Grinning, the man motioned toward a bench, under a broad shade tree. "Sit with me, mister. Have a smoke."

He wanted free of this strange man, clad in a blue tee shirt and dirty brown shorts, out of which extended his white, spindly legs. Now he was offering him his own cigarettes!

The man ferried him to the bench "Who'd you come to see, mister?"

Although he seemed harmless enough, Harry shifted away. "A client."

"Where you from?"

"Downtown." The man looked at him blankly. "Toronto," Harry added.

"Nice car." The man motioned toward the lot. "How much you pay for it?"

"Thank you. It's not that expensive." Harry sought to end the interrogation politely. "I really must go. My client's waiting." Stubbing out his cigarette, he started for the path. The man straggled behind with a hitching sort of limp.

"What you work at, mister? You're not from the government, are you?"

"I'm a lawyer," he said.

The man stood dead still. Suddenly, he clutched his head in his hands and screamed, "A lawyer? Not a lawyer!" He began to run in circles. "Fuck! I hate lawyers. Dirty, tricky … all of them! Lawyers put me in here!"

Harry hurried up the path, but the man grabbed his sleeve. Together, they made a ridiculous pair jostling each other along the path to the hospital. Finally, Harry shook himself free. The man dropped back among the shrubs near the steps.

"A lawyer, by God! That's the devil himself," he screeched from behind a tree.

Harry swung open the screen door. Briefly, he contemplated latching it, but the man had disappeared. No wonder Norma complained about the place. Madness erased all boundaries.

The infamous Mrs. Burke scurried into the lobby, her pincer like hands outstretched.

"Donald!" she screeched.

Harry met her head on. "Mrs. Burke, I am not your son. I'm Harold Jenkins." He thought better of announcing his profession.

Mrs. Burke stopped dead in her tracks. Storm clouds seemed to be gathering about her, but to his relief, she smiled with great sweetness and drifted off toward the now darkened dining room.

At the desk, he asked for Mrs. Dinnick.

"She's in play therapy."

Harry's eyebrows shot up. Visualizing Norma with plasticine and paint, he chuckled. Undoubtedly, she would call such activities *idiotic.*

"You're not her great-nephew, are you?"

"No. She doesn't have any relatives."

The woman shrugged and set to her typing.

Harry persisted. "I'm her lawyer, and I'd like to see her."

"Lawyer, are you?" She peered sourly at him.

Harry stiffened. "Yes."

"You can wait for her in her room. Number 306. They'll bring her up in about ten minutes."

The elevator clanged upward to the third floor, and Harry stepped into the corridor, crowded with wheelchairs. Slumped to one side or the other, the occupants stared up at him with ghastly expressions. As he walked toward Norma's room, a forest of arms stretched upward to catch his hand.

One woman brandished a teddy bear and chanted, "Johnny, come home." Holding his breath, Harry found Norma's room. No wonder she hated it here.

He was surprised to see her sitting by the window. She acknowledged his presence with a brief nod.

"I thought you were at some kind of therapy," he said, setting down his case.

"Me? Hardly! It's worth my life to run that gauntlet of wheel-chair lunatics."

Harry held up his hand. "I know, Norma. I had to get past them too."

Suddenly, she was on the verge of tears. "How can you leave me in this place?"

"There's *no* choice!" Then he continued more quietly, "Norma, you must be here. You *know* the alternatives." He pulled up a chair. "Listen, we've got business to discuss."

"Yes?" She pursed her lips.

"I've been approached by someone claiming the money I'm supposed to find."

Norma was alert.

"He says it was raised specifically for medical research."

Norma remained silent.

"His name is Dr. Robert Hawke."

Norma recoiled as if he had slapped her. Instantly, her mind reeled off in recollection of Venice, where she had first met Robert Hawke. She turned, vacant eyed, toward the window.

"Norma, do you know a Robert Hawke?"

When she did not reply, he feared he had lost her.

At last she said weakly, "Yes. I have met a *Mr.* Robert Hawke, but he's no doctor."

Norma saw herself at a café on a terrace overlooking the Grand Canal in Venice. The sky and water blended into a shimmering sheet of white. With the sun burning through, the buildings on the far side of were deep in shadow. *Timeless*, she had thought.

Arthur and she were having cocktails when they first saw Robert, crossing the broad piazza with languid strides. Robert's thin, straw-colored hair was plastered across his brow, like a school-boy's. His clothing gave him a dandified air—white suit, cream silk shirt, and a bowler hat in hand.

"What a pleasure, Mrs. Dinnick." Robert gave a courtly bow and removed his white kid gloves.

He sat down next to Arthur. In the dying sunlight, Arthur squinted up at him. At first, Robert's manner was smoothly diffident, but soon his soft features appeared to coarsen. Norma lost herself in a study of the stripe-shirted gondoliers below.

Robert's soft lisp broke into her reverie. "Mr. Pappas asked me to see you, Arthur."

A breeze picked up from the sea, and the shadows along the canal deepened. Norma shivered slightly. Arthur sat absolutely still. To Norma, the waiters were only dark, silhouetted figures swirling about the terrace like apparitions.

"Yes?" Arthur said.

Robert smiled pleasantly, but his tone was formal. "He is awaiting your report. I trust it is forthcoming in the next few days."

Arthur sipped his drink. Only after he had carefully set it down did he speak. "The money is quite safe, Mr. Hawke. I'm working on the accounting."

Robert's blue eyes hardened and bore into Arthur's.

"There are only a few items yet to be allocated," Arthur added.

Robert continued to stare at him across the table. "When will it be ready?"

"As soon as we return home. Late next week."

Robert shook his head slowly. "You must understand that Mr. Pappas wants more than an accounting. He wants the *money*, my dear man."

Norma had concluded that the plump, soft-skinned man was, as she put it, one of *those people*.

Norma jerked around from the window. "Harry!" Norma spoke with great distaste. "He was a homosexual."

Harry looked uncomfortable. "So I understand," he said. "But that has nothing to do with what we're up against. Hawke says that the money is now desperately needed for research into

Alzheimer's. He claims his company is close to a cure, and that the money was always intended for that purpose."

Harry peered into Norma's eyes, which had grown flat and unseeing. She had already drifted back to the piazza in Venice, where Arthur had tried to disguise his tremors by shifting about in his chair.

Arthur's voice cracked. "*Of course*, Robert. George will receive the money, along with a *full* accounting, on my return."

Smiling sadly, Robert reached across the table and patted Arthur's arm. "I certainly hope so, for your sake, dear boy." He stood to kiss Norma's hand. "Arthur, I shall convey your words to Mr. Pappas, who will consider them a solemn undertaking."

He sauntered across the piazza and down the steps to where the boatmen waited. As he stepped into the gondola, he bowed and raised his bowler hat to them in a cheery salute.

Surfacing from her reverie, Norma tossed her head back indignantly. "Harry, that money was stolen by Pappas and Hawke. Archie was in on it too."

"Well, you can't lay claim to funds obtained by fraud."

"Neither can they."

Of course, she was right. Neither party could legitimately claim profits from a fraud. And, there was no Statute of Limitations for fraud. The money would escheat to the Crown, meaning the government would get the loot. Bureaucrats and flunkies would declare, in officious tones, that proceeds from fraud fell into the black pit of government coffers. *A duly sanctioned fraud in itself,* he thought!

"Norma? You must think very carefully. Do you know where the money could be? Can you think of *anything* else … any clue at all?"

Norma Dinnick frowned. "I've told you everything I can think of.…"

"Hawke has made a proposal. He's suggesting that, since neither of us knows where it is, we join forces to find it, and *then* determine its ownership in court."

Norma grasped his hands and gazed intently into his eyes. "The trail begins in Venice. You must go there first."

"Venice? I thought I was to start in London."

"No. The first bank is in Venice. That's where Arthur went. And then someone went to London." Then Norma was off again. Her features clouded over as she slumped back in the chair.

"Norma!" He shook her shoulder as gently as possible. "Are you sure about Venice?"

With distant eyes, she looked over his shoulder. "You must beware. They are getting closer now, Harry. Many wait on the path for you to stumble."

He grasped her hand. "What the hell? Norma, you must tell me who else there is."

Norma closed her eyes and bowed her head.

Damn! It's as if she's speaking in tongues, he thought.

As her breathing slowed, she began to give little snorts and whistles.

Harry could never predict Norma's trips into madness. *Where* did she go, he wondered? And what might bring her back?

At last, she spoke in a distant monotone. "Harry, you must not be fooled by Hawke. Such a charmer! He may seem safe, but he is deceptive and not to be trusted. He has no honor and will steal from me." She blinked her eyes hard, as if trying to recollect something. "Arthur always said the puzzle was in two pieces. The first piece is in Venice. At least that's where the money is. Only paper is in the box in London."

"So the numbers you gave me are definitely for bank accounts in Venice?"

"They must be...." Her voice trailed off as her eyes darkened. "Puzzle pieces fitting together," she said with finality. "It's all so long ago, and Arthur was too clever by half."

"Where is the key to the box in London?"

"At the bank in Venice." Her chin slumped onto her chest, and she began to snore gently.

Harry knew he could open the box, even if the key were lost, provided he could prove entitlement.

He patted her hand to rouse her. "Whose name is on the box, Norma?"

"Why Arthur's and mine, of course. On both boxes." She smiled at him vacantly.

Harry rose to go. He reviewed the documentation he would need—Arthur's death certificate, the court probate of his will naming Norma his executrix, and the order appointing himself as her guardian. Such a neat paper trail established his authority over Norma's millions, but it also led to a potentially dangerous showdown with Hawke. While Norma's instructions were not binding on him, he would be foolish to ignore her warnings. Although Hawke's offer had its attractions, Harry knew he could never trust him. He sighed, knowing he would get nothing more from Norma.

As he packed up his case, a tap came at the door. A nurse entered and closed the door softly behind her. "Mr. Jenkins, I'm so glad to see you." She moved swiftly to Norma and took her hand. "Her great-nephew came to visit last night."

"Great-nephew? But she doesn't have one."

"He introduced himself as John, and Mrs. Dinnick asked, *Betsy's John?*"

Harry looked heavenward. "She must have been hallucinating. She never had any brothers or sisters. No children, either."

The nurse looked uncertain. "Well, whoever he was, Mr. Jenkins, Mrs. Dinnick bit him."

"What?"

"Yes, she bit right into his hand." Perplexed, she shook her head. "She's never done anything like that before. I've let the doctor know, just in case it's her medications."

"Did you actually see her bite him?"

"No. But I saw the teeth marks. The cut was bleeding and when I offered to bandage it, he started swearing. Quite a frightening man!"

"What did he look like?"

The nurse paused. "He was tall and quite heavy. In his late twenties, I think. One of those big, bodybuilder types."

"You didn't get his name?"

"No, he ran out." Frowning, the nurse shook her head. "But it's odd. Once he'd left, Mrs. Dinnick said he was Betsy's son, John, and that he needed money."

Harry closed his eyes and sighed. Likely, one of Hawke's men had come to bully information out of her. But he had to chuckle at the thought of Norma's biting him.

At the door, he said, "I'll tell them at the desk not to let any visitors in. Please call me if he returns, or if she has *any* other visitors."

All the wheelchair people had disappeared from the corridor. Harry hurried to his car, afraid he might meet the man with his cigarettes. Madness indeed blotted out the borders of normalcy.

Driving back into the city, Harry could not shake the sense that Norma knew far more than she had let on. But how much was reality and how much paranoia? Her recollections, like stars in the cosmos, were crystal clear one moment, and simply gone from sight the next. She and Arthur had outsmarted a lot of very dangerous and angry people. *And so,* he thought, *many people wait on the path for me to stumble.* Beware of Robert Hawke, Mrs. Deal and now Betsy's John, probably Mr. Deal. Legions must lie in wait.

When he marched into his office, he collided with Miss Giveny. Pink phone messages fluttered in the air. He stooped to retrieve them for her.

"Now I've got to change all my travel plans!" he grumbled.

"Good thing you're back. There've been some important calls for...."

His look silenced her. "Do you mind?" He tossed his airplane ticket on the desk. "Get the travel agent on the phone. Please. Cancel Saturday's flight to London, and book something else to Venice."

"Venice?"

Harry stiffened. "Yes. Venice."

Miss Giveny rose with the dignity she employed when most angry. "Certainly, Mr. Jenkins. I'll attend to it right away."

Suddenly, his cloud of fussing lifted. He stopped and smiled. What was wrong with Venice? Mentally, his destination for the past week had been London, but he'd been there many times. Venice was something new. Visions of ancient pink and gold palazzos on dark canals floated before him.

Five minutes later, he snatched up the receiver. "Miss Giveny? Get the agent to find me a place to stay, will you?"

"You're booked into the Bellini."

"Oh." Harry was pleased. "Is it central?"

"Right on the Grand Canal, next to the train station."

"Excellent. And thank you!"

Maybe I can convince Natasha to come to Venice with me. Much more romantic!

He called her. Not at the office, on her cell, nor at home. He left voice mails everywhere.

As he was heading for the kitchen to find some coffee, the reception door swung open. Harry turned to see Dr. Hawke.

"Sir?" Harry shook his out stretched hand. "What can I do for you?"

"My dear boy," began Hawke. "I just dropped in for a progress report."

Harry guided him down the hallway to the library and closed the door.

"I said I'd call you once I'd seen Mrs. Dinnick."

"I know. That's why I'm here. I decided to save you the trouble of phoning."

Harry sat down heavily. "How did you know I'd been to see her?"

Hawke smiled benignly. "It came to my attention."

"How?"

"My personal assistant, Mrs. Deal, knows the head nurse at the Mercer. You've met Mrs. Deal, haven't you, Harry? Lovely woman, isn't she? I think you'd like her if you got to know her."

Harry unbuttoned his jacket and sank further into his chair.

"Aren't you going to offer me a drink? Coffee, at the very least?"

Harry rang for Sarah. Moments later, she arrived with two coffee cups.

"Yes, I delivered your message to Mrs. Dinnick."

"And?" The doctor's eyes flickered, as he tasted his coffee.

"Who is John—Betsy's John?"

"Pardon?"

"Someone using the name John visited Mrs. Dinnick last night."

Hawke smiled benignly. "I'm sure your client has many visitors. Perhaps of the imaginary variety?"

"He certainly was not imaginary. The nurse saw him and told me about the visit."

The doctor shrugged. "I have no idea...."

Harry smiled broadly. "Well, sir, whoever he was, Norma bit him."

"You think that is amusing?"

"It was certainly deserved. Apparently, he was there demanding money."

Hawke shook his head sadly. "Terrible places, these nursing homes. Someone is always stealing from the inmates."

"Anyway," Harry continued, "Mrs. Dinnick remembers you, or she thinks she does."

Hawke's smiled slightly. "I am very glad to hear that, in her delirium, she has not forgotten me."

"She says you, Pappas, and Archie acquired the money by fraud."

Hawke chuckled. "Dear boy, that money was raised for medical research."

"According to Norma, there was no charitable intent whatsoever."

To Harry, the man's eyes seemed to shift their focus. His voice grew harsh. "If she believes such nonsense, then she is no more entitled than I." More quietly, he said, "We seem to have a problem, Harry."

"We have a difference of opinion, sir."

Hawke sat in silence, measuring the extent of his opposition. Harry remained still.

"I understand access to the Mercer is shockingly easy, Harry," Hawke said softly.

"Are you threatening my client? Surely not John again?"

"Of course not, dear boy." Hawke's hands fluttered upward, and he sighed. "You see, Harry, you do not quite understand that we are unwilling partners in this mess." Hawke's soft lips twitched. "On the one hand, Mrs. Dinnick is overcome with greed. She wants the money all for herself." He shook his head in wonder. "How she can need it cooped up in an asylum, I cannot fathom." He shrugged and held out his hands in an expansive gesture. "On the other, my pharmaceutical company desperately needs the funds, which were raised for research."

"Dr. Hawke, I'm bound to protect Mrs. Dinnick and her interests."

"Did you deliver my offer to join forces to find the shares?"

"Yes, and she was noncommittal."

The doctor's face darkened. "I am quite sure that your appointment as her guardian allows you to decide such matters without her consent. After all, having been committed, she can scarcely be expected to make rational decisions about such important matters."

"I'm bound by the terms of the court order, which require me to seek her instructions."

Hawke touched his arm lightly. "I'm sure you have discretion to act, Harry," he said genially.

Instinctively, Harry recoiled. Of course, he had discretion to decide whether to join forces. *But not with a snake!*

Turning to go, the little man waved cheerily at the door. "Take a day or so to think about it, Harry."

CHAPTER 12

▼

The police laughed at me! Dorothy silently screamed. Armed with Richard's diaries and Armand's description of the angry husband, she had expected to be taken seriously, but Sergeant Welkom's ugly, smirking face mocked her. In patronizing tones, he suggested she talk to her minister, relatives, or friends. In other words, anyone besides the police. *He thought I was crazy!* she raged. Then, all over again, she despised Richard. She pulled open the door to Eaton's Department Store.

Once inside, she breathed more easily, finding calm and purpose in the cosmetics and jewelry departments. With every kind of lotion and mask, she had tried for years to make herself attractive or at least *presentable*. But why? Richard had never taken notice. The worn down lines could be covered, but she could never disguise the yawning cavern of emptiness within.

She moved on to the jewelry counter, where the clerk displayed watches for her, each one encased in rows of diamonds. Finally, she chose the most expensive one and rang it up on the charge card. The clerk wrapped it in a small gold box, and she, without another thought, dropped it into her purse. Next, she purchased a slip in the lingerie department and some butter tarts in the food court in the basement. The clock over the subway entrance read almost four. She crossed the street and entered the Arcade for the Tea Room.

Posters for the Caribbean, in a travel agent's office, caught her eye. She hated Christmas and now, with Richard gone, maybe she should take a trip. Then she remembered last winter, when he had left her alone.

"What shall I do when you're gone?" she had asked as she finished packing his case.

"Whatever you wish." He turned to study himself in the mirror. "There's plenty of money in the account. Draw on it as you like."

Wearily, she sat down on the bed.

"Have your sister visit, if you're lonely," he suggested.

"But where are you going?" She trembled under his stare.

"Down south on business. I have to investigate a tax haven for a client."

Richard had trained her that secrecy was essential in all his business affairs. *Solicitor client privilege is a fundamental principle of law,* he had always insisted. How typical of him to hide his lechery behind a facade of legal ethics!

Sometimes, she felt adrift on frightening and unfamiliar waters, unable to decide even the simplest matters.

"Should the shrubbery be cut back?" the gardener had asked that morning. She did not know how to answer him. When she botched up the premiums on the house insurance, the agent had to straighten out the mess. Richard's most wretched legacy was her all-pervasive sense of incompetence. Secretly, she was becoming relieved at the absence of his hectoring presence. But worst of all, for several nights, she had awakened to the sound of a crying baby.

In the dwindling light of the Arcade, she was struck with a thought. *Perhaps he went down south with Q.* If so, he might have used this travel agency, which was close to the office. She pulled open the door.

"Excuse me, sir?"

"Ya?" the young man mumbled, scarcely tearing his eyes from the computer screen.

"I'm hoping you can help me."

Tapping his keys, he asked, "Where d'you want to go?"

"Nowhere," she replied.

The man frowned and bit his nail.

"At least not yet. I'm looking for information."

"Where you *thinking* of going?"

"Down south."

The travel agent rumpled his hair. "In June?"

"No. At Christmas." She sat down wearily. "Do you know any good tax havens, young man?"

"What? I'm no lawyer, ma'am."

Dorothy sighed, "I'll come straight to the point. I think my deceased husband might have booked a trip through your office. He went down south in February last year."

"So?" The young man looked bored.

"I want to know where and with whom he went."

"Listen, lady, that information is confidential."

Although she had no idea what constituted a sufficient bribe, Dorothy took out one hundred dollars from her purse.

The man eyed the money. "What's your husband's name?"

"Richard Crawford."

He held out his hand. "For that," he said holding out his hand, "I'll look it up. But you gotta understand, there's no guarantee."

Dorothy handed him the bills, which he stuffed in his pocket. Peering intently at the computer screen, he tapped on the keys. After several clicks, he shook his head. "Nah! Nothing here, Mrs. Crawford. He didn't book anything through us."

"I could be wrong on the dates," she said faintly.

His eyes narrowed. "I could do a general search, if you want."

"Yes, please."

"But that'll cost you more."

"How much?"

"Fifty."

When she counted out the money, the travel agent shot forward in his chair and furiously tapped the keys.

"Here we are! Crawford, Richard. One ticket to Nassau, February 21."

"Only one?" she asked weakly.

"Ya. Just one, lady. You can look if you want." He turned the computer screen around.

Dorothy, about to cry, shook her head. Quickly, she gathered up her purse and hurried from the shop, back into the Arcade.

One hundred and fifty dollars gone for nothing, except the knowledge that Richard might have been telling the truth. Now she had only fifty dollars left for Armand. From a nearby bank machine, she withdrew another two hundred dollars, in case he should need help in remembering.

Pulling open the Tea Room door, she stepped inside. A waiter appeared at her side.

"Tea, madam?"

"Is Armand here?"

"No, madam, he just left."

Dorothy began to sink. Alarmed, the waiter caught her elbow.

"It's very important I speak to Armand immediately," she insisted. "It's a matter involving family."

The waiter's eyebrows shot up. "His wife has not taken a turn for the worse, I hope?"

Unable to comprehend, Dorothy shook her head. "Please, tell me if he's coming back," she begged.

The waiter did not wish a scene. "No, he finished his shift." To him, the woman seemed very distraught. He lowered his voice. "I will tell you where he is, but you must not tell his wife."

Wondering what secrets Armand kept, she nodded.

"He stops in at the bar before going home. It's called the Billingsgate, just down the next hallway."

Dorothy quickly found the Billingsgate, but she hesitated before entering. She had never been inside a bar, except once, in London. Several men burst from the door, almost knocking her down. With great solicitude, they steadied her and then went on their way.

Inside, it was dark and noisy. Immediately, the bartender spotted her tiny, lonely figure. "May I help you?" he asked.

"I'm looking for Armand. He works in the Tea Room."

"Armand!" the bartender called out above the noise. "Lady here to see you."

At the back, Armand, tall and gaunt, rose from a table to make his way to the bar.

"My dear Mrs. Crawford! What are you doing here?"

Dorothy immediately regretted intruding on his privacy. But she grasped his hands and said, "Armand? Please, I must talk with you!"

As he took her arm, the crowd opened and made way for them.

Armand asked. "Would you join me in a drink, Mrs. Crawford?"

"Yes." She did not want a drink, but it seemed rude to decline. "I'll have a...." She stopped to think for a moment. "Sherry. Yes, thank you, a sherry."

When the drinks arrived, Armand said, with a lopsided smile, "So, you have learned of my guilty pleasures, Mrs. Crawford."

She was embarrassed. "I didn't mean to invade your privacy."

He shrugged. "You are very upset. How may I help?"

"About my husband, Armand."

"What more can I tell you? Mr. Crawford was a very good customer. Always a gentleman."

"How often did he come in?"

Armand sat back, focused in recollection. "Perhaps two, maybe three times a week."

"Was he always with someone?"

"Usually, but sometimes he came alone." Armand smiled slowly. "I think on those occasions, he really was expecting someone, who failed to show up."

"Did he see anyone in particular, more often than others?" Dorothy reached for her handbag.

"It is embarrassing to say, but your husband had quite an extensive group of ladies."

Dorothy withdrew one hundred dollars from her wallet and spread the money on the table.

Armand's face darkened. "Mrs. Crawford, you should not display money in public."

Unaware of the protocol of bribery, Dorothy was flustered. "It's for you Armand. To help you remember."

Armand's twirled the stem of his glass between his fingers. "Put it away," he said quietly. "I will not take your money. I will tell you whatever I can remember."

She touched his arm. "I am *so* sorry if I've offended you, Armand. Please tell me anything you can."

For a moment, he stared at the ceiling. "You will recall I spoke of a man and a woman and an argument. That woman had been in the Tea Room many times before with just your husband. They seemed quite—how shall I put it—intimate and friendly? But frequently, they seemed to be silently arguing. You understand me?"

Dorothy nodded. "What did she look like?"

"She was not a large woman. She had a small, round, almost childlike face." Armand searched carefully for the right words. "Not childlike. Innocent—and conniving—all at the same time." Armand seemed abstracted. "I never believed her for a moment. She was no innocent. Underneath was a streak of guile and deception." Armand nodded in satisfaction with his description. "Like a spider—waiting."

"A spider waiting?" Trying to picture such a person, she shook her head. "Did he use her name?"

Again the waiter studied the ceiling. Then he snapped his fingers. "Yes, he called her Queenie."

Dorothy burst into tears. A tiny piece of information had fallen into place.

Armand was alarmed. "What has so distressed you, Mrs. Crawford?"

Despite his attempts at comfort, she continued to weep openly in the bar. She rested her head on his shoulder.

"Please, madam. Try to collect yourself. I was only providing the information you requested. Now I have upset you."

"It's not that," she sniffled into his collar.

He held her away from him and looked into her eyes. "Then what is it?"

His tenderness made her sob even more. Something was sliding away inside her. It was too hard to be brave without Richard. "Everything! He's left me so alone." She held a napkin to her nose raw with sniffles. "I ... oh, Armand! I just don't know how to live anymore."

Armand patted her arm gently and broke away. "I am calling you a cab to take you home. I will escort you to the street. Come, please."

He rose and held out his arm for her. Together, they left the bar. Once outside, Armand hastily found a taxi and deposited his charge into it. As she waved good-bye, he thought her a very sad lady.

In the cab, she could not escape Armand's vivid image of the spider waiting, which had assumed gross proportions in her mind.

How can I defeat this spider, who poisoned Richard? I'm not clever enough, not fast enough to catch her. All trickery and deceit! I cannot.... She drifted off for a few minutes.

Home at last, Dorothy realized she had not eaten since breakfast. In the kitchen, she made a sandwich and ate at the table overlooking the garden. She shivered at the disgusting, wild profusion of weeds poking through the flagstones. *How many spiders are creeping in the underbrush waiting to bite—to poison?*

Although she only nibbled on the edges of her sandwich, the food seemed to stick in her throat. Maybe she had cancer. She hoped it was the quick, inoperable kind that would be over in a matter of weeks. She drank some juice, but still the food stuck in her throat. Leaving most of the sandwich on the plate, she started upstairs.

The last rays of evening sun filtered through the windows as she climbed slowly upwards to the bedrooms above. At the top of the stairs, she heard the baby crying again. Cocking her head, she strained to listen. Now, it was more like a whimper. Opening the spare bedroom door, she saw the room just as it had always been: the old double bed with the patchwork quilt, the chintz curtains. Suddenly, she listed to one side but reached out for the doorknob. Her left leg dragged, but then, she righted herself. The cry was coming from the closet, but when she opened the door a crack, she saw nothing but a few old dresses on hangers. Then from behind her she heard a giggle, more like cooing, chortling, happy sound.

In the middle of the room, Dorothy cried out, "Please, come out, wherever you are!" She startled when a shadow passed above the dresser, but then she laughed. It was only herself in the mirror. *The baby has gone back to sleep*, she thought. *But whose baby? Marjorie Deighton's? The golden-haired child? Or mine, which disappeared in a torrent of red?*

With tears and laughter, she drifted into the bathroom. She almost hoped to hear Richard's hectoring voice *You always get confused over the simplest things. Why can't you be more ...?* And on and on. Smiling in the mirror, she opened the medicine chest.

Taking the bottle of little, pink sleeping pills and a glass of water, she returned to her own room and sat on the bed. There were more than enough pills to do the job. But what if they didn't?

Her once furious determination to find *Q* was remote as a childhood memory. At last, she succumbed to the golden-haired daughter, letting her laugh and dance in her mind. She had never felt colder.

In the fading light, she picked up the glass of water and swallowed six pills at once. It would be like falling into the deepest sleep of her life. Forever. She lowered her head to the pillow and waited.

Richard's photograph stared accusingly at her from the dresser. Her eyelids drooped. No wonder women succumbed to such a handsome, domineering man. Armand's face floated before her, to be replaced by a black spider with extraordinarily long, wavering legs. She could hear Richard's voice calling her Queenie. *Underneath was a streak of guile and deception, like a spider.* The perfect challenge for Richard. She felt herself sucked downward into darkness. Her eyes flew open, and she struggled to sit up. She *had* to find Queenie. Sliding from the bed, she stumbled to the bathroom.

Dear God! Don't let me die, she whispered. *Not yet.* Over the toilet, she stuck her finger down her throat and retched. The poison was gone.

The knocker crashed against the front door. Pulling her robe about her, Dorothy rushed down the front stairs to answer it. Before her stood Mrs. Boyd, the next-door neighbor. Dorothy could not understand why the cursed woman looked at her so strangely. Then she realized she was still clutching the empty bottle of pills.

"Mrs. Crawford, are you all right?"

Nosy woman! Dorothy stuffed the pill bottle in her pocket.

"I brought over some mail. The postman—he's new—delivered it to my place." Uninvited, Mrs. Boyd stepped into the front hall. "Now, I know, dear, you're just settling back in after all your travels, but I baked some muffins for you." Mrs. Boyd produced a brown paper bag. "I'll just come in and make some tea for you."

Horrified, Dorothy watched Mrs. Boyd march through the dining room and into the kitchen. She called out cheerily, "I hope you're eating, dear."

Damn the woman, thought Dorothy, but she was too weak to stop her. She trailed into the kitchen and slumped into a chair. Without thinking, she set the pill bottle on the table.

There appeared to Dorothy to be two Mrs. Boyds floating about her kitchen, looking for tea things and mouthing words in a strange language. Dorothy's head swam and she decided, after much thought, that the pills must still be affecting her.

Her face darkening, Mrs. Boyd snatched up the pill bottle. "Dear, you haven't taken too many of these, have you?" she asked carefully.

"Only enough to do the job." Dorothy said sweetly.

Mrs. Boyd gasped. "The Bible says it is a mortal sin!"

"What good has the Bible ever done me?" whispered Dorothy. "If I can't find the killer, I want to die." Dorothy would have teetered from the chair, had Mrs. Boyd not righted her.

"You're talking utter nonsense, Mrs. Crawford," she said sternly, as she phoned for the ambulance.

Drained of color, Dorothy leaned back against the wall. Within five minutes, the paramedics crowded into Dorothy's tiny kitchen. Quickly, they set up the intravenous and placed the oxygen mask over her face.

"Any next of kin?" asked one of the men.

Mrs. Boyd shook her head. "Not that I know of. Her husband just died." She found a listing for Harold Jenkins, Barrister and Solicitor, and gave it to the paramedics. She shook her head as they loaded Dorothy into the ambulance. *Suicide is a mortal sin!*

CHAPTER 13

▼

"Phil? I need to see you as soon as possible." Dr. Michael O'Hearn breathed heavily into the telephone. "Is now okay?"

"Not the best time, really." Philip Glasser glanced at his book. "I can see you around one."

"Not any sooner?"

Glasser pulled on his goatee. Michael was a brilliant research scientist, but he bulldozed through life as if every person were an obstacle. "All right, come down now."

Philip had received calls from four board members: Kilbarry, Stanhope, Junger, and Swan, all outraged at Michael's incessant demands to know why his presentation had been postponed. His junior could destroy a promising career if he didn't acquire some diplomacy. Although he might be on to something about the Hawke Institute, there was nothing concrete.

Michael's knock shook the glass window of his door.

"Please come in, Michael." The scowl on Michael's face surprised even Philip, who was used to his sense of drama. "Pull up a chair."

Michael dragged a metal stool toward the desk, but remained standing. "Phil, I'm sure someone was trying to suppress my report to the board."

Glasser held up his hand. "Just a minute! It could have been a legitimate mix-up."

Michael perched on the stool. His trouser leg flapped as he nervously jogged his leg. "Somebody telephoned me at one-thirty on Thursday afternoon saying the board couldn't meet until the morning. Then I find out the decision's already been made." Michael threw his hands up. "What else should I think?"

"Who called?"

"Some woman from the administration office."

"She said so?"

Michael paused to reflect. "Yes, she did."

"You didn't check?"

"Why should I? If word comes from Tasker's office, you follow it."

Philip stretched back in his chair. "I think it's an administrative screw up, not some dark plot."

Michael looked disgusted. "You know I'm no paranoid, Phil. It just seems so convenient."

Glasser shrugged. "Michael, you can't go off half-cocked like this! You've got a promising career ahead of you, but…."

"I *had* hoped for your support."

Phil held up his hand. "Okay! The real issue is the validity of the research."

"You saw my report. At best, the work is in its most preliminary stages. There's not enough data to conclude much of anything."

"Aren't we supposed to determine its validity? Partners in the research?"

"That's not what I'm hearing."

Glasser removed his glasses and set to polishing them. "What are you hearing, then?"

"Hawke wants complete control of the clinical trials, beginning to end." Michael rose to pace. "We're just to sit by and, at the end, give our stamp of approval."

"Then, why bother with the Queen Mary at all?"

Shoving his hands in his pockets, Michael marched in front of the desk. "We give them a legitimacy they wouldn't otherwise have. We approve of everything, regardless. They ride on our reputation, and we get the money for the geriatric wing and a percentage of the profits from the sale of the drug."

"What? Who said that?"

"Bradgate, the junior on the board."

"That kind of deal wouldn't be in the Board minutes. How does Bradgate know?"

Biting his lip, Michael straddled the stool. "He says he overheard Hawke and Tasker in private conversation."

For Glasser, one piece of the fantastic story rang true. The very political Dr. Tasker was not above making a deal for his own aggrandizement. But Michael, with his zeal, could have misinterpreted the situation—especially with second hand information. "You have to be extremely careful, Michael. You can't accuse Tasker or anyone else of anything, unless you can prove it."

"Well, that's what Bradgate said."

Philip reached for the phone.

"What are you doing?"

"Setting a meeting with Bradgate, of course."

"Really?" Michael was pleased.

There was a tap at the door.

"Come in." Glasser set down the receiver.

A man in jeans and a black tee shirt, with a courier bag slung over his shoulder, stepped into the lab. "Is Dr. Glasser here?"

Philip rose. "Yes, I'm Dr. Glasser. Something for me?"

"Do you have any identification, sir?" The courier smiled tentatively.

Glasser handed him his card and signed the weigh-bill. "Great name for a courier company," said Philip, gesturing at the lettering across the man's tee shirt, which read: *As The Crow Flies Courier*. "But, you're not the usual delivery service for the hospital."

The man nodded and quickly backed out of the room.

"Must be the lab studies I ordered from Atlanta," he mumbled as he returned to his desk. "Just a second, Michael. I'll take a quick look."

Philip put his reading glasses on and began to open the envelope.

First came a brilliant flash of searing heat, and then the detonation. It rocked the desk and blew Philip against the wall and Michael onto the floor. Flames shot upward, and Philip's screams filled the room.

"My hand! Oh, God, my hand!" shrieked Glasser, writhing on the floor.

Michael vaulted across the room. The hand spurted blood. Michael tore the sleeve off a lab coat and applied a tourniquet. He hit the emergency button. Glasser began to shake.

Paramedics were in lab within minutes and put him on a stretcher. With the doctor's cries echoing along endless tiled corridors, they raced to the emergency department. Quickly, Doctor Glasser was anesthetized.

Michael rushed back to the lab. He found the tips of two of Philip's fingers on the far side of the room, blown almost beyond recognition. The courier envelope and its contents were now charred ruins, but he managed to write down the return address. Coughing in the acrid smoke, he called 911. The police found him seated in the middle of the room on the small metal stool staring at the devastation.

His thoughts were so scattered he could scarcely speak. He handed them the remains of the envelope. After several moments, he managed to give a relatively coherent report to the officers. At last, he said, "The name of the courier company is *As The Crow Flies.* I never heard of them before." Michael knew he was still in shock and said nothing of his suspicions.

CHAPTER 14

▼

Harry drank black coffee and juice at his kitchen counter. Since the divorce from Laura almost a year ago, he could not concentrate on domestic matters sufficiently even to prepare a real breakfast. He tossed the remains of his toast in the garbage. He had moved downtown after she left just to get away from the myriad reminders of her and their marriage. Still, he found the silence of the new house oppressive. He longed to shout, just to make some human noise.

Not long ago, he had asked Natasha about living together. *Let's not rush,* she had said. He was trying to give her all the time she needed. The telephone rang.

"Mr. Jenkins?" The voice sounded officious.

"Yes, speaking."

"This is Abigail Forrester at the Queen Mary Hospital. We've admitted a patient last night, Dorothy Crawford."

"Oh ... oh. What's the trouble?"

The woman hesitated. "Could you meet with her doctor this morning?"

Harry checked his watch. "Yes. What time?"

"Say around ten. Dr. Winter will be doing rounds then."

"But what's the trouble?" Harry asked again.

"I'd rather you discussed that with Dr. Winter. We're calling you because you're the only contact we have for her."

How sad, thought Harry, hanging up the phone. *To whom does one turn in old age?* Wiping the crumbs from the counter, he warmed in the sunlight illuminating his garden and in thoughts of Natasha. He tried to visualize her years from now. As she grew in grace, her beauty would shine all the more brilliantly. Consumed by his need for her, he prayed they would be together forever, both in health and in sickness.

To reach the Queen Mary, Harry drove along Harbord Street, which ran through the center of the University of Toronto. Soccer players in blue and gold uniforms dotted the back playing field of University College. Memory was strangely seductive and intensely poignant. Instantly, he could place himself in the very moment, twenty-five years ago, talking with Laura underneath the stone arch of the Hart House Chapel. He could see her squinting up at him in the sun as he bent to kiss her.

In memory, it was only a moment ago. Day by day, time seemed so arbitrary and demanding yet, in an instant, he could erase those years dividing him from the past. And now, Natasha inhabited his being, and he knew he would always carry her within him, on into the future. Perhaps, when all moments—past, present, and future—came together, that was eternity.

Soon he was circling Queen's Park Crescent to reach University Avenue, where the hospitals stood row upon row. The Queen Mary was the largest and oldest hospital in the city. As

Harry drew into the parking lot, he saw a large, new sign. *Future Site of the Hawke-Tasker Geriatric Wing.*

Good grief, he thought. Hawke had wasted no time with the board. Puzzled, he could not recall where he had heard the name Tasker.

Dorothy was on the fifth floor of the south wing. White-coated doctors, with interns in tow, whisked along the main corridor and passed in and out of patients' rooms.

"I'm looking for Dr. Winter and Mrs. Dorothy Crawford," Harry announced to group of nurses at the desk.

"Dr. Winter is on rounds," said a woman without looking up, "and Mrs. Crawford is in 403 down the hall on your right."

Harry knew better than to interrupt doctors on rounds. Obediently, he headed for Dorothy's room. Upon entering, Harry blinked in the dim light. There lay Richard Crawford's widow, in a tiny, bird-like heap on the bed.

"Dorothy?" Touching her shoulder, he spoke close to her ear. She stirred as if from the deepest realms of sleep. "Dorothy? It's Harry Jenkins. The hospital called and asked me to come."

"Harry?" she murmured, still disoriented. After a poor night's sleep she recalled only dreams infested with spiders.

"Yes. What's wrong?" He was pleased to see she could shift herself onto her back No broken bones.

She smiled weakly. "I've had a bit of an accident, Harry." She struggled to hold her eyes open. "By accident, I mean I took too many pills."

"What kind?"

"Sleeping pills."

"How did that happen?" Harry sat on the edge of the bed and took her hand.

"It wasn't exactly an accident. But, partway through, I changed my mind." She regarded him sleepily. "You see, after I took the pills, I realized I had a *real* reason to live."

"I'm glad of that!"

She squeezed his hand slightly. "Richard was murdered. I have to find his killer."

"Any more thoughts on who might have poisoned him?"

"Actually, Harry, I *do* have more information now." She spoke so sleepily, Harry feared she might drift off. "You remember Richard wrote in his diary about *Q*?" Harry nodded. "Well, *Q* stands for Queenie, and I have a description." Dorothy closed her eyes in concentration. "She's a small woman with a round, innocent face, but not innocent. From what I've been told, she ought to be called *Queenie, the dissembler.* Like a spider."

"A spider?" Harry tried to picture such a person, without success. "How do you know this?" he asked.

"Armand—he's a waiter at the Tea Room—described her and said Richard called her Queenie."

Dorothy seemed to drift off. Moments passed, but when Harry stood up, she reached for his hand. "Please don't go yet. I'm so alone," she said.

Harry sat on the bed again. "I understand you talked to the police."

Dorothy groaned. "Yes. I met the most awful sergeant. What was his name?"

"Welkom," Harry smiled. "Sergeant Nick Welkom."

Dorothy's eyes flew open. "Yes. That's the one. All he did was laugh at me. Thought I was some batty old lady with nothing to do but make trouble."

"He took you seriously enough to call me."

"He did?" Dorothy sounded pleased.

"I could only tell him what I personally know—that Richard died of a stroke in my office and that you were concerned about poisoning."

Dorothy sighed. "At least you didn't say I was crazy."

Harry chuckled and patted her hand. "Of course not, Dorothy. But what can I do to help now? Seems your doctor wants to speak with me. Is that all right?"

"Yes. Tell him it was an accident. I have to get out and track down Queenie."

"I'll find him and tell him so." Harry rose again to go. He was pleased at her new determination. If suspicions of murder gave her reason to carry on, all the better.

"Harry? Do you think I should hire a private detective?"

"Yes, I think so. If you do decide to, call me and I'll find a good one for you."

Harry found Dr. Winter at the nursing station. He was pleasant and effusive.

"What shall we do with our Mrs. Crawford? You're her lawyer, aren't you?"

"Yes, and actually, her deceased husband was my partner."

"You know her quite well, then?"

"Yes," Harry spoke authoritatively. "She's quite upset. Legitimately so. She thinks, not without reason, that her husband was murdered."

The doctor's eyes widened. "And *you* think?"

"It's obviously not impossible. Before his death, he wrote in his diary that he thought he was being poisoned."

The doctor consulted the chart. "She took an overdose of barbiturates."

"And has thought better of it, since she now has something to live for."

"Which is?"

"To find her husband's murderer. She's already been to the police, and she's thinking of hiring a private detective."

The doctor scribbled down some notes and closed his file. "We'll get a psych consult, Mr. Jenkins. If it turns out as you say, we'll send her home with some follow-up in place."

"Good," said Harry, handing him his card. "And thank you doctor. If you need me, just call."

The two men shook hands and parted.

Harry arrived at his office just before eleven o'clock. On his desk, neatly bundled up, were his airline tickets and confirmation of his hotel booking in Venice. Lounging back in his chair, he clasped his hands behind his neck and smiled. Glimmering blue waters and ancient buildings, golden in the setting sun, floated before his eye. In grade school, his social studies book had contained a dark, mysterious photograph of the Bridge of Sighs, over which were marched those condemned to execution in the yard of the Doge's Palace. From that moment on, Harry had determined to see as much of the world as he could. Funny how little things made huge impressions and stayed with you throughout life. On Saturday night, he would be on his way to Venice.

The telephone interrupted his reverie, which had progressed to floating past Piazza San Marco in a gondola. "Yes?"

"Ms Boretsky on line one."

Harry drew a deep breath of pleasure and pressed the first line.

"Hi, darling," she said. "What are you thinking about at this very moment?"

"Of carrying you off to Venice and ravishing you there."

There was a low chuckle, and then she said, "Venice? I thought you were going to London."

"Change of plans. Want to come?"

"Yes, I *really* do want to, but...."

"What's the problem?" Harry sat up straight and reached for his ticket. Maybe he could book another one.

"When do you leave?"

"Saturday night." Harry held his breath.

"Damn." Natasha's laugh was low and musical. He loved her voice. "I can't get away until Tuesday or Wednesday at the earliest."

"Cancel everything, Natasha," Harry said grandly. "Sweep your calendar clear for us."

Natasha sighed. "You know, Harry, I'd love to, but I am right in the midst of negotiations on a big commercial deal. But, with any luck, it will close on Tuesday. And then, there's Stratford and Sheila." She paused thoughtfully. "But maybe I can do that sometime this weekend."

"Come afterwards. I'll wait for you. *Very* romantic—a tryst in Venice."

She was silent for a moment. Harry prodded. "Probably by then, I'll be finished my work. We'll have some time alone." Immediately, he could visualize Natasha lying naked under a cool sheet in bed with him. A light breeze would stir the curtain to the balcony overlooking the Grand Canal.

"I will *try* my very best, Harry," she said at last. "Where will you be staying?"

"At the Hotel Bellini. I'll get you the number, so we can arrange it."

Silence hung between them. Harry feared a coolness was settling over their conversation. "Natasha?" His voice betrayed his anxiety. "Is that okay?"

"Yes, Harry." Her voice made him sink with desire. "There is no one in the world I would rather meet in Venice. I shall do my very best."

I love you. I want us to marry. It was on the tip of his tongue, but then she was saying good-bye. "When can I see you?"

"Come over Friday night." She sighed. "I've got an important call coming in. Bye." Then she was gone, leaving Harry grinning foolishly into the receiver.

Again, Miss Giveny buzzed. "Courier delivery for you, Mr. Jenkins," said his secretary frostily. The closer he got to his departure date, the more difficult she was becoming.

"Well, have Sarah sign for it at reception."

"The courier insists it must be delivered to you personally."

"What on earth is it?"

"How should I know? Sarah says it's big."

Impatiently, Harry strode from his office to reception. On Sarah's desk, sat a large box, approximately three by four feet. The courier held out the weigh-bill to him for signature.

Harry glanced at his shirt. "Great name for a courier company—*As the Crow Flies!*" Lifting the edge of the box carefully, he asked, "What on earth is in it?"

The courier shrugged and quickly backed out the door.

"Is it heavy, Sarah?"

His receptionist shook her head. "No, Mr. Jenkins. But there's been some funny sounds coming from inside."

"What?" Harry bent to listen. Miss Giveny crowded in.

"Almost like a faint scratching. But I'm not really sure," she said.

"I'll take it to my office and open it." Both Sarah and Miss Giveny followed him down the corridor.

"Look." He set the box on the coffee table. "There are tiny holes all around the top." He began to cut the tape.

Miss Giveny caught his hand. "Be careful! We don't know what's inside."

Sarah backed away. "Maybe it's a bomb, sir."

"What? The box is light as a feather." Harry began to chuckle.

"Letter bombs aren't heavy," Miss Giveny warned.

Harry put his ear to the box. "I do hear a scratching. For God's sake! It's something alive." Swiftly, he cut the tape around the box and pulled back the lid.

Within, he saw a brass cage. "Good Lord!" He tore at the box.

White wings flapped and beat with great strength. The two women shrank back. Harry lifted the cage free of the box.

He stood in open-mouthed amazement.

Biting hard on her knuckle, Miss Giveny stifled a shriek.

"It's a pigeon!" Sarah was aghast. "Who would give you a dirty bird like that?"

At last Harry spoke. "It's not a pigeon, Sarah. It's a dove."

Miss Giveny's voice pitched into a wail. "What are we to do with a bird? Whatever kind it is, it's dirty."

Never taking his eyes from the cage, Harry lowered himself into a chair. "A dove is a symbol of peace," he said quietly. "Sarah, give me the envelope that came with it."

Only one person would think of such a grand gesture. Smiling, Harry slit open the envelope and read,

My Dearest Harry,

I regard you as a most worthy opponent. However, I believe you will agree it is far more expeditious to cooperate in locating the missing funds than to engage in a futile battle. Although Mrs. Dinnick does not believe in the rightness of the Hawke Institute's cause, perhaps you and I, as gentlemen of reason and intelligence, can agree to fight our battle in the courts of law. I sincerely reiterate my offer of joining forces to locate the funds. Please accept this gift as a small token of my great admiration for you. I await your response.

With Sincerest Regards,

Robert Hawke.

"Who sent this filthy thing?" Miss Giveny demanded.

Harry gazed at the dove, which was now puffing and preening its feathers. "Why, our friend, Dr. Robert Hawke, of course."

"What do we do with it?" asked Sarah, quite reasonably.

Harry was at a loss for an answer.

"Send it back," snapped Miss Giveny.

"But it doesn't say where it came from," said Sarah.

Harry laughed. Only now did he consider the practicalities of the situation. "Call some pet store and ask if they want it." He pondered Hawke's letter. Having comprehended what lay behind the gesture, he had to consider the offer carefully. Certainly, Dr. Hawke was desperate to join forces.

Visualizing Hawke's soft face, he could hear his lisping, conciliatory words. Coolly, he debated the dangers of speaking with the doctor. With almost no information to give, Harry considered he would run no great risk. Since he needed whatever help he could get, he hoped he might learn something valuable. He reached for the phone and dialed the King Edward Hotel.

In the suite, Mrs. Deal answered. "He's unavailable at the moment, Mr. Jenkins, but *both* of us are *very* much hoping to meet with you."

Harry flushed slightly at the intimate tone. "Please thank him for the most unusual gift, and ask him if we can meet this evening."

"I *know* the doctor would be delighted if you could join him for dinner in the suite, say, about seven."

"All right. I'll be there." They said good-bye. Harry had hoped for a more neutral and less private setting, but the arrangement would have to do.

Shortly before seven, Harry took the elevator to Hawke's suite. Mrs. Deal greeted him at the door. After pouring him a drink, she settled on the chesterfield beside him. A small, round table of white linen was set for two in the bay window.

While not an especially attractive woman, Mrs. Deal's engaging presence ensured she would be remembered. Her mouth was just slightly too wide, and her nose a trifle long. But her cheekbones were fine, giving her appearance a certain grace.

"I'm sorry if I seem distracted, Mr. Jenkins."

"Harry. Please." He sipped his drink and waited for her to continue.

"We're really very excited here tonight."

Harry's eyebrows rose.

Her voice lowered in a conspiratorial fashion. "We've just had more results from the clinical trials in San Diego."

"Trials?" Harry was trying to concentrate on her words, but she had moved within six inches of him.

"Yes. The ones for Alzheimer's. The most recent reports are very promising."

"Excellent." Harry shifted slightly in his seat and said, "The Institute has high hopes, then, for success at the Queen Mary?"

Smiling broadly, Mrs. Deal nodded.

Harry remembered the sign announcing the construction of the Hawke-Tasker Wing over the parking lot entrance. "Who is Tasker?" he asked.

She looked blankly at him.

"I saw his name in connection with Dr. Hawke's at the hospital," he prodded. "Something to do with building a geriatric wing."

"Oh, yes," Mrs. Deal said vaguely. "He's the chief administrator of the Queen Mary."

"There's money for construction, as well as research?"

"We certainly hope so, Harry." She brushed his hand as she reached for his empty glass. "But money troubles are everywhere. It would be a shame if the research stalled for lack of sufficient funding." Mrs. Deal then nodded toward the door on the far wall. "He works absolutely tirelessly. For him, it's a calling."

"Dr. Hawke is here now?"

She nodded. "Just finishing up a few calls." Taking his glass to refill it, she suddenly asked, "May I ask you a favor, Harry?"

Harry was surprised. "Certainly." He was only being polite.

"Please consider Dr. Hawke's request for help very seriously. He needs as much support as he can get." She continued in worried tones, "I'm afraid he's at the breaking point of exhaustion."

"What do you think *I* can do?"

"He's leading a great cause. If you can assist in any fashion he asks, I implore you to do so."

Harry was surprised at her zeal. For her, Hawke must be the messiah of pharmaceuticals. He simply nodded.

The far door bumped open. Mrs. Deal rose swiftly. Two slippered feet appeared at the door as the wheelchair nosed its way out.

"Good evening, Harry," said Robert warmly. "I'm so pleased we could have this time together."

Harry stood up to shake hands. Only days ago, the man had marched about the St. George's Club like a ringmaster. He took Hawke's hand, offered like a limp and boneless fish.

Hawke looked up expectantly. "So, Harry, you liked my little gift?"

Harry hesitated. "It was most unusual, Dr. Hawke."

"That's all?"

Harry smiled. "The gesture was very impressive."

Robert Hawke chuckled. "I'm glad you think so. Obviously, Harry, I want to set aside our futile disputes."

Hawke spread his hands in a gesture of conciliation. Harry folded his hands and remained silent.

"Mrs. Deal?" said Hawke abruptly. "See to the delivery of the dinner and then leave us, please."

His assistant called for room service, and then turned to him. "It's on its way, Dr. Hawke,"

As she left the room, Hawke reached up and patted her hand. "Thank you, my dear." Then staring at Harry, he continued, "Mr. Jenkins and I will have an interesting conversation."

Within moments, two waiters entered with a trolley. The meal was set out.

"Push me over to the table, will you, Harry?"

Harry obliged, and then took his own seat.

After the waiters served a cold leek and potato soup, Hawke dismissed them. "My friend will look after the rest of the service." The waiters bowed and disappeared.

"Sorry to put you to work, Harry, but I'm sure privacy is important to you as well." Robert dabbed his lips with his napkin. "I'm so glad you liked my little gift. I put a great deal of thought into it."

"It was very clever," Harry conceded.

"I wanted to convey two things. First, the sincere offer of rec-onciliation from one gentleman to another in hopes of forming a bond of cooperation." Harry was about to interrupt, but he was silenced when Hawke raised his hand. "Secondly, to express my deepest and most heartfelt respect and admiration for you."

Harry flushed. He could think of no response.

For a moment, Hawke continued to spoon his soup, then once more dabbed his lips. His fastidiousness fascinated Harry.

"You are a man of integrity, Harry. One doesn't find that much anymore," the doctor said wistfully.

Harry was becoming embarrassed. "Dr. Hawke, why don't we get down to business?"

The doctor looked shocked, as if his dinner companion had seriously breached a rule of etiquette. "Why, Harry, we haven't even gotten to the main course!"

They ate in silence for some moments. Then, Harry rose to remove the soup bowls and set out the main course, which con-sisted of filet mignon and charred vegetables.

"As I was saying, I admire you greatly. You have an energy and reserve which is really quite magnificent." Hawke cut his meat and chewed thoughtfully. "You see, dear boy, I would much rather have you as an ally than an adversary. We are just on the point of a major breakthrough in the treatment of this scourge."

"Alzheimer's, you mean?"

"Yes," breathed Hawke, as if his spirit were escaping.

"And you want me to lead you to the money, so that it may be used to fund your research?"

Hawke reached for the carafe of wine and held it up. "Will you pour, Harry. Just for yourself. I find that wine sometimes interferes with my medication."

Dutifully, Harry filled his glass and took a sip. "Is that the general idea, Dr. Hawke?"

"Of course not, Harry. I'm proposing that we join forces to find the money as expeditiously as possible. Once it is found, I am ready and willing to submit the issues to a court of law."

"In your view, what are the issues?" Harry knew a court application could be so worded as to ensure the outcome.

"My lawyers would work with you in developing the questions. I believe an agreed statement of fact would be appropriate to narrow the issues."

Obviously, thought Harry, *the man has already received legal advice or has had prior litigious experience.* He sat back and sipped his wine. "What facts do you think we agree upon?"

"The initial sum raised. The intent of the consortium...."

"You see, right there, we have a problem...."

Hawke held up his hand. "Of course, there are differences, Harry. And the court is the place to air them. I'm only saying why not get the money first and then argue the merits?"

Harry waited.

"If it would make you more comfortable, you can have it all in writing."

For a second, Harry was moved by the supplication in the doctor's damp eyes.

Harry set aside his plate and leaned forward. "What do you have that I need, Dr. Hawke?"

Hawke smiled slowly. "You are very astute, sir. I understand that Arthur Dinnick hid the money in a very clever fashion. In order to access the actual cash, you must first have something else. I do not know what that is. On the other hand, I have a key for a box. Rather like two pieces of a puzzle."

"Really? You have the key to the box?" Harry was not about to let Hawke think his bargaining chip was not useful. "And what do you think I have that will help?"

"I have only the most fleeting perception of the puzzle. You are privy to Mrs. Dinnick's thoughts. I am not. You have Mrs. Dinnick's legal authority. I do not."

"Unfortunately, due to her condition, she can be little help." Once again Harry sipped his wine. They finished the first course, and when Harry poured the coffee, he felt the room spin for a fraction of a second.

Hawke tossed down his napkin. "Wheel me back to the chesterfield, please."

When they had settled, Harry felt a dull ache at the base of his skull. Faint, yet annoyingly persistent.

"What do you think of my proposition, Harry?" Hawke asked softly. He withdrew a small cigar and commenced to light it.

Harry took a cigarette, but did not light it. "All right, Dr. Hawke. Have your lawyer call me first thing in the morning. I will only agree to look at an agreement. Nothing more."

"Excellent, Harry. I knew you'd see the reasonableness of my proposal."

"Just to look at ..." Harry shook his head. He thought he saw clouds rolling into his line of vision.

"Of course. We are, first and foremost, gentlemen and men of honor," Hawke declared.

The last Harry saw was a smile slowly crossing Hawke's pudgy face. He wondered at the pressure at the back of his neck. Then, all was black. Harry slumped sideways onto the chesterfield. Within moments, Mrs. Deal appeared from the far doorway. Swiftly, she lifted Harry's feet to the cushions and removed his shoes.

"Help me take off his jacket, my dear." Hawke and Mrs. Deal sat Harry up and removed his jacket. As he set the jacket aside, the doctor stroked the fabric appraisingly and then sank to the wheelchair. "Our Mr. Jenkins certainly has good taste." His voice grew hoarse. "Now, loosen his tie and open his shirt to the waist."

Puffing on his cigar, Robert Hawke looked on with pleasure. Then he stood up from the wheelchair and unbuckled Harry's belt and unzipped and loosened his trousers.

Standing back, he said, "Now, when Mr. Jenkins awakes, he will fear he has been violated."

"But why do you want him to think that?"

"His fear is the greatest and most sensitive chink in his armor. Call it a test for my trial of one."

CHAPTER 15

▼

Chez Marcel was a small restaurant near High Park in the west end of Toronto. Veronica Deal preceded her brother, Garth, through the door to see prints on the wall of Parisian streets, bistros, and gardens. She was pleased. In the dim light, she saw the room was small and intimate. Tables, set with white linen and tiny lamps, were close together, making it a perfect spot for eavesdropping. Except for two women at a table against the wall, the room was empty. Brandishing menus, the waiter seated them nearby at the window.

The plan had worked well. Although Veronica thought Garth had taken far too much pleasure in terrorizing Harry Jenkins with his Jeep, he had found out that Harry was seeing Natasha Boretsky. Simple enough to find out Natasha's dinner plans with her friend Erma.

From near the window, Veronica had an excellent view of both women, who were conversing intently over glasses of wine. To hear better, she signaled Garth to remain silent. That suited him fine, and he stared out the window, cracking his knuckles.

Over the top of her menu, Veronica studied the two. The woman closest to her was definitely Natasha. Veronica's appraisal was quick and dispassionate. Natasha's best features were her broadly set, dark eyes, and her mane of glossy hair. Although the makeup was minimal, Veronica appreciated her artistry. Her figure was good, and she knew how to accent it with elegant but subdued clothing. Harry Jenkins certainly had good taste.

The other woman, at least ten years older, was slowly acquiring a sunken appearance, particularly beneath the eyes and the cheekbones. Her black shirt and slacks accentuated her thinness. On both wrists, she wore chunky silver bangles. *An odd pair*, Veronica concluded.

"So how's Sheila these days?" she heard Erma ask.

Natasha leaned forward, elbows on the table. "Angry, I guess," she said with a frown. "That pretty well sums it up."

"About what?"

Natasha's eyes narrowed. "Me … us … everything, it seems. We're arguing all the time. She's possessive. I'm claustrophobic. I'm feeling like the faithless bitch because she wants me to commit to living together, and I simply can't."

Erma sat back. "Wow! You two are on a rocky road."

The waiter approached to take their orders.

"She's *so* manipulative, Erma," said Natasha, twirling her wine glass reflectively. "But I really feel badly for her."

"Tell me about it! People can be manipulative, but only if you let them. Believe me, I *know!* Playing on sympathies is a favorite tactic. The most gorgeous young men arrive at my door and wheedle their way in with all kinds of sad stories. Starving artists, begging for food, drink and a warm bed for just *one* night. Then they camp out forever either in the house or at my studio." Erma sighed. "I have such a penchant for strays." Then she laughed softly and asked, "What's *really* bothering you, Natasha?"

"I've met someone, Erma."

"Male or female?"

"Male. His name is Harry Jenkins."

At her table, Veronica lowered her menu.

"And?" Erma asked.

Natasha gave an elaborate shrug. "It seems I've fallen in love with him." Her tone was serious, but then she could not prevent a broad smile.

"How long have you been seeing Harry?" asked Erma, smiling back. She could see that far away look in her friend's eyes at the sound of his name.

"About a year. It's getting quite serious. We've been talking about living together."

"Sheila knows?"

"Oh, yes. She knows about him, but not the living together part. She met him the other night. And after he'd left, she said that if *that* was the competition, she wasn't worried."

"Well, of course! She's bound to be jealous." Erma stared at her friend. "Does Harry know about her?"

Natasha shook her head. "I don't think he *knows*. At least, I've never told him."

Erma grinned. "Listen, sweetie, some men think it's a turn on."

With a rueful smile, Natasha looked heavenward. "Oh, my God! And some want to join the fun." She sobered. "But, Harry is different...." she said quietly.

Erma smiled. She knew the sounds of a woman *in love*. The waiter placed salads before them.

Veronica could see Natasha's attractiveness to both sexes. *Not unusual*, she thought. For her, it was natural and no great matter. But Robert had a sick fascination with what he coyly termed *duality*. He loved to find the weak points of his victims. Any bit of information might be stored away for some future use. But he remained so secretive about his *trial of one* and plans for Harry Jenkins. Nonetheless, she was obligated to pass this extra information on to him.

"But here's the problem," Natasha continued. "Sheila is demanding that I make up my mind."

"Maybe not such a bad thing?" Erma offered, as she passed the salad dressing.

"She makes me feel like some sort of freak. With her, I end up dividing myself up with a big fence down the middle. One side is for her, and the other for Harry. Then, whichever side I'm on, I feel like I'm betraying one or the other of them. And, Erma, she does think in terms of *sides*."

"That's ridiculous! People aren't like that!"

"I know that, and so do you. But Sheila doesn't."

Erma shook her head sadly. "You shouldn't have to live like that."

"We're driving each other crazy! She thinks she'll win me over to her *side* permanently." Natasha paused to catch her breath. "But to do that, I have to pack a very large part of me up and pretend it doesn't exist. Honestly, Erma, I can't live that way."

"Nor should you have to!" Erma knew how possessive Sheila could be.

"Then she calls me a faithless bitch who can't be true to any-one."

"Honey, you can't let her go on like this. She's doing *real* harm to you."

The waiter came to remove the bowls.

Natasha looked glumly at her picked-over salad and pushed it away. She said, "I can only commit myself to whoever wants the real me, not some torn apart, cut up creature."

"Listen, Natasha. You know you *are* going to have to decide."

"Of course!"

"Is Harry ready for this?"

"That's the problem. He's everything I want in a man and a whole lot more. But I'm worried that he'll think, like Sheila, that I can't be faithful to him."

"Can you?"

"Yes, I can and I think it is time to choose. I just don't know if he can accept all of me … and trust me."

Both of them had ordered veal, which was now set before them. Natasha grew reflective. "But, I do still love her. We've been through so much together, and she was absolutely won-derful about my brother, Josef."

"That was a long time ago, Natasha. Things change: people grow."

Natasha poured more wine. "Damn it, Erma! I just can't help seeing it from her point of view. I really am the faithless bitch, keeping her on tenterhooks."

"She's being very unfair, Natasha. Maybe Harry *really* is the better person for you."

Natasha pushed her food about on her plate. "I suppose, but I can't help seeing she's right in so many ways. I keep thinking of Josef."

Erma sighed. "It was horrible what happened to him."

Natasha shook her head. "True. But what he did in the space of twenty years was amazing, at least to me." Smiling in recollection, she continued. "Did I ever tell you he wrote poetry?" She rushed on, her eyes sparkling. "About things most people never think of. About seeing the divine in a drop of rain or sensing the sublime in another person. He could see and feel how everything is connected." Then, more quietly, she added, "Most people thought he was a little crazy."

Erma nodded sadly. She knew how Josef had died.

"Everybody thought he was just a dreamy kid. But he taught me so much, and he said, "If you ever find that special *thing* in someone, if you ever—even for an instant—find someone who opens your inner eye to meaning, don't let them get away."

"What he *did*, Natasha, was amazing too. He wasn't just a dreamer. Everybody likes to think they'd be brave enough to risk their own life for another, but how many actually would?"

"I know. Everyone thought Josef had his head in the clouds. But in an instant, he sacrificed himself for a complete stranger." Momentarily, Natasha fell silent. "I was with him in the pub that night. When they started beating the other boy, he just leaped on them in a second. And then they dragged him out in the alley and stabbed him to death."

Erma asked: "For you, Harry has this special "thing" or quality, and Sheila doesn't?"

Natasha fiddled with her wine glass and then looked up. "Yes," she said quietly. "It's what Josef was talking about—opening up the inner eye to experience how everything really is connected."

"Sounds like you love the man and feel obligated to Sheila."

Natasha nodded slowly and then spoke, "Well, I do love Sheila, or at least I care deeply about her, but…."

"But it's a different sort of thing with Harry?"

Natasha looked away, trying to catch the right words for her thoughts. "Yes. The first time I actually spoke with him—it was only briefly—was at a funeral, of all places. Funny thing, when I saw him everything, everyone else in the room just seemed to fall away." She shrugged. "I just *knew*. And to this day, it's the same."

"You're very lucky, Natasha. That sounds like the real thing."

"There's only one problem. Sometimes I feel like his fantasy woman. That he doesn't see past all that to a real person with all the usual baggage. And so, can I ever be the real me with him? He has me on a very high pedestal."

"Perhaps you need to climb down and let him see the real you. You've not been exactly forthright with him."

Natasha shrugged. "But who is the *real* me? Sometimes, I feel like two different people. There's the me when I am with Sheila. There's the me when I am with Harry. Until now, it hasn't been too difficult to live in both worlds but…."

Erma wanted to shake her friend. "Wake up, Natasha. You've just said Sheila's made you feel that way. You are *not* a divided soul." Disturbed by Natasha's frame of mind, Erma poured more wine and continued, "Sheila *really* has done a number on you. Keep that kind of thinking up and she'll make you schizophrenic! *All—every bit of you—is the real person.*"

Natasha relaxed and sipped her wine. "I know! I just seem to go around in circles. First, I feel all chopped up, and then I remember that's just Sheila talking in my head."

After the waiter cleared away the plates, they ordered coffee.

"I'm thinking of meeting him in Venice, Erma."

At the other table, Veronica set her fork down and strained to listen.

"Thinking?" asked Erma, open-mouthed. "What's to think about?"

"Harry is going Saturday night. I have a real estate deal to close, but I could get away next Tuesday or Wednesday and meet him there."

Erma sipped her wine. "What does Sheila say?" she asked.

"If you go, don't expect to come back to me."

Erma examined the dessert menu. "That's plain enough. Maybe now is the time…." She paused while the waiter poured the coffee. "Listen, maybe it sounds trite, but you *do* have to go with your heart. You do have to think of what's right for you."

The two women sat quietly for some moments. Erma sympathized with Natasha's predicament. Simply put, that was her nature. Either she chose or worked something out with both of them. *Or,* she ended up alone. Sheila was digging her own grave by forcing Natasha to choose. She knew the depths of her friend's passion.

There was another aspect. Erma knew that Josef had, in a few short years, permanently shaped Natasha's life. Her friend was struggling with two kinds of love standing head to head: passion and compassion. She had *already* chosen Harry. Her real dilemma was how to avoid hurting Sheila.

"But a trip to Venice?" Erma smiled brightly. "Why not? Where would you stay?"

"Harry mentioned the Bellini, right on the Grand Canal."

"Perfect view of all those gondoliers! Sounds *very* romantic."

Veronica motioned to Garth to pay the bill. An excellent evening! Harry Jenkins was off to Venice Saturday night to stay at the Bellini. Robert would be pleased. They rose to go.

Natasha and Erma drank more coffee. "After all," Erma persisted, "Isn't it time you had a little fun in your life?"

Smiling, Natasha said, "I think you're right, Erma."

CHAPTER 16

▼

Back home from hospital, Dorothy was filled with purpose and energy to find the mysterious Queenie. The simplicity of one ad in the Yellow Pages drew her eye: *Samuel T. Baxter, twenty-five years experience in all fields of investigation. Reasonable rates.* She set the appointment for the next day. Dorothy's preconception of a private detective was a big, beefy man, exuding a world-weary cynicism.

When she opened the door next morning, her hand flew up to stifle a tiny cry. An apparition stood before her. Mr. Baxter bore such a close resemblance to Richard that she almost fainted. The puzzled detective entered.

He chose the far end of the dining room table, where her husband used to sit. Almost as small as Richard, he had the same fineness of features, and when he spoke, Dorothy could pretend Richard was still alive.

Samuel T. Baxter took out his pen and notebook. "What service may I provide, madam?" Even his phraseology was courtly, like Richard's.

She decided to enjoy the similarities. "Mr. Baxter, my husband is dead. I have reason to believe he was murdered."

"Have you been to the police, ma'am?"

Tears sprang to her eyes. He gazed at her impassively.

"Yes!" She shook her head in disgust. "But I got absolutely nowhere, Mr. Baxter."

A small sigh escaped the detective. Much of his business depended upon either the indifference or ineptitude of the police. Deciding to get directly to the point, he asked, "Why do you think your husband was murdered?"

"It's all here." She pushed the diaries across the polished table. "Before he died, he wrote in his diary about visits to somebody called *Q*. Every time he went there, he was sick. He thought she was poisoning him."

The little pile of dog-eared books did not look impressive to Mr. Baxter, but he opened them and placed his reading glasses on the tip of his nose. With great care, he ran his finger down each page. Dorothy waited ten minutes in silence for his verdict. At last, Samuel Baxter removed his glasses and put them in his breast pocket. He regarded her with pale, dispassionate eyes, which she mistook for kindness.

"Is that everything you have?" asked Baxter, who liked tidy bundles. He had the soul of a bookkeeper, not an investigator.

Dorothy gaped open-mouthed at him. "No, Mr. Baxter, there is much more! Armand—he works in the Tea Room downtown—says my husband frequently came in with a woman called *Q*."

The detective's eyes flickered with interest. "You're husband was seeing other women?"

The question hung in the dining room. Foolishly, Dorothy wished Richard were there to defend himself. *Or Harry should be handling this*, she thought.

She scarcely recognized her own voice. "Yes, my husband, Richard Crawford, was a notorious philanderer!" She was shocked. Never had she said such a thing out loud. Through her tears, she plunged on. "I always thought he'd had a few affairs, but when he died, I found that he had strings of women." She almost choked. "And the worst is, he had a child … a daughter … a bastard child, and I had none!"

Sam Baxter's eyebrows curved upward. "If he was murdered, madam, perhaps it was by an angry husband."

Dorothy grew livid. "But Richard is accusing this woman *Q*." She snatched the diaries back. "It's right here, in February and March."

Baxter hated unpleasantries, but he forged ahead. "I believe, madam, that he mentions you in his diaries as a potential…."

"He was completely mad! I was loyal to him throughout forty years of marriage."

The detective retreated. "Of course, Mrs. Crawford. Fear can cloud a man's mind. I'm only suggesting that we not limit ourselves to looking for a woman."

In surprise, she said, "Then you believe me?"

"You do have *some* evidence," Baxter said grudgingly. A bloodless sort, he did not understand the rage of passion in the human breast. He feared unaccountable forces drove Mrs. Crawford. "But you do need a great deal more," he concluded.

"More? Yes, Mr. Baxter. I can give you more," she cried out.

"Yes?" he asked mildly. Her zeal was beginning to disturb him.

"I asked Harry Jenkins for all the files beginning with Q, which my husband opened in the last year."

"Who is he?" The detective readied himself to take a note.

"My husband's law partner of almost twenty years. He opened three files: Quentin, Quance and Quill," Dorothy said defiantly. "I want you to follow up on them."

Baxter paused to make his note.

"Mr. Quance was an incorporation. Mr. Quentin, a divorce, and Mr. Quill had some business in making a will," she said. "All of them were men."

"And you want me to interview these people," he concluded with satisfaction.

Mrs. Crawford nodded vehemently. Undoubtedly. Richard had called one of the women Q. From Q, it was a short hop to *queen of my heart* or Queenie. Her husband was never without a clever endearment, except for her.

The detective was perplexed. "If your husband was such a …" he paused, consulting his notebook, "notorious philanderer, why do you want to find his killer?" For Baxter, something did not add up. "Why not simply say he got what he deserved, and leave it at that?"

Dorothy was shocked. How could this man, whose every movement called forth Richard's ghost, ask such a stupid question?

She tossed her head angrily. "And leave his death unavenged?" Rising swiftly from the table, she said hoarsely, "He may have humiliated me with his affairs. He may have left me alone countless days and nights, wondering where he was, whom he was with, and what he was doing. And yes, he fathered a child with another woman." Her voice broke off, and she began to weep. Through her tears, she whispered to herself, "I hate you, Richard. I am *so* alone now!"

The detective waited patiently for her to collect herself.

At last, she said, "But, Mr. Baxter, do you understand nothing? He is still a human being who has been murdered!"

It did not tally up in Baxter's estimation. *How could such a scandalous libertine be so loved?*

"I have a description of her, Mr. Baxter," she muttered, dabbing her nose with a Kleenex. "She had a round, childlike face and seemed like an innocent. But she was no innocent. She had a streak of guile and deception underneath, *like a spider waiting*." She peered at the detective. "That's what Armand, the waiter in the Tea Room, said."

Frowning, Baxter made his note, and then cleared his throat discreetly. "Mrs. Crawford? I think we should discuss our potential business relationship." Discussion of fees usually brought most clients down to earth.

"You mean, you'll take the case?" Dorothy looked up hopefully.

"Certainly, madam," he said with a chilly smile. "The charges are two hundred dollars an hour with a retainer of five thousand dollars."

Dorothy shrugged and quickly wrote the check. "What is your first step, Mr. Baxter?" she asked.

"I'll start with Quill, Quance, and Quentin." He took the proffered check and inserted it in his wallet. "Then I'll talk to

Mr. Jenkins and the waiter Armand. Maybe they can give me more background."

Dorothy nodded. "Harry's always been a great help to me. I'll tell him you'll be calling." She rose from the table. "And I'm sure Armand will tell you anything he can."

On his way out, Baxter wondered: *why would the woman instigate a search for a murderer, if she were a potential suspect, having motive, opportunity and means?* Shaking his head, he knew he would never understand women.

After the detective had left, Dorothy sat in Richard's chair in the living room. *The man seems honest enough*, she thought, but he was a cruel parody of her husband.

CHAPTER 17

▼

Harry did not stir for more than twelve hours. At six o'clock in the morning, Mrs. Deal entered the suite. Harry, his head tilted back on the cushions, was snoring lightly. She touched his brow and then checked his pulse. Gently, she smoothed the blanket and studied him. In their few meetings, she had sensed his energy and generosity of spirit. Robert was certain deep conflicts drove him. For whatever purpose, Robert intended to crack him open. Immediately, she understood Harry's attractiveness to women. He was an accepting man, in whose presence one could be oneself. Natasha Boretsky would need someone like him. She drew the curtains open a fraction of an inch and left.

The sun began to burn through the haze over the lake. A dull light seeped into the suite. Groaning, Harry shifted on the chesterfield. Still half-asleep, he rubbed the back of his neck and stretched. His eyes flickered open to see only the dimmest outlines of a room.

Where, in God's name, am I? He stared at the ornate clock on the mantle-piece, but could not make out the time. His mouth was so dry, his tongue felt pasted to the roof of his mouth. His head was throbbing so painfully, he scarcely dared move. Not since law school had he had such a violent hangover. As he lay perfectly still, the remnants of the prior evening crept into his mind.

This must be Hawke's suite, he thought dully. *How could I have drunk so much?* When he tried to sit up, his head reeled, and the edges of the room darkened. He looked down to see his shirt was open from collar to waist. Carefully swinging his legs to the floor, he tried to stand up, but his pants threatened to slide to the floor. *My God! The zipper is torn.* He sat down abruptly. He could remember nothing.

The room began to swim, and a dry retch escaped him. He envisioned Hawke's face looming from the shadows as they talked about … what? He saw Hawke's hand fluttering toward him. Jesus! Did he touch him? How did his clothes get into such a state? He closed his eyes as sickness welled up within him.

A knock at the door jolted him. Stumbling to his feet, he did up his belt and tried to fasten his shirt.

"Room service, Mr. Jenkins," came the voice from the hallway. When he opened the door, a smiling waiter wheeled in the breakfast table.

"Good morning, sir. Shall I set this by the window?"

Nodding, Harry reached for his wallet, but the waiter said, "Dr. Hawke has taken care of it, sir. The breakfast is in the warming oven. Please enjoy it at your leisure."

The thought of food sickened him. In the bathroom, he blinked in the light to see acres of gleaming marble and brass.

Fluted columns framed both tub and shower. Thick, gold-colored towels and a robe were hung over the back of a chair. Harry could hear the midmorning traffic through the open window.

It couldn't just be the wine, he thought. He stared at the sink, which looked like an obscenely huge flower blossom. Next to it rested a note. Searching for his reading glasses, he found them in his shirt pocket and read:

Dear Harry,

Thought you might like to freshen up this morning after last night. You are a man of many dimensions. Relax and enjoy your breakfast. By the way, my lawyers will be in touch with your office by noon today.

Sincerest Regards,

Robert.

Harry sank into the wicker chair. *After last night? What the hell did he mean?* Through his fogged brain, he remembered the part about the lawyers and agreeing to *look* at the proposed agreement. But he shuddered at the thought of what *dimensions* he was talking about.

Pitching the note into the wastebasket, he began to undress for the shower in a stall the size of a walk-in closet. Steam billowed as he soaped his chest. Despite his most concentrated effort, he could not recall anything beyond sitting on the chesterfield and agreeing to look at the proposal. But wait? He had felt sick, and his neck had hurt like hell. In frustration, Harry massaged the base of his skull. He couldn't recall a damned thing more.

In front of the mirror, he put on the terry cloth robe and reached for the razor, shaving mug, and brush. When he peered in the mirror, he flushed. The question formed in his eyes. If Hawke had done anything with him ... *to* him, *surely*, he would remember. A vision of Hawke's pudgy hand and narrow, little eyes flashed before him. Not until his cheeks were as smooth as possible did he stop shaving.

Harry reached for his clothes. Only when he pulled on his pants did he remember the broken zipper. And then there was the shirt and the missing buttons. For God's sake, he couldn't go directly to the office! Clutching his shirt around him, he marched into the bedroom. He would call down for the car and go back home to change. As he lifted the receiver, a knock came at the door. Harry answered it.

A bellman stood before him with a black suit bag over his shoulder. "Mr. Jenkins? Dr. Hawke asked me to deliver this to you."

Without a word, Harry tipped him and shut the door. He lay the bag on the chesterfield. There was a note attached.

Dear Harry,

I thought that after last night, you might need a new shirt and trousers. I trust these will be satisfactory. My admiration for your energy and reserve has grown immeasurably.

Yours,

Robert.

Jesus Christ! Harry threw down the note and tore open the bag. There lay a fine white shirt, a tie and a suit. Harry fumed. Of course, it was of the finest quality.

Suddenly, he stopped and looked about the room. Every need had been anticipated. Preparations had been made to satisfy all his desires, even before he was aware of them. He rushed to the breakfast table and removed the covered plate from the warming oven. His stomach turned at the heartiness of the bacon, eggs, and toast. He poured a cup of black coffee. Only then did he see yet another note beside the creamer. Angrily, he ripped it open.

Dear Harry,

After last night, you may not feel like all this breakfast. First try the hair of the dog in the refrigerator. Hope you're feeling better.
Good luck,

Yours,

Robert.

[PS: you really are an intriguing enigma. So sorry I am detained on business this morning. I am usually a much better host.]

Harry threw open the refrigerator. There stood a frosted glass of tomato juice, no doubt with a hefty shot of vodka in it. He slammed the door and returned to his coffee. As he sipped his cup, he looked about, feeling like a very comfortable laboratory rat. No opportunity for suggestion or innuendo had been missed.

He returned to the refrigerator. With a spoon, he stirred the drink, and then tasted a drop. Of course, it was good.

Sitting at the window, he drank the vodka and tomato juice down. Within moments, he felt his muscles relax and his headache clear. Undoubtedly, it was the best remedy for a hangover. But he did not recall drinking more than a glass of wine last night. His watch read almost eleven-fifteen. He would dress and go straight to the office. Likely Hawke's lawyers had already called. In the bedroom, he began to dress. The shirt felt smooth and cool on his skin. The suit hung in precisely the correct fashion.

Examining himself in the mirror, he felt naked, as if Hawke were privy to every detail of his life, mind, and body. It must have been knockout drops. No resistance. No memory. In the mirror, he saw the fear in his eyes.

The telephone rang. "Mr. Jenkins?" a pleasant voice asked. "Your car is ready for you at the front. The keys are at the concierge's desk."

"Thank you," said Harry quietly. How did someone know he was ready to leave at just that moment? He glanced about the ceiling of the bedroom and the living room, but he could spot no hidden cameras. Quickly, he collected his things and left the suite. In the corridor, the chambermaid smiled and asked if the suite were vacant. He nodded. As far as he could tell, it was.

Twenty minutes later, as he entered his office, Sarah asked, "New suit, Mr. Jenkins?"

Harry stopped in mid-stride at her desk. Sarah was young and pretty, a lovely addition to any office. *Not flirting*, he thought wistfully. Probably just complimenting a middle-aged divorcee out of kindness. But he enjoyed every second of her attention.

"Yes, as a matter of fact," he smiled.

"Oh, indeed. You look very handsome."

Miss Giveny bustled from the back room. "What are you doing here?" she demanded.

"Pardon?"

"I thought you'd be off around the world by now."

Harry continued toward his office. "You know I leave tomorrow night. You booked the tickets."

Gladys Giveny paid no attention. "Well since you dropped in, perhaps you'd like to review some messages."

He glared at her as she slid past him in the doorway. "Yes, I will, Miss Giveny." His head was beginning to hammer again. "Do we have any coffee?"

"I put a pot on about an hour ago, so I don't know if it's fit to drink." Miss Giveny sat down heavily and set out the messages. "We weren't expecting you."

So, go and get it yourself, he thought grumpily, heading back down the hall. The carafe contained an inch or so of weak-looking brew. He poured half a cup and returned to his office.

Miss Giveny began, "Dorothy Crawford called. She's hired a private investigator named Samuel T. Baxter."

Wonderful, he thought. *Even if it takes suspicion of murder to rouse her!* "Does she want me to call her?" he asked.

"No. She just wants Mr. Baxter, her private eye, to look at the Q files."

Harry shook his head. "It'll have to wait until I'm back. I can't let somebody come in and rummage through the files.

Tell Dorothy I'll be glad to meet with her by...." Harry checked his agenda. "By the twenty-ninth or so."

Miss Giveny scratched down the instructions, then rose to leave.

"You can reach me anytime at the Bellini," he offered as she shut the door.

Damn woman, he thought. She could not imagine any serious work being done *trotting about the globe*, as she would say. The entire face of the legal world had changed beyond recognition, but not for Miss Giveny. He suspected she would bring out the quill pens in his absence.

What in hell is wrong with me? I should be happy with a trip to Venice, especially if Natasha comes. He picked up the phone to call her. The receptionist said she was out until mid-afternoon. He left his number.

Miss Giveny's peremptory knock came at the door. "Mr. Jenkins? You'd better look at this fax, which just came in."

He read a letter from the law firm, Oates and Comstock.

Dear Mr. Jenkins

RE: HAWKE and DINNICK

We are the solicitors for Dr. Robert Hawke, who has instructed us to write to you with respect to an agreement between you, as the legal guardian of Norma Dinnick, and the Hawke Institute. We have been advised by Dr. Hawke of the following:

1.] That the two of you have agreed to share information and cooperate in the locating of a fund of money initially raised in1963 by George Pappas, Archibald Brinks, David Parrish, and Arthur Dinnick for medical research.

2.] That neither of you will take any steps to locate such fund without the full knowledge of the other and that each of you undertakes to keep the other fully advised of any efforts in this regard.

3.] That upon locating the said fund, both of you undertake to submit the determination of the ownership of said fund to the Supreme Court of Ontario in accordance with enclosed draft statement of claim.

Please review the statement at your earliest convenience and let us have your comments.

Yours very truly,

John Q. Oates, QC.

Harry flipped through the twelve pages attached, the gist of which was contained in paragraphs 15 and 16.

15.] That commencing in January 1963, the consortium comprised of the said George Pappas, Archibald Brinks, David Parrish, and Arthur Dinnick raised, by share offering, the sum of approximately five million dollars for medical research into diseases responsible for memory loss in the aged. All members of Elixicorp Enterprises [herein referred to as the consortium] were agreed as to the purpose of the fund. The Hawke Institute is the legal owner of the fund because the said George Pappas, Archibald Brinks, and David Parrish assigned all their right, title and interest in the fund [for good and valuable consideration] to the Hawke Institute. All members of the consortium are deceased.

16] That the said Arthur Dinnick invested the fund, as he was authorized to do by the consortium, but he did not advise the members of any details of the location or nature of the investment or investments. Upon his death, the widow of Arthur Dinnick has, without color of right, claimed ownership of the said fund and has refused to provide the Hawke Institute with the details of the investment, claiming that such is unknown to her.

Without color of right, mused Harry. That was a legal euphemism for theft. Although Norma had more than a few versions of her story, she vehemently insisted they had invested only their share. Arthur, of course, had been a genius at investing! She denied the money had ever been raised for medical research, and if it had been raised for that purpose, the whole business was a fraud played upon the naive of Toronto.

So, what was the defense to Hawke's claims? The best position was the hardest to prove—that the money claimed by Norma was only Arthur's share and was not obtained by fraud. Both parties would deny any scheme to deceive, because fraud was fatal to both sides. The Supreme Court justices would most certainly cast a jaundiced eye upon such reasoning. To have any hope, Norma would need to prove the money came strictly from Arthur's investing talent.

But wait! The statement of claim said that George Pappas, Archibald Brinks and David Parrish—everybody *except* Arthur Dinnick—had transferred his interest in the shares to Hawke. *Bonanza!* If that were true, then Norma had a legitimate reason to resist Hawke's claims because her husband had never signed over his interest to Hawke—because he was already dead! Harry grinned. It was the best news he'd ever had about the case.

Quietly, he said, "Miss Giveny, take a letter, please."

His response was short and noncommittal. They were misinformed. He had *not* agreed to any such terms, but merely to look at a proposed agreement. Further, he could only sign after consulting with his client. As her guardian, his authority from the court required him to raise issues with her to the extent that such was possible. By Dr. Hawke's own admission, Arthur's interest in the shares had never been transferred to the Institute. And so, Norma's claim was justified. Once Miss Giveny had prepared the letter, he signed it and had her fax it.

As he worked through files that afternoon, he could not rid himself of thoughts of the doctor. A clear plan was essential. In Venice, likely it would not be hard to locate the branch where the fund had been deposited. *But why Venice,* he wondered? Norma maintained that Arthur had died in Florence. He must have traveled to Venice at some point to make the deposit, maybe to throw Pappas off the trail. The shares, needed to access the fund, must be somewhere in London. Why go to Venice first? Either Norma had forgotten or he needed something from the bank in Venice to get the shares in London. Much work to be accomplished without alerting the watchful Dr. Hawke! He faced a formidable adversary, whose presence clung to him like a cold, dense fog.

CHAPTER 18

▼

Natasha, dressed in tailored khaki shorts and a white shirt, tossed her case in the trunk of her convertible. She would pick up Sheila, drive to Stratford for an evening performance, and then stay overnight. *Hamlet. How appropriate! To act or not to act? That is the question.* Her conversation with Erma seemed locked in another distant time. Although her determination to choose was ebbing fast, she knew she couldn't remain on the fence. She parked outside the house where Sheila rented an upstairs flat. Two cats stretched and yawned on the tiny veranda as the sun broke through, illuminating the riot of flowers spilling from boxes and urns.

When Sheila backed out the front door with a large suitcase, Natasha lowered her sunglasses. *How long does she think we're going for?* Instantly, regret suffused her. *How can I be so awful?* Sheila was true, loving, and kind. *Like a puppy dog!* As her friend struggled down the steps with her case, bleakness settled upon Natasha.

"Hi." Sheila spoke breathily, with anticipation.

Natasha took her case and set it in the trunk. When she briefly kissed Sheila's cheek, the words *the kiss of a traitor* flew into her mind. Sheila gathered her long paisley skirt about her knees and settled into the passenger seat.

Natasha smiled at her friend and her fiery red mass of hair, which always reminded her of centuries-old paintings of Botticelli virgins. Her skin was pale as alabaster with patches of freckles from the sun. Resisting the temptation to reach out and touch her hair, Natasha shifted into first gear and pulled away from the curb.

"You're keeping the top down?" Sheila asked lightly.

Natasha nodded. "Have you got a scarf for your hair? If it starts to rain, I'll put up the top."

Without further comment, Sheila put on a scarf and her sunglasses. Soon they were on the expressway, which skirted the lake to Hamilton. With the wind making conversation impossible, both of them were left in their own worlds.

Since she has demanded I choose … Natasha's thoughts trailed off. Glancing over at her friend, she suddenly warmed. *She's so afraid of losing me, but….* She gripped the steering wheel. *We can't keep on like this. Everything postponed, and nothing resolved.*

An unbidden image popped into her mind. Patches of lifeless grass appeared matted under melting snow. Tall headstones stood over dead, muddied leaves. Beyond the grave markers fell shadowy shapes she could not discern. Of course, it was Josef's grave, the last time she had visited it. Natasha felt frozen on the edge of a dark precipice.

Sheila stewed. Although she clutched her scarf around her head, she was determined not to object to being blown about by the wind. *If she goes on about her damned freedom to choose and her nature, she can go to hell. Maybe it's time I started looking for somebody new … maybe Rhonda.* Holding her scarf in place, she glared at Natasha. But given the set of her jaw, Sheila knew there was no use in needlessly opposing her. Besides, letting her have her way gave Sheila pleasure she did not understand. Pursing her lips, she thought, *She can't just go off with Harry. Not after all this time.*

Red taillights popped up ahead. Natasha geared down swiftly and smoothly. Stopped in traffic, they felt the wind pick up from the lake. At Sunnyside, the swimming pool, with its Grecian columns and stone balustrades, was silhouetted against the gray water and sky. Soon the traffic moved, and they picked up speed on the open highway.

Within an hour, they were turning onto Highway 8, which wound up through the Hamilton Mountains and on to Stratford. Lost in thought, Natasha caressed the gearshift stick and, once on the straight road, shifted back into fifth. Suddenly, she was swept by weariness, familiar to those who desired control. With Harry, she could relax her need to order life. Sheila brought out her protectiveness and also an unpleasant passion to dominate.

Natasha glanced across at her friend, who was watching her out the corner of her sunglasses. Smiling, she took her hand, and when she said, "We need to talk while we have this time together," she heard Sheila's sharp intake of breath.

At first the car swerved only slightly. Feeling a tug at the right rear, Natasha grasped the steering wheel tightly. Next she felt a drag and then heard a thumping sound.

"Shit," she said quietly.

"What's wrong?"

"We've got a flat," Natasha said, steering the vehicle onto the gravel shoulder, where the road turned sharply upward to the left.

"Oh, God, Natty! What'll we do now?"

Natasha brought the car to a stop and turned off the engine. They sat in silence, listening to the wind sweep across the fields of grass. Once more clouds had gathered in the sky blotting out the sun.

"We'll change it." Natasha got out and opened the trunk. "Come and get your bag out."

"Can't we call somebody? I don't know how to change a tire."

"Do you happen to see a phone booth anywhere? Do you think we *can't* fix this?"

Sheila's lip trembled.

"I'm sorry," Natasha muttered. "I forgot my cell phone." Taking their bags from the rear, she unlatched the compartment for the spare.

"Have you ever changed a tire before?" asked Sheila, as she tried to get a signal on her cell phone.

"Always a first time, my dear." She smiled brilliantly at Sheila and wished for only a moment that Harry were with her. Studying the instruction sheet, she realized the vehicle had to be on a level surface.

"I'm going to let the car down to the bottom of this hill." Climbing back in, she got into reverse and gently rolled the car backwards, until she judged it was on the level. She got out and saw that Sheila had retreated to a nearby rock.

"You're just going to sit and watch?" Natasha pushed back a strand of hair and glared at her.

"Well, tell me what to do. You're *always* in charge."

"Help me lift the spare out of the trunk."

Obediently, Sheila helped her remove the spare. She struggled with the jack, only to drop it on her foot. Groaning, she limped back to the rock and resumed her seat. "If you didn't always have to prove something, Natasha, we could flag somebody down for help."

Natasha ignored her and began organizing the pieces of the jack. After ten minutes of intense concentration, she managed to fit it in place under the rear bumper and raise up the car. Red-faced, she rose and slowly walked up the hill to Sheila, still seated on a rock.

"You see," Natasha began, trying to check her anger, "all we have to do is take off the nuts, put on the spare, and screw them back down in place. Then we're done."

Sheila smiled and spoke softly. "I'm sorry, love. I wasn't trying to start anything."

Natasha was momentarily mollified. But then she said, "When I'm finished, we have to talk." She looked down to see her shirtsleeve was blackened. Silently cursing, she returned to the car.

Unable to bear the suspense, Sheila followed her and stood nearby as Natasha squatted down with the wrench. Each nut she fired into the hubcap made an angry clang.

"It's about Harry, isn't it?"

"No," Natasha replied, continuing grimly with her task. After a few moments work, she lifted the tire off.

Sheila's voice rose to a whine. "Yes, it is! I can tell. You've been seeing him all the time now."

"Help me lift the spare on. Please."

Together, they struggled in silence to match up the holes of the spare to the bolts on the axle. At last, they succeeded, and Natasha quickly spun the nuts back in place.

"See if there's a spanner in the back to tighten those nuts."

Sheila searched and returned with a small wrench. "This it, Natty?"

"No." Natasha found the spanner in the grass and set to work. Five minutes later, she was done. She rose and wiped her brow. "Let's get the flat into the trunk. Then we'll take a break and put the jack away afterwards."

Once finished, they retreated into the field and found another rock out of view of the road.

After moments of silence, Natasha spoke, "It's not really about Harry, darling. It's about us. We're arguing all the time." She sighed and reached for her hand.

"If Harry weren't taking up all your time...."

"It would still be the same." Natasha's heart sank as Sheila sniffled. "I'm not very good for you," she blundered on. She looked up to see mountains of clouds seemingly gathered as witnesses. *Where are the right words? Can I ever solve the riddle of passion and compassion?* She wished Josef could tell her.

Sheila could not speak. With the familiar lump rising in her throat, she put on her sunglasses, although it had almost completely clouded over. To her, Natasha was unfathomable. They had been friends and lovers for years, and now she was going to trash everything just because of Harry. *Just wait! Given enough time, men always show their true colors.* But her heart ached with her need for her.

Natasha, knowing she had to be honest, stared off at the horizon of fields. "It's just me, the way I am." Then she sighed deeply and said, "No, it is *partly* to do with Harry—the kind of person he is."

"You can't be both, Natasha. At least, not in the real world, where other people count for something." Sheila hunted in her purse for a Kleenex. "We've been through this a million times. Why *can't* you decide?"

"Believe me. I am *trying* to decide." She saw Sheila's lip tremble. She forged on. "With us, I feel like I have to cut myself into pieces and hide half of me."

"Natasha? What do you mean? I love and want all of you." Sheila cried out.

"But you make me feel like half of me is suffocating."

"Natasha!" Sheila began to cry. "You're just a traitor. Men are pigs. You know that. All they want is their own pleasure. Men have always subjugated women. Made them live in fear!" Sheila jumped up to pace in circles about the rock. "How can you …?"

Natasha reached up and caught her hand. "Not all of them are like that, sweetheart."

"What about *us*? You said we'd live together!"

"I *never* said that!"

"You said you'd think about it." Sheila snatched her hand back and retreated several paces backward, almost tripping over another rock.

Natasha's face darkened. "Maybe I did, but that was over a year ago."

Sheila could not help more tears. "Look what I put up with! All these years, whenever you've gone off with someone, what did I do? I tried to make a new life for myself, and then, you'd come back. I'm just a doormat to you. *Please come in, darling Natasha. Walk all over me again!*"

"You know I only left once! That was because you were seeing...."

Sheila cringed as if Natasha had slapped her. "You know, I was only trying...."

Natasha threw up her hands. "You don't treat someone you love like that!"

They sat in silence, with their backs to each other.

At last, Natasha spoke very quietly. "Sheila, this can't be love, not when we're hurting each other this way, this much."

Swiveling around, Sheila shouted. "You can't be true to me or anyone else. And, for sure you won't be true to Harry." Then the significance of Natasha's words came over her, and she whispered, "but I *do* love you, Natty."

Shielding her eyes against the sun, Natasha gazed at her but did not speak.

Sheila dropped to her knees. With uncharacteristic passion, she placed her hand around Natasha's neck and kissed her mouth for a long moment. Natasha was angered, not by the kiss, but the flash of desire within.

She pulled away. "Look, I'm sorry. It's no use talking. I can't seem to work this out with you."

Hands on hips, Sheila towered over her. "And do you *really* think Harry's going to accept you? That's a laugh! You think he's going to put up with this crap?" Stepping back, she began to mimic her. "Darling, please. I *simply can't* make up my mind. At the age of thirty-six, I don't know who or what I am!"

"Stop it, Sheila!"

"I'll tell you what you are! You're mean and cruel. You don't give a damn about anyone else except yourself." Sheila started to cry again. Natasha reached out for her, but Sheila pushed her away and started off down the hill.

Suddenly, they heard a creaking noise and then a loud snap. They ran to the road in time to see the car slowly roll off the jack and, with increasing speed, bounce down the grade into the ditch.

Neither of them spoke. In silent agreement, they started walking back along the road.

"I'm pretty sure," Natasha said. "I saw a garage back this way."

They walked single file along the shoulder. Sheila stopped and, turning back on her, said, "You know, Natasha, you can get away from me if you want. But you'll never get away from your screwed-up self."

Natasha stood still in the hot sun. Her gaze encompassed the lush, green, rolling farmland, the copse of trees, and the brook that split over a rock into two streams before winding around and down the hill and into the ditch. No matter how fast or slow or in what direction the water broke over the stones, branches, and twigs, its current always ran deep and steady. *It really is all from one source*, she thought, glimpsing for an instant a sort of form and order to life. But then, the sense evaporated, and her life, once again, seemed fragmented. With a chill creeping through her, she acknowledged that duty and pity, not passion and love, bound her to Sheila. Slowly, she caught up with her to walk single file along the road. *Everything postponed. Nothing resolved.*

CHAPTER 19

▼

After visiting hours, Garth Deal hid in the stairwell on Norma's floor until the nurse disappeared down the hall into a room. He was disgusted with the easy access to the Mercer. With no questions asked, any idiot could walk in, and any lunatic could walk out. But the weird sounds from the rooms, like animals snuffling and little birds screeching, spooked him. He opened Norma's door. The old lady lay asleep in the rose-colored lamplight. As he approached, her eyes flew open, then narrowed in suspicion.

Ronnie had coached him on how to handle the old biddy. Drawing up a chair, he smiled and gently took her hand. She blinked, and then smiled in recognition.

"John?" She tried to sit up. "Betsy's John?"

Garth nodded as he stroked her hand, with ugly veins standing out. But the softness of her skin amazed him. "Ya, it's me, John. How ya doing, Grandma?" He was careful to keep his hand away from her mouth. The bite marks were almost healed up.

Norma continued to gaze at him fondly. "How are Betsy and Peter, dear?"

"Fine, Grandma. Just fine." Ronnie had said to go along with whatever game she wanted. He took the jackknife from his pocket. "They treating you okay here, Grandma?" He patted her hand and let it rest on the cover while he pried open the knife beneath the sheet. Gazing trustingly at him, she winced only slightly when Garth held her fast by the wrist.

He drew the blade lightly across three of her fingers at the first joints, saying softly, "They cut Arthur's fingers off, one at a time, Norma." A small line of blood popped up on two of the fingers. He made another cut, just a little deeper at the second knuckle of the index finger. With a sharp cry, Norma tried to snatch her hand back. He slapped his hand over her mouth.

"I'm gonna cut yours off, too, if you don't tell us where the money is."

Norma bit hard.

"Fuck! You stupid old bitch!"

When he pulled back his hand, she began to howl. At first it was a low, keening wail, but soon it rose to a sharp staccato of screams.

Garth kicked over the chair. Knife in hand, he rushed out to the corridor, where he could hear the nurse calling out. He raced for the red-lit exit sign at the far end of the hall. The howling echoed as he ran all the way down the stairwell. Within moments, he was at the ground floor, running for the Jeep.

In her mind, Norma was no longer at the Mercer. "Arthur!" she screamed. "Watch out!"

The nurse found her on the floor, blood seeping from her hand.

Once again, Norma was in Venice. She remembered the lunch at Harry's Bar near San Marco. The gondolier, standing high up in the boat behind her and Arthur, had sung romantic songs. As if in a dream, the golden palaces on the Grand Canal floated by. Turning into the shadows of a narrow canal, their gondola swept under bridges and past tall, red-and-white-striped poles. Arthur, in weary silence, surveyed the Calle Vallaresso. Lulled by the voices of the gondoliers, Norma closed her eyes until they were there.

The entrance to the bar was hard to find, because it was tucked away down a narrow street. Behind the intricate grill-work of the door, the gold lettering read *Harry's Bar.* Arthur pushed it open.

Wooden nautical motifs of anchors and compasses dotted the walls and made Norma think she was on a small ship. The little wall lamps set the room aglow. Behind the bar stood two white-coated bartenders, who smiled and briefly nodded toward a table at the back. Robert Hawke, resplendent in a suit of white, beckoned them. Arthur guided her by the elbow past the round tables of pale yellow linen.

Hawke bowed formally. "Arthur … Norma. I am so delighted you could come to my little luncheon." He shook Arthur's hand heartily. Then, bowing again, he clicked his heels together smartly and kissed Norma's hand. When he pulled out her chair, a strange shiver coursed through her. In a merry fashion, Robert questioned them about their stay in Venice and recommended sites they had not yet seen.

"This bar has such an interesting history," he exclaimed. "The European aristocracy frequents the place." He waved his hand to encompass the room. "All sorts of literary types come here as well." His enthusiasm drove him on. "Did you know Ernest Hemmingway named one of the drinks they serve? It's called the Montgomery."

Norma and Arthur looked about in silence. Suddenly, Robert stopped and gazed at Arthur thoughtfully. "Shall we order?" He waved, and a waiter was at his side. Norma and Arthur picked up their menus.

"You simply must try a Bellini. It's the specialty of the house," said Robert.

"What's in it?" asked Norma suspiciously.

"Peach juice," smiled Robert, holding up one finger. "But only from white peaches, my dear."

Norma had never heard of white peaches.

"And Prosecco, a fine Italian champagne. A pure delight!"

Arthur nodded, and then studied the menu.

Robert touched the waiter's sleeve lightly. "My dear boy, bring us three Bellinis and three of your fabulous chicken sandwiches." The waiter collected the menus and departed.

"Mrs. Dinnick," Hawke began in a friendly fashion, "have you enjoyed your little holiday in *Serenissima*?"

"Pardon?"

"The Most Serene Republic." Looking vaguely disappointed with her, Hawke continued, "It's an old name for Venice."

"Yes, of course," she sniffed. "But I'll be glad to get back to Toronto. The garden will be going to rack and ruin."

When the drinks were set down, Robert raised his glass to them. "A little toast, my friends. To good health and long life in beautiful places."

Arthur and Norma sipped cautiously and then, when the sandwiches arrived, they ate sparingly.

Finished eating, Robert dabbed his lips with his napkin. He placed his hand over Arthur's and gazed at him intently. Usually, Robert's eyes were hard as sapphires. Now, they were soft and pleading. His companions did not move.

"Arthur, I am so *terribly* worried about you."

Instantly, Arthur's body became rigid.

Robert began to stroke Arthur's fore and middle fingers of his right hand. "You see, George Pappas can become quite irrational if thwarted. He was by no means satisfied with your undertaking." Next, Robert spread each of Arthur's fingers out on the tablecloth. "He demands the money at once."

Now ashen, Arthur let Robert continue stroking his hand.

"Only through my small powers of persuasion have I been given one last chance, dear boy, to save you." Reaching across the table, he grasped an ivory-handled butter knife. He gazed at Arthur with limpid eyes, and then gently drew the knife across the tops of Arthur's fingers.

Arthur froze in place. The stroke of the dull blade was a deadly caress.

Tears formed in Robert Hawke's eyes. "If Mr. Pappas does not have the moncy by noon, tomorrow, they will find you, wherever you are, and they will cut off one finger for each day you are late."

Arthur did not move.

"You have the hands of a nobleman, Arthur. Such a shame to see them injured in *any* way."

In silence, Arthur continued to stare at the charming, yet utterly brutal man before him.

"Not only your hands could come to harm. I would hate to see that." Robert placed his hand over Arthur's once more and stared into his eyes. "You are a man of such attractive and exciting energy, my friend. Please have the money in time. Mr. Pappas does not give extensions."

After lunch, Robert paid the bill, and they left. Norma spent the afternoon alone in the hotel while Arthur did some banking. The next morning, they took the train for Florence.

That night, Harry dreamt of Natasha. Her phantom presence teased him, and he called out her name from the depths of his sleep. The telephone jangled, destroying his pleasure.

"Hello?" he croaked, struggling to capture fragments of his dream.

"Mr. Jenkins? It's Mrs. Godfrey calling from the Mercer."

"Yes?"

"It's about Norma Dinnick. I'm her night nurse."

Harry swung his feet to the floor. By now, Natasha had fled.

"She's been howling, Mr. Jenkins."

"Howling? What do you mean?"

"Screaming, crying out. She's demanding to see her *protector*. I assume that's you."

"Does she say what's wrong?"

"No. She's quite disoriented. The doctor could increase her medication, but he wanted you to see her first, just in case she has something important to tell you."

He peered at the bedside clock. A quarter to five. "Tell her I'll be there within the hour." Harry hung up and hurried to the shower. In twenty minutes, he was backing the car out the drive.

With no traffic, he arrived by five thirty. The Mercer was bathed in a cool, clear light, and the crows were swooping and circling high above the lower field. Harry half-expected to find Norma sitting on the front step with her bag packed.

Walking through the main entrance, he was met by Mrs. Godfrey, the nurse.

"Is she quiet now?" he asked.

The nurse nodded and walked briskly to the elevator. "Once we said you were coming, she settled down. That, plus Doctor Menzies prescribed a mild sedative."

Norma lay peacefully in her bed.

"What on earth has happened to her hand?" Harry stared at the bandaged fingers and then at the nurse.

"That's the part we can't understand. She has a cut on each of her fingers on the left hand. They aren't deep. Not much more than scratches."

"Has any one been with her?"

Mrs. Godfrey shook her head. "No one has been in to see her. At least, not that we know of."

Harry sat down and touched Norma's arm. "Norma?" he spoke gently. "It's Harry."

Norma's eyes opened. In the dim light, it took a moment for her to focus. Then a smile of great sweetness passed over her face. "Oh, Harry! Thank heavens you've come."

She sank back into a doze. Harry tapped her arm once more. Her eyes flew open in alarm. "They've cut Arthur's fingers off, Harry."

"Arthur's? But Arthur is dead, Norma."

Norma shook her head. "One by one, they did."

He had to orient her back in the room. He took her hand. "What happened to your fingers?"

Norma examined the bandages and then began to weep. "See? They were so cruel. They cut them off with a butter knife."

Another of Norma's flights into the past! He asked softly, "Norma, did you dream about Arthur? I know it can seem so real."

She focused on him. "No, Harry. They cut off his fingers."

The door opened. A short, rotund man entered. His smile was pleasant as he held out his hand to Harry. "I'm Dr. Menzies, Mr. Jenkins."

Howling, Norma shrank back and began rocking side to side. "Fingers! Arthur ... cut his fingers!"

In Dr. Menzies, Norma saw the young Robert Hawke of Harry's Bar. When Harry tried his best to comfort her, she clutched at him. "Harry!" she whispered urgently. "Be careful. Listen to me."

Harry held her arms and stared into her eyes. "I'm here Norma. I'm listening."

She spoke in dark tones. "Harry, you are much too trusting. They meet at night, under cover. They're plotting against us … working together … they never stop." She ran her hands over his face and gave him a knowing glance.

"I understand these things, but you do not." She glared at Dr. Menzies. "Men like him are very charming but very dangerous. They listen on the phone and…."

"Norma, that's Dr. Menzies. He works here at the Mercer," said Harry, glancing over his shoulder. The doctor moved closer.

Norma shrank back and then began to cackle. Her eyes beheld another frightening world.

"*Don't* let him fool you!" she hissed, pointing a bandaged finger at the doctor. "He will steal Arthur's money from us. They will stop at *absolutely* nothing!"

"Did anyone come to see you tonight, Norma?" Harry asked.

She shook her head and then sank back on the pillow. For a moment, it seemed Norma might slide into exhaustion and sleep, but suddenly, she grabbed Harry's sleeve. "And you must…." Her words became the mad prattle of paranoia. "Beware of the brute. He is huge and strong … very strong! His name is John."

Harry felt her frail body shudder. "You are destined to be defeated." Her sobs grew to a howl.

As Dr. Menzies moved to the bed, he looked at Harry with great curiosity. "Does any of that mean anything to you, Mr. Jenkins?"

"A little bit, perhaps," he said carefully.

"We thought her paranoia and psychosis were under control with her current levels of medication." The doctor shrugged and made a note. "Nurse, increase her medication to three milligrams twice a day. But give her an injection of Haldol now."

When the doctor turned to go, Harry asked, "Dr. Menzies, how can we find out what happened to her hands?"

The doctor consulted his notes. "She had no visitors last night. Could be another resident, I suppose. He shrugged. "Or maybe self-inflicted."

Harry could not imagine Norma harming herself. Puzzled, he said, "I'll be out of town for a week or so. I'd like to leave you my phone number."

"Sure. Where are you going?"

"Venice."

"Ah, lucky man!"

"Yes." Harry smiled weakly. "I'll give the number to the nursing station. I'd like you to contact me, especially if she starts asking for me."

"Certainly. Not a problem," said the doctor as he left.

After the injection, Norma lapsed into a deep and serene sleep. Harry collected his case and headed for the car. Seven o'clock and traffic into the city was building rapidly. Within thirty-six hours, he would be off to Venice.

Troubled, he tried to make sense of Norma's words. The doctor's appearance had triggered something in her. At first, she seemed seized with the gift of prophesy, and then she had become sphinx-like. It was the business about his trusting nature and defeat being his destiny that disturbed him the most.

CHAPTER 20

▼

Waiting all day for Mr. Baxter, the detective, Dorothy's anticipation grew. Convinced of her Q theory, she was certain the golden thread to Richard's murderer would emerge, now that she had a description of the woman. She sat on the edge of her chair in the dining room, as the detective opened a very thin file containing several pages of scrawled notes. He polished his glasses and cleared his throat.

An accountant, thought Dorothy.

"As discussed, Mrs. Crawford, I have contacted Mr. Quance, Mr. Quentin, and Mrs. Quill." The little man popped a mint into his mouth and ran his finger down his scanty notes. "Mr. Quance, a bachelor, consulted your husband on the incorporation of his drainage business. And Mr. Quentin, a widower, had a dispute with a contractor." Baxter looked up at her bleakly.

An unaccustomed sharpness rose in her voice. "That's all you have? What about Quill?" To Dorothy, he no longer resembled Richard in any way.

Baxter held up his hand. "I was coming to that. Quill is dead. But I visited his wife at a nursing home, where she has resided since 1985." Baxter spoke slowly, as if trying to make the most of meager results. "Apparently, she suffered a severe stroke back then and has been unable to communicate ever since. Mr. Quill visited her faithfully every day for almost twenty years, until his own death a year ago." Samuel Baxter shuffled his papers, tipped back in his chair, and regarded his client.

"Nothing more?" she began in a quietly tremulous voice.

Baxter blanched. "The Q's do not seem to be a significant lead, Mrs. Crawford."

"You mean I have spent one thousand dollars to be told utterly useless information?"

"Well, now...." fumbled Baxter. "We now know that none of the Q's had wives—capable ones—at the relevant time."

"That much is obvious, Mr. Baxter." Stunned by the surge of righteous anger, she gasped at its unfamiliar power. "You have wasted my time, sir, and my money, which my husband earned through hard, honest work!" Her entire being quaked with fury.

Samuel Baxter peered cautiously at her. "May I ask a question, madam?"

"What?"

Baxter blinked for a moment, then said, "Mrs. Crawford, you have indicated that your husband had ... ah ..." He struggled for the right words. "A number of affairs, and that they caused you considerable torment."

"Your point, sir?"

"Then why on earth would you wish to pursue a course which can only deepen your obvious pain?"

Dorothy remained perfectly still. Only briefly wondering at the question, she rose from the table, nearly knocking a teacup to the floor.

Her voice rose shrilly. "Murder? Unresolved?" She advanced upon the detective, who shrank back. "Obviously, Mr. Baxter, you understand nothing! Despite my husband's unfaithfulness, I will not let his death go unpunished!"

"But you have so little to go on, madam."

An unknown person was leaping within her, one hidden for a lifetime. How had such a furious soul remained so quiescent? She rapped her knuckles on the table.

"Yes, my husband was unfaithful a hundred times over. Yes, he caused me the greatest pain, but he was an honorable man, respected by his profession! He wrote treatises cited by judges throughout Canada. He was a good and steady provider. His clients revered him." Dorothy, having risen to her full height, now wavered over the little man. "I'll have you know, Mr. Baxter, that despite his philandering, my husband was a fine and respected man. In fact, he was a Queen's Counsel."

Her voice cracked in cold fury. "His murderer must be brought to justice!" Dorothy burst into tears.

Mr. Baxter threw up his hands in futility. "Mrs. Crawford, you need far more to go on."

"And I shall find it myself." She opened the front door. "Consider our relationship terminated, sir! Send me your bill and the balance of the retainer in the mail."

Baxter shrank down the front steps. She slammed the door shut. In his car, the detective shook his head at the irrationality of women.

Dorothy sank into Richard's chair in the living room. Maise, the cleaning lady, hung in the doorway.

"Mrs. Crawford?" she asked softly.

"Yes, Maise? I left your check on the kitchen counter, didn't I?" To Dorothy, Maise was no more than a child who had worked for her for several years. A child from Jamaica or was it Trinidad?

"Yes, ma'am. Thank you." Still, Maise remained at the door.

"What is it, dear?" she asked more kindly.

Maise hung her head. "I was wondering if you'd come to the church service with me tonight?"

"Church service?" Dorothy could not imagine what had gotten into the girl.

"Ma'am? Ever since you gotten back, you seem so sad … real sad." Maise twisted her hands under her apron. "I was just thinking that, maybe, if you came, you could pray with us. I talked it over with Pastor Jones, and he said the church would welcome you."

Open-mouthed, Dorothy stared her. Not for years had she been in church. Richard occasionally took her, but only for business reasons such as a funeral or the wedding of an important client. But someone else within her said, "I'd be honored, Maise. In fact, I'll drive you to your church."

Maise's face broke into a shy grin. Dorothy hunted down the car keys. She had driven only rarely during their marriage and not since her husband's death. Richard had always taken the wheel. The twilight was deepening as she backed the immense Ford LTD from the garage. Maise waited at the curb. At first,

Dorothy had trouble getting the gearshift from reverse into drive, but soon she got the hang of it.

What have I ever found in a church? She never remembered what the minister said, but she was comforted by the beautiful music and the familiar cadences of the liturgy. But whenever she tried to think of God, an austere image of Richard appeared in her mind.

Maise climbed in and gave her directions. "It's the Church of the Redeemer just off St. Clair, ma'am."

Time for an adventure, thought Dorothy as she drove very slowly down the street. She jumped when a car honked at her and then roared past. Nearly scraping a parked car, she prayed she would soon get used to driving. By the time she reached St. Clair Avenue, she began to feel more comfortable.

Maybe prayer will help. She imagined quiet pews lined with members of the congregation, their backs turned in a solemn wall of silence. *Surely, God would want me to find a murderer? I will ask him to give me the strength and the will to do so.*

They arrived at the church, which was a plain, flat-roofed building crammed in between rows of tiny houses. What had she imagined? Surely, a real church should have a steeple and stained glass. When Maise opened the front door for her, the pulsing beat of a bass guitar overwhelmed her. She could feel the vibrations throughout her entire body. The inner door was opened by a man who grinned at her from ear to ear. A sea of black faces turned to greet her. Hundreds of people threw their arms heavenward and swayed to the music. What had she expected?

Maise, smiling beatifically, led her to a pew near the very front. Open-mouthed, Dorothy sat down. Within moments, the preacher, in his white robes, ascended to the pulpit. Somewhere outside herself, she realized that the man was shouting. And he shouted for the next half hour. As best as Dorothy could tell, the whole congregation would be sent straight to hell after the next rousing song. *Hell fire and damnation.* All of it was poppycock!

Dorothy's church was quiet and orderly: hymns were followed by the sermon and then the collection. The congregation sat facing the front, each man, woman, and child an island of calm. A fierce and alien spirit roved about this church.

In a daze, Dorothy was led up to the pulpit. Maise nodded encouragingly. The preacher rested his hand on her head and, rolling his eyes to the heavens above, asked God to relieve Dorothy's soul from suffering. *Amen and hallelujah!* shouted the congregation. She burned with shame at the spectacle they were making of her. *Fire and brimstone here on earth!*

There is no God in this madhouse. He is not here to help me. The preacher looked down upon her sorrowfully. Desperately, Dorothy turned away. The preacher made the sign of the cross as he watched Dorothy, a tiny white and wizened figure, hurry down the main aisle of the church. The congregation looked upon her with such sympathy that Dorothy began to cry. For her, the exit seemed miles away as she stumbled in her rush. Hands shot out to help her, but fearing them, she continued her pace.

They must not touch me, she thought. She concentrated only upon the door and the light beyond. At last, she was outside in the flickering twilight. For long moments, she sat shaking behind the wheel.

No one's God can help me. At last, she opened all the windows and drove slowly down the street. Soon she was back at Avenue Road. Turning south, she came to the leafy, winding crescent of Queen's Park and beyond it, the parliament buildings, imposing in their red, Romanesque style.

What good did the law ever do me? I cannot call upon God in his church, or justice in the courts. I must do this myself. Then, quietly at first, she began to hum. *What was that song*, she wondered? *Glory, glory hallelujah!* The most stirring hymn imaginable! Tossing her head back, she envisioned herself marching on toward … what? She neither knew nor cared. Her hair, held stiffly in place by spray, began to loosen and rise up in the breeze. She opened her mouth and sang out, "Glory, glory hallelujah!" By the time Dorothy had reached Lakeshore Boulevard, she was singing out as loudly as she could.

Once she emerged from under the railway bridge, she made a sharp right turn, only to realize she was headed steeply upward to the expressway, with no turning back. She had not driven on the highway since the 1940s. Traffic swept by her as she tried to edge into a lane. Horns blared as she almost hit the concrete abutment. Terror stricken, she hunted for an exit.

With the dark, empty buildings of the Exhibition Grounds in view, she managed to turn around, only to find herself on another up ramp. Creeping into the highway lane, she screamed when a horn blasted her. Sounding like a train, a tractor-trailer bore relentlessly down on her, flashing its headlights. With its brakes screaming, the truck pulled sharply back in front of her. Clutching the steering wheel, she quaked.

But then, she caught her breath. With the truck gone far ahead, the lights of Toronto and the waterfront spread before her like a beautiful honeycombed curtain of light. *A marvelous tunnel, leading me on and on, but to where?* she wondered. The expressway arced around and about the tall buildings so closely, she thought she might peer into the windows. It was a breath-taking city that she did not know.

She tossed her head back and laughed. Her hair fell loosely about her head and blew in the wind. Suddenly, she felt herself letting go. Again, she sang, "Glory, glory hallelujah!" As she picked up speed, the wind and the thousands of lights signaled freedom she had never known before.

Eventually, she got off the expressway and followed city streets up to the Danforth, that part of town where much of the Greek population lived. After several attempts, she parked the car on the street. The lighted storefronts and throngs of people entranced her. With energy flowing through her, she walked past fruit stores and meat shops, bakeries and restaurants, all open to the night time crowds. Strange sounds—foreign tongues and music—led her on for blocks.

She was hungry. Stopping outside a restaurant, she read the menu filled with names of unfamiliar, foreign foods. When she entered, a waiter, with a white beard and twinkling eyes, gave her a courtly bow and then seated her at the window. At first, it seemed strange to sit alone, and she wondered if she should pretend she was waiting for her husband. But no one looked askance, and the waiter was kind and explained the items on the menu.

The aromas wafting from the kitchen were delicious. With confidence, she ordered *souvlaki* and determined she would like it. A glass of white wine was placed before her. She could not remember ever having eaten alone in a restaurant before. Soon the plate was set before her filled with rice and little roasted potatoes and bits of lamb on skewers. The meat was succulent—not like the dried out Sunday roasts she was used to. And the two starches! An unheard of gastronomical extravaganza! When the waiter inquired if she were enjoying the meal, she nodded with enthusiasm. She washed the food down with the delicious white wine. Seeing her reflection in the window, she raised her glass in a toast and drank down the last drops.

She finished off the meal with a steaming cup of strong black coffee. With her first sip, she felt the warmth radiating throughout her body. Smiling, she acknowledged the rising pride within her. If she could drive on the expressway and explore the city, she could solve the mystery without Mr. Baxter. She did not need a man to help her.

CHAPTER 21

▼

Waiting for Harry, Natasha paced the lobby, lost in thought. Would he fear her nature meant she could never be faithful? Or was that just Sheila's claim?

Approaching Natasha's building, Harry saw the lake glimmering in the brilliant sun, low on the horizon. Odd to think that very same sun would, in a few hours, rise over Venice, where he hoped they would soon meet.

Just as he was about to park, Natasha appeared at the side of his car. She slid into the passenger seat and kissed him.

"Such a beautiful evening, Harry! Let's go for a walk down at the lake."

Agreeing, he put the car into reverse. Riding along Lakeshore Boulevard, they spoke in soft, familiar murmurs about the happenings of their days. She said nothing of her sense of urgency to see him and did not mention Sheila. They parked under some broad shade trees, near the Sunnyside pool.

In silence, they began to stroll. Shadows filled the cavernous stone archways leading to the pool within the white stucco building covered with a red-tiled roof. On a padlocked iron gate, a sign was posted. *Pool closed for cleaning*, it read. Harry began to wonder at her quiet mood.

Natasha's tension began to lift as they walked arm in arm around the enclosure and into the red, setting sun. She concentrated on him, liking the feel of his arm in hers. She loved his air of thoughtful attentiveness, which enveloped her. Weary of endless arguments with Sheila, she yearned to go to Venice with him.

They sat on a picnic bench.

"So," he said, "We won't see each other again before Venice?"

She reached for his hand. "I don't think so."

He caught her hesitant tone. "Something troubling you?" he asked.

She tossed back her hair and looked into his eyes. "No, darling, but we should talk."

"Sure," he said cautiously.

She picked up a twig and began drawing figures in a patch of sand. "Remember, some time ago, we talked about living together?" She looked up at him keenly. "And about love."

He stopped up and said carefully, "Yes? Have you thought more about it?"

She nodded slowly. "I was not being completely fair to you."

"How do you mean?"

They got up to walk along the shoreline where seagulls swooped and cried.

"You've been the *most* patient man in the world." She caught his hand and drew him closer. "Remember, we agreed to give ourselves time to really get to know each other?"

Harry nodded.

"About loving each other enough to let us be our real selves?"

He cleared his throat. "Yes. Have I passed the test?"

"Oh, indeed!" She grinned slyly at him. "With flying colors!" Gently, she touched his cheek. "But sometimes, I think I'm still your perfect fantasy woman."

He grinned and wrapped his arm about her waist. "Then it's all your fault. Can I help it if my seductress ignites my imagination? I mean, would you want it any other way?"

"Perhaps you could lower the pedestal an inch or two."

"Done!" he laughed. "But surely you like it just a little bit."

She laughed but then grew serious. "Harry? Sometimes we've talked about our childhoods."

"Yes?"

"I was just wondering … do you think all the people you've been in the past—the child at different stages, the student—that they're still inside you?"

Harry laughed. "I'm living proof of that! Remember last year about my father? There I was, a full-fledged adult—or so I thought—trying to look after a helpless, but ornery old man. But it was really my injured, eight-year-old self trying to cope."

"That's exactly what I'm talking about. You had to let him be himself."

Natasha stopped and leaned against a wrought-iron railing. Silhouetted by the intense evening light, her face remained in shadow. "I was reading somewhere that our fundamental nature is already determined at birth, and that it forms your destiny."

Harry nodded. It was refreshing to think of something other than the usual machinations of modern-day law practice.

"Do you agree?" She looked at him keenly.

He hesitated. "Yes, I think so, at least to a degree." To the extent he had thought about it, Harry believed in free will.

"Sometimes, I feel like there is a core person inside, someone who's always been there and always will be."

Suddenly, it occurred to him that their conversation was not just a casual exploration of philosophy. He felt at sea, trying to understand where her questions led.

"Natasha, are you talking about us? Is there something you want changed?"

Not answering him at first, she stared out onto the waves. Suddenly, she thought—*Why am I making this into such a problem?* Then she saw both of them from outside herself and at a distance. She knew she had her answer.

He was a kind, thoughtful, insightful, and intelligent man, who truly loved her with his passion and life. She glimpsed, if only for a fleeting moment, what lay inside him, the source of the attraction. Josef might have called it the spark or essence of life. She smiled, knowing that she could trust it, whatever its name.

As if light were spreading over every part of creation and past all time, it came to her that her nature did not divide and trap her. It was a gift that unified and freed her. She breathed deeply and felt its vast scope, power, and strength. Sheila's demands to choose one sort of life over another had cut deep, dark chasms within her where none should ever have existed. Now she could simply leave the torment behind for, in reality, it was and always would be the choice of one kind of *person* over another.

"No, my darling!" she said, winding her arms about him and kissing him deeply.

She took his breath away.

"I want you, and I want us to be exactly as we are."

"Will you come to Venice?"

"I will move heaven and earth to get business taken care of. Then I'll be off to see you by Wednesday."

"Will Sheila mind very much?"

"I've already talked to her, Harry." She took his wrist and glanced at his watch. "We need to get going. I've got a ton of paperwork to deal with, and *you* have to pack."

Parked in front of her condo, she took his hand and, one at a time, slowly kissed each finger of his hand.

"Let me come in?" he whispered urgently.

When he held her, she felt herself slipping, sliding, and opening up to his entire being.

"Yes," she said.

Hours later, Harry drove home across the Bathurst Street Bridge, which spanned the desolate railway lands below. He was not sure what had come over Natasha, but he grinned and started to hum. His mind raced to count the days until she was in Venice with him. Surely, he could get Norma's business taken care of quickly.

Further up Bathurst Street, he passed the Wheat Sheaf Tavern, once a student hangout where he and Peter Saunderson, his roommate from law school, sometimes had a beer.

Peter was the so-called *friend*, who had framed him twice. Years back, he had painted them as homosexuals, resulting in the end of his very first serious love affair with Katrina. Last year, Peter had used him to frame his lover, Roger, and his wife, Bronwyn. Peter, one of the flunkies for Pappas, had tried to find the very shares he was now tracking down. Because he had failed, Peter committed suicide rather than face the wrath of George Pappas.

Harry's house was jammed in between two much larger homes. Edging the car down the laneway, he entered through the rear door. Inside, it was stifling hot. He stripped off his jacket and turned on the air conditioner full blast. He found a beer at the back of the fridge and searched for sandwich makings.

While he was slicing the tomato, a question confronted him. Why did he respond so negatively to Hawke's advances? It wasn't simply that the guy was creepy. Some said that such reactions betrayed buried desire. Spreading the mayonnaise on the tomato and ham, he tried his hardest to imagine the attraction. It simply was not, nor could it be, there. Natasha had put her finger on it. The basic, immutable core could not be changed. He ate his sandwich and then began to pack.

CHAPTER 22

▼

After rushing all next day to get to the airport, Harry found his flight was delayed almost two hours. In the passenger lounge crammed with noisy families of straggling children, he closed his eyes. As he drifted off, his chin sank to his chest, and the din of voices grew into white noise. Images of Norma and Hawke, arguing outside a café on a palazzo, floated before him in a golden light. When he began to snore slightly, a little girl grabbed her mother's hand and giggled. He heard nothing. Visions of water, arching bridges, and flocks of birds had swept him away.

"He's got a gun!" screamed a voice.

Harry startled from his reverie. At the collective gasp, his eyes flew open, and he lurched forward.

A dark, cloaked figure stood before him. Harry started away.

The figure climbed up on the seat across from him.

"Stay!" the figure commanded Harry.

The man reached for something bulky under his coat. Harry edged away, and the gate area began to clear. The figure withdrew a package and waved it above his head.

Harry heard more shrieks. "A bomb!"

Passengers scattered. His heart thudding, Harry froze in place. *Not yet,* he thought! *No one can be after me so soon.*

Then the hood of the cloak fell away to reveal a man's grizzled face. "The Lord sees all! The Lord God sees into your very souls!" the man began intoning from above.

The mother screamed and clutched the little girl, who cringed against her.

At once Harry saw, in the man's eyes, the glint of madness of another world.

Waving the package high, the looming figure shouted and pointed at Harry.

"Yea! Though mine enemies surround me, I am protected by the Lord God, my savior." Spittle flew from his lips as he cried, "The righteous God shall fling mine enemies into the cauldrons of hell!"

"Sir?" Harry began cautiously, "I am not your enemy." He edged further from him.

Four uniformed guards sped across the concourse. Leaping over seats and landing full force upon the man, two of them knocked him to the floor. The others surrounded him, stamping their boots on the hand holding the package.

"Sweet Jesus!" he screamed. "In the face of mine enemies, I turn the other cheek!"

"Good God! He's just an old man," whispered Harry.

Ripping open the package, they found a leather-bound Bible. They tore off his hooded cloak to reveal a shock of white hair and his blotched skin. A tooth was missing, and blood streamed down his cheek. As if he were weightless, they marched him from the lounge, his spindly legs dragging on the floor. Trembling, Harry sank back to his seat. He did not know whether the crazed old man or the security police had frightened him more. Murmuring, the other passengers settled into their places.

Within moments, it was as if nothing had happened, and normality reigned once more. Harry's heart still pounded in his chest. Breathing deeply, he acknowledged the silent fear within. His plan to track down Norma's bounty required vigilance and caution, not paranoia.

Glancing at his watch, he saw that only five minutes had passed since the incident. Still shaken, he decided to find a drink in the bar overlooking the runway.

Just as he was ordering a beer, a man in jeans and a tee shirt brushed hard against him. Harry shied away and then jumped when the man grasped his arm to apologize. Taking his beer to a far table, Harry wondered, *Is this how Norma lives? With paranoid delusions? I can't be looking over my shoulder the whole trip!*

To distract himself, he watched the planes circling above in holding patterns as they waited to drop from the night sky. Tiny baggage carts scurried across vast distances to reach the aircraft whose red lights blinked on the tarmac. He knew the hooded figure had nothing to do with Hawke, nothing to do with him.

Garth Deal entered the room and sat at the far end of the bar. He ordered a scotch and, cracking his knuckles, spotted his quarry. In his pocket, he had stuffed his ticket for the same flight to Frankfurt and then Venice.

The old man, thought Harry, who was thrown to the floor and kicked, was a crazed religious zealot. He knew that gleam of paranoia in his eyes. He thought of Norma, trapped in her maze of confessions. Incarceration in a mental home was the price of her madness, genuine or not. Then he considered his adversary, Robert Hawke, who sought to seduce him with charm, intelligence, and wit. *And* he made him question himself. Finishing his beer, he sighed and stared out at the yellow and green pinpoints of light on the dark runways. Madness seemed to surround him.

Then he headed back for the gate, looking over his shoulder to see … what? He did not even know what to look for. Fortunately, the flight was not too crowded, and he got a window seat with no one beside him. After dinner, he fell into a fitful sleep. Next morning, the Frankfurt airport and the dash for the next plane to Venice blurred in his mind.

In less than two hours, the small plane banked, and Harry glimpsed Venice rising like a golden mist from the sea. Glittering domes and spires floated upward from brilliant blue waters, wafting through the city. With a tilt of the wing, the vision was gone, but like a kiss from a lover, the sensation remained. Enchanted, Harry immediately knew the power of his captor.

At Marco Polo Airport, he boarded the water taxi. As he approached Venice, he craned his neck to see the domes and spires from the mouth of the Grand Canal.

He stood in awe. Two thoughts collided. Instantly, he knew the beauty of Venice was at once ephemeral and immutable. It mirrored the human soul and, perhaps even his own, with great intimacy. The vision from the plane was only an insubstantial dream compared to the reality now laid out before him.

Bridges arced over glistening water, and soft-colored walls of pink, yellow, green, and white hung above the dark, impenetrable doorways just above the water. From shadows, gondolas swept past marble balustrades, and then emerged into light. The indistinct cries and song of the gondoliers rose up to him.

Riveted, as if beholding a painting of great beauty, he longed to reach out and touch the view simply to assure himself of its reality. Excited, his imagination drew him both inward and outward in the same instant. Like an artist, he labored before the scene to fix its essence within himself and yet laughed at the impossibility.

At last he was at the landing for the Hotel Bellini. Not until he entered the lobby, was he aware of the cacophony outside. Any sound within the grand reception hall was muted like soft whispers in a church of vaulted ceilings. As Harry walked across the expanse of red carpeting, the clerk glanced up with a half-smile. He handed him his reservation confirmation.

"We are delighted to have you as our guest," the man said in perfect English. He tapped the computer keys, and then such a cloud of sorrow passed over his face that Harry paused in taking out his passport. Excusing himself, the clerk disappeared behind the velvet curtain at his back. Harry took out his credit card. Although too weary for real annoyance, he was ready to blame Miss Giveny for failing to ensure proper reservations. Within moments, another man appeared from behind the curtain with the clerk.

"Welcome to the Hotel Bellini, Mr. Jenkins. I am the manager, Signor Fantino." The small, round man bowed formally and shook Harry's hand. Then, muttering in Italian, he bent over the computer. Angry whispers from the manager brought defensive chattering from the clerk.

"Forgive me, sir," Fantino began with an unctuous smile. "It appears someone …" he glowered at the clerk, "has mistakenly given the beautiful room set aside for you to another guest." The manager tapped more computer keys. "It appears that we are fully occupied."

Irritation flared up in Harry. "Listen, I made the reservation more than a.…"

The manager beamed and touched Harry's sleeve. "Please, sir, we will upgrade your accommodation to our very finest suite overlooking our beautiful canal." He spread his hands in a gesture of grandeur. "At absolutely no additional charge to you."

Harry was more than mollified. He was delighted. "That's excellent, Signor Fantino. Thank you very much," he said, handing over his credit card.

The manager waved and bowed again. "It is our pleasure. We had one of our very best rooms reserved for you. But, alas.…"

Once registered, Harry found a bellman at his side to take his bag. The key was the old-fashioned heavy kind, which he would remember to leave at the desk. The elevators were set along a corridor running from the main hall. Slowly, they rose to the top floor and stepped out. Soft breezes swept from windows at either end of the corridor and billowed the sheer curtains. The bellman opened the double doors to the suite.

Harry's eyes took in the immense room. The mahogany four-poster bed was a scroll of fantasy. Gilt-edged mirrors hung high on the wall with vases of flowers set underneath. His feet sank into the expanse of plush cream carpet, broken only by an oriental rug of red and gold. Tall glass doors led to a stone terrace, and beyond that lay the Grand Canal.

Immediately aching for Natasha's presence, he closed the hall door. She would revel in such luxurious elegance. After a hot shower, he lay on the bed. Before sleep swept over him, he envisioned Natasha curled beside him, and then Norma appeared, smiling into the sun in a field of crows at the Mercer.

In the hotel next door, Garth Deal stood at his window with a perfect view of Harry's suite. While his quarry slept, Garth smoked and read the English papers he had bought at the newsstand in the lobby. Following Jenkins about would be an easy enough job but, with Ronnie's restrictions, not much fun. He tipped back in his chair and began to doze.

At seven o'clock, Harry blinked open his eyes and gazed at the chandelier in the center of the ceiling. He studied the doors to the terrace. With cries of the gondoliers rising up, he imagined the canal and bridges below. Struggling to sit up, he reminded himself he was there on Norma's business. In the telephone book, he found a listing of banks. With only the account numbers, he needed a central source, like a banking association, to locate the transit numbers. There it was! He copied down the number of the *Banco Associonne*. Hungry, he decided to find a restaurant and then stroll about the city.

The elevator descended with the solemnity of a funeral cortege. At last, the brass gates heaved open, and Harry stepped into the corridor leading to the main hall.

Upon seeing Harry, the clerk waved him over. "Mr. Jenkins, there is something for you." Withdrawing an envelope from a pigeonhole behind him, he handed it to Harry.

"For me? Thank you," said Harry, surprised. Wandering away from the desk, he slit the envelope open. Inside were two tickets to a performance of Vivaldi's *concerto grossi l'estro armonico*, for tomorrow night at San Marco Basilica. Turning back, Harry said, "Are you sure these are for me?"

"Oh yes, sir. Compliments of the management," smiled the clerk.

Near the potted ferns, Harry spotted the manager, Signor Fantino, bowing at him. His smile was impish and so full of secret merriment that Harry almost expected a wink. But why such a gift? Surely, the new quarters more than made up for any confusion over the reservation.

Harry loved the seductive pull of great music. Leaving the hotel, he tried to remember his last concert, and he reflected life rarely gave him much pause for pleasure. He strolled down the cobble-stoned pathway to the bridge and found a café, over-looking the canal. Seated on the terrace, he was happy to be alone. In the deepening dusk, light from lamps along the canal speckled the black waters with shimmering gold. The more intense his gaze, the more elusive the essence of the city became. He studied the menu and sipped his wine. When the waiter appeared at his side, Harry ordered the *picata di vitello al limone*.

A shadow formed on the periphery of his vision. Behind him, a chair scraped on the flagstones. A low, musical, English-accented voice replied to the waiter's attentive murmurs. Harry turned back to his view of the canal to watch the vaparetto glide to the landing and disgorge its passengers. After dinner, he would board the boat for a ride along the Grand Canal. His dinner arrived.

"Good evening," the English voice said. Harry assumed the woman at the table behind him was addressing someone else. Paying no heed, he began to eat.

"Isn't it beautiful here?" Harry wished only to be left with his thoughts, but the voice intrigued him. Not wishing to be rude, he half-turned in his chair.

In the shadow, it was difficult to make out her features. But her smile was pleasant. "How long have you been in Venice?" she asked.

"Just got here today," he said politely, returning to his meal.

"So have I," she said. Harry only nodded. Moments passed in silence.

"Are you visiting for a while?" the woman asked.

Harry shook his head. "Just a few days." Despite his need for solitude, he found her accent charming. Not to be surly, he continued. "Have you been in Venice before?"

"Indeed. I come here at this time each year."

Harry set down his fork and turned. "I'm sorry. We ought to introduce ourselves." He stood and extended his hand. "I'm Harry Jenkins."

"And I am Margaret Rutherford." She nodded graciously and took his hand.

Momentarily indecisive, Harry asked, "Would you care to join me, Mrs. Rutherford?"

She seemed embarrassed. "Oh really … no. I wouldn't dream of intruding. I only meant …"

"Please," he said, holding out a chair.

In hesitation, Mrs. Rutherford twisted her napkin. Then smiling almost shyly, she came to his table. He pushed her chair in for her.

After they had exchanged formalities, her dinner arrived. A companionable quiet settled over them, until she began, "Venice is an incomparably beautiful city. Are you here for pleasure or business?"

"A bit of both." He was determined to stay clear of his purpose. "You said you come here each year at the same time?"

Mrs. Rutherford, her face clouding with sadness, fixed her gaze on the distant palaces. "Yes, Mr. Jenkins, I come each year in hopes of finding my son."

"Really?" With her expression, their conversation had swept to a far more personal level than he expected.

Her voice took on an uncomfortable intensity. "You see, my son was estranged from his father some years ago." She set down her fork and stared at her hands. "He—his name is Eric—is different from other boys."

Harry knew it was a mistake to ask, but, as if in a play, he filled in his lines. "Different? In what way?"

"My husband was a captain of industry. You know the type, Mr. Jenkins." An edge of bitterness crept into her tone. "Always right about everything. Up at six—cold shower—off to run three miles and then put in a fourteen hour day." Gently, she pushed her plate away.

Harry did not stir. He could picture the type so vividly that a sense of voyeurism swept over him. "And no room for Eric?" he asked quietly.

"Exactly, Mr. Jenkins." Her smile was caustic.

He could not resist asking, "And they argued?"

"Indeed. The clashing of opposites! Eric was a poet. He sees beauty in the world. His father sees only financial opportunity."

"You say he *was* a poet," Harry said carefully.

"Oh, I'm sure he still is … somewhere." Her eyes glinted in the light.

"But you return each year to look for him. Why do you think he's here?"

"Sometimes, he writes to me from Venice. He sends me his poems, but no return address." She bowed her head. "His father does not know."

At once, Harry understood her pain, and yet he found no words.

"But, Eric is my son," she said, "and I love him dearly."

Harry did not miss the defiant tilt of her jaw. He reflected sadly upon such pain. Indeed, a mother caught between husband and son lived in a cruel house. At last, he said warmly, "Mrs. Rutherford, I wish you the greatest luck in your search."

"Thank you very much. You're very kind." She looked up brightly at him and asked, "Do you enjoy music, Harry? I've heard there's a wonderful performance of Vivaldi at the San Marco Basilica on Monday evening."

"Yes, I *do* enjoy music, but I believe that performance is sold out." He stood and shook her hand. "This has been most enjoyable, but I must go." He hesitated, and then asked, "Where are you staying?" He wondered at his question.

"The Garibaldi Hotel."

He nodded, and then stepped away from the table.

"Are you on a search of your own, Mr. Jenkins?"

Surprised, Harry shrugged. "Perhaps. Why do you ask?"

"Just a sense. I think most people, who come to Venice, are looking for something."

He smiled slowly. "Yes, in many ways, I suppose I am." He shook her hand again and left her on the terrace.

In London's Mayfair Hotel, Robert Hawke slunk, like a restless beast, around his top floor suite. Below, Oxford Street flowed like a river of light in the evening.

"A spectacular view isn't it, Robert?" Veronica handed him a drink.

Accepting the glass, Hawke grunted. "What about Jenkins and that brother of yours?"

"Garth did call when you were in the bath."

"And?" Hawke, with his back turned to her, steeled himself for a litany of excuses for her brother's ineptitude.

She opened her notebook. "Jenkins is at the Bellini, and Garth has a room across the way at the Artimede, looking directly into his room."

"So the up-grade worked?"

"Yes. Fantino was very pleased to comply."

Hawke gave a little smile, not more than a slight upward pursing of his lips. "Very good. So Fantino remembered me?"

"Yes. And he will be at your disposal should anything else be required."

"And Garth …?"

Evading the question, Veronica continued brightly, "Fantino spoke very warmly of you and remembered your stay at his hotel."

Robert rubbed his hands together with pleasure. "Enrico is a good man. He will do as I ask without the slightest question. What about the concert tickets?"

"Two for Monday night. Compliments of the management."

"And will our Mrs. Rutherford accompany him?"

Veronica shook her head. "We don't know yet."

Robert's face turned a violent red. "And why do we not know?" he spluttered.

Veronica looked down at her notes and said quietly, "Garth did not see him at dinner. And I haven't heard yet from the woman—Mrs. Rutherford."

"What?" he whispered hoarsely. "You mean that idiot brother of yours lost him? He couldn't even follow the man out to dinner?"

Veronica used her most soothing tone to quiet him. "Robert, you cannot follow Jenkins that closely. He'd catch on in a minute."

"Jesus!" Hawke paced in front of the window, his bathrobe draping open. "Some people do know how to shadow, Ronnie."

"Now, Robert, please don't start."

Throwing up his hands, he shouted, "Start? I am asking a simple question which deserves an answer!"

"Robert, please! Do up your robe properly."

Robert stood over her shouting. "That brother of yours was a most difficult child, was he not? Put away in an institution for beheading the neighborhood cats?"

Mrs. Deal jumped at the sound of shattering glass. Robert had flung his glass against the fireplace, the shards splintering on the hearth.

"No parental control or discipline!" he raged, continuing to let the robe drape open.

Calming Robert too soon was like throwing gasoline on a fire. When his fury returned to a simmer, she said, "There was a call from Davenport in San Diego this afternoon."

Robert turned abruptly with a broad smile. "Really? Good news, I trust?"

"Some patients are showing very promising test results," she said, nodding enthusiastically.

"Ah! Wonderful, Ronnie. I'm *so* glad." Covering himself modestly, he relaxed in a chair. "It's such an exciting little project."

"I wish you'd tell me what you're really up to with Jenkins. I need to know, so I can be sure your instructions are properly carried out."

"Me?" Hawke grinned slyly. "I'm not up to anything, my dear. Officially, the plan is to kill Jenkins as soon as he leads us to the money."

"Then why are you setting up all these little tricks of yours?"

Hawke became cool. "Little tricks? I have no tricks, Ronnie."

"What about the Vivaldi tickets and Mrs. Rutherford?" Veronica frowned in recollection. "Didn't you hire another man named Angelo?"

"Ah … you see through me." His sarcasm was delivered in a pleasant, lilting voice. He reached to stroke her hair. "My sweet," he said softly. "I confess, I do have a few little plans for our friend, Mr. Jenkins. Call them tests, if you like."

"Is Garth to be a part of them? I just want to know so I can tell him exactly what to do."

"I understand your concern completely. I am doing my utmost to maintain a compassionate attitude toward a moron, because of *you*, Ronnie." He kissed her cheek. "Honestly, I *really* want him to succeed—for his sake, for yours and of course, the plan.

The doctor took his seat once more and primly crossed his legs. "But you must make one thing abundantly clear to Garth, if that is possible: under *no* circumstances must he harm our Harry in any way, unless he has been so ordered by me. *And*, Ronnie, he must keep him in view at all times *without* being spotted." He looked at her beseechingly. "Surely, that is not too much to ask?"

Harry boarded the vaparetto and took a seat outside near the bow. Garth Deal sat inside the cabin, running his fingertip along the edge of the knife in his pocket. He enjoyed his work, but long, drawn-out missions frustrated him.

Lost in thought, Harry stared at the inky shadows in doorways. As if in a dream, cafés glittering at the water's edge, and palazzos bathed in hazy light drifted past. Laughter and music came softly to him across the water.

He smiled in recollection of Norma's insistence. *The gondolas are far too expensive, Arthur. We will see this Grand Canal just as well from the vaparetto.* She was right. A ride in a gondola could cost two or three hundred American dollars. About to hide five million, Norma would not have squandered a cent on luxury or pleasure. A clever woman, but where did she go when she slipped beyond his reach? The psychiatrists saw only her sweet vulnerability, just before a sphinx-like mien slipped over her, engulfing her in an autistic trance. They missed that intervening moment of lucidity, that instant of cunning intelligence before the flight into madness.

Norma claimed to have murdered Archie Brinks, a Toronto stock trader, by arranging his execution in a courtroom. She insisted she had intentionally exhausted her lover, David Parrish, by dragging him up to the top the Statue of Liberty, where he suffered a heart attack. She swore that George Pappas had so greatly enraged her that she had plunged a knife between his shoulder blades. But Harry knew she could not have killed Pappas. He died of a gunshot wound to the back of the head, gangland style, within days of her confessions. Doubtless, she wished to have the credit. As far as he knew, Dr. Robert Hawke was the only current pretender to the riches, but there could easily be plenty of others.

Garth Deal shifted impatiently in his seat. His instructions were to follow Jenkins and keep Ronnie advised of his every move. But, with the guy playing tourist, the job was too boring to keep his full attention. He amused himself with remembrances of his old game. As a kid, he had derived special pleasure in killing all kinds of bugs by slowly cutting off their wings and legs with his jackknife. He would let them flail and squirm until, in a godlike rush of power, he would slowly squish them with a rock.

He moved onto the outer deck, taking a seat not five feet from Harry. In his youth, Garth had spent many afternoons behind the shed in the backyard capturing field mice for cats to tear apart, but soon the thrill was not enough. Jenkins was just like those mice—pitifully weak and unaware of danger. Lost in his own world, he made a perfect quarry.

Harry decided to get off at the next landing. Garth Deal followed. As he walked beside the canal, Harry considered Margaret Rutherford's situation, which seemed to confirm Natasha's thought that *your nature was your destiny.* In the Rutherford household, the natures of father and son were in such cosmic opposition that Mrs. Rutherford's destiny was to be trapped in the conflagration.

Thinking of his own father, Harry continued to stare out onto the water. After his sister Anna died, the man sank into a black hole and remained there for years. Was it his nature to be so greatly affected by her death that he could not communicate with his wife and only son? Perhaps another man would not have been so affected. Thank God, last year they had begun to talk, but now that was becoming almost impossible. Was Natasha saying that a person's nature—at least some parts— could never be changed? *If so*, he wondered, *is acceptance the only way for love to flourish?*

Excited by his new game, Garth cracked his jaw and knuckles. He popped a piece of gum into his mouth and chewed rapidly. Fun to see how close he could come to Jenkins without being noticed. The guy wasn't even checking over his shoulder, so he figured he could come right up behind him and then with his knife…. Garth began to whistle.

Harry stopped. Garth dodged behind some people strolling beside the canal.

Drawing a deep breath, Harry thought of Natasha. She had been almost certain she could come to Venice. Surely, it would happen.

Unbidden, a childhood memory of butterflies cruelly pinned to a cloth to preserve their beauty, arose before him. Even then, he had known that the animation of their wings increased their loveliness tenfold. Sometimes when he came too close, Natasha seemed to close up and drift off. He knew he had to let her be free. Otherwise, he would surely extinguish their life and love. The enigma of her held him fast. But some change seemed to have occurred on their last night.

Reaching the Bellini, he paused at the front door and looked about. He shook his head as if to dispel a strange sense, which had overcome him. *I must be imagining it,* he thought, glancing behind himself. Seeing no one who looked remotely threatening, he went inside and picked his key up from the night clerk. An envelope was waiting for him. In the elevator, he opened it and unfolded the single sheet. It was a faxed note from Natasha.

Harry,

Sorry I can't come to Venice. I've been delayed on my deals. Call me when you return,

Natasha.

Harry unlocked his bedroom door and stepped inside. He stared at the letter. *What? No "Dear Harry"? No "Love Natasha"?* He crumpled the single page and tossed it into a wastebasket.

Garth Deal watched him from the window across the way. He saw Harry's dead white face in the dark and watched him smoke two cigarettes on the balcony. At last, Harry rose to go in. He did not bother to undress. He simply lay down on the bed and gazed out the window until sleep finally came.

CHAPTER 23

▼

Dr. Michael O'Hearn pocketed the tickets for the play at the Royal Alexander Theater. The lights of the marquee sparkled, illuminating King Street and the theater crowds. He scanned the billboards advertising the play *Lovers Entranced.*

Janet, his wife, drew him close. "Now, don't go drifting off to sleep," she warned, squeezing his arm.

He nodded absently. The hospital never left him, particularly since Phil Glasser's fingertips had been blown off. Yesterday, over drinks at the St. George's Club, he had laid out his suspicions for all the hospital board members. The San Francisco address of Brahma Pharmaceuticals had turned out to be false. No listing for the courier, *As the Crow Flies Courier*, could be found anywhere, but still, he was convinced of a connection between Hawke and Brahma. The board members were enraged. Michael could understand now. The doctors, seated in the bar of the club, were obsessed with self-interest. The Hawke Institute had them in its clutches.

Janet tugged his sleeve. "See? Jonathan Coatsworth is playing the lead."

"Who's he?"

"Oh, Michael, he's on television all the time. You've seen him before."

Michael shrugged. The crowds moved toward the door.

"We've got great tickets. Fifth row, center on the main floor," she told him. "Coatsworth plays an old curmudgeon in his eighties, smitten with lust." She winked at him.

Once they were seated, Janet flipped through the playbill. Michael fumed about the afternoon at the police station. Unable to make a definitive connection between Hawke and Brahma Pharmaceuticals, he had failed to impress the detectives, Worrell and Zammit. But wasn't it *their* job to get the evidence? He had given them a lead to pursue, and there it had ended. A benign disinterest floated about the room. Shifting in their seats, they asked what the board of directors of the hospital thought. Michael knew about stonewalling.

Now, he folded and refolded his program until it was nearly ragged. His wife reached over and rested her hand on his. The lights went down, and the audience fell silent.

A beam of light followed an old man in striped pajamas, strolling from stage left. With his formal bow to the audience, the lights went up, and a kitchen was revealed. A backdrop of a darkened window appeared with a stove and fridge from the 1940s standing stage right. The man lounged on the edge of the kitchen table and spoke in a conversational tone.

"Good evening, ladies and gentlemen." Coatsworth smiled broadly. "Tonight, I play the fool." When the actor swept his arms upward, all the lights in the house brightened. The voice of a woman came from the back of the theater.

Marching purposefully down one aisle, the woman laughed, "You certainly are a damned fool, Peter!" She climbed the steps to the stage and headed for the refrigerator. "A grown man like you should be able to look after himself." Coatsworth cringed. Muttering, she heaved open the refrigerator and stuck her head in. Her rear end bumped about as she foraged.

Swinging around, she fixed Coatsworth with such a look of dismay that the audience chuckled. "Where's the food?" she demanded.

Michael sat absolutely still, his eyes fixed on the old man.

The woman began to scold. "Your fridge is empty except for this old jar of mustard and pickles!" She held out the jar and laughed, "You're hopeless without someone to look after you." With his back turned to the audience, Coatsworth tossed his arms out as if beset by an interfering troublemaker. Everyone laughed.

"You need a woman to keep house," she berated him. "Now that you're entering your dotage."

Huffing with annoyance, Coatsworth turned back into the spotlight.

Michael peered at the actor, and then flipped through the program to find Coatsworth's biography. Now he was certain. The actor was Andrew Jefferson, fresh from his appearance at the St. George's Club. Unbelievable! Hawke's finest example of the success of his clinical trials was an actor!

At intermission, Michael spoke with the manager. Settling back into his seat, he whispered to his wife, "We're going to try to meet Coatsworth after the play. I told the manager you're a great fan of his."

The lights went down. Janet stared at him in the dark.

At the play's end, the manager tapped Michael on the shoulder. Coatsworth had acceded to the request. They were led up narrow, winding stairs and through arches closed off with heavy red curtains. At the sound of a muffled "come in," the manager swung open the dressing room door. Michael pulled Janet by the hand into the room.

Coatsworth, still wearing his pajamas, stood before a mirror removing his makeup.

Michael held out his hand. "Hello, Andrew," he said. Janet shook her head, ready to correct him. Frowning, he touched her arm.

"Pardon?" The actor turned.

Smiling, Michael sat on the edge of the chesterfield. "You played Andrew Jefferson."

Coatsworth frowned in concentration. "And when might that have been, dear boy?"

"One week ago, at the St. George's Club."

Disturbance clouded the actor's eyes. Hastily, he grabbed more cotton balls and turned to the mirror. "I'm afraid you're mistaken, mister …?"

"Dr. Michael O'Hearn. This is my wife, Janet." Janet smiled in confusion. "I was in the audience for Dr. Hawke's show. I shook your hand."

Coatsworth glanced at him in the mirror and smiled vaguely. "Ah, well … yes." He straightened up and faced Michael. "Well now you've found me out, what can I do for you?"

"Tell me about Dr. Hawke."

The actor shrugged. "I know nothing of the man. It was a strictly professional engagement."

"You didn't know it was all a hoax?"

Waving his hairbrush, Coatsworth smiled broadly. "Of course, dear boy! That's what theater is."

"But you must have known it was a fraudulent claim," Michael insisted.

With a patient air, Coatsworth set down his brush. "It was a professional engagement, sir. Would you like to see my statement of fees? Of course, I was paid, quite handsomely too."

"Who paid it?"

The actor began rummaging through his wallet. "Yes, here it is. Paid by Hawke Pharmaceuticals." He squinted in the light. "A division of Brahma."

Michael felt his heart thud. *Bonanza!* "Mr. Coatsworth," he said very quietly, "would you please let me have a copy of that invoice?"

Coatsworth squinted up at him. "Why?"

At first, Michael had no answer. He gazed into Jonathan Coatsworth's eyes. At last, he said simply, "It would be a very great help to me."

The actor hesitated, and then smiled with great sweetness. "Well, if it would please you *that* much, dear boy, I suppose I could give a copy." Lowering his eyelids, he said "Simply as a memento of an evening that you so greatly enjoyed." He touched his arm lightly and handed him the invoice. "Take it to the manager. I'll call and ask him to make you a copy, Dr. O'Hearn."

Michael nodded. "I'm very grateful, sir."

Rushing down three narrow flights of stairs, Janet followed her husband. "Michael? What on earth was that all about?"

With a grin, Michael looked upward at her. "Tell you later, darling. I want to get this copy made before he changes his mind."

Jonathan Coatsworth poured a glass of sherry and, before lighting his cigar, he struggled to open the dormer window. Rain spattered into the alleyway, cooling off the evening heat. The bottom of the twisting fire escape was lost in the mist below. Jonathan fingered the invoice, which an usher had returned to him from the manager's office. He shrugged. *Just another professional engagement that had been reasonably well received*, he thought.

A soft tap came at the door. Coatsworth set his cigar on the window ledge and opened the door. Hepple, the janitor, stood before him, bucket in hand.

"They'll be turning off all the lights soon, Mr. Coatsworth." Jonathan was fond of the little man who smiled shyly up at him. Almost every night for thirty-five years, Hepple had closed up the theater.

"Don't worry. I shall be gone in a few minutes."

The janitor sniffed, and then a slow smile of conspiracy passed over his features. "Don't be leaving any ash about, sir."

Coatsworth, as he had many times before, gave a wink and said, "I shall be most careful, my good man."

As Hepple turned to go, he said, "Just remembered, sir. A man was asking for you after the play. Wanted to know if you was still here." He shook his head fiercely. "But I told him, I didn't know."

"That's good," said Jonathan absently. Although he was pleased by the occasional autograph seeker, he preferred as few intrusions into his private life as possible.

"Big man, he was." Hepple spoke reflectively. "Not the kind of person you usually see here."

"How so?" Jonathan mumbled, wanting to get back to his cigar.

Hepple shrugged. "A bit of a ruffian, I'd say, Mr. Coatsworth. Didn't look much like a playgoer."

"I suppose he's gone?" Jonathan started to close the door.

"Oh, indeed. I sent him off. Saw him walk west along King Street."

"Thanks, Hepple. Good night." Jonathan closed the door.

Perching on the window ledge, he puffed on his cigar. He could see along the alleyway to the street, where the lights of the marquee gave the few passersby a sickly neon glow. He sipped his sherry and wondered at his reflective mood.

For years, he had played the butler or some minor walk-on part. Now at sixty-eight, he had his first lead in a play, albeit a half-baked comedy. He dropped his cigar out the window and watched the ember spark and twirl into the alley below. What had happened to the old dreams of the Shakespearean stage? He jauntily saluted his reflection in the mirror. Such hopes had died years ago. He hurried down the endless flights of stairs. As he left the theater, he gave a quick bow to Hepple, who was sweeping the sidewalk.

Jonathan strolled back up the alleyway misted by the rain spattering on hot pavement. Tonight, understanding of life weighed far too heavily upon him. *Time*, he thought, *for a drink at the bar the next street up.*

Just past the fire escape, Jonathan saw a figure barreling toward him with a huge, black umbrella. As he flattened himself against the wall, a gloved hand, from behind, seized his windpipe. His elbows flailing out, Jonathan tried to peel away the fingers clutching him, but he was no match for such strength.

As his body sagged, his spirit strove upward, lost in tag ends of Shakespearean sonnets. Trumpets sounded from nowhere. Before he slipped to his knees, a knife blade was thrust between his ribs and into his heart. Jonathan collapsed in the rain puddles and garbage. A black-heeled boot seemed poised above him forever, until it smashed down into his face. The actor was left dead, heaped at the side of the theater.

Ten minutes later, Michael O'Hearn's Jetta spun out of control on Bayview Avenue, just below the Bloor Street viaduct. On the curve, slick with rain, the car careened into the high, wire fencing and ripped out a hundred feet of it. Then the car flipped and smashed into a concrete abutment. Michael and his wife died in an instant.

CHAPTER 24

▼

By morning heavy, humid air had crept over Venice, muffling the cries of the boatmen unloading boxes of fruit and vegetables at the landing. The sun glared through layers of cloud and blanketed Harry's suite in stifling heat.

In the light, Harry's eyes hurt. He retrieved Natasha's letter and smoothed it out. Still the same telegraphic message!

Harry,

Sorry I can't come to Venice. I've been delayed on my deals. Call me when you return,

Natasha.

The words settled heavily upon him. He rose unsteadily and looked out. Beneath him, the Grand Canal lay black and turbid. Sourness descended upon him.

There had to be some mistake. Her curtness made no sense. Or had he missed something the night before he had left?

Do the job and get the hell back home, he thought. Norma's mission was no longer an intriguing case, just an annoying duty to be done quickly. But he must not minimize the obvious danger. He had to keep a step or two ahead of Hawke.

But Natasha would not leave his thoughts. He picked up the phone and dialed her number. Remembering it was the middle of the night in Toronto, he slammed the receiver down.

His eyes wandered to the hotel across the canal. A man was staring into his room. His bulk loomed with menace. Harry backed away. Immediately, he thought of the Jeep, and bile rose at the back of his throat. The man swiftly withdrew into shadow.

At the buffet downstairs, Harry's stomach churned. He took juice, a croissant, and black coffee from the buffet and sat in the formal dining room. At first, he doodled irritably on his yellow legal pad. Why no explanation? Was she dumping him?

That could *not* be right. He could not describe it well, but the last night in her apartment had been different. Few words had been spoken between them, but he had sensed that some reserve—some inhibition or impediment—had floated off, and they had regarded each other with new eyes. *There must be a mix-up. But what?*

He *would* send her a fax. He paused to consider his tone. Warm? Upset or calm and reasoned? A touch of humor seemed appropriate. At last, he wrote:

Darling Natasha!

I am disappointed! But wait, I can stay in Venice till you get here. No rush. On the other hand, I'll go to London, Paris, and Rome ... Berlin ... Afghanistan [but would you come?] ... Mount Kilimanjaro [need I go on?], just to be with you. You name it, and I'll be there.

He watched the waiter pour more coffee into his cup—rich, black liquid filling a perfect, round circle of white. Pausing, he looked about the still restaurant. In the dim light, frail and elderly tourists at breakfast seemed trapped forever, like faded figures in a centuries-old painting. Without hesitation, he finished off the fax.

I love you and need you. I want to be with you always. Please try to come. Please! Let's get married in Venice.

All my love, Harry.

Smiling, he finished his coffee, and then hurried to the front desk to find Fantino on duty.

"Bonjourno, Signor Jenkins!"

Harry nodded. "I'd like to send a fax, please."

"Certainly, sir. Please ..." Fantino held out his hand. "I will give it to the clerk, who will...."

"I'd like to do it myself, right away."

Fantino inclined his head and smiled briefly. "Since it is an urgent matter, I will cut away all red tape!" he said grandly. Snatching the paper from Harry's hand, he continued, "I will send it from my private office." Before Harry could object, the manager had disappeared behind the velvet curtain.

Once in his office, Fantino set aside Harry's declaration of love and marriage proposal. In its place, he inserted a blank sheet of paper. The fax to the lady, whom Fantino understood to be most attractive, would have no words of love and marriage. It would have no words at all.

Harry fidgeted with the newspapers at the reception desk. *Where in hell is the man?* He calmed himself with thoughts of Natasha. That last night there had seemed no need for words, as if she had truly given herself over to him—to them. It was no passing affair. They would meet, if not in Venice, then somewhere else. They just needed some time away together.

Whistling, the manager carefully stapled the fax receipt to Harry's letter and returned to the lobby. "Please, Signor Jenkins. The letter has been sent as instructed."

Harry checked the fax sheet to ensure her home fax number had been correctly stated. Then he turned to go.

Laying a hand on Harry's arm, Fantino asked, "May I assist you in any other way, Signor Jenkins?"

Harry backed away slightly. "No, thank you, but if you have a map ..."

Fantino's eyes widened, and then he quickly said, "Of course, signor, I will give you a map. But it would be my greatest pleasure to give you directions or provide you with a private guide."

The intrusion set Harry on edge. "Just the map, thank you."

"Certainly, Signor Jenkins." The manager bowed and was about to spread a map on the desk. "If you tell me where...."

Harry took the map from his hand. "Thanks very much, but I'll be fine on my own." He pocketed the map and turned to go. Over his shoulder, he saw the manager dial the phone at the desk.

Outside, Harry swore. Fantino was doing everything in his power to follow him. And then, there was the huge hulk shadowing him. He stopped to study the map. After intense scrutiny, he found the location of the Bankers Association. Hurrying across another bridge, he forged on. Within moments, he knew he had made a wrong turn.

Duty had struck Harry blind to the beauty of Venice. The gondolas, so enchanting yesterday, now appeared to float aimlessly about the landing, their black curved prows seeming to touch, as if engaged in conspiratorial conversations. Darkened passageways, once so enigmatic and charming, now yawned like dangerous labyrinths ready to suck him in. Stopping in the shade, he studied the map.

Garth Deal stepped into a doorway and cracked his knuckles. Being ambidextrous was a great advantage. His left arm was as strong and agile as his right. From behind, he could cut Jenkins' air off with his right arm and thrust in the knife, high up on the left side between the ribs, straight into the heart. His excitement mounted. Sometimes, it was almost better than sex.

Harry caught sight of the familiar, bulky shape crammed into a doorway. Stopping, he peered around a stone gargoyle. Definitely, it was the man in the hotel window across the way—Hawke's emissary. He turned into a shop and bought a package of cigarettes. On his way out, he saw the same man in the next shop with his back turned, examining cheap masks and china models of the Rialto Bridge.

Speeding up, Harry started down another cobblestone path, which narrowed to no more than an alleyway. As he progressed, the air grew fetid, and the shadows thickened. In the growing heat, he had difficulty breathing. Undoing his collar, he glanced over his shoulder.

The man's looming form blotted out the entrance to the narrow passage. Knowing his direction had been a mistake, he sought escape. But maybe he should approach him? Any confrontation should be in the open, with lots of people around, not down some dark alley. No. Better keep moving! When he started to jog toward beams of sunlight up ahead, he heard rasping in his chest.

In his hurry, he stumbled on broken cobblestones and nearly toppled into the canal. Loud, off-key singing and then laughter filled the ever-narrowing passageway. From above came a clatter of tins. Suddenly, a torrent of dirty water poured down not a foot away from him.

Abruptly, he turned back and, with labored breathing, rushed deeper into another maze of twisting alleys. Again his pathway narrowed, then ended abruptly at the next doorway. He froze, trapped in a dead end!

To his left was the canal. One step, and he would be in the water! Over his shoulder, he saw the shadow of the ominous bulk not ten yards from him and heard his whistling. Rivulets of sweat ran down Harry's face. Touching a doorknob, his hand twisted it open. He stepped inside a deserted stairwell, where it was cool, musty, and silent. In the gray interior light, he leaned against the wall and breathed as quietly as possible. Maybe the man had not seen him. Harry must have waited ten minutes.

When he looked outside, Hawke's man had, like an apparition, simply disappeared. Harry edged out of the doorway and heard the echo of muttering voices. Forcing himself to retrace his steps back up the alleyway, he saw only a few black-cloaked women carrying baskets of laundry. The huge man was no longer in sight.

Hawke's plan was crystal clear. Track him until he found the money, and then kill him. On top of that, they were toying with him—wanting him to know he was in their sights. Harry shivered in the heat and began retracing his steps. He had to check out of the Bellini as soon as he got back.

At the next turn, he stopped. Before him lay the Bridge of Sighs, brooding morosely over black waters. In an instant, his childhood dream of romantic adventure dissolved. Now the gloom and terror of prisoners clutched him. He sank to steps leading down to the water and shook his head at the collision of dream and reality.

Recollections of a visit to the Tower of London swept over him. Utter dread had emanated from the Tower as if carried on the air from its blood-soaked soil. Here too, the bloody past whispered cries to all who would listen. Slowly, Harry rose and turned away.

Right in front of him was a sign, which read *Associonne d' Banco*. He grinned in relief as he opened the door. Inside, he stepped up to the marble counter with a brass lamp and green shade. He realized he was still trembling. A young woman looked up. When she smiled and pushed back a lock of hair, he thought of Natasha.

"Bonjourno, signor. How may I help you?"

Harry took out his pad of paper. "I'm trying to locate some bank accounts. I've got the account numbers, but not the transit numbers. Could you tell me what bank they might be at?"

She leaned over the counter to see his note. He could not avoid noticing the swell of her breasts.

"Why do you wish to know?" She gazed directly into his eyes.

Harry shifted slightly further away down the counter. "It's a confidential matter for a client."

"I cannot give out such information, signor." She moved closer still. "If you allow me to copy down the numbers, I will see what I can do."

"No, signora," Harry said. He could feel her breath in his ear. She reached forward so that her breast brushed his hand.

"If I am to assist you, sir," she said, drawing back slightly, "I will need to make several calls. Then I could have the information when you return tomorrow."

"Tomorrow? Why not telephone whomever, and I will speak to him?" He stared back at her.

Suddenly, the girl shrugged and returned to her stool. "Then I cannot help you, signor."

Reaching into his wallet, he took out a fifty euro note. "Would this help?"

Fear filled the girl's eyes. She did not move. Just as he was about to take the money back, her hand shot out and grabbed it.

"Signor. Please. Speak to no one about this."

Harry nodded. She stuffed the bill in her pocket.

Trembling, she said, "The bank you are looking for is the Banco Franco. There is only one, close by the Rialto."

"Why are you so afraid?"

"Go!" she hissed. "And please, tell no one that I gave you the information."

Harry nodded and left without further word. In the back office, the girl dialed the Bellini Hotel.

"Signor Fantino?" she whispered into the phone. "He has left. He refused to give me the numbers and, of course, I gave him nothing whatsoever."

Fifteen minutes later, Harry found the bank, just where she had said. A musty odor overcame him as he entered. Through high windows, light tried to permeate the dank atmosphere. An elderly man, wearing green visor, sat on a stool.

"*Scussi*," Harry said. "Is the manager in?"

The old man squinted up at him. "The manager is in a meeting. Come back another day."

Harry craned his neck to look into the main office. Behind the desk, sat a man dressed in a formal looking suit. The office appeared to be empty.

"There's no one in there with him." Harry said. "I'll wait. Please tell him that I am an *avocati* and wish to discuss a mutual client's business."

Regarding Harry suspiciously, the old man edged off his stool and entered the manager's office. Harry could understand no part of the conversation, but within a moment, a somber looking man emerged to shake his hand.

"I am Signor Allegrini. It is an honor to have you here, sir. Please to come in." Wheezing, he ushered Harry inward. Once seated, he began, "And how may I assist you with this mutual client?"

"I'm Harold Jenkins, an *avocati*. I represent a Mrs. Arthur Dinnick."

Allegrini laced his fingers over his protruding stomach. Harry withdrew his notes from his case.

"I understand her late husband, Arthur, had an account at this branch of your bank."

The manager waved his hands in the air. "But signor! I can only speak with the legal owner of the account."

"Of course, I have documentation that will...."

The telephone rang and, when Allegrini answered, he spun himself about to look out the window. He spoke rapidly into the phone. "Che documenti, signor? Che dinero?" Then he listened intently for several moments.

Harry froze. *Is that Fantino calling? Are spies everywhere?*

Allegrini hung up. "Do you have account numbers and documents that establish your authority?"

Harry had to trust him. He handed him the list.

With glasses perched on the end of his nose, the manager examined the papers, and then said gravely, "I shall have my assistant, Paulo, find this information. They are, sir, very old accounts. The records will be in the vault out of the premises."

"How long will that take?"

The manager shrugged. "A day or two, perhaps, signor."

"The matter is extremely urgent," said Harry. "Couldn't we speed matters up?"

The manager's eyes narrowed. "In that case, I could send Paulo downstairs to check our records."

"I thought they were stored off premises."

"We do have *some* old records downstairs." He called in his assistant. "Paulo? Go to the basement vault." Paulo nodded. "See if we have a record of these accounts in the name of Arthur Dinnick."

Paulo turned a ghastly white. "Dinnick?"

"Si. Dinnick." said Allegrini.

The little man began to tremble. "They are very old accounts, signor. Too much bad history."

"What? You know them?" The manager's eyebrows curved upward.

Paulo shook his head rapidly. "No … no!" He hurried off.

Harry and the manager chatted until Paulo arrived with a file. The old man bowed his way out, shutting the door tightly behind him. Allegrini opened the file and spread out a letter. Minutes passed as he read.

At last he wheezed, "Signor Jenkins, there are some complicated instructions here."

"What kind of instructions?" Harry asked.

"First, I must ask under what authority you operate."

Harry slid Arthur's death certificate and probated will across the desk. "Arthur Dinnick died on the twenty-eighth of August 1985, leaving his entire estate to his wife, Norma." Harry flashed the gold court seal on the probated will.

His breath coming in short puffs, Allegrini examined the will and death certificate, and then nodded.

"This is the court order," continued Harry, "appointing me as Mrs. Dinnick's legal guardian. Also, my own passport."

Allegrini took his time examining the documents. At last, he rasped, "Before I tell you what else I need, you must open this envelope in my presence."

Harry saw his own hand tremble in anticipation as he reached for the envelope. The hunt was almost over. He slit the envelope open. The brief note was signed by Arthur Dinnick. It read:

> *Dear Norma/or whomever may be acting on your behalf,*
>
> *You must go to London and present Barclay's Bank in Cromwell Road, London, with the following code in order to gain access to the Elixicorp share certificate.*
>
> *The code # is: AD.082885*
>
> *Once you have the share, bring it back to the manager, who will then give you the funds, payable in any form directed by you or your legal representative.*

Arthur's plan was an elegant puzzle, thought Harry. If he had started the search in London, as originally intended, he would immediately have hit a dead end. Although he might have satisfied the requirement of entering the safety deposit box, he would not have been able to remove the shares without the code. Without Norma's disjointed recollections, he would never have guessed that the trail began in Venice.

"Do you have a document entitled Elixicorp Share Certificate?" the manager asked.

"No, sir. But I know where to find it. I'll be back in a day or two to give it to you."

Allegrini regarded Harry benignly. "May I assist you in any other way, signor?"

Wary of some trick or delay, Harry studied the manager's face, but could discern nothing from his bland expression. After shaking hands, he strode from the office.

Outside, Paulo leaned against the balustrade of a bridge. Appearing gray and sickly in the shadows, he caught Harry's sleeve.

"Signor Jenkins? Please to talk with you. It is urgent." The quaking voice made Harry stop.

"What is it, Paulo?" he asked.

"The Dinnick file." The man glanced up and down the canal. "I remember the day Signor Dinnick came to the bank. He was very frightened that day."

"Frightened? Of what?"

"A man was following him."

"Did you see him?"

"Si." Paulo nodded frantically. "He come in just after Signor Dinnick leave the bank." Then the old man jabbed a finger at his eye. "The man, he have the bad eye. No ... no, the evil eye. I see him, and I cross myself."

"What did he look like?"

Paulo paused to consider. "He was not tall. He was round and soft, and his clothes, very good clothes. He was young man."

"Did he have a lisp?"

Paulo looked up at Harry with incomprehension.

"Did he speak softly?"

Paulo concentrated, then nodded rapidly. "He talk soft—like a woman. Si."

For Harry, Paulo had painted a picture of the young Dr. Robert Hawke.

"Thank you, Paulo. I think I know the man."

"His softness hides much, Signor Jenkins. But the evil eye tells all."

Harry patted the old man's arm and turned to go.

"Signor Jenkins, I tell more."

"Yes?"

"I hear them talk. Signor Dinnick and the other man. He threaten him with death if he does not give them the money." Paulo began to stutter. "I read in the newspaper. Signor Dinnick was found dead two days later in a hotel room in Firenze."

"He died of a heart attack."

Paulo shook his head frantically. "No. Signor Dinnick was murdered with poison."

Harry shivered in the dank chill surrounding him. "How do you know he was murdered, Paulo?" he asked quietly.

The old man tapped a bony finger next to his eye and whispered hoarsely, "The man was evil. He kill Signor Dinnick, because he hide the money."

Harry regarded Paulo carefully. If the man were right, then Hawke had shadowed Arthur's every move. When the money disappeared from view, Arthur had been murdered.

"I'll be back in a few days, Paulo. We will talk again." Harry turned away and walked rapidly to the landing for the vaparetto.

CHAPTER 25

▼

Mrs. Deal spread the blanket on the grass in Hyde Park. Opening the picnic basket, she glanced furtively at Robert. She hadn't yet given him the latest report.

"I do hope you brought cold chicken?" Robert asked. "And potato salad, too?"

She checked the basket. "Yes, everything."

"What about the wine?"

"That too." She held up the bottle of French Chardonnay.

"Excellent, Ronnie!" Stretched out on the blanket, he clasped his hands behind his head. "When I was a child …" A wistful smile crept over his face. "Mother would take us for a picnic on Sundays."

Veronica wondered what version of mother was coming. Sometimes she was a saint, who fed her children sweets and took them to the seaside. Other times, she was the harridan who locked her children out of the house and raged at them from upstairs windows. But perhaps Mother had her side of the story. Robert was likely the kind of child who should have run off to the circus.

"My happiest moments," he sighed, "were when my brother, David and I played on the swings. Sometimes the little bugger would knock me off and we'd roll around in the dirt till we were black." Robert chuckled. "Mother would get *so* cross!"

"Here's your plate." Veronica knew his imaginative interludes usually spelled trouble.

Robert nibbled daintily on his chicken leg. "See that little boy and girl with their nanny?" A boy of about six, dressed in gray flannel shorts and a long sleeved white shirt, ran swooping through the grass. His older sister lumbered after him, shouting.

"That little fellow is chasing the birds. What fun he's having!" Robert laughed. "Just look at the imp! Even though he'll never catch them, his pleasure is in the pursuit."

"Robert, would you like to hear the latest report?"

"Not now! I want to watch these children. His older sister's a bit dull."

"Dull?"

"Don't you know anything about children, Ronnie?" Then he added crossly, "Well, what about the report, then?"

"Harry has found the bank."

"So now it's *Harry*, is it?" Robert's eyebrow curved upward unpleasantly. "Not feeling for our adversary, are we, Mrs. Deal?"

Veronica shook her head.

"Good. And has he gotten my money yet?"

"We don't know."

"Garth's asleep at the switch again?"

She hesitated. "No, he could hardly walk into the bank with him, could he?"

"What else has your brother not done?"

"Nothing, but Jenkins has moved out of the Bellini."

"Why?" Robert's gaze returned to the children. "Look! They're off to the swings. Such a charming little fellow. That sister's no match for him."

"We're not sure why he moved."

"Our Mr. Jenkins has much energy and intelligence, rather like our young man on the swing. No doubt Garth's been breathing down his neck."

"Garth's been quite careful …"

"Look at him, will you?" Hawke spoke in delight. "The child is swinging so high, he must think he's in the treetops."

Veronica followed his gaze. The boy wriggled to the edge of the swing. "He's going to jump off!" she said.

"Risk taking is bred in his bones, my dear, unlike his doltish sister."

As the boy hit the ground, he rolled onto the grass, just avoiding his sister's kick.

"Stupid and vicious little girl!" Robert declared. Turning back to Veronica, he asked, "Any other news?"

Veronica began gathering up the plates and cutlery. "Unfortunately, there's been a death."

"Whom did Garth murder now?" he asked sharply.

"An old man at the bank."

"Great God in heaven! Not the manager, I trust?"

Veronica shook her head. "No, the manager's assistant."

"Jesus, Ronnie! Can't that brother of yours go back to beheading cats or terrorizing mice?" Robert focused his attention on the children running off to the teeter-totters. "Where is the body now?" he asked.

"It was dumped into one of the canals."

"Is there anything to connect Garth?"

She shook her head.

"We'd better get to Venice as soon as possible," he muttered. "Our Mr. Jenkins must be on to something, if he's still there. At some point, we will have to confront him."

Hesitating, she then asked, "Robert, are your plans for Mr. Jenkins any more specific?"

The boy wriggled off the teeter-totter just as his sister reached the top.

Robert laughed. "See! He's going to get her back."

Slamming to the ground in a heap, the girl wailed. The nanny grabbed the boy and shook him.

Robert was outraged. "Look at that ridiculous woman! She sits reading her magazines, oblivious to the real events, then descends upon the boy." Tears glinted in his eyes. "Just like Mother!"

Recovering, he spoke more quietly, "You see, my dear, I do have a very precise plan for Harry, of which I've already spoken. Once he's found my money, I will take it from him and kill him. But don't misunderstand me. I'm in no hurry."

"Why the delay?"

"I want to observe our Mr. Jenkins to see what stuff he's made of. After all, he just might qualify for my trial of one, which," he chuckled, "by its name, suggests only one suitable candidate."

"And what is this "trial of one" all about?"

"The ideal candidate is a man of high intellect and intuitive powers. He must also combine daring with an edge of cunning, just like that young man over there." Hawke brightened with a new thought. "Ronnie, I suppose Garth's like that boy's slow-witted sister?"

Veronica, struggling with the picnic hamper, determined to ignore him.

"Besides, I have another test for Mr. Jenkins. Do you think he is an honorable man? Although he refused my completely reasonable suggestion that the court decide the ownership of the funds, I still think he is a man of integrity. After all, he *is* a lawyer."

Annoyed with the musings of an empty-handed man, she asked, "Shouldn't you help me with this blanket and basket?"

"What? Oh yes, of course, my dear." Gazing about the park, he lifted up the picnic hamper. "Wait! The children are back. I'm going to buy them ice cream." At a rapid pace, he set off toward the little boy.

"Robert, stop!" Veronica cried out. Robert turned back. "You can't do that."

Hawke was astonished. "Why ever not?"

"You can't buy ice cream for children you don't know."

His lips tightened in stubbornness. "Why not?"

"People will think you're a child molester." She could scarcely believe he could be so stupid.

"Me? A child molester? That's ridiculous. I am merely admiring a very fine young boy and want to reward him."

Veronica shook her head slowly in disbelief. "Honestly, just trust me. That nanny will call for the police. Then where will you be?"

The thought of the police sobered him. Yet he could not believe the simple act of buying an ice cream could be so vilely misinterpreted. At last, he said, "All right, Ronnie. If you say so." Wistfully, he glanced back at the boy, then started out of the park. Veronica struggled up to the street with the hamper.

Barreling through the doors of the Bellini, Harry almost slammed into Fantino.

"Signor Jenkins? A letter was delivered for you this morning," said the little man.

"A letter, not a fax?"

"Si." The manager retrieved an envelope from the pigeonholes behind the front desk.

Harry did not recognize the handwriting on the envelope. "Signor Fantino? I will be checking out this afternoon."

The manager's face darkened. "But, sir! Are your accommodations not satisfactory?"

Harry shook his head. "They're fine, but I've had a change of plans."

"You will leave a forwarding address, in the event that we receive a response to your fax?"

"I'll check back to see if there's anything." Harry said abruptly.

In his room, he took off his shoes and undid his shirt. No one was watching from across the way. He opened the envelope.

Dear Mr. Jenkins,

If you are alone in Venice, I wondered if you might care to join me for dinner this evening. I found Sunday evening very pleasant, and I trust you did as well.

Sincerely,
Margaret Rutherford,

Garibaldi Hotel.

Suspicious of everyone and everything, Harry tossed the note aside, but almost immediately retrieved it. The woman was undoubtedly one of Hawke's spies. Why not see the woman? Perhaps he might glean some useful information. Or better still, use her to throw them off the trail. With no Natasha, he had to acknowledge the pull of loneliness. Picking up the phone, he called Marco Polo airport and asked for the next flight to London. Nothing until the morning. Hawke's thug was dogging his every step. Probably, he should keep on the move but suddenly, he realized how weary he was.

Wandering out to the balcony, he saw a crowd had gathered at the bridge. At least ten men were trying to drag something from the canal. Several had dived in to drag what looked like a sack from the water.

Harry jumped when the telephone rang. The clerk downstairs wanted to confirm he was vacating the room. Glancing about, he realized it would take only moments to pack. *Man on the run*, he thought.

"I'll be out in half an hour."

"May I call you a water taxi, signor? If you tell me your destination...."

Harry was about to cut him off, but then he said, "Can I get a train to Rome from here?"

"One leaves in about an hour at four o'clock. Shall I phone and reserve a ticket for you?"

"Yes, please. Tell them I'll pick it up at the station."

After paying the bill, Harry carried his luggage out the front door. Maybe Fantino and his stalker would think he was on the train to Rome. It was a short walk to the train station. Inside, he picked up his ticket, and then he wandered around to lose himself in the crowd. After a trip to the washrooms, he found the tourist accommodation bureau down a corridor.

"What hotels have vacancies?" he asked the clerk.

"The Grand Hotel is near the station, signor, and it is also clean."

Harry checked the map and saw the hotel was near The Garibaldi, where Mrs. Rutherford was staying. Outside, he took a circuitous route to The Grand.

At the landing, the divers had opened the sack dragged from the canal. Inside it, they found the body of an elderly man with a deep knife wound in his back high up on the left side, straight into the heart. They hoisted him into the funeral coach.

CHAPTER 26

▼

Dorothy Crawford backed the immense Ford LTD from her narrow driveway and drove downtown for her appointment with Miss Giveny. *Maybe she will have some clues as to the identity of Q,* she thought.

What does Mrs. Crawford want now? fretted Gladys in the office. One of Merle's late night weeping attacks had kept her up most of the night. It was beyond her to imagine what her sister had to weep about. But, this morning, with curiosity overcoming her exhaustion, she had agreed to see Mr. Crawford's widow.

On her arrival, Gladys whisked Mrs. Crawford into the library. "What can I do for you?" she asked abruptly.

"I need some information, dear." Dorothy had decided to employ the warm, trusting approach used by Richard when he wanted something very badly. "I think both of us cared for Richard a very great deal."

Gladys' mouth went dry. Like a cornered animal, her eyes darted about the room. "I worked for your husband very hard for thirty-five years." Gladys sniffed.

"I know, and he appreciated your efforts far more than he let on."

Suspicious, Gladys said stiffly, "He was a fair employer, Mrs. Crawford."

"I'm sure he was, dear. By the way, I smell coffee. Could we have some together?"

"All right." Gladys headed for the kitchen.

"Let me come too. I'll help carry things."

Before Gladys could object, Mrs. Crawford was halfway down the hall with her. The cups rattled in her hands as she set up the tray.

Back in the library, the two women regarded each other. Dorothy smiled. Gladys blinked, determined to reveal as little as possible.

"I am hoping you can help me," Dorothy began.

"How?"

"You know that I've been asking Harry about files beginning with the letter Q."

"Well you can't look when Mr. Jenkins isn't here." Gladys was determined not to be tricked by widow's entreaties.

"I realize that, Gladys, but would you like to know why I wanted to see them?"

Curiosity overcame her. "Why?" she asked.

"Because Richard was murdered!"

"What?" Miss Giveny's mouth hung open in disbelief. "That can't be!"

"I'm afraid so. Richard kept diaries where he talked about eating at Q's house and feeling sick." With tears in her eyes, she said, "He ate there just a few nights before he died."

"But he died of a stroke in the office."

Dorothy spoke coolly. "Brought on by poisoning—probably arsenic administered over a long period of time."

Gladys' mind reeled and then she remembered Mr. Crawford kept milk in the refrigerator and a stash of antacids in his drawer. Near the end, it seemed as if something painful was eating away at him. She burst into tears.

Dorothy rushed to take her hand. "Please, Gladys. If there's anything you can do to help find Richard's killer?"

Gladys knew who *Q* was. On the Norma Dinnick files, Mr. Crawford had always drawn a pink *Q*. She bunched her Kleenex to her lips and stared at Mrs. Crawford.

"*Q* poisoned Mr. Crawford? That can't be. He loved her."

"You know who *Q* is?" Dorothy asked softly.

Gladys always knew someone had to protect Mr. Crawford from women. Despite her secret passion for him, she had missed the real danger he was in. Grief stricken, she said, "I loved your husband, Mrs. Crawford. I should have protected him."

Dorothy remained composed. After all, what woman didn't fall under Richard's spell? "You mustn't blame yourself! But will you help me find his killer, Gladys?"

Gladys nodded tearfully and blotted her cheeks. "*Q* is Norma Dinnick," she said solemnly.

"Is she still alive?"

"Yes. But she's confined to the Mercer Mental Hospital," Gladys spoke as if this fact were evidence of just punishment.

"Is she incompetent?"

"Yes, officially. But she's too clever by half." Gladys sniffed.

"You mean she's not really incompetent?"

"Sometimes she's completely lucid. But when it suits her purposes, she can get completely mad." Gladys pursed her lips. "Mr. Jenkins doesn't see through her."

"Is she allowed visitors?"

"Oh yes. You can walk in any time."

"Thank you, dear. You've been a very great help to me," said Dorothy.

Exhausted by her revelations, Gladys bowed her head and said, "You won't tell anyone I said this, will you?"

"Of course not. It will be our secret." Dorothy collected her purse and left.

Gathering up the coffee cups, Gladys thought how foolish she must look, like a wasted old maid confessing a schoolgirl crush.

Dorothy drove directly to the Mercer. Her motivation in hunting down Richard's killer was now crystal clear. She was no different than Gladys, who had spent her life loving the man from afar, even though he scarcely noticed her. She, the ever-dutiful wife, had also been scorned and ignored. But despite his faithlessness and cold contempt, Dorothy finally admitted that, inexplicably, she still loved Richard and always had. She and poor Gladys had much in common.

She found Norma in her room, just finishing her lunch. Immediately, she recognized the tiny, round face and the sharp, darting eyes from the funeral. She was just as Armand had described her—a black widow spider. The woman was cunning and deadly. Danger had always been an aphrodisiac for poor Richard.

"Mrs. Dinnick?" asked Dorothy.

Norma looked up from her tray with an innocent and open expression. "Who are you?" she asked.

"I'm Dorothy, Richard Crawford's wife."

"How is Richard? I trust he's well." Norma said sweetly.

"He's dead," Dorothy said flatly. She caught the hesitation before sadness swept over Norma's eyes.

"Oh my dear, I am *so* sorry." Norma dabbed her lips carefully with her napkin.

Dorothy pulled up a chair and sat down. "He's been dead more than a year."

"Really? I was not informed of his passing."

"Richard was murdered, Mrs. Dinnick."

"Oh dear goodness no!" Her hand flew to her lips. In shock, she whispered, "But who would do such a thing? He was such a fine man."

Gladys was right. Norma was too clever by half. Dorothy knew this kind of woman, who had the perfect mix to fool Richard. Like a pretty lace curtain, sweet vulnerability masked shrewd and sharp cunning.

"Yes," sighed Dorothy, "Richard died a slow and horrible death."

"Oh, my dear," Norma reached out her hand. "I am so very sorry."

When Dorothy saw a tear slide down Norma's cheek, she checked her anger. "Did you know Richard well?" she asked.

"He was Arthur's lawyer, mostly." She gave Dorothy a knowing glance. "Husbands," she smiled, "always keeping their wives out of their business."

"Richard always told me everything," said Dorothy.

Norma retreated slightly. "Well some do, of course. Only to say that I had little to do with Mr. Crawford until Arthur died and we had to settle his estate. Of course, Richard was a wonderful help then." She dabbed her cheek with a Kleenex.

"I need your help, Norma," Dorothy said warmly.

"I'd like to, dear. But I can't see what I can possibly do. I'm just an old woman confined to a nursing home." Norma's voice trailed off as she looked keenly at her visitor.

"You can give me information, Mrs. Dinnick."

"What sort of information?" Norma's eyelids began to droop. Dorothy touched her hand to waken her. "I must find Richard's murderer. He kept a diary, Mrs. Dinnick."

Norma's eyelids flew open. Her gaze sharpened. "He did? What did he say in his diaries?"

"He suspected that he was being poisoned."

Norma knotted her hands together. "The poor man!"

"Yes. And it was extremely painful to him."

Dorothy had practiced her lines for whatever moment of truth came. "Mrs. Dinnick, I've always known about Richard's countless affairs. Just before his death, he was eating meals at a woman's house. He called her *Q* in his diaries." Dorothy watched for a flicker in the old woman's eyes, but saw none.

Norma smiled sadly. "I'm sure you're distraught about his death. But I know nothing of it. Richard never mentioned anyone with the initial *Q.*"

"That's what I thought at first. But I think *Q* stood for a pet name, a term of endearment—like Queenie."

Norma sagged over the remains of her lunch. "Still," she murmured, "I never heard him say anything like that."

Dorothy knew she must hurry. Soon the conniving woman would be feigning sleep, or worse, madness.

Prepared for angry denials, she said, "I know you had an affair with Richard, while he was seeing Marjorie Deighton." Counting on jealousy, Dorothy expected fury when she said, "And he fathered a child with that woman. Her name was Suzannah."

Instead, almost knocking her tray from the table, Norma rocked with laughter. Red-faced, she sputtered, "Me? An affair with Richard?" She choked with another spasm of mirth. "Why, my dear Mrs. Crawford!" She struggled for composure. "Richard was a devoted lawyer, but never attractive to me." Again she suppressed a laugh. "Far too stiff and proper, like a military man."

Although Dorothy had counted on being right, she knew that passionate affairs were not the only motive for murder. She took a chance.

"Was there a problem with the estate or some other legal matter?"

Norma's eyes became distant with recollection. "Yes," she said softly. "There were many problems and lots of money. Too much, I think. Almost a curse."

Dorothy nodded her encouragement.

"George Pappas was the main problem."

"Who was he?"

"George? He was a very handsome—but dangerous—man, my dear. My husband had very carefully invested money that was rightfully ours. George, Archie, Robert, and even David were all trying to take it from him. But Arthur had invested it very safely, just for the two of us."

Jabbing her finger in the air, Norma continued, "Now, that was not right!" She shook her head. "Somehow, Richard got the crazy notion that the money came from some sort of fraud years ago. I tried to convince him—it didn't matter what I said—he was so sure of himself. He simply would not listen."

"Did Richard want you to give it to them?" Dorothy knew that, although Richard was a cheat when it came to women, he was highly principled in his legal advice.

"Yes! Can you believe it? Utter madness, I told him. You cannot expect me to just hand over what is rightfully mine. He didn't know how hard Arthur worked for that money. Would you believe he wanted to settle it in court?"

Norma peered intently at Dorothy and said, "He would have brought in the police, or spent it all in court applications." Norma drew herself up. "And he was wrong. Dead wrong."

"Did you try to stop him?"

Norma looked at Dorothy as if she were crazy. "Well, of course I did. We'd have lost everything we'd worked for, Arthur and me."

"So you put something in his food?"

Norma nodded triumphantly. "Yes, I did. Otherwise, I would have lost everything." Then she blushed. "You know, I think Richard did rather have a *pash* for me. He used to call me his Queen."

Pulling on her gloves, Dorothy rose to leave. "Thank you Mrs. Dinnick." Almost too weary to speak further, she turned at the door and said with a warm smile, "It's been wonderful to talk with you, Mrs. Dinnick. We've had such a lovely visit."

Norma gazed vacantly at her and said, "Do come again, dear."

CHAPTER 27

▼

Natasha and Sheila had gone for a drink at the bar of the 360 Restaurant at the top of the CN Tower. A carpet of city lights lay beneath them. A sullen silence hung between them.

Tossing a lock of hair from her face, Natasha stared into her drink. *Harry must be settled in Venice by now,* she thought. *I can still book a flight for Wednesday night.*

Sheila was growing morosely stubborn. "You can't live in both worlds at once. You *have* to decide."

"What is the big deal about a trip to Venice, Sheila? Why are you drawing the line there?" Then Natasha thought, *I may not be able to get away because of the Cornish deal.*

"I should have drawn the line ages ago! You have no concept of loyalty or friendship. You just act as if no one else had any feelings. What about me?"

Natasha was so sick of the constant haranguing. She felt as if a door were closing swiftly and silently behind her. "All right, Sheila. I won't go, if it means so much to you."

"Oh, no! Don't play the martyr with me. You'll end up staying and hating me."

"Listen." Natasha rapped her keys on the bar. "I can't please you, no matter what I do. If I go, you'll mope about. If I stay, you'll think I'm blaming you." Frustrated, Natasha threw up her hands "I can't satisfy you."

"Go, Natasha! You damned well better go." Sheila was becoming tearful. "It's what you *really* want!"

Reaching for her purse, Natasha tugged Sheila's sleeve. "Let's get out of here."

As soon as they stepped out of the bar, Sheila took Natasha's arm. "I want to show you something over here."

They walked across the carpeted floor to a tiled area. Beyond that lay a shimmering glass floor. Drawing Natasha to the edge she said, "Look down. Isn't it beautiful?"

Glancing downward, Natasha wavered at the precipice. Instantly, she closed her eyes. Her stomach lurched. More than a thousand feet below, cars formed a ribbon of light along Front Street as far as she could see.

Natasha grasped Sheila's arm. "My God!" she croaked, pulling back.

Sheila, in her loose floral skirt, spun out into air across the glimmering glass. "Come on out, Natasha. It's amazing!" Laughing, she danced further away, then back again. She took Natasha's arm. "Come, dance with me in thin air," laughed Sheila.

Frozen by fear, Natasha was rooted to the spot. Neither her arms nor legs would move. Light sparkled above and below, disorienting her. "No. I can't. No, please, Sheila!"

"My dearest Natasha," she smiled. "You're standing on the edge in more ways than one. Just look down! If you go to Venice, do not expect me to be waiting for you. If you intend to stay, you better be happy with the choice." With an elaborate shrug, she concluded, "Do whatever you want. It's on your own head!"

Nodding, Natasha backed away. "I'll think about it." Satisfied, Sheila let her go. Sinking in spirit, Natasha rode the elevator down the tower with Sheila.

They drove back to Sheila's apartment. "Stay the night, Natasha. You've got enough stuff of yours at my place."

Natasha was too tired to object.

Inside the flat, Sheila said, with trembling lip, "I really didn't mean what I said. I really do care, Natasha, what you decide." Pouring glasses of wine, she suddenly cried, "You make it so hard! After all, how do you think I feel when you're off with Harry, knowing what you're doing? And then you tell me how wonderful he is and that you love him. That's supposed to make me feel better? I could understand a fling, but...."

As she accepted a glass of wine, Natasha murmured, "It's something I think about all the time. But it's not as simple as you make it sound."

"Why? Why isn't it simple, Natasha? We either love each other or we don't. And that means being faithful to each other."

"If people love each other, they work things out. They give each other space, not cut off their air supply."

Sheila stood before the living room window looking out upon rooftops bathed in the moonlight. Her shoulders were shaking. "I really *do* love you, but you don't seem to understand how much this hurts. Don't I count for anything?"

Natasha put her hand on her shoulder. "I know you *think* you love me, but if we don't accept each other as we are, how can it be love?" Retreating to the couch, she continued, "You've known about Harry for a long time. Why make an issue of it now?"

"Because it hurts! Why can't you understand how much it hurts me?" Sheila cried out, hunting down a Kleenex. Then she flung herself down on the couch and laid her head on Natasha's lap.

Natasha stroked her hair and stared out the window. "Shall I go home now?"

Sheila shook her head furiously. "No, please don't, Natty."

"All right, I'll stay if you want." Natasha continued to gaze out the window. *She is in so much pain, but so am I."* Then she said softly, "We can't go on like this. We're hurting each other too much."

When Sheila had quieted, Natasha rose from the couch. "I'm just going to check my e-mails. I've got an early morning, so we ought to get some sleep."

Sheila struggled to sit up. "Sure, Natty," she said, wiping her nose.

In the den, Natasha checked her inbox and printed out a few messages for the next day. Glancing at a sheet in the printer tray, she caught her breath. She read:

Dear Harry,

Although we've met only once, I feel I know you. You need to know—this is for your own good—that Natasha and I have been lovers for many years. No doubt this will be a surprise to you, but she's incapable of being *true to either of us. Thought you'd want to know before you get further involved.*

Regards,

Sheila.

Natasha's hand flew to her lips to stifle a cry. Paper in hand, she rushed to the bedroom. "Sheila?"

"Yes, darling?"

Natasha shook as she held out the paper. "Did you send this to Harry?"

"Send what?" Sheila took the paper. Growing pale, she whispered. "Please, Natty ... please believe me. I didn't send it."

Natasha continued to stare at her. Her lips moved, but no words came out.

"I was just letting off steam." Sheila smiled uncertainly. "You must believe me!"

"And you call *me* a traitor?"

"No ... I never sent it."

"But you wrote it. You were going to send it," Mouth agape, Natasha backed away and hurried down the stairs.

Sheila sank to the top step and watched Natasha struggle with the front door to get out. Resting her head on her knees, she rocked back and forth. *Please Natty! I didn't mean it. I love you so much!*

Natasha was stunned. In a dead, cold fury, she drove two hours east of the city to Sandbanks Park, where the family cottage was. Josef and she had had their last real conversation there before he died. At almost midnight, Natasha's car bumped along the road—a path, really—cut through a farmer's field. Her high beams illuminated the stalks of early green corn, waving lazily against the black sky. The wind off Lake Ontario was unceasing.

Up ahead, she saw the cottage, exposed and listing to one side. Its frame was gray with age. She stopped and, lowering her window, listened to the sweep of the wind through the open fields. In the distance, she heard the waves crashing onto the beach.

When she entered the cottage, she immediately went into the living room, with its scatter rugs, worn couch, and armchairs. From the window, she saw huge clouds fly up against the moon, blotting out any chance for a view of the beach. Night closed in. The bed in her room was high and lumpy, and the sheets smelled musty. She had expected to have trouble sleeping, but when she lay down, she fell exhausted into a deep sleep.

It was nine o'clock when she woke the next morning. After coffee, a fried egg, and toast, she walked down the path choked with a grotesque profusion of weeds and onto the beach. The sand was so soft and deep that, with each step, her calves ached with the strain of walking. She watched the gulls circling above, calling out in eerily human voices. Strangely, the pain in her legs made her aware, not only of her own body, but of every living thing surrounding her. With the stiff breeze, the huge lake still heaved and waves broke upon the beach. She walked with ease along the hard, wet surface at the water's edge. One gull landed not twenty yards ahead and eyed her from an ancient piece of driftwood.

Nearing the sand dunes, she felt Josef's presence. Although dead for almost twenty years, he seemed to be always with her. Hearing his voice within, she warmed at his imagined smile and pretended he was there. She squinted in the blinding sun and picked up a stick. As she walked, she knocked shells away toward the water.

Sheila, you have betrayed me, she thought, amazed at her calm.

Far down the beach, a dog barked and ran about in circles. A man followed at a distance, then turned away from the lake and disappeared among the dunes. Soon, the dog was gone too.

Her helpless fury was spent, leaving her with an unaccustomed feeling she could not name. She had expected to pace the beach in anger. In her usual analytical fashion, she might have tried and convicted Sheila for her treachery. But she understood that Sheila's actions were borne of pain and suffering.

Instead, Natasha walked along the sand slowly, lost in a growing sense of unity within her body, the sand and birds, the water, and the sun. It was just the way she had felt with Harry before he left for Venice. She strove to keep the sense alive in her.

The perception of being a part of everything grew swiftly within her. *It must be real*, she thought. And then, piercing through her like a flash of light, was another revelation. Being a tiny part of everything, everything was within her. There was no meaningful distinction between the life inside and outside her. She, Sheila, Harry, the gulls, and the dog down the beach all came from the same place, the same source. Some all-powerful force lay underneath, unifying not just her, but *everything*. And with that realization, the last of the divisions within her fell away like the waves receding from the shore.

Natasha gazed out onto the gently undulating lake, seemingly encased in a silver sheen. She could hear Josef saying, *If you ever find that special "thing" in someone, if you ever—even for an instant—find someone who opens your inner eye to meaning, don't let them get away.*

Then she turned and walked slowly past the riot of weeds and up to the cottage. Soon she would drive back to the city. She knew Harry was her passion, the one who had awakened her to herself. But she still heard Sheila's cry—one of all humanity—*because it hurts!* Sheila's pain, from fear of loss, was a pain shared by the whole world. She did not reach it by reason, but she knew there was only one thing she could do—act with love, care, and compassion. At once, she knew Josef was still with her.

CHAPTER 28

─────────▼─────────

Harry found the Hotel Grand on a narrow canal of fetid water. *Not up to the Bellini standard,* he thought as he heaved open the door. The wallpaper in the lobby was a design of rustic red brick. A small counter top served as the reception desk. No one was in sight. Setting his case down, Harry tapped on the bell.

A young man, wearing light blue eye shadow, appeared from behind a curtain. Upon seeing Harry, he lowered his eyelids and smiled. Harry had never seen such long lashes. He reached for his wallet.

"Signor?" In the dim light, the clerk's face was the palest and smoothest white.

"I called earlier. You have a room for me. I'm Harry Jenkins."

The clerk ran his finger down a short list and found Harry's name. "Si. You spoke to me." Taking his credit card, he registered Harry.

"Is the Garibaldi Hotel nearby?" Harry asked. Suddenly he was weary. Upstairs, he would soak in a long, hot bath.

The clerk smiled with an expression Harry could only describe as shy. He was no more than a boy. "Si. Just three doors along the canal, signor."

He handed Harry a key. "Room twenty-four. It is our very best room. I hope it will be satisfactory," he said doubtfully.

"I'm sure it'll be fine," Harry replied. Most of all, he wanted to get upstairs and shut out the world for a few hours.

"Do you need help with your bag?" The boy wavered slightly behind the counter.

Harry shook his head and picked up his bag. The lift, a simple mechanism constructed in a well of circular stairs, clanked upward to the second floor. His room was down the hallway at the front of the hotel.

Opening the door, he saw that the room was no more than eight by ten feet. He pushed his bag to one side, and sank onto the narrow, lumpy bed with a sigh. *It's only for one night*, he reminded himself. A chipped sink hung crookedly from the wall next to the chest of drawers. When he opened the only other door in the room, he found a closet. *For God's sake*, he thought dully. *No bathroom.* He found it down the hall.

After carefully locking the bathroom door, Harry filled the tub and lay in the tepid water. At least, he was safe from prying eyes. Disconnected thoughts floated in and out of his mind. Having seen Hawke's thug, he knew whom to watch out for. Was Natasha's reply waiting for him at the Bellini? Surely, his declaration of love could not be met with silence. He hunted down the soap and set it in the wire dish.

Climbing out of the tub, he wrapped a towel around himself and started to shave. As he lathered his beard, the image of the boy downstairs appeared in his mind. *Such diffident charm,* he thought. In the mirror, he saw a tiny smile appear on his lips. In an instant, that smile was replaced by shock. He picked up his razor and began to shave, nicking himself several times.

Back in the bedroom, while he dressed, he debated calling Mrs. Rutherford. There was no real evidence to connect her with Hawke, and the prospect of an evening alone depressed him. He dialed her number and was surprised to get her on the first ring.

"Mrs. Rutherford, it's Harry Jenkins. I got your letter, and I'd be pleased to join you for dinner."

"Wonderful." She spoke briskly. "You're done with your business then?"

"For today, at least."

"When are you free?"

Harry checked his watch. "Would six do? I'll pick you up."

"How kind! But really you needn't. We could meet somewhere."

"No trouble. I'm not far off."

"Oh, you've moved then?"

Harry bit his lip. "No. The Bellini isn't that far from you."

Harry thought he heard her sigh.

"All right, I'll see you here at six."

After hanging up, Margaret Rutherford dialed the Mayfair Hotel in London. "Mrs. Deal, I think Dr. Hawke should come to Venice now. I'm having dinner with him tonight at six, and then the concert, I hope." She paused to listen. "Yes, he has the tickets, but he hasn't asked me, at least not yet. And by the way, he's moved into the Grand Hotel just a few doors away. No, I haven't seen Garth."

After concluding the call, Veronica Deal carefully reported her conversation to Robert, who looked as if he might explode in yet another furious tirade. But rationality struggled with madness and finally won out.

Breathing deeply, she collected herself and asked, "When are we going to Venice?"

"This afternoon, Mrs. Deal!" he hissed. "But first, I shall take my bath!" He slammed the door.

Veronica was not feeling quite herself, not ill really, but her ability to resist Robert was strangely diminished.

Hawke, seated on the edge of the tub, watched the suds rise to his calves. He had seen Ronnie's vacuous look of love upon hearing Harry's name. If they weren't lovers already, they soon would be. Fury at her betrayal flamed within him. As for Harry, he had his own plans for him. Harry was made for him, not Ronnie.

On the way to Heathrow, the cabbie drove past the Tower of London.

Black clouds blew off, and sunlight dappled the stone walls with light and shadow.

Robert suddenly became conversational. "Such a shame we have no time today for the Tower! But some day, Ronnie, I'll take you there."

"It's certainly a grim looking place," Veronica said, gazing up at the thick Norman walls and towers where three huge black birds circled in ever-widening arcs.

"Once you pass through the Traitor's Gate," he said, glancing darkly at her, "you come to the White Tower, built by William the Conqueror. It has marvelous facilities for the most exquisite torture in the Dungeon of Ill Ease. There, a prisoner can neither stand up straight nor lie down." Hawke's grin was impish. "Most inconvenient after being on the rack, don't you think?"

"You've been to the Tower before?" she asked.

He sighed pleasantly. "Many times, my dear. It is one of my favorite London haunts. In the aviary at the Tower, they always keep six black ravens in a cage. In ancient times, it was prophesized that should the ravens ever leave the Tower of London, the monarchy would collapse. The King, the Queen, and all princess and princesses would die most horrible deaths, and blood would run in the streets for eight days. And so, even today, the gathering of ravens presages a disturbance of the natural order."

"Why was the Tower built?" Veronica asked.

"It was a symbol of power—bloody power—where political prisoners were tortured and beheaded. Some struggled with the guards to escape. Their wailing was most desperate, but...." he shrugged and smiled, "quite useless."

"What an awful place!" she muttered, staring at the gates.

Robert said quietly, "Before we leave for Venice, we must discuss our plans for Mr. Jenkins." He saw a shiver pass through her at the sound of his name. *Traitorous shrew*, he thought!

He visualized Ronnie laughing in Harry's arms. And what about the man himself? Robert had thought Harry worthy of trust, had treated him well, and had even given him gifts. For his pains, the man had betrayed him, slipping away on his treacherous plot to steal the money. Such perfidy would be justly punished.

"I will tell you a story, Ronnie," said Hawke in a friendly fashion. "On June 17, 1535, the Lord Great Chamberlain, Thomas Cromwell, pronounced sentence upon the *traitorous* John Fisher, Bishop of Rochester, whose misguided conscience would not permit the doctrine of royal supremacy over the Church. Guess what his sentence for treason was, my dear Ronnie?"

Veronica gaped in fear at him.

Hawke spoke merrily. "That he be led back to prison, laid on a hurdle, and so drawn to the place of execution: there to be hanged, to be cut down alive, his privy members cut off and cast into the fire; his bowels burnt before his eyes; his head smitten off, and his body quartered and divided at the King's will."

"Good Lord, Robert! You keep such grotesque things in your head?"

Robert grinned impishly at her. "That and much more! Many who were imprisoned and then beheaded wanted to know the details of the actual ceremony, such as where to lay one's head, the proper way of kneeling, and how to signal one was ready for the sharp slicing of the axe."

Veronica stared in disgusted fascination at Robert. She could find no reply.

"Such executions were very popular. Begging for mercy and flailing about always increased the crowd's pleasure immeasurably. After all, my dear, they came to witness not only the blind and hopeless struggle for life, but also the exquisite moment of final submission. Then they stuck the dripping heads on poles and paraded them about."

Veronica shifted away and stared out the other side of the cab.

"Do you understand *blood lust*, Ronnie?" Hawke asked quietly. "It is an ancient human emotion. But until you feel the tug of it in your own gut, you cannot comprehend its power and attraction. Just for a moment, picture some poor wretch wailing for mercy, struggling uselessly with his captors, and begging piteously. Wouldn't that be a real show for giddy pleasures? History tells us that's what people really want."

"I don't want that! What happened to civilized behavior?"

Robert patted her hand. "It is but the thinnest of veneers." Then his lips turned downward in disgust. "We must still discuss our friend Harold Jenkins."

Veronica was alert. "What about him?" she asked cautiously.

"He has betrayed me."

"Because he …?"

Hawke's eyes grew hard. "That treacherous fool promised me his cooperation."

"But, Robert, he never did agree …"

"Don't you contradict me!" He was enraged. In his mind, he saw the two of them lying in bed, laughing, smirking, conniving. "You, whom I have treated so well, have also betrayed me."

Veronica froze. Robert was accusing her of plotting with Jenkins. Dragged to the Traitor's Gate! She saw the cold stare of paranoia in his eyes.

"How have I betrayed you?" she demanded, knowing she had to challenge him.

Hawke's eyes darted blindly heavenward. "You have lain with Jenkins, have you not?"

Astounded, Veronica managed to croak, "What? I've met him only once or twice. How can you even *think* that?"

"Maybe not yet. But you will. I can see it in your eyes. I can hear it in your voice at the sound of his name." He turned on her ferociously. "I have no doubt you will, you simpering, sluttish female!"

"Robert! Stop this instant," she hissed. Fighting back was her only chance of regaining any control. "Neither Jenkins nor I have betrayed you. It's your own sick imaginings at work. As for Jenkins, he never agreed to anything. And just look at what you've done to him!"

Robert shrank back at her harshness.

"Look at all the stupid tricks you've played on him—making him think you've had sex with him, sending faxes to destroy his relationship with this woman, Natasha—trying to seduce him with Mrs. Rutherford and the boy at the hotel. What has that got to do with getting the money back?"

"They were not stupid tricks!" he insisted with the stubbornness of a small child. "Oh, Ronnie!" He looked at her with damp eyes. "You do not understand. I will have the money back, but I have another plan for our Mr. Jenkins."

"Which is?"

Hawke's eyes grew hard again. "I want to capture the essence of the man."

"And just how do you intend to do that?"

Robert's smile was beatific. He lounged back in the cab. "My dear, it is a psychological experiment." He dabbed his eyes.

"One best understands the essence of a man in that moment hanging between life and death." Hawke rubbed his palms together. "It is the moment of truth, when all pretense is torn away, and we descend into the raw animal state. All the prisoners at the Tower went to the block with the greatest trepidation of the inevitable. And how did they conduct themselves? Most with disappointing grace and dignity, born of hopelessness. A few renegade souls fought against their fate, but ultimately they recognized their resistance was quite useless—*and* they submitted."

Hawke was silent for a moment, imagining what he could devise for *his* Harry. Then he asked, "At that moment, what do you think Harry will do?" He did not wait for her answer. "He will fight for life with every cell in his body. He is a renegade soul!"

"So you want to prolong his death and create the greatest amount of pain and torment?"

"How else will I capture his essence?" asked Hawke in an entirely reasonable tone.

"Do you need to kill him?"

He looked at her keenly. "Are you begging for his life?" His eyes danced, but there was no mirth in his laugh. "He is a most attractive man."

Wary of another trap, Veronica shrugged.

"I would *so* like you to beg for his life, Ronnie," he breathed, patting her hand. "Just a little?"

"I think you should just get the money from him and disappear with it. Why kill him?" she said flatly.

"Not so good at piteous imprecations are you, dear?"

"I hardly know the man."

"Well, I do! He is a magnificent specimen. A true and unified spirit." Hawke leaned forward and spoke earnestly. "Our Mr. Jenkins *will* be in my trial of one."

After speaking with Mrs. Rutherford, Harry looked glumly about his room, which was beginning to resemble a cell. The narrow window let in only the thinnest rays of light, illuminating the shabby dresser, chair, and bed. Peeking out the window, he checked to see if anyone might be looking in. Nothing to be seen for the moment! The smell of dirty laundry and cooking rose upward. He closed the window, but soon decided he could not remain in the oppressive room.

With no particular plan, he took the stairs to the lobby. He was surprised to find a tiny, but pleasantly comfortable bar at the end of one hallway. He sat on one of the stools facing the door to the kitchen.

From behind a swinging door, the boy appeared with a tray of glasses in hand. He seemed surprised to see Harry.

"You would like a drink, signor?"

"Yes, please. Scotch with ice. Just a drop of water."

"You have just arrived in Venice?" he asked pleasantly when he brought the drink.

"No, but I've only been here a few days."

The boy began polishing the bar.

"I didn't expect to find a bar in this hotel."

The boy nodded and smiled. "No, it is not a five star accommodation." He continued his polishing and said, "Your room—it is the best we have—is not very comfortable." This was said as a statement of fact.

Harry nodded and sipped his drink. "What's your name?" Harry was only slightly surprised at his question.

"Angelo."

Harry turned back to his drink. Angelo began polishing the glasses.

"Are you from the States?" the boy asked.

"No, I'm Canadian. Toronto, actually."

"Really? I have many relatives in Toronto." Angelo's eyes sparkled. "Someday, I will go there to visit."

Harry smiled. "I'm sure you'd like it. There's been a large Italian population in Toronto for many years. In fact, people from countries all over the world live there."

The boy regarded Harry. "You look like a businessman. A banker, no?"

Harry was surprised. "No, not a banker. Avocati." Of course, the boy would be wondering why a lawyer would stay at his hotel.

Angelo stopped polishing the glasses. His eyes narrowed. "Interesting!" He shrugged. "Just a game I like to play." He touched Harry's hand lightly. "I like to guess the work the guests do." Then he laughed. "We do not have many avocati here."

"Some would say the two occupations aren't that different. So maybe you're close." Harry began to relax with the small talk.

"Do you come to Venice on business or pleasure, Signor Jenkins?"

Harry shook his head. "My business is just about done. So, I'm really just enjoying the city. I have to get back to Toronto soon."

Angelo began putting the glasses away. With his back turned, he said softly, "If you wish, I could come to your room later."

At first Harry was uncertain he had heard the boy correctly. "Thanks," he said rather stiffly. "But, no." Suddenly, he was annoyed. First Hawke, and now this. The boy's shoulders sagged. Harry strove to lighten the moment. "Look, I'm sorry, but I'm engaged to be married." He fumbled for words. "It's not my sort of thing."

"If you have not tried it …" Angelo laughed lightly, "how do you know?" He gazed into Harry's eyes.

Harry finished his drink and slid off the stool. "Look, Angelo …" Harry knew his face was flushed. "I'm about as straight as they come. No offence …" he concluded lamely.

Angelo smiled as Harry fussed with his wallet to pay the bill. Harry was conscious only of his own heartbeat.

"I will embarrass you no further, Signor Jenkins."

Harry almost sighed in relief.

"But, if you change your mind, I'll be here."

Harry hurried out the front door of the Grand and began walking back to the Bellini. Stopping at a phone booth, he called the hotel. Yes! They did have a fax for him.

"Please leave it at the front desk." Harry could only grin. Moments later, he was in the hotel. Fortunately, the lobby was crowded with guests checking in. With any luck, Fantino would not see him. The clerk handed him the envelope. Garth

Deal watched from behind a newspaper. As he left, Garth rose to follow.

Outside, Harry squinted. The late afternoon sun had burned through the layer of cloud hanging over the city since the morning. On the piazza, in front of the train station, he found a café, where he ordered an espresso. With his chest constricted, he stared at the envelope and at last slit it open.

Harry ... Good. I'm glad you agree that it's best not to come. Natasha.

What in hell? The response was nonsensical, completely absurd! What about his marriage proposal? Setting down the paper, he stared out onto the canal.

Then he remembered Fantino, the trickster, had taken his love letter into his office. How easy to send something else to Natasha and simply attach the receipt to his letter—unsent! This fax was a photocopy and, at the top, it looked as if the sender's address had been whited out. Smiling in relief, Harry decided to phone her as soon as he returned to the hotel.

Sipping his coffee, he reviewed his plan. Tomorrow, he would go to London. Then, with the access code, he would get the Elixicorp share certificate and be back in Venice in time for the bank. By Thursday, at the latest, he could be in Toronto with Natasha *and* the money. The faster he moved, the better.

So disturbed had he been to read Natasha's fax, he almost missed the other note in the envelope. He opened it up and spread it on the table. Good Lord! It was from Dorothy Craw-ford.

Dear Harry,

I am writing to let you know who Q is. I suppose you felt that you could not breach a solicitor-client privilege, and I respect that. However, I have met Q, who turns out to be your client, Norma Dinnick.

Harry caught his breath. Holy God! Not Norma! He read on.

I visited her and she said she poisoned Richard because he was trying to make her give herself up [or some such thing] … something to do with money from a fraudulent scheme, in which a George Pappas, David, Archie, and Robert were involved. I've gone to the police, and at last, they are taking me seriously.

Regards,

Dorothy.

Harry blinked in stunned amazement. *Utterly wicked* were the next words, which came to mind. Norma had murdered his partner, Richard? Unbelievable! Quickly, he rose and retraced his steps back to the Hotel Grand, followed closely by Garth.

Angelo was not at the desk. Harry took the steps two at a time up to his room, where he dialed Natasha's cell. No answer. He left a message. "I think there is some big mistake. I …" The connection was lost. He tried several times again without success.

Only then did he look about the room to see the closet door ajar. Through the crack, he saw his suitcase had been hastily shut with some clothes sticking out. First, he thought that Angelo had been in. But why? The boy had only made a half-hearted proposition. Was he part of some grand scheme to thwart him? Of course, everyone was after the code from the bank.

He phoned Dorothy at home.

"Dorothy? Harry Jenkins. I got your fax."

She sounded frightened. "Harry, I'm not supposed to be talking to you."

"Who says?"

"The police. Sergeant Welkom."

"Did he say why?"

"He thinks you're involved."

"Me?" he said, only slightly surprised. Welkom was the cop who had suspected him of money laundering and murdering his own client, Marjorie Deighton. "You saw Norma Dinnick?"

"Yes. I accused her of having an affair with Richard, and she laughed at me. Then I asked if there had been any legal problems with her husband's estate. That's when she started talking about murdering Richard because he knew about some fraud."

"She said she was *Q*?"

"Yes. Well," she said—"he used to call me his *Queen*."

For years, he had thought of Richard as not much more than a lecherous old goat. *And* the one who had kept him in the back room, as his *very* junior partner. Here was proof that the man had acted nobly, on principle. A slow and painful death had been his reward.

"Harry? Are you still there?"

"Yes." he muttered. "Dorothy, I didn't mislead you. I didn't know who *Q* was. But you're right. As Norma's legal guardian, I'll have to defend her. So, we shouldn't talk further."

"No, Harry. I know you didn't, but Sergeant Welkom is suspicious."

"When I'm back, I'll see Norma immediately."

"You'd better, because they're likely charging her with murder very soon."

"What's the point? She could never stand trial."

"I don't know, but that's what the Sergeant says." Dorothy was silent for a moment. "Harry, I'm sorry if this is causing you trouble, but I had to find out."

"I know you did, but we shouldn't talk further. At least not now."

After hanging up, Harry remained on the bed for a long time. Norma had confessed to Richard's murder! Until now, he had pitied her and felt he must do his duty to protect her. But this time, his partner had been the victim. Furious anger at her treachery burned slowly within him. *The shares must be cursed,* he thought! *How many dead bodies are strewn in the wake of the hunt for them? And now poor, noble Richard is added to the list. Surely to God, some good can come from this!*

He knew Richard had been fond of citing the *clean hands* doctrine. "With tainted hands," he would argue, "one could expect neither justice nor equity from the courts." He would have urged Norma to be honest and forthright, and to submit any issues to reasoned argument in open court. Norma would have fought every bit of his advice with cunning and zeal. With his uncompromising views, Richard would have been just as stubborn. *Two people locked in mortal combat! And look who won—and look what Richard got for his principles!* Harry lay back on the pillow and stared at the ceiling. He now stood exactly where Richard had, not much more than a year ago.

A soft tap on the door wakened Harry from his dozing. "Who is it?" he called.

"Me. Angelo."

"Angelo, I already said …" He tried to keep the annoyance from his voice.

"No … no, Signor Jenkins. A letter has been delivered for you."

"Letter?" He was suspicious. "I'm not expecting any letters."

"Still … it is here. I slip it under the door for you?"

Harry stood up and checked his watch. Five-thirty already. "No. That's all right, I'll open the door."

Angelo stood before him, dressed in black leather pants and open white shirt. "Here is the letter." He handed Harry the envelope and turned to go.

"Wait a minute, Angelo. Did you see who delivered this?"

The boy shrugged. "I did not see him very well. He left when I came to the reception desk. I think he was very tall and very large."

"Thank you, Angelo." Harry closed the door and opened the envelope. The note was brief.

Dear Harry,

I am very disappointed. I was convinced of your integrity and honesty. I will be in Venice shortly, and I would like to arrange a meeting with you.

Regards,

Robert Hawke.

They had found his hotel. He tucked the note of the code for the shares into a pocket in his belt and hurried downstairs. The boy was at the desk.

"Angelo? I may have a visitor tonight—a small but rather portly man. He's usually dressed rather oddly, sometimes in a white suit."

Angelo's eyebrows shot up.

Harry shoved a one hundred euro note across the counter. "If he comes for me, please tell him I have checked out."

"What about the very big man?"

"Same thing, please."

"You do not need to give me money for such a thing."

"Please. I want to. It's very important."

Angelo frowned, but he pocketed the money. "Signor Jenkins, if you do not wish to be alone tonight … I would not bother you."

Harry regarded the boy more closely. Suddenly, he felt a pang. Was it envy for the boy's youth, his freedom, his attractiveness? He caught a glimpse of himself in the mirror behind the desk and felt about a hundred years old. He nearly sank with weariness. "Thank you, Angelo. I'll be fine."

Mist rose from the canal, and a stench hung in the air. With only a few lamps lighting his path, shadows in doorways tricked his eye, and he almost lost his footing on the slick cobblestones. Soon, he and Hawke would meet face to face.

The warm lights of the Garibaldi Hotel drew him inward. Suddenly, he realized, in his loneliness, how intensely he craved female companionship. Even if she were one of Hawke's people, he would give nothing away. Perhaps he might learn something useful.

Mrs. Rutherford sat in the lobby, leafing through a magazine. She was younger and more attractive than he remembered. Perhaps the serenity of her gaze and the glow of the intimate lobby gave him a fleeting sense of safety. When he shook her hand, he caught the scent of her perfume.

"Mr. Jenkins, I'm so glad you could come," she smiled. Immediately, he relaxed.

He gave her his arm and together they stepped outside. "Any particular restaurant in mind?" he asked.

"How about Capani's? It's just a few canals over."

Harry nodded. "Have you contacted your son yet?"

She shrugged helplessly. "Not yet. But I've spoken to a few of his friends." Since her tone suggested reserve, he decided not to pry.

Opening the door to Capani's, Harry immediately felt comfortable. The bartender waved them toward a quiet table at the back where they ordered wine, and a waiter lit the candles.

"How long will you stay in Venice?" he asked. In the candlelight, he thought she could hardly be forty. But with a grown son, that hardly seemed likely.

"Possibly another week, Mr. Jenkins."

Harry waved his hand. "Please! If we are to have dinner together, you must call me Harry."

"And you shall call me Margaret."

Harry smiled and picked up the menus.

"Do you believe in free will, Harry?"

Harry had scarcely expected a philosophical debate. Her sudden seriousness hung like a shadow over them. In the mood for chitchat about weather and travel, he did not want to have to concentrate too much.

"I like to," he said simply, reasonably sure his answer was safe. "Why?"

"I suppose, when you come to Venice, those sorts of questions occur." The wine arrived, and orders for dinner were taken. "You see, I don't."

"Really? I would have thought you might," he said, not having given the matter much thought.

"Why?" she asked.

Her intensity flustered him slightly. "I don't know. Just because you're here on your own, doing as you please."

She leaned forward and rested her elbows on the table. With her jacket draping open, he became aware of the gentle swell of her breasts. "Perhaps free will is just an illusion, and we go day to day, unaware of the forces *really* driving us."

Unsure of her direction, he became wary of some subtle trap. "I don't know that I follow...." If she were Hawke's emissary, she would be after any information about his search for the shares.

"Let me tell you more of my story." She stared into her wine glass. "From the moment of his birth, my son was the person he is today."

"And that is?" Harry asked carefully.

"My son is a precious and sensitive flower," Margaret Rutherford sighed.

Harry tried not to wince. No man would care for such a description, especially from his mother. Perhaps Mrs. Rutherford was a major part of whatever family problems there were.

"It is his destiny to remain as such." She smiled brilliantly at Harry. "In a way, it is wonderful, because he can give the world his beautiful poetry." Her eyes glittered with pride. "But otherwise, he must pay a heavy price all his life."

"Pay? How?" he asked.

"He must always be the outsider looking in. But then," she hesitated, "perhaps that is the lot of poets and visionaries."

Harry was getting lost, but he thought better of interrupting. He drank his wine.

"But," she continued, "despite such sorrow, I still think that a son links one to the future. Do you have children, Harry?"

"No," was all he said.

She continued. "His father—as I said before—is a captain of industry. He was born a cold and authoritarian soul. Because he can never free himself of his materialistic nature, he also must suffer. He is a victim of his own nature, which traps and estranges him from himself and his family. Neither of them will ever change."

Mrs. Rutherford's depth of passion seemed increasingly manic. Harry asked, "And where do you fit into the equation?"

Her laugh was self-deprecating. "I, Harry, am the woman in the middle. My nature is to keep the peace. Not that there is any to keep, but it suits my nature to be the buffer. And so I, too, am bound."

"So, you believe that we all have our roles, which are predetermined, at birth, by our nature."

She nodded, tears forming in her eyes.

"It seems very bleak," he said quietly. "Is there no way out ... no room for change of heart or improvement?"

For moments, she seemed lost in thought. "Perhaps the lucky few have a chance." She shrugged. "I think we are all engaged in a search, the nature of which is not necessarily clear. We seem to wander through our lives not even knowing that we *are* searching. Faint hope that we can change sends and keeps us on our search."

The dinners arrived. Both of them began to eat. For Harry, her thoughts contained an echo of Natasha's the other night. Had she been saying that she felt bound by her nature? Perhaps that was what had bothered him. But then, her mood had seemed to shift, and he thought she had truly given herself over to him and to them.

"You seem to be a very troubled man, Harry."

He set down his fork. "I do?" He heard his own defensiveness. In his view, he had plenty to be troubled about—Natasha, Hawke, and Norma Dinnick. Love, danger, and madness.

"Yes. Are you on a search of your own?"

"Perhaps," he said uncomfortably. "I agree in the sense you say—that life itself puts us on a path."

"After coffee, I will read your palm, if you like." Her soft laughter was enticing. Only once had his fortune been told, when he was a law student and madly in love. "I'm quite good. It's not just a parlor trick."

"All right." Mrs. Rutherford's intensity was starting to grate on him, and he began looking for a way to end the evening. At least, a palm reading would be a game.

The coffee arrived in a silver carafe. Margaret Rutherford poured. "Now give me your hand, Harry."

Harry obliged. Mrs. Rutherford's face darkened in the candle light. "Your major task in life is great, Harry."

Harry smiled in amusement. If only his dinner companion knew *how* right she was.

"Two parts of your soul are at war. You must eventually integrate them, if you are to have any peace."

"What parts are at war?"

"Only you can answer that. But don't forget! All opposites are illusory."

Harry frowned.

"But perhaps, if you told me more about yourself?"

Harry shrugged. "There's not a lot to tell."

She looked at him closely. "You are one of the fortunate ones, Harry. You are capable of great success, provided you ask for help in your search."

He smiled. "Very good. I'm impressed." *At last*, Harry thought, *she is putting her plan into effect—to get me to confide my problems in finding the money.*

"And I am the sort of person who is always called upon to help. Destiny is at work here."

Pretty heavy-handed! Now it *was* time to go! Next she'd be pumping him for information under the guise of mending his psyche. "Well, Mrs. Rutherford, this has been most enjoyable, but I'm pretty tired."

She continued to hold his hand. "You are a man far too closed in. You must learn to trust, and...."

His irritation rising, Harry removed his hand. "No search. Just a very tired man." He waved at the waiter for the bill. "We should get going."

Outside, he took her arm. Together, they walked back to the Garibaldi Hotel.

"Would you come in for a drink?" she asked.

"No ... really," he said, checking his watch. "It's late, and...."

"Well, good night, then. I hope I didn't upset you with my palm reading."

Harry smiled. "No, not at all." He shook her hand and watched as she entered the hotel.

He was only twenty-five yards from his own hotel but, as if to shake off a growing sense of gloom, he crossed a bridge and wandered into a maze of calles. Peering into a darkened shop window, he saw a Pinocchio marionette surrounded by strange objects: an ancient globe, an unclothed figure looking more like a fetus than a doll, and a black-and-white Mardi Gras mask. In the light rain now falling, he shivered.

From the corner of his eye, he caught an immense shadow blotting out his entire pathway. He turned around sharply, but too late: he saw an arm shoot upward. Instinctively, he recoiled. The gloved fist smashed down on his shoulder, driving him onto the cobblestones. He felt his body slump backwards. His cheek was scraped raw by the stones. A boot smashed hard into his forehead once, then twice. He felt warm blood trickling down his face, as he tried to cling to consciousness.

Garth Deal bent over Harry and searched his pockets one by one. He rummaged through his wallet and tossed it to the ground.

"Can't find a fucking thing!" he muttered.

Just before he drifted off, Harry saw a woman join the man and heard their frantic whispers.

Harry lay unconscious on the slick stones for more than five minutes. At last, his eyes flickered open. A familiar face hung in the light above him. The person was trying to help him to his feet.

"Angelo?" Harry muttered. "Where did you come from?"

Angelo struggled to raise Harry to his feet without success.

Waiting for the flight from Heathrow to Venice, Veronica began to appreciate the enormity of Robert's tangled mind. Before leaving the Mayfair Hotel, he had demanded all her credit cards and, except for a few coins, all the cash. With no money, she was trapped.

Now he was in an expansive, bragging mood. "Have I ever told you about Brahma, Ronnie?"

Immediately, her concern grew. "No. Tell me."

"Brahma conducts the *real* research near San Diego." Hawke waved his hand dismissively. "Hawke Pharmaceuticals, where the Alzheimer's program is carried on, is just window dressing for the real project."

"What is the real project?" she asked cautiously.

"My trial of one is carried out at Brahma, where we are attempting to find the cause of the disease by actually inducing it."

"Not in humans, Robert!"

"How else?" he smiled in merriment. "I want my Harry to be in the trial of one because, with his much finer mind, there will be a far greater chance of success."

Visions permeated Veronica's imagination. Scores of vacant-eyed souls wandered high in the hills of San Diego, ravaged by Robert's experimentation. Harry Jenkins would be the next victim in his trial—the best mind yet to be destroyed. Robert's tales of beheading and thumbscrews were children's games compared to his projects at Brahma.

"I need to go to the ladies' room, Robert."

He waved at her cheerily. "Don't be long, my dear. It would never do to miss our flight."

She had only one chance. Rushing to the pay phones outside the washroom, she dialed the Artimede Hotel. "Garth Deal, room 409," she whispered hoarsely.

"Not here," came the reply.

"Can you take down a message? Tell him his sister called. Dr. Hawke instructs him to stop at once. Have you got that?"

One pudgy finger lightly touched the telephone hook. The line went dead. Veronica bowed her head and said quietly, "I'm sorry, Robert."

"Your cretinous brother cannot help you." His words dripped like acid. "Why would you think he could, when he can scarcely cross the street himself?"

Veronica said nothing. Slowly, she settled the receiver back on the hook.

He took her arm. "Now let's get back to the gate. They'll be calling our flight any minute."

At the gate, she asked, "How many have you experimented upon so far?"

"Only five."

"What shape are they in?"

Robert shook his head sadly. "Not too good, Ronnie. They do not have Alzheimer's, but they no longer really have any minds to speak of. So, it is rather difficult to judge the results."

"So you want Harry as your next guinea pig?"

"I *was* right. You do love him." Strangely, Hawke seemed pleased with this conclusion.

"No. I just think the whole business is so god-awful."

"Ronnie, please understand." He still spoke patiently, but a note of menace had crept into his voice. "Such experiments are not without precedent. Lobotomies have been done in the name of science—electro-shock and biochemical therapy, too."

"But those were terrible! Besides, the patients were ill. No one took a perfectly normal person off the street and tried to give him a disease."

Hawke's eyes grew hard and flat. His breathing was sharp. "I am sorry, Veronica, that you seem not to understand the most simple matters." He rose and walked swiftly to the gate. Veronica followed slowly behind. For the first time, she was truly frightened.

CHAPTER 29

▼

Blood flowed from a deep gash in Harry's forehead. Angelo tore off his tee shirt and bent over him. When he turned his head on the pavement, Angelo groaned at the amount of blood. Trying to stem the flood, he bunched up his shirt and pressed it against the wound.

"Harry, are you okay? What happened?" He tugged at Harry's arms and cursed at the almost dead weight. Grasping him under the arms from behind, Angelo dragged him to his feet. Breathlessly, he stumbled along the pathway from one street lamp to another until they reached the Hotel Grand.

"Jesus! Mother Mary of God!" he whispered once he had dragged Harry into the elevator and up to the bedroom.

"Harry! Wake up. You cannot go to sleep. Somebody has beaten you." Panting hard, he heaved him onto the bed. With great care, he loosened Harry's collar, shirt, and pants so that he could breathe more easily. Harry did not stir.

Angelo switched on the lamp illuminating the room in a dull, yellow light. Now he could see clearly. "My God, Harry, who did this?" Still the blood flowed. His tee shirt was soaked. Soon the pillow would be drenched. He rushed to find more towels. Harry groaned and blinked his eyes open, but only for a moment. Angelo pressed gently on the wound to staunch the endless flow. *Rivers of blood*, he thought.

Again, Harry's eyes opened. He was conscious only of the light and the naked expanse of chest above him. His hand rose to touch his cheek, which was warm and wet, and then he touched the flesh above him. He wondered vaguely who was with him and why his head was throbbing. Then, he lapsed back into darkness.

For five more minutes, Angelo worked steadily. But when he lifted one towel as gingerly as he could, the skin stuck to it, and the wound gaped open. Blood was oozing out again. Only stitches could repair such damage. From the room, he telephoned the hotel doctor, who was only a few doors away. Thank God, when he reached him, the doctor agreed to come.

Harry stirred and muttered in his confusion. "Norma ... Natasha...."

Angelo smiled. Not surprising that this man had more than one woman. He soaked a towel in warm water and tried to clean off his left cheek, which was only scraped.

Harry jerked his head away. The face before him regarded him solemnly. So familiar was it that Harry struggled for a name. The skin was so smooth and pale, the nose and cheek bones so thin and graceful.

Harry reached up to touch the face and asked, "Who are you?"

The face frowned. The lips said, "Angelo. The clerk at the hotel. Don't you remember me?"

"Ah, yes, of course...." Harry could feel himself drifting away. He had to keep his eyes open.

Angelo shook his shoulder gently. "Please Harry, do not go to sleep. You've been hit hard on the head. You have a concussion, I think."

Harry's eyes flew open. Memory was returning. The looming figure had followed him and attacked him from behind. The pockmarked face with small, mean eyes had hung above him as he lay on the cold pavement. He could feel the hands roughly frisking him every part of him. And the woman, Mrs. Rutherford, had been there.

When the door opened, the boy rose swiftly. "Dr. Zenobio, thank God you are here! He is bleeding very badly."

Shuffling to the bed, the old doctor lowered himself carefully onto its edge. Whispering to himself as he examined the gash, he suddenly turned on the boy and, "Who has done this?"

Angelo's eyes widened. "I do not know. He is a guest of this hotel, and he was out walking. I did not see what happened."

"Who will pay for the stitches?" the doctor asked.

"I am sure he will. He has a credit card."

The old man shook his head. "No credit. Cash." He rubbed the tips of his fingers together.

"How much is it?"

"Ten euro for each stitch," He examined the gash once more. "Ten or twelve stitches. Look in his wallet." He applied a blood pressure cuff and shook his head. Waving a needle in the air, he said. "Also, it costs another twenty-five euro for the anesthetic."

Angelo looked doubtful, but he reached into Harry's jacket for his wallet. "He has plenty of euros. Much more than you need."

The doctor pursed his lips and nodded. "That is good."

Angelo looked out the window as the doctor set to work.

"He has lost a lot of blood," Zenobio said. "But he will be okay."

With gnarled fingers, he injected the anesthetic and prepared to suture. Throughout the procedure, he hummed an aria.

Angelo went to the lobby to change the euros. When he returned, Zenobio was just finishing up. "If he was not robbed," he asked severely, "why was he attacked?"

"I do not know, doctor. I did not see…." Angelo stammered.

He shook his head and wrote out a prescription. "He has also a concussion. Wake him every two hours to be sure he's all right." He looked sternly at Angelo. "Be sure not to bother him otherwise." He turned slowly for the door. "And get this prescription filled. It's an antibiotic so the wound does not become infected."

After the doctor left, Angelo dabbed Harry's scraped cheek. This time, Harry did not stir. "Harry, listen to me." When he shook his shoulder gently, Harry muttered and then cried out, but he did not waken. "I am taking your wallet to get the prescription filled at the farmacia. I will be right back." The boy left, silently closing the door behind him. Outside, Angelo rushed to the farmacia, where the lights were still on.

The door of Harry's room creaked open. He did not hear Mrs. Rutherford enter. Standing at the foot of his bed, she saw the blood was seeping and spreading rapidly to soak the bandage. Holding her breath, she rummaged through his jacket pockets, hoping to find the paper with the bank code. Nothing. In desperation, she yanked open the dresser drawers to find nothing. She could not fail. Dr. Hawke dealt severely with the unsuccessful.

With the medicine and more bandages in hand, Angelo ran across the two bridges back to the hotel. So much blood frightened him. The man who gave him the money to seduce Harry might be the attacker. When Harry had shown up, he'd been happy to try. But no one had said anything about beatings. *The hell with the man*, he thought, and shuddered at his bravery. He only wanted to protect Harry, but could not say why. He had never met anyone like him before.

As Margaret Rutherford frantically searched Harry's luggage, the door swung open. For long moments, she and Angelo stared at each other.

"What are you doing here?" Angelo asked, moving cautiously into the room.

"I was worried about Harry. I heard he'd been attacked."

"Why are you looking in his bag?"

"For his passport to contact any of his relatives."

"I do not believe you." Angelo took the bag from her.

Blood had begun dripping into Harry's right eye. He turned his head on the pillow and asked, "Who's there?"

"Me, Angelo. And the lady you had dinner with."

When Harry blinked his eyes open, he saw Mrs. Rutherford smiling tentatively at him.

"Harry, I was so worried about you! I came as soon as I heard."

"Did you see who attacked me?" he asked.

She shook her head. "No, I'd gone into the hotel before he came."

Harry remembered clearly. As the man had stood over him, she had been there. "Get her out of here, Angelo," he said at last.

Angelo took Mrs. Rutherford's arm and opened the door. "Do not come back," he said. "I will see you out of the hotel."

Returning from downstairs, the boy moved swiftly to the bed. "Harry? What is going on? She was going through your luggage." He touched Harry's forehead. "You are bleeding so badly. I have to make a new bandage. The doctor's stitching is not so good."

Harry only murmured as the boy gently peeled off the gauze. "I think it will be okay. The blood is slowly stopping." He dressed the wound as carefully as he could.

"Thanks, Angelo," Harry murmured.

"It's okay. Here is your medicine." He held out a glass of water and two pills. But Harry could not lift his head. The boy reached under his neck and raised him up. Conscious only of the warmth and gentleness of the boy's touch, Harry gulped down the pills and sank back.

Angelo stood at the window, his back turned to the room. "Harry? I must tell you something. That big man came to the hotel and paid me to seduce you."

"What?" Harry tried to sit up.

"He did not say why I was to do this. But they wanted me close to you to learn something. The lady going through your bag—I think she was paid too."

Harry tried to sit up. "I have to get out of here."

Angelo's face darkened. "Harry, I will look after you."

Everything the boy had done since the attack caused Harry to trust him. "No. I trust you, Angelo. You have been so kind, but they'll be back, and I have something I must do."

"What?"

"I have to get to London."

"But you cannot travel like this, Harry."

"I know, but tomorrow."

"It will take a few days. The doctor said you have a concussion."

"It's a short trip. Just overnight."

"I will hide you until you can travel."

"Where? Not in the hotel."

The boy shook his head. "In my apartment. It is close, and you will be alone." He saw the hesitation in Harry's eyes. "I promise I will not trouble you. I only want to help."

Harry believed the boy. He sank back on the pillow with his head throbbing.

"I will not move you tonight," he said, "but I will stay here with you."

Harry was grateful. He did not want to be alone.

"Besides," he continued, "the doctor says I am to wake you every two hours because you have a concussion."

"Thank you, Angelo," Harry murmured as he dozed off.

At midnight, Angelo checked the hotel and locked up. Back in Harry's room, he moved the chair near the bed to put his feet up. First, he tried to read the papers, but found his eyes drooping. At the sink, he held a cold, wet cloth to his face. At one o'clock, noises outside made him spring to the window. He smiled. Only some people with too much wine!

Sitting in the chair, he gazed at Harry. Although only twenty, Angelo had had many partners, but it was only sex. He had never wanted to look after anyone before—never really cared for someone. Harry was different.

At two o'clock, he shook Harry's arm. "You okay? Please say something to me."

Only briefly did Harry open his eyes. He smiled slowly and patted Angelo's hand. "Thanks, Angelo. I'm all right." He could not remember such kindness. He drifted back to sleep.

When he woke him again, just before dawn, Angelo was pleased to see Harry's eyes were clear and steady. With his finger to his lips, he said, "Do not make a sound. I am going to move you to my place, while it is still dark."

Harry nodded and began to sit up. Groaning in pain, he knew he could not travel far.

"I will not turn on the lights, so you must be careful. A friend is at the back of the hotel in a gondola. He will take you to my place. I will bring your bag later."

In the hallway, Harry stumbled toward the lift. Angelo shook his head. "It makes too much noise, Harry. We must take the stairs."

They descended the back staircase very slowly. With each downward step, Harry's head throbbed with pain. The early light, breaking through the small windows on the landing, illuminated their way. Grasping the banister, Harry gingerly made his way from one step to another. Angelo supported him under one shoulder, but with every step, the pain from the gash hammered his forehead. Harry gasped in pain for air.

When the knocker crashed at the front door, Harry sank to the last step. Angelo held his breath and prayed. The buzzer sent shock waves through the hotel.

"Stay here, Harry. I will answer it." Feigning sleepiness, he stumbled through the lobby and angrily threw open the front door. No one was there.

Harry saw a shadow cross the window of the back door. Nearly blacking out with pain, he slithered to the floor and sat with his back against the door. Now back at Harry's side, Angelo motioned him into the broom closet. Then he opened the back door. The huge man stood before him.

"What in hell do you want at this hour?" Angelo's jaw jutted out.

"Listen, you little faggot, where's your boyfriend?"

"Which one?"

"You know who! Harry Jenkins."

"Gone. Checked out last night."

Garth slammed Angelo against the wall. "I'm looking around, pretty boy." He took the steps two at a time to the main floor.

Angelo sagged with relief. "Harry!" he whispered, "Get out the back door!"

Harry opened the door a crack.

Garth loomed at the top of the stairs.

Instantly, Harry hid in the shadows.

Garth bellowed at the boy. "What'd you say, you little queer? I oughta beat the shit out of you!"

"Nothing." Angelo started up the stairs toward Garth. "I was just admiring your … ah …"

Confusion passed over Garth's face. He wavered above Angelo. "Come here," he shouted. "You're showing me around!" He marched Angelo into the lobby.

Harry nearly retched as he scurried, crablike, across the floor. Pushing the door open, he crawled out onto the steps. Just as Angelo had said, the gondolier was there to lower him into the boat. As the sun was breaking over the rooftops, the man covered him with a tarpaulin and pushed off. Harry was lulled by the soft lapping of the water as it broke over the prow.

Garth Deal cocked his head. He twisted Angelo's arm and marched him back to the rear door. "Motherfucker!" he cursed. "If he just went out the back door, I'm going to break every fucking bone.…" Shoving Angelo against the wall, he flung open the back door. The canal was still and empty. The gondolier had already slipped far into the shadows.

Later that morning, Robert Hawke and Veronica checked into the Garibaldi Hotel. They could find no trace of Mrs. Rutherford. "That stupid, conniving woman has betrayed me!" the doctor growled.

At noon, Angelo left the Hotel Grand for his apartment, leaving Sylvia Rialto manning the desk. She was intrigued when Angelo asked her to call if anyone came looking for him or Mr. Jenkins.

"What are you up to, Angelo?" she asked, raising her eyebrows and smiling.

"Nothing. Just looking out for a friend."

Sylvia smiled and lowered her eyes. "Ah … Angelo … so Mr. Jenkins is at your apartment?"

"Listen, Sylvia. Mr. Jenkins is in very great danger. He was so badly beaten last night, I had to call Dr. Zenobio."

"I did not know you were so rough, Angelo," she laughed.

The boy blushed. "Don't be ridiculous! He was attacked just outside our door. I brought him in and took him to his room."

"Whatever you say, Prince Charming." She loved to tease the boy and make him stammer. When she shrugged, as if the truth were of no consequence, Angelo slammed the door and was gone.

At his apartment, he wakened Harry. "How are you feeling?" he asked.

Harry groaned, "A little better, but my head still hurts like hell."

"I brought your bag and your medicine." Angelo checked his watch. "It's time for you to take it."

Harry popped in two pills and drank from the glass of water, swallowing hard. "Why are you doing all of this for me, Angelo?" he asked.

Embarrassed, the boy shrugged. "You are badly hurt and so …"

Although it hurt his face, Harry smiled. "Well thanks. If you ever need your life saved, I will try to return the favor."

"Do you really have to go to London?"

Warily, Harry asked, "How do you know I'm going to London?"

Angelo said worriedly, "Because you told me so last night. You do not remember, Harry?"

Slowly, the conversation came back to him. Although he had told Angelo his destination, he didn't now feel concerned. He realized that he instinctively trusted the boy. "Yes. I remember now. If you have a phone here, I'll call and arrange a flight."

"Sure, I have a phone. Here's your wallet. I took it last night to pay the doctor and get your medicine."

Harry took out his credit card and dialed the airport. Within five minutes, he had booked a flight leaving at eight o'clock that night.

"That man is very frightening and dangerous. My friend, the gondolier, will take you to the taxis for the airport. Are you coming back?"

"Yes. I'll just be overnight."

Angelo grinned. "You can stay here again."

"Thank you, Angelo," Harry said quietly. "I will." Realizing he was drawn by the boy's closeness, he struggled to get up. Angelo held out his hand to assist, but Harry shook his head. "No, thanks. If I'm going to London, I've got to be able to move around on my own."

Harry moved to the window. "I see you've brought my bag."

Angelo nodded.

Harry rummaged about in his case and found clean clothes and a package of cigarettes. "Do you smoke, Angelo?"

"Sometimes," he replied, as he moved toward the window. "Sometimes, when I'm feeling down." He took a cigarette and sat on the bed. Harry moved to a chair.

"Harry, you're jumping around like a nervous cat. I said I would not harm you. Don't you believe me?"

Harry lit his cigarette. "Yes, of course, I believe you. It's just that I have a bit of a hang-up, an extreme reaction, if you will...." His voice trailed off.

"That is too bad, Harry." The boy drew slowly on his cigarette. "But I know it's just the way it is. Some people are made like you, and some like me."

For the first time, Harry wondered if there were no middle ground, and for a fleeting moment, he wished there were.

The boy stubbed out his cigarette and stood up. "You should sleep this afternoon. I will arrange to get you to the airport, and come back to wake you." Harry nodded and lay on the bed. Angelo left. An unaccustomed restlessness kept Harry from drifting off immediately.

He had to deal with Robert Hawke. His only hope was to stay one step ahead of all of them. If Hawke thought he had the money, he would stop him before he left for London, but if he believed the job weren't finished, he would not close in. To buy time, he had to let Hawke think he was still unraveling the puzzle. With his head growing thick and fuzzy, he frowned to think of Richard and Norma, the noble philanderer and the murderous fraud. At last, he drifted downward into sleep, only to find Angelo waiting for him in a dream.

When Robert Hawke entered the Hotel Grand, Sylvia looked up from the desk. Instantly, she knew what Angelo had meant. The visitor was dressed in a white suit and black shirt. The woman with him sat down in a chair. He laid his white kid gloves on the counter and tapped his cane.

"Signor?" she said.

"Do you have any accommodations?" he asked. He pursed his lips and looked about.

"Si. We have two rooms left. Would you like to see them?"

Hawke nodded. He took Veronica by the arm, and together the three entered the lift. Sylvia showed them Harry's room.

"This one needs to be made up, of course. It was vacated early this morning."

As if he had smelled a distasteful odor, Robert Hawke wrinkled his nose and motioned Veronica out.

Robert said, "Look at the other room with the lady, dear." He dabbed perspiration from his forehead with a handkerchief. "I'm feeling a little under the weather. I'll meet you in the lobby."

Veronica would not try to escape, because the drug had made her compliant. He smiled a ghastly smile and started for the lift, saying, "Take your time. Don't rush." Once they were gone, Robert returned to Harry's old room. Methodically, he searched the bedding, the drawers, and the closet. Nothing. Of course! Harry would be too careful to leave anything important behind.

When Angelo returned to the hotel, he came face to face with Robert Hawke on the staircase. Recognizing him from Harry's description, he quickly ran back to the apartment.

He shook Harry's shoulder, saying, "He's here. The man you described."

Harry was instantly awake. "Hawke's here?"

"Not here, but back at the hotel."

Harry sat up. "Does he know I'm here?"

Angelo shook his head.

"Can you get someone to deliver a letter to him?"

"Sure. I can deliver it."

"No, Angelo. It's too dangerous. Someone else.

"The gondolier will."

"I need to write a note."

Angelo handed him a pen and paper. Harry stared out the window at the rooftops. Hawke was playing no gentlemanly game of chess. At the back of his mind, he sensed the doctor had another, unknown agenda that was not determined by reason. First, he had to buy time. He wrote:

Dear Robert,

You are a most admirable adversary, sir. I accept your proposal, as a gentleman, to submit our dispute to court, provided we call an immediate truce.

I must advise that I have not yet obtained the funds, but I expect I shall have them within a few days. Any interference in my activities will result in my canceling this agreement.

If you agree to this proposal, please leave a note at the front desk of the Grand Hotel. In several days, I will contact you there.

Sincerely,

Harold Jenkins.

He folded the note and sealed it in an envelope. "Angelo, please have your friend deliver this to the man at the hotel."

The boy took the note and hurried downstairs.

CHAPTER 30

▼

Promptly at five o'clock, Harry slipped out the back door and onto the dock. He climbed into the gondola and lay down. The tarp was pulled over him. In darkness, the gentle rocking of the boat nearly lulled him to sleep. Within fifteen minutes, the tarp was torn back, and he was lifted onto another dock and escorted to a taxi. From the rear window, he saw Venice fade to a glow on the horizon. The trip to Heathrow passed in a haze of disjointed recollection. It was almost ten o'clock in the evening when he checked into his hotel in London, on Cromwell Road.

Angelo returned to the Grand Hotel shortly after Harry had left. Garth Deal was in the lobby.

"So, where's your lover boy?" Garth sauntered over to Angelo and towered over him.

"Which one, dear?" Angelo lisped and batted his eyelashes in parody.

"Jenkins! You asshole." Garth squeezed the boy's shoulder hard. Angelo almost sank to his knees. Garth smirked. "That was just a love tap. Where's Jenkins?"

"I don't know. He left yesterday," Angelo gasped. "Gone back to Toronto."

"Toronto?" Garth shoved him against the desk. "Don't give me that shit!" He dreaded having to tell Dr. Hawke he had lost the quarry.

In his hotel room in London, Harry was able to dress his wound himself. Although the bandage kept slipping down his forehead, he thought it not too bad a job. In the morning, he would go to Barclay's Bank down the street, get the shares, and be gone. Once the nightmare chase for the money was over, he could get back to normal. Leave it to the courts to sort out the claims of both Norma and Robert to the money. Before getting into bed, he tried to reach Natasha. No luck. Thoughts of her were all that kept him sane. Maybe he could dream about her, if he tried. Sleep came swiftly, but his dreams were disturbing. Once again, only Angelo appeared. As if tortured, Harry cried out several times in the night and woke in a sweat as the light broke through the curtains.

Garth approached Hawke's door cautiously and knocked. When Veronica answered, he was stunned at his sister's appearance—worn out, stupid, and dazed.

He entered the room. "What's with you, sis? You look like hell. You got big circles under your eyes."

"I'm okay. Come in." Veronica did not know what was wrong with her. For the past two days, she had dragged around as if she were walking on the bottom of the ocean. Maybe Robert was giving her something else to make her sick.

Hawke emerged from the bathroom, dressed entirely in black. He sat down and crossed his legs. For a moment, he attended to brushing his pant leg. "Your report, Garth?"

Garth cracked his knuckles. "Dr. Hawke, I saw the little faggot at the hotel." Seeing his employer's expression, his grin faded. "I mean, Angelo, the desk clerk."

"And?" Hawke uncrossed his legs and stretched out.

Clenching his fists, Garth continued, "Says Jenkins has checked out and gone back to Toronto."

"What?" Hawke's tone was low and incredulous. "You let him get away?"

Garth did not move. If he had to, he could snap the fat little neck with his bare hands.

"You idiot!" Hawke sprang to his feet and spluttered, "Can't you even follow one man without losing him?" His jowls turned purple with rage.

"I'm sorry, boss," Garth muttered. "He just kinda slipped away."

"Too smart for you, eh?" shouted Hawke, furiously pacing in circles. "Serves me right for hiring a moron!"

Garth's face darkened. "What do you want me to do, Dr. Hawke?"

"Jenkins didn't go to Toronto, you idiot."

"Really?"

"He just sent me a note. He says he hasn't got the money yet."

"So what do I do?"

Hawke shook his fist under Garth's nose. "Follow the boy! Find out where he lives, because Jenkins is either there, or he's coming back!" Rage had exhausted the doctor. He muttered, "Get going, moron. Get the hell out of my sight."

Garth left quickly and started back for the Grand.

The next morning, Harry hungrily ate breakfast in his room. Looking out the window, he watched the sunrise, creating patterns of light and shade on the white-faced buildings across the road. The code for the bank was in his wallet, and all the necessary documents were in his case. Soon the Elixicorp shares would be in his hands. The quest seemed to have lasted forever, but now it was coming to a close. Surprised at his calm, the moment seemed strangely anticlimactic. In the bathroom, he fussed with a new bandage in hopes of looking somewhat normal. At last, he was ready.

At ten o'clock, he left the hotel and walked the several blocks to the bank in Cromwell Road. Suddenly, the question presented itself. *Who had actually executed the scheme?* Norma must have opened the box in London, because Arthur was already dead. *A dangerously brilliant woman!*

He continued past mothers with small children and prams strolling on the street lined with fruit shops and bakeries. As far as he could tell, no one was following him. He stopped at a door with lettering on frosted glass. It read: *Barclay's of Cromwell Road.* He imagined Norma scurrying through the door thirty years or so ago, needing the manager's assistance immediately. She had always been expert in playing upon the sympathies of all who crossed her path.

The branch was small and elegantly appointed. He approached a teller.

"I'd like to see the manager, please." Although he hated banks, Harry always tried to be polite and circumspect within their vaulted chambers.

"Certainly, sir," said the young man, as he showed Harry into an empty office. With a cheery wave, the teller concluded, "The manager will be with you in a moment."

As he waited, he half-expected Hawke or his shadow to emerge from some darkened corner. But everything had gone smoothly so far! After a ten-minute wait, he was less optimistic. Finally, a woman in a red dress entered and slid into the leather chair.

She reached across the desk to shake hands "What can I do for you, mister …?"

Harry found her smile delightful. She did not seem alarmed at his bandaged forehead.

"Harry Jenkins," he said. "I'm a solicitor from Canada, instructed by my client, Mrs. Norma Dinnick, to obtain certain shares from a safety deposit box at this branch."

"You have the key, Mr. Jenkins, and evidence of your authority?"

"Indeed." Harry pushed the key across the desk to her along with the documentation. "Before we go into the box, you need the code from a bank in Venice."

"Let me check the card catalogue." She opened a drawer at the side of her desk.

Harry prayed there would be no hitch.

"Yes, you do need a code. Do you have it?"

The paper from his wallet was wrinkled. Harry spread it out and handed it to her. He would not be surprised to see Hawke, wearing his fedora and kid gloves, march in and rap his cane on the desk.

"Your documentation?"

Harry handed her the gold-sealed court order. "I'm her legal guardian. She's very elderly and incompetent."

The manager examined everything carefully. Harry offered another prayer to whatever powers might be in operation this morning.

At last, she smiled. "Everything seems to be in order, Mr. Jenkins. I'll have the vault clerk let you into the box."

"Thank you." He rose and shook her hand.

Harry and the clerk entered the vault. Row upon row of thin, stacked metal boxes confronted him. He could picture Norma inserting the key—the very key he now held—and locking up the box. The clerk used her key and left. Harry inserted his.

Carefully, he carried the box to a small cubicle in the far corner. Only when he sat down, did he realize how heavy his breathing was. Slowly, he pulled out the drawer. He saw only one white envelope. He slit it open and took out the stiff, ivory-colored paper.

There it was—*One Common Share in Elixicorp Holdings.* He knew it was the real thing, having seen copies before. Admiring the red, scrolled lettering, he caressed the edges and corners with his fingertip. Finally, the first part of the puzzle was solved. Harry could not wait to confront Norma.

Very carefully, he folded the share certificate and put it in his case. Scarcely believing how smoothly the meeting had gone, he hastened to say good-bye. Outside, he checked his watch and grinned. Time enough for a stroll and lunch before catching the plane back to Venice.

CHAPTER 31

▼

Garth Deal saw Angelo leave the hotel at noon. By sliding into doorways, he managed to remain unseen by the boy as he crossed the two bridges to his apartment.

Garth called Dr. Hawke on his cell phone. "Sir?"

"I trust, for your sake, you still have him in sight," Hawke breathed into the phone. He and Veronica were seated at a café on Piazza San Marco.

"He's just left the hotel. Going over a bridge …" Garth hurried not to lose him. "He's going in some building, but there's no sign on it."

"Probably he lives there. Perhaps he's going home for lunch, Garth?"

"Yes, sir."

"Stay there until he comes out, then call me."

Pocketing his cell phone, Robert fumed, "Honestly, Ronnie. I have to hold his hand every step of the way."

Veronica had stopped eating in Robert's presence and was feeling much better. With neither brute strength nor stamina, she was certain Robert had relied upon a fleet hand to feed her drugs. Just his style—effeminate and weak. But she continued to feign stupor and compliance.

Half an hour later, Garth called back. "He's come out and gone back to the hotel, I think."

"Tell us exactly where you are in relation to the Grand, and we'll meet you there."

Garth did his best to explain. In another twenty minutes, Robert Hawke was on the steps to Angelo's apartment.

"Garth? Bring the boy back from the hotel." Hawke put his finger to his lips and tittered. "Don't let him distract you from your mission. I hear he's most attractive."

Infuriated, Garth started back to the hotel. He was no pansy, and if Hawke wasn't his employer, he would have kicked his head in.

Robert reached for Veronica's hand. "Come, my dear. Let's have a look around."

The door to the apartment swung open easily. Robert smiled. "Such a pitiful little place! Not much more than the Dungeon of Ill Ease, Ronnie."

Looking for traces of Harry's presence, he entered the bathroom. He wrinkled his nose at the brown stained sink, almost hanging from the crumbling wall.

"I sense Harry will be returning shortly to this humble dwelling." He glanced about in genuine despair. "Harry deserves far grander than this. When he returns, we will persuade him to come with us to San Diego, where he will have only the finest accommodations."

Veronica looked upon Robert with dull incomprehension.

On his flight back to Venice, Harry was beset with images of a sweetly smiling Norma Dinnick, which were swiftly replaced by her sphinx-like visage. *How could she have poisoned Richard?* Chomping into his cold chicken sandwich, he stared out onto the banks of clouds. In memory, he could see Richard collapsing at his feet, mouthing his lascivious fantasies of Marjorie Deighton. His prim, proper self was the perfect disguise to hide all manner of sexual escapades, but even so, he had died trying to convince Norma to do the *right* thing.

In Venice, he arrived at the bank just before it opened for the afternoon. He sank to the bench where Paulo, the bank clerk, had insisted Arthur had been murdered. The sun descended behind the rooftops, making shadows spill out of doorways to fill the narrow calle.

A huge, hulking figure rose in the mist and passed over a small bridge. *Surely to God, he isn't back!* thought Harry. Jumping to his feet, he was ready to hide from sight. His head throbbed so violently, that he knew he could not withstand another attack. But the figure reappeared, leading a small child by the hand back across the bridge. Together they sang and laughed and then disappeared into a doorway. Harry sank back in relief.

When the bank opened, Harry entered. Dull light seeped downward from high, narrow windows. Swept back in time, he envisioned Arthur furtively glancing over his shoulder for the young Robert Hawke as he ferreted away the funds. Harry marched across the blue-and-white terrazzo tiles to the wickets. He glanced up to see a shadowy figure in the cage.

He addressed the teller. "Is Signor Allegrini in, please?"

"Si." The teller smiled. "Your name, please?"

"Harry Jenkins. I saw him several days ago."

With eyes flitting about, wariness crept over the youth's face. "The manager is out. If you make an appointment, he will see you tomorrow."

Harry peered in the direction of the manager's office. Quickly, the door was shut.

"But his door just closed."

"He is on the phone," the boy said stubbornly.

"Then I'll wait." Harry marched over to the manager's office and rapped sharply. Although there was no reply, Harry could hear wheezing within. He pushed the door open.

"Signor Allegrini, I must see you about the business we discussed...." Harry's voice trailed off.

Allegrini paled as if confronted by an apparition. "Please, Signor Jenkins!" he pleaded, waving his hands. "Go away." Drawing himself up to his full height of five feet, he spoke in short, wheezy breaths, "Paulo was right. That file is cursed."

"What on earth do you mean?"

"Paulo is dead," he whispered.

Harry sat down. "Good Lord! What happened?"

"He was murdered just after you left the bank. A customer saw a huge man force Paulo into an alleyway." Allegrini looked up with damp eyes. "They found his body in the Grand Canal." Holding a handkerchief to his nose, he blew hard. "He was stabbed in the back. After more than thirty years of service."

Stunned, Harry did not speak for several moments. "I am terribly sorry," he began. "How very shocking for you. Have they caught the man?"

Allegrini shook his head sadly. "No, he got away without a trace."

"Is there anything I can do? Go to the police?" Harry offered, shuddering to think the man who stabbed Paulo was, undoubtedly, his own attacker.

The manager threw up his hands in a gesture of futility. "Nothing can be done."

"Then to business, signor? I have the Elixicorp share certificate with me." Half-expecting Hawke to appear, Harry glanced over his shoulder. "It's the last document you need. If you can transfer the funds, as we discussed, the whole matter will be out of your hands."

Allegrini eyes narrowed. "That is very wise. I would like to see the end of it."

Harry withdrew the share certificate from his case. "You need this to release the funds to me as Norma Dinnick's legal representative."

Rummaging through his cabinet, Allegrini muttered, "The file was here the other day, but where is it now?" His wheezing quickened as he dug deeper.

A shadow passed over the glass-paneled door of the office. Harry stiffened.

With a bird like cry, the manager slammed the drawer and threw up his hands, exclaiming, "It is gone, Signor Jenkins! Paulo *was* right. It is truly cursed!" He sank to his chair, his features pale and twisted. "Holy Mother of God!" he whispered, crossing himself.

Panic choked Harry. Did Hawke snatch the file at the very last moment? It contained the account numbers and the letter of instructions. If true, now each one of them had a piece of the puzzle, but neither could act without the other.

Harry rounded the banker's desk. "That can't be!" he nearly shouted. "Please, sir, let me look." With his heart pounding, he threw open the cabinet and tried to search methodically. He saw his trembling fingers rooting among the files. Hawke and his men could do anything. Poor Paulo! Dragged from the canal!

Allegrini quaked in fear. "Paulo was right. The evil eye has cursed the file!" Nearly stumbling, he rushed to open the door. He called out, "Vincenzo! Come quick!"

Within moments, the young teller was at the door.

"The Dinnick file! Where has it gone?"

The teller frowned and shook his head. "Paulo's file? The one he had before he was...."

"Si ... Si!"

Standing up straight behind the desk, Harry exhaled sharply. "Have you seen it?"

Again, the teller frowned. "I think so ... on Paulo's desk." He turned sharply and rushed off. Harry and Allegrini stared at each other. They could hear the teller's whispered curses and the shuffling of papers on Paulo's little desk in the next office. After long moments, he was back with an old, dog-eared file under his arm. He held it out to Allegrini. "This is it?"

Sighing in relief, the manager sank to his chair. "Si," he whispered. "But why did Paulo have it on his desk?"

"He said he was going to burn it. That only terrible trouble could come from it." The young man lowered his eyes. "But he was shaking so bad, he went outside for a smoke and then," he hesitated, "he was murdered."

"Thank you, Vincenzo. You may go now, but please get the key so I can lock my door," said Allegrini quietly as he opened the file.

Weak with relief, Harry took a seat.

The teller returned with the key. The manager locked the door and settled behind his desk to examine the file and the Elixicorp share certificate. At last, satisfied, he wheezed, "There is a great deal of money involved."

"How much?"

"Fifty million American dollars."

A staggering sum! Harry had known there was a lot, but never just how much. Fingering his bandage, he reflected upon the unimaginable violence and carnage along the path to the spoils. *And* Paulo was murdered just before he could burn the file.

"I'll give you a written direction to transfer the fund into my solicitor's trust account in Toronto." Quickly, he wrote out the instructions.

The little man stood and wobbled toward the door. "I will take care of this immediately."

The manager was gone ten minutes.

What on earth is keeping him? Harry's concerns about some last-minute technical hitch mounted. Fifteen minutes passed. Worried that Hawke or his henchmen had entered the bank at the very last moment, Harry rose to hunt for the manager. Would he find him heaped in a corner—stabbed to death?

Opening the office door, he glanced toward the heavy wooden front door with its glassed windows. Light filtered inward illuminating dust motes hanging in the still afternoon air. No sound and no movement.

Looking upward to the mezzanine, he suddenly envisioned dark figures shifting silently behind the rows of columns. He struggled to bring his imagination in check. Ridiculous! No one was there—or could be there. And then he heard faintly, rapid footsteps ascending a staircase from somewhere deep within the bank. At last the door to the teller's cage flew open and Allegrini emerged—breathless. Head bowed in a study of an envelope, the manager scurried across the tiled expanse of the foyer. Together, they entered his office.

"It is done, Signor Jenkins. Here is your receipt," he wheezed.

At last, the job is finished! thought Harry.

The manager remained standing.

Harry shook his hand. "Thank you, Signor Allegrini."

Without another word, the little man nodded and solemnly showed him the door.

Weak with relief, Harry stopped on the Rialto Bridge and breathed deeply. His thoughts spun in his head. How horribly ironic! Had poor Paulo not been killed, he would have burned the file, and the money would not be under his control.

In a blind stupor, Harry stared onto the Grand Canal. Above the din, he heard a rich contralto voice singing an aria, accompanied by the yearning strains of violins. From around a corner floated a barge, festooned with garlands of flowers and strings of tiny, twinkling lights. On the deck, a statuesque woman in a silver gown stretched out her arms, tossed back her head and sang.

Exquisite melodies soared from the violins of her four accompanists in evening dress. As if suddenly awakened from a dream, Harry felt his senses quicken and life rush in on him.

His first glimpse of Venice had stirred unrealized perceptions lying deep within him. At times, he thought, the world brimmed with such clashing and conflicting forces, that only chaos ruled. But, at this moment, he sensed an invisible, unified life force mysteriously holding the world together. *Beneath its riotous surface, Venice is a living, breathing soul.*

Now, in the late afternoon, the parade of musicians bathed in an ethereal, golden light seemed a suitable celebration of his victory. For an instant, he grasped once more that the significance of existence could be known in each and every fleeting moment. Each ray of light illuminated the soul, and at any moment, the past, present, and future—all in one—lay before him. He watched the barge disappear. At last, the job was done! Time for a breather.

From the brilliance of the Grand Canal, he dove into the dark labyrinth of calles leading to Angelo's. Almost immediately, he made many wrong turns and lost his sense of direction. Blind alleys and dead ends confronted him, and his earlier moments of joy and satisfaction were blotted out.

Norma's mocking face beset him. How she had manipulated him! By God, she would not keep the money. But then, who *should* receive it? Several turns took him to a small canal snaking off in an entirely different direction. Suddenly, he was back at the Rialto Bridge.

Disoriented, he struck out again to find his route. Over his shoulder, he saw only empty passageways with sunlight pooling on cobblestone walks. All was silent. Alone, he smiled tentatively and began to relax. Once he was safely at Angelo's, he would have a hot shower and shave. The boy had saved his life. How could he even begin to repay him?

Harry was sure he was in the right neighborhood, but he had difficulty finding the front door to the apartment. After circling over several bridges and retracing his steps, at last he looked up to see a sign that read: *A. Canaletto #2*. Smiling, he took the steps two at a time to the darkened landing and found the key under the mat. The door swung open easily.

"Welcome back, Harry." Although he spoke cheerily, there was underlying menace in Robert Hawke's tone. His grim face was shaded by his black fedora, tilted at a severe angle. He sat on the only chair in the room. Veronica Deal rested on the bed. A huge man blocked out the light from the window.

"What the hell are you doing here?" Harry inwardly breathed a sigh of relief. *At least the money is safe.*

Hawke ignored the question. "I'm sure you've met my Mrs. Deal before, Harry. And I would like to introduce her brother, Mr. Garth Deal, the one who has been following you with limited success." Gesturing with his cane, Hawke continued, "And that lump over there is Garth's assistant, Lennie."

Garth loomed over him. Definitely, he was the man in the Jeep and across from him at the Bellini. Rat-faced Lennie grinned at him from the bathroom door. Harry felt the tiny room close in on him.

"I thought you'd wait for my call, Robert. How did you know I was here?"

Hawke tapped a finger on the side of his nose. "A little bird, Harry," he chuckled. "You'll see in the kitchen," he added unpleasantly.

With cold seeping through him, Harry asked, "Where is the boy?" He brushed past Lennie and stuck his head into the kitchen. Angelo was seated on a high stool, staring out the window. A jacket was draped over his arms.

"Angelo … you told them?" he asked softly.

Pain spread across the boy's face. "Si," he said.

"But …" Harry stiffened. "What did they do to you?" he asked, fearing the answer.

Hawke spoke liltingly from behind him. "Actually, Harry, your lover tried *very* hard not to tell."

Harry swung around. "He's a friend, not a lover." Instantly, shame at his disavowal of Angelo engulfed him. For a moment he was speechless. Angelo's eyelids only flickered, and Harry looked away.

"What happened?" he asked. Angelo hung his head. Edges of fear pressed in on Harry. "What do you mean, *'Tried very hard not to tell?'* He saw the proud tilt of the boy's jaw and feared the worst. "What have you done to him?"

"We tried all civilized manner of persuasion, Harry. But it was quite impossible." Slowly, Hawke removed his kid gloves. "You see, he's quite helplessly in love with you."

"Tell me now, Robert!" Harry demanded.

Hawke nodded curtly at the boy. "Remove the jacket from your arms."

Staring out the window, Angelo lifted up the jacket with his right hand. His left hand was bound in bandages from the elbow to knuckles. Blood had seeped out a little at the wrist. For the first time, Harry noticed the smears of red on the floor, as if they had been cleaned up in haste. Sickness of foreknowledge seeped into him.

"Hold up your left arm, Angelo," the doctor commanded.

Angelo raised his left arm. His hand dangled uselessly at the wrist. His shoulders shook and tears trickled down his face.

"Now, raise your hand," said Hawke.

"I cannot," said the boy. Tears coursed down his cheeks.

Harry reached out and took Angelo's hand, which flopped and swayed at the wrist. "What *exactly* have you done to him, Robert," asked Harry, his anger mounting.

"Just a little operation on the tendons, Harry. We absolutely begged him to tell us." Hawke shrugged. "He was advised of the consequences, but alas, he refused. He left us no choice, you see."

Harry stood outside himself. He saw himself, a middle-age man, gently touching a young boy with love. With great care, he lifted Angelo's hand to his cheek and wept.

"Dear God, Angelo! You did this for me?"

Tears glinting in his eyes, Angelo nodded and settled his head on Harry's shoulder.

Harry held the boy gently in his arms and kissed his forehead, where his damp hair was matted. The moment seemed to last forever.

Thoughts, tangled in words, flew through his head. *All existence and all time, eternally, forever ... its meaning and truth captured in this fleeting moment. Love and nature are destiny. And yet, such a terrible collision of love and madness have wreaked the most hideous consequences.* Yet, through embrace, through touch with hands, arms, lips, and fingers, the words tumbled in upon him: *At last, a son!*

Harry's tears dried. He turned from their embrace. With cold and murderous fury engulfing him, he swung hard, sharply catching Hawke on his pudgy chin. Pain flashed from his hand to his shoulder. Hawke sprawled on the floor, and Harry leapt upon him. Under his thumbs he felt the little man's windpipe. Incredible how puny he really was! He lusted to crush out the life of the horrific being now in his grasp. Like ocean waves, fury swept him up and carried him on its crest. He was nearly helpless to stop. With unknown strength, he dug deeper and ever deeper with his thumbs. The face beneath him grew a violent purple, and the eyes bulged hideously.

From a thousand miles away, he heard Angelo cry out. "Harry, stop! You will kill him!"

Then Harry was lifted into the air by Garth and Lennie and thrown to the floor. A boot jammed into the back of his neck, and darkness swallowed him up.

Moments later, Harry woke to the knowledge that murderous blood lust coursed in his veins. He lay panting on the chesterfield. Angelo sat on the floor, his head bowed.

Quivering with excitement, Hawke bent over Harry. "How wonderful, Harry! You have passed the test with flying colors! You are indeed the candidate for my little trial of one." Then he spoke icily. "You *do* have the money, don't you?"

"Yes."

Hawke smiled indulgently. "That's better. A little cooperation would be most helpful." He straightened up and continued, "How much is there?"

When Harry tried to sit up, Garth shoved him back down.
"Fifty million American dollars."

Beaming, Hawke sat beside Harry on the chesterfield. "Oh,
that is absolutely wonderful, dear boy." He rubbed his legs in
excitement. "Do you have it with you?"

"Of course not," Harry muttered. "Do you think I'd carry
that kind of money around in my wallet?"

Hawke's face darkened. "Where is it, then?"

"In my solicitor's trust account, back in Toronto."

Hawke's eyes bulged and his hands trembled with rage. "Are
you telling me, Mr. Jenkins, that you are not giving it to me?"

"Why should I? We were going to submit the issues to
court." He took perverse pleasure in watching Hawke's swift
transformation into madness. *Like gentlemen,* I believe those
were your words."

Clenching his fists, Hawke spluttered, "That money is mine!"

Harry could not resist goading him. "But, sir, it was your
proposal. We were to join forces and then, when we found the
money, battle its ownership out in court. Like gentlemen."

Garth's fist slammed into his face. As Harry sank back, he
nearly choked on warm blood gushing from his cheek and lip.

Hawke paced rapidly about the tiny room in circles. He
shouted, "You betrayed me! You slithered out to find it for
yourself and that lunatic, Dinnick."

"Why would I trust you?" Harry asked weakly. "You followed me and had me beaten by your henchman over there.

Then you've destroyed Angelo's wrist. God knows what else you've done!"

Hawke was in such a tirade, he did not hear Harry. "And you betrayed me with her!" Hawke swung around, pointing at Veronica.

"What are you talking about? Mrs. Deal? I've only met her once or twice."

Veronica sat up on the bed but did not speak.

"Look at her! You could not resist her."

Harry could not fathom Hawke's brain. "I've had nothing to do with her," he maintained. Garth drove his fist into his other cheek. He could scarcely see for all the blood. Through his swollen lips, he managed to say, "You can beat me, Doctor Hawke, but that won't get you the money."

Hawke grabbed Harry's ear and pulled him close. "I have something more persuasive for you, Harry. We're going to San Diego. Now."

"San Diego? Why?"

"You will see soon enough."

Garth and Lennie dragged him from the couch. In that instant, Harry knew it wasn't just the money. There was another plan.

"Kill the boy." Hawke ordered.

Lennie grabbed Angelo's arms and held them back. Eyes ablaze, Garth unsheathed his knife.

Harry struggled to his feet. "For God's sake, Robert! You can't...."

Carefully, Hawke dusted off his suit. "Why Harry! Love can be such a powerful sentiment, can't it?"

"You can't harm him. He's just a kid, who's had nothing to do with this mess. You can have half the...."

"No, Harry!" Angelo shouted. "Do not bargain with him!"

With an impish grin, Hawke turned to Veronica. "You see, my dear? I do enjoy this little drama. Mr. Jenkins is going to beg for his lover's life."

"Stop it, Robert!" Veronica rose from the bed. "You can't have blood on your hands. If it ever came out, it would completely destroy everything you've worked for. When you're on the verge of a breakthrough, you're going to throw it all away?"

Hawke looked keenly at her and said slowly, "How very wise of you, Ronnie." Then he shrugged. "All right. Just tie him up and put him in the closet." He turned on Harry. "Besides, Mr. Jenkins, half the money is *not* nearly enough!"

Disappointed, Garth put his knife away. Together, he and Lennie bound Angelo's hands and feet together. Then they wound tape around his mouth and eyes and hoisted him into a closet. Next, they grasped Harry under the arms and lifted him off the chesterfield.

"What's in San Diego, Robert?" Harry asked.

"Ah ... Harry. I can hear the trepidation in your voice. At last you have a glimmer of understanding. Yes, I do want *every* last cent of the money, but there is something even more important than money." Hawke motioned his men to take Harry down the back stairs. Clutching Veronica by the arm, he followed. His words echoed ominously in the stairwell. "On the way to the airport, Harry, I will tell you about my trial of one and what's in store for you."

"If we're leaving the country, why not let the kid go? He can do you no harm."

"My dear Harry. You are a very noble sort." Hawke's chuckle was ugly. "Pleading for your little slut right to the end! Don't worry. I'm sure one of his many lovers will rescue him."

CHAPTER 32

▼

On the dock, Veronica did not look at Harry, but she touched
his hand. Dizzy, he wavered at the water's edge as the motor-
boat pulled up. The trip across the water was short. A long
white limousine awaited them. Harry was shoved in back
between Lennie and Garth. Hawke and Veronica took the seat
on the side.

"Care for something?" With a genial smile, Hawke held up a
crystal decanter from the bar.

Although he could not bear the thought of liquor, Harry
hoped to engage his captor enough to talk. He nodded, and the
doctor filled two glasses with a finger of scotch.

"To your health, Harry." They raised their glasses as the limo
sped off.

"We're going to Marco Polo Airport, where my helicopter
will fly us to Florence. From there, we will take my private jet to
San Diego."

Harry sank back into the leather seat between the two massive sets of shoulders. Although his stomach was lurching, he
managed to ask, "What's in San Diego, Robert?"

Hawke considered the question carefully. At last he said. "Harry, I have always said I am very attracted by your energy. Do you know what I mean by that?"

Harry shook his head.

"My God! Think, man! It's not just sexual. That is only one small part of a man. It is your spirit, your essence." Leaning forward, he continued excitedly, "It is your mind and spirit that hold the fascination for me. And when you proved instinct could govern you, you passed the test with beauty and grace. Just think! If Garth and Lennie had not been there, you would easily have crushed the life out of me."

"Robert, I'm only a lawyer with a modest practice. There's nothing special about my mind."

Hawke stared at Harry. "Do not sell yourself short! Most people are no more valuable than laboratory rats. Would you not agree?" Not waiting for an answer, he rushed on. "I am engaged in research of the greatest import." His flushed face betrayed his zealotry. "But sadly, the quality of the human brain varies greatly. Yours is one of the finest I have come across."

Harry was beginning to sense the depths of his danger, but he asked mildly, "Are you conducting experiments in San Diego, Robert?"

Hawke's eyes gleamed with paranoia. "How did you know that? Have you been spying, or perhaps," he turned on Veronica, "you two have been talking?"

"Of course not," Harry said in as soothing a tone as he could muster. "Ever since we talked over lunch, I've been fascinated by your research. Alzheimer's is the scourge of the twenty-first century."

Robert slapped his hands on his thighs. "How right you are! You see, Hawke Pharmaceuticals is conducting the usual research on curing Alzheimer's, even trying to reverse its effects." He leaned close to Harry. "But the *real* research is in San Diego."

"Really?" Harry's head was beginning to spin again. By concentrating on Hawke's face, he might avoid passing out. "You're pursuing a new angle there?"

Beaming, Hawke placed his hand on Harry's knee. "Unless you know what causes a disease, how can you hope to cure it?"

Understanding burst upon Harry. Of course, all sorts of unconventional medical experimentation had been conducted by the mad. The goose-stepping intelligentsia of the Third Reich had conducted hideous trials in the name of medical science.

But he shook his head. "I don't know. Tell me."

Robert giggled like a small child. "Simple. By trial and error. You try to induce the disease."

Harry spoke carefully. "Have you had success inducing the disease in humans, Robert?"

"What intelligent questions you ask, dear boy!" Hawke exclaimed. "Yes and no." Intense concern passed over his face. "I cannot say with any certainty that Alzheimer's has been induced."

"How are your patients faring?"

"Physically, quite well."

"But mentally?" Harry prodded.

Robert shook his head and rushed on. "Here's the problem. The minds which I have used are really ..." He threw up his hands in disgust. "substandard, you see."

With frightening clarity, Harry saw his danger was immediate.

"You, Harry, will be in my trial. You have a first-rate mind and a truly expansive spirit. Since the experiments are so very new, it will be a trial of one."

Harry stared out the window. The horror of secret research in the empty hills surrounding San Diego overcame him.

"Only one thing, Harry," Robert began quietly, "is as important to me as my research. It is the money. You see, if you give it to me, I will be able to set up alternative methods of experimentation, and I will not need you. If you give me the money, which is rightfully mine, I will deliver you home unscathed. You have my word as a gentleman."

The words rang in Harry's mind. *As a gentleman.* Were he not so desperate, he would have laughed. For Harry, it was an impossible deal with the devil. He could purchase his own safety at the cost of fifty million American dollars. But then Hawke's madness would spread, and who knew where it would go next? The money seemed destined to poison humanity forever. Only time could give him any chance for escape. He decided to stay in the game.

"My mind is worth fifty million American dollars to you?" Harry hit the right note of incredulity.

Just for an instant, Hawke appeared doubtful. "Well, the research is at a critical point."

Harry interrupted. "Let me think about it, Robert. I'd like to see your facilities in San Diego, and the results so far, before I commit myself. I have a real interest in the diseases of the elderly, given my clientele *and* my father of whom we spoke."

Hawke regarded him shrewdly. "Very good, Harry," he breathed. "I'm so glad you're intrigued with my little project."

At the airport, they were ushered from the limousine into a low, one storey building, with only a waiting room and a small office. The staff greeted Dr. Hawke warmly.

Within moments, they were instructed to stay in a group and walk quickly to the helicopter. Harry squinted in the brilliant sun as he was marched across the tarmac by the henchmen.

In the distance, perched on the horizon like an alien species of bird, the helicopter whirred. As they neared, the fury of sound from the engine and twirling blades engulfed them.

Silhouetted against the bright sky, the ground crew waved the party in a wide circle around the tail of the helicopter. Hawke and Veronica were only a few feet behind Harry. The tail blade spun with such speed, it was nearly invisible. Harry turned back to say something flattering to Robert about the aircraft. Veronica caught her shoe on some cables. Robert turned back to hurry her. Crouching down to struggle with her heel, she lurched and then fell full force against Robert.

Losing his balance, the pudgy man stumbled. Desperately, he reached out to right himself. Veronica stayed clear as he clawed at the air to keep his balance. The ground crew, waving frantically, ran toward him. Their shouts could not be heard above the deafening roar of the engines. Within seconds, Hawke fell and was caught in the invisible spin of the tail blade.

Rooted to the spot, Harry watched the horrific scene unfold. With sickening, thudding sounds, the human form of Dr. Hawke exploded in a torrent of red, hideously bisected against the brilliant sun by the spinning blades. Remains were splattered far across the tarmac.

Undamaged, Hawke's fedora was lifted upward in the wind, free of the blades. It sailed with ease across the sky like a black bird of prey to settle on the tarmac thirty yards away. For Dr. Hawke, there was no time for fear and none for pain. When the pilot cut the engines, screams—frantic at first—soon died in the wind sweeping through grasses at the edges of the runway. Silence grew as the whir of the blades died.

Like dogs without a master, Garth and Lennie screamed and ran in circles. At last, they stopped and sank to their knees as if waiting for instruction.

Veronica, crawling to her feet, shouted, "Run, Harry! Get away!"

Sickened, Harry tore himself away and ran toward the main building. With sirens blaring, the ambulance raced onto the tarmac. Rushing through the waiting room, he glanced over his shoulder to see Veronica, Garth, and Lennie huddled together beside the now still helicopter.

At the road, he found a taxi back to Venice. Slamming the door shut, he nearly retched at the memory of the malevolent force spewed across the field of tar. Sinking back in the seat, Harry began to shudder. Tears rose as he sought to erase from his mind the grisly blast of flesh he had witnessed. Thank God, Mrs. Deal had brought an end to Hawke's madness. His mind spun in circles.

He lurched forward. *Dear God, Angelo!*

Immediately, he envisioned his dim apartment with its gray walls of peeling paint. Above his bed, next to a cracked mirror, hung a crucifix. Mute in his defiance, Angelo would have been dragged to his sacrifice. But now, locked in the closet and bound with tape around his face, hands and feet, he would be unable to breathe. Harry stuffed fifty euros into the driver's hand and begged him to hurry.

Settling back, he heard a high-pitched whine, almost like mosquitoes. He twisted around and looked out the rear window. No cars were in sight—only black dots on the horizon, dipping and swaying from side to side like a swarm of locust. He squinted in the light. Within moments, he could tell they were helmeted riders on motorbikes.

Surely to God, Garth Deal would not be in pursuit. He only did Hawke's bidding and Mrs. Deal would prevent any further action. But *were* the bikes following him? Soon, the riders were almost on his tail. The wheel of one bike just grazed the rear of the taxi. Not more than a tap or a faint thud.

Rolling down his window, the driver cursed into the wind. Then the bikes—there must have been six of them—stormed past the cab, heaving up gravel and dust behind them. Harry sank back in the seat.

At last, they reached Tronchetto, where he could catch the vaparetto into the city. Once out of the taxi, Harry sprinted to the landing for the boat to San Marco. Venice passed by him unnoticed. From the San Marco landing, he ran through narrow calles to Angelo's apartment. Up against the wall leaned a motorbike.

Flinging open the outer door, Harry nearly sank with fear. A pale moon-shaped face wavered in the darkness. But the man only shuffled to one side to let him by. A young girl, seated on the steps, gazed blankly up at him.

"Change, signor?" she asked.

Harry tossed her a coin and dashed up the stairs. Angelo's door gaped open. He ran in.

"Angelo!" he shouted. The apartment was silent in the gray light.

He wrenched the doorknob of the bedroom closet. "Angelo? Are you in there?"

The door gave way, and Harry saw a form huddled, in perfect stillness, against the wall. A lifeless arm was sprawled out from under his jacket.

"Angelo!" Harry sank to his knees. "Please, God, no!" he whispered. "Don't let this be."

He gently touched the boy's hair, which was damp and matted down. Thank God, he was still breathing. Or was he? With all his strength, he heaved the lifeless body from the closet and onto the middle of the floor.

Harry shook his shoulder. "Angelo, please! Wake up!"

The boy did not stir. Finding scissors in a drawer, he worked carefully to cut the tape from his mouth. Only once did he stop to wipe the sweat dripping from his face. At last, he peeled the tape from his mouth. A faint bluish tinge circled Angelo's lips. Harry cried out in frustration and tried to position his head for mouth-to-mouth resuscitation.

But then Angelo sighed and began to breathe shallowly.

"Angelo! You're breathing! Can you hear me?"

No response.

Next, when Harry carefully stripped the tape from his eyes, the lids flickered open.

"Harry?"

"Yes, Angelo." Afraid the boy would lapse into unconsciousness, he lifted up his shoulders and cradled him in his arms. Faint color was returning to his face. "Keep your eyes open, Angelo. Come on. I'm going to lift you to the bed."

With his heart thudding, Harry dragged the boy across the floor and propped him up against the bed. The body began to list precariously to one side, and Harry shoved him back up again.

"Angelo!" Harry tapped his cheek. "Please help me! I can't get you on the bed without your help."

At last the boy stirred and struggled onto the bed. Harry worked rapidly to free him from the tape at his wrists and ankles.

Angelo stared up at Harry and, for the first time, seemed to recognize him. "Thank you," he said weakly. He rested his hand on Harry's leg.

Harry rose. "I'll get you some water. How do you feel?"

Angelo moaned. "I almost died...."

In the kitchen, he could not find a clean glass. He took one from the sink and washed it. He had to get Angelo help.

Returning to the bedroom, Harry was relieved to see the boy still awake.

Angelo's eyes darted about the room. "Where are those men?"

"Gone," was all Harry said. "They won't be coming back."

Harry sat on the edge of the bed and held the glass. As the boy reached to drink, his hand began to shake. Soon his whole body was trembling, and Harry feared some unaccountable seizure from the deprivation of oxygen would overtake him.

"I cannot hold the glass," Angelo wept as he wound his arms around Harry's neck.

They sat on the bed for some moments in the room with its tall, gray walls. Harry looked out the window upon the tiled rooftops.

When he had been married to Laura, more than anything, he had wanted a child. Either she did not, or they had simply never made the time. He thought of his own father, his hands turned under and useless, who had never showed affection. Now, more than ever, he wished there had been time for children. Then he held the glass to Angelo's lips and let him drink. The boy slurped the water eagerly. Amazed at the gentleness creeping over him, he dried the tears from his face with a towel.

"Let me look at what they did, Angelo." Harry reached out to take his wrist.

"No!" Angelo pulled away and turned his face to the wall.

"But why?"

"You cannot undo the bandage."

"But it's almost falling off."

"No!" Like a child, the boy scrunched himself up, knees to chest.

Fear seeping into him, Harry said, "But it should be looked at by a doctor."

Angelo did not respond.

"What did they do to you? Please tell me."

"I do not know."

"What do you mean. You must have seen…."

"They put me to sleep. I know nothing." Angelo insisted.

"How?"

"They held a cloth to my face. It made me sleep."

Harry reached out to touch his arm. Angelo cried out.

"But you *are* in pain! I can see blood seeping out." Harry rose in frustration. Then he reminded himself Angelo was not much more than a child. "It will get infected if it is not treated," he said more patiently.

Angelo scrunched himself further against the wall. "Leave me alone."

Harry sighed deeply. He had to ask. "Why did you do this for me, Angelo?"

At last, Angelo turned to face him. He spoke shyly. "Because I love you."

"But we scarcely know each other."

"Love does not need a *reason*, Harry." With Angelo's smile, a quiet radiance filled the room.

How stupid am I? Harry wondered. *How many times must I learn that the heart has an eloquence all its own—far greater than the mind?*

Pondering the vast dimensions of love, Harry gazed at the young man sprawled on the bed. Gentleness crept over him. He could find great love and gratitude, stunning admiration for the bravery of sacrifice. But, although he saw his attractiveness, desire was not there.

Angelo shrugged. "It's okay, Harry. I expect nothing in return."

At last, Harry said, "You're more than twenty-five years younger than I am, Angelo. I know I can ... I do ... love you as a son."

Angelo smiled. "Then that will have to do. That pleases me." He paused. "In fact, I have no father."

"What happened, Angelo?" Harry asked quietly.

The boy shrugged. "It was a long time ago. He was a gondolier and was killed in an accident. I was three years of age."

The room was growing stuffy in the late afternoon. Harry rose to stretch. He stood at the window and wondering whether he could help. *A boy with no father—a man with no son.*

Angelo sat on the bed, his head bowed.

"Forgive me Angelo if my question is too personal." He knew his phrasing would be awkward, but he knew no other words. "Have you ever had a girlfriend ... ever liked a girl?"

The boy shrugged. "Sure, lots of times."

Harry saw the proud tilt of his jaw and the flash of defiance in his eyes. He knew he must be careful with such tender pain.

"I've had lots of them, but I like guys much better."

Harry was surprised that he had reached the outer limits of his own knowledge. He did not know what else to ask.

Suddenly, Angelo sprang from the bed in fury. "You think I can change, don't you? You want to cure me." His breath was sharp and shallow. His voice was filled with anger. "Because I had no father, you think ..." He broke off in frustration. "Why can you not understand? It's me—who I am. And I *like* being me."

Harry had not expected anger. He stepped back. "I *am* sorry, Angelo."

"You think you're better than me! I'm sick but you're normal!"

"I didn't say that at all...." Harry faltered.

"Harry, you do *not* understand. To me it feels right. I am *made* this way. You are *made* your way. We are not going to change." Angelo glared at him until his lip began to tremble. "It has nothing to do with my father!" He turned away sharply and lay on the bed. "And I want people to like me the way I am," he said softly into the pillow.

Harry realized the boy was silently sobbing. He sat on the bed and rested his hand on his shoulder.

"Get the hell out of here!"

"Angelo, don't. I was only trying to help. It's just that I've never known what to do or say."

The boy shifted around to face him. "You understand *now*, Harry?"

Harry nodded. "Yes, at last."

"Good! We cannot change, but you have not the right to look down on me."

In that moment, Harry realized the boy's simply stated truth, and he was ashamed at his own arrogance. Some aspects were immutable. Nature was destiny. How puny was intellectual understanding compared to that of the heart. Angelo's love and sacrifice had taught him many lessons. And look at how he had repaid him!

Gently taking his wrist, Harry said, "Angelo, I am truly sorry. You have taught me much."

Angelo surveyed Harry's face with momentary suspicion. "I believe you, then." Suddenly, he grimaced in pain. "Harry? Pour us some Grappa? It is in the cupboard under the sink."

"Of course." Harry brought the bottle and two glasses back to the bed and poured.

In one gulp, Angelo drained the glass. "More, Harry, please."

Angelo drained another.

When he saw the sweat forming on Angelo's brow, Harry frowned. "Angelo, you're in a lot of pain." He moved closer. "We have to do something about your wrist."

"Nothing can be done."

"You don't know that," Harry said. "They can do all sorts of things nowadays."

Angelo shrugged. "I have no money."

"I do."

Angelo shook his head angrily. "No, Harry! I will *not* take your money."

"It's my fault. None of this would have happened, except for me."

"Still...."

"I want to take you to the hospital, Angelo. Have the doctors look at your wrist."

"I will lose my job and not be able to find any work," Angelo said sadly.

"Then come to the hospital."

"You have a lot of money?"

"Yes, I do."

"Then I will go—sometime."

Harry nodded. It was the very least Norma could do with her many millions. If the money could make some wrong into right, maybe it might break the curse. "You need a doctor now, Angelo. What about the one who stitched me up?"

Angelo lay on the bed, breathing heavily. Fear flickered in his eyes.

"Okay. I will call Zenobio. Give me the phone."

Harry waited while Angelo dialed. Although he spoke in Italian, he could hear his frightened tones.

Angelo hung up and, closing his eyes, whispered. "He will come. But when he does you must leave."

"Why?"

"Because I want you to.…"

Fifteen minutes later, they heard the doctor, in the stairwell, humming an aria. Harry let him in. Shaking his head, the old man shuffled into the bedroom and closed the door. Harry stood staring out the window and then began pacing the tiny room.

Half an hour later, the doctor came out, closing the door behind him. He only glanced at Harry and tipped his hat. Before he left, he turned back, whispering, "*Che monster questo a lui?*"

Indeed, thought Harry! A true monster had cut Angelo's wrist. *And it is my fault!* He went into the bedroom. Angelo sat at the window.

"What did the doctor say?" Harry asked.

Angelo smiled bravely. "It's nothing," he shrugged. "But you were right, Harry. He gave me some pills so that it does not become infected and for the little bit of pain."

"He asked me what *monster* did this to you."

"What?" Then the boy laughed. "Sometimes Zenobio … he's a crazy old man. He makes much out of nothing."

"Please let me look at it, Angelo. This is my fault. You must let me help."

"No! The doctor has just bandaged it up properly. I will not undo it."

Harry shook his head in frustration. "All right. Will you promise to go with me to the hospital in the morning?"

"Maybe."

Harry sank to the chair. Within moments, he heard the sputter of a motorbike outside. He sprang to the window.

Angelo frowned. "They do not allow bikes in the city."

They heard the engine die and saw a figure walking the bike across the bridge and out of sight.

"Well, he's gone now," said Harry, checking his watch. "Let's have dinner. We should stay at a hotel tonight, just to be safe."

"Those men will come back?"

"No. I'm sure they are gone. But I'd feel better if…."

Angelo nodded. "Okay. At my hotel?"

"No. Somewhere else."

Harry booked a suite at the Hotel Monaco on the Grand Canal. They ate in the restaurant overlooking the water. The boy sat on the edge of his chair, his pant leg jiggling. For an instant, Harry was struck by the sensuous curve of his lip and the proud cast of his features. Quickly, he looked away.

"I am sure they can attach those tendons, Angelo," Harry began as the waiter served the wine.

"An operation is too expensive," Angelo brooded.

Harry shook his head. "Listen, I can and want to pay for it."

"It will be at least a five thousand euros! You have that much?"

"Yes," Harry smiled, "and much more. As soon as I'm back home, I will put the money into the account at the hospital to pay the doctors. And I'll send you money until you're well enough to work again."

Angelo looked nervously about the restaurant. At last he said, "I will think about it."

Partway through the meal, Angelo set down his fork. "Harry? Why are you afraid of me? You are nervous like a cat."

"What?" Harry was alarmed. "Of course, I'm not."

The boy gazed into Harry's eyes with an intensity he had not seen before. "Do you still look down on me?"

"Good God, Angelo! No!"

"Because, if you do, I cannot accept your offer."

Harry set down his wine glass. "What can I do to convince you, Angelo?"

The boy shrugged. For the first time, Harry noticed the thinness of his shoulders.

"I spoke in ignorance, Angelo. It's just that I don't know much … don't understand these things very well. I suppose it's where I came from."

"Where *did* you come from?"

Harry could think of no answer. But then, he heard himself talking, words tumbling out on top of one another. "Angelo, I grew up in Toronto. My father could not express his love … his feelings. Everything in my world told me that men must not feel, men must not cry, or touch, or love one another. And if they did, they were weak or sick. They were sissies … laughed at … mocked. And sometimes, if people found out, they were beaten up. Sometimes even killed."

"Do you believe that is right?"

"Jesus, no, Angelo, I don't! I cannot understand such cruelty in the face of love. *Especially* now! I never understood how it could cause such vicious reactions. Love is love … it is good … no matter who's involved. But I always felt, for me, it was uncomfortable, like it just wasn't *me*."

Angelo smiled sadly. "Harry, I am truly sorry for you."

"How so?"

"You are so frightened and lonely. Closed off in yourself."

Harry found nothing to say.

After dinner, they went upstairs. At the door to the room, Angelo was careful to stand apart from Harry.

As Angelo entered, his entire left side throbbed with the pain of the incisions. Zenobio was right. A mad butcher had mangled his arm. In the bathroom, when he tried to loosen the bandage, it began to unravel. He saw the wounds and groaned.

Harry heard the boy and opened the bathroom door.

"Good God, Angelo!" The slashes on his wrist and up and down his arm looked like bloody carvings. The black stitches looked like huge, ugly insects sucking at the wounds.

Harry was staggered. "Angelo, I did not know. Please forgive me. They did this to you because of me?" He reached out and took the boy in his arms.

Locked in an embrace, they stood together for long moments. As if something inside were breaking open, Harry could feel the throb of life within. In that moment he could, at last without fear, understand the need and feel the desire. It was so simple. It was the flow of love and life—all life.

Angelo shoved him hard. "Get away, old man!"

Harry was astounded. "But, Angelo, I was...."

"Stay away from me! I like young, not old!" Angelo threw open the door and flung himself on the bed.

"Angelo, why on earth?" Harry saw his shoulders were shaking. He sat beside him on the bed.

Angelo wrenched around. His face was stained with tears. "You pity me. You feel you owe me. It is no good that way, Harry. I do *not* love you!"

Harry feared to speak, as if anything he said or did would only cause more harm. At last, he said, "Then you *must* accept my help. You will need plastic surgery to reconstruct your arm."

"I need my arm to work." Angelo said flatly.

"I know. And it needs to look okay, too."

"If you promise, Harry, that you really have enough money, I will take your offer."

Harry smiled. "Don't worry, I have plenty of money for whatever is needed."

Harry lay still in the dark, until he heard deep breathing from the other bed. His mind reeled at the sacrifice that had been made for him. Sometime later in the night, he heard little cries from across the room. He switched on the light to see Angelo shifting onto his side, trying to protect his arm in sleep. He got another blanket and covered him up. Left with his own thoughts, he contemplated the now still Grand Canal and marveled at the myriad gifts of love he had received from Angelo.

In the morning, they had breakfast on the terrace of the hotel overlooking the water, and then they walked slowly to the hospital. Angelo was admitted at once due to concerns about infection. The doctors were optimistic, assuring Harry that they could restore function to his arm.

Harry arranged for the surgery, a private room, additional nursing care, and therapy. Angelo was taken into the operating room at eleven o'clock. Harry strolled about the city until one o'clock, when he returned to the hospital and was advised of the success of the operation.

He found Angelo in his room with nurses at his bedside. Harry took his hand.

"Angelo?"

The boy only murmured, but then he opened his eyes.

"Angelo, the operation went very well." Harry stopped to clear his throat. "You'll be able to work in about four weeks after therapy."

Angelo smiled weakly and began to drift off.

"I have to catch the next flight back to Toronto, but I will call you here at the hospital."

Angelo began to snore lightly. Harry smiled and bent to kiss his cheek. "I love you, Angelo," he said. "You have taught me more than you can imagine." Then he hurried back to the hotel for his luggage.

CHAPTER 33

▼

Spinning the steering wheel smartly, Dorothy Crawford slid the Ford LTD into a parking space at Harry's office building. Only one piece of the puzzle remained. Where was Richard's golden-haired daughter, Suzannah Deighton? Likely, Gladys would know.

The child must be a forty-year-old woman by now and had probably never known her father. Did she resemble him in any way? *The whole truth will make me free*, she decided.

Entering the office, she saw no one, but heard sniffles and then a loud honk. *Miss Giveny must have a terrible cold*, she thought. After tapping on the brass bell, she waited until the secretary poked her head out of an office door. Dorothy was alarmed at her pallor.

"Yes, Mrs. Crawford?" asked Gladys abruptly.

"My dear, whatever is wrong?"

"Nothing." Gladys muttered. "Just a head cold."

"But, you've been crying…."

Bursting into tears, Gladys scuttled back into her office.

Astonished, Dorothy followed. "Please, Gladys. What is the trouble?"

"Merle, my sister," Gladys groaned. "She died. The funeral was yesterday."

"But then, why are you here? You should be at home." When Richard had died, she was stunned. Shock had carried her through the funeral and then later, the real pain began.

"Mr. Jenkins isn't back yet. Someone has to be here," she wailed.

Dorothy took Gladys' hand. "You were very close to your sister? Tell me what happened." When Richard died, everyone was so kind for a week or two, but then the sympathy shriveled up, just when she needed it most.

"Merle never had much of a life, Mrs. Crawford."

"How do you mean, dear?"

"Something was wrong with her. Everybody knew it, but nobody knew what it was."

"You mean she was sick?"

Gladys blew her nose again. "No. I guess you'd just call her simple."

Dorothy frowned.

Gladys rushed on. "She wasn't too quick. Never did anything with her life, except depend on me."

Dorothy caught the note of resentment.

"But she never did anyone harm, either. She was sweet and kind, but she just never did *anything*." Gladys searched Mrs. Crawford's face as if it might contain the answer to the puzzle of Merle's life.

A life, stillborn, even at death. An existence empty of any apparent purpose, thought Dorothy. "You were responsible for her?" she asked.

"She was like a little child all her life," she murmured.

"Gladys, you must get out of here. I'm taking you for lunch. My treat."

Gladys shook her head. "I can't leave the office."

"Surely, you take lunch?"

Gladys thought of her tuna salad sandwich in the fridge. Balefully, she glanced at the telephones. "All right," she said.

"We'll go to the Tea Room in the Arcade," Dorothy said, holding the door open for her.

"The Tea Room?" Gladys trembled. She had never eaten there before.

From the blinding noontime light, they sought the shadows of the Arcade. In the Tea Room, a young waiter seated them promptly.

Gladys peered worriedly about, as if in fear that Mr. Crawford might appear and order her back to her desk. Dorothy immediately felt Richard's presence but no hectoring, authoritarian voice rang in her ear.

She began carefully, "Gladys, I know how hard it is when you lose someone you love." Since Gladys looked as if she might burst into tears, Dorothy changed the subject, "This was a favorite place of Richard's."

Gladys nodded and sought her Kleenex.

"Richard brought his ladies here."

Gladys nodded solemnly. The waiter took their orders: a tuna fish sandwich for Gladys, and a club salad for Dorothy.

"You were so helpful about Queenie. I'm hoping you might help me with another little problem."

Gladys wondered what the nosy woman wanted. She had no experience with intimate conversation. She had no friends and it was pointless to tell Merle anything. Her sister never understood much of anything. Gladys felt extremely uncomfortable.

"I found some letters at home between Richard and a Marjorie Deighton. Apparently, Richard fathered a child named, Suzannah, with her."

"Oh?" Gladys choked.

"I'd like you to tell me how to contact her."

Instantly, Miss Giveny's throat dried, but then she spoke the truth. "Mrs. Crawford, I don't have the slightest notion."

"But there must be some clue, some lead?"

Tears welled up in Miss Giveny's eyes. "I told you about Norma Dinnick. Isn't that enough?" Her voice began to rise into an unfamiliar register. "It's only decent to let *some* things alone!"

In shock, Dorothy stared at the tight-lipped, grim face before her.

Suddenly Gladys burst into tears. "I loved him too, but always from a distance. Always hoping for a kind word or smile, which would make my day." Gladys rummaged for her Kleenex. "How do you think it feels—always keeping your feelings secret and hoping for just a few crumbs?"

Dorothy bit her lip. "Gladys, please. I'm *so* sorry ..."

"I was loyal to him when others weren't. I kept secrets for him and protected him." Her face raw, she looked at Dorothy in disbelief. "Don't you see? All because I loved him so terribly...."

"I know how difficult Richard could be, but ..." Dorothy said soothingly. From the corner of her eye, she could see the waiter approaching cautiously.

"And *now,* Mrs. Crawford, you want to dig up trouble?"

"I *am* sorry, Gladys. It was wrong and stupid of me even to ask."

"Why do you want to keep after the poor man? Let him rest in peace. He's *dead,* you know!"

Dorothy felt her heart heave. Despite the hopelessness of Gladys' love, she had more respect for his memory than she.

They sat in silence, waiting for their lunch. Gladys sniffled. Dorothy stared into the corner. She could almost see Richard charming his ladies at the far table. She looked down at her wedding ring, which she spun on her finger. She regarded the secretary, still hopelessly in her love with her husband. Gladys had led her to Norma Dinnick, from whom she had learned that he died for a principle. Why not leave it at that? Nothing could be gained from finding Suzannah. Forget the philandering. In her heart, she knew it was his nature. He could not help himself.

At last she spoke. "Gladys, thank you. You're right. I will let him rest."

When the lunch was served, they ate in silence, with Gladys wondering why Mrs. Crawford had changed her mind so suddenly.

"After lunch, why don't I drive you home?" asked Dorothy. "You must take some time off."

Gladys nodded. But when they were finished, she was suddenly overtaken by an unfamiliar recklessness. Charged with a sense of possibilities, she realized she needn't rush home—Merle wasn't there. Stifling a tiny sob, she decided she might look around the stores or even go to a movie. She said to Mrs. Crawford, "Thank you, but I won't need a ride. I think I'll stay downtown for awhile."

CHAPTER 34

▼

Natasha geared down sharply on the ramp into her condominium-parking garage. Her neck was so stiff that she could scarcely turn her head. And, a migraine was beginning to throb. This afternoon, she had lost the Cornish deal, which would have netted her at least fifty thousand dollars in commission.

Sheila's involvement was clear. Having retained her to appraise the commercial property on Ryan Street, she had naturally given her access to the vendor's private land use reports. Now those reports had gotten into the prospective purchaser's hands. And then, of course, with insider information, the purchaser had walked away from the deal. She only wished to get home and lie down in a cool, dark room, alone. *How could Sheila have done this?*

She opened the door to her apartment. There sat Sheila on the chesterfield.

"How did you get in?"

"You know … with my key." Sheila rose to kiss her. "I came to apologize for the other night, honey." Her casual tone masked her growing nervousness. Natasha remained silent, her face darkening. Sheila began to plead, "You *have* to believe me, I *never* sent Harry that email."

Natasha turned on her angrily, "Did you give Rhonda Franks those land use reports on my deal?"

Sheila's hand froze in midair. "Me? No ... Natty, I didn't. I'd never do that," she said uncertainly.

"Don't lie to me, Sheila. It only makes it worse."

"Who said I did?"

"Nobody. But you're the only one who had the information."

"All right, I did! But it was only because Rhonda said you authorized it." Sheila was verging on tears.

"And you never thought to check with me?"

Sheila's tone became wheedling. "I didn't think she'd lie, Natty. *Really* I didn't. Not about something like that!"

"How can I trust you or anything you say?" Natasha began to pace. "Do you realize you've just lost me fifty thousand in commission?"

"No! But how?"

"Corinth walked away from the deal this afternoon."

"They can do that?"

"Of course, they can! You knew the deal wasn't firm." Natasha was certain Sheila was trying to ingratiate herself with Rhonda, the one with innumerable lovers of dubious character.

Rushing to her, Sheila sank to her knees. "Please, Natty! Don't be cross. I'm so sorry. I didn't mean for that to happen."

Natasha was thunderstruck. "Cross? Sheila, that doesn't come close to describing how I feel. This is not love. It's betrayal beyond belief!" In fury, she yanked the curtains closed.

Sheila drew back. "Well, if you won't accept my apology...."

In an instant, Natasha saw her with new eyes. The woman was a manipulative child, with neither character nor any understanding of love.

Why have I wasted the past year debating between the two of them? In a way, she thought, *it has little to do with me.* The issue was not which sex she preferred, or to which one she could be true. Again and again, it came home to her. The question was far more fundamental. *What kind of person could she love and trust?* For years, Sheila had held her fast, distracting her with the false issue of her divided nature. Now, Natasha was breaking free of that blinding habit of mind and sense of obligation.

She saw herself walking along the shore of Lake Ontario near the cottage. That vast body of water, powerful and impersonal, ceaselessly rolled and dashed upon the sand and rock. *We are,* she thought, *but a minute fragment of that total natural energy.* With the tremendous force of new realization, she was swept with understanding that love just existed—like that energy. Real love needed no reason, explanation or justification. But if love were not true, no amount of rational thought or talk could ever make it right. *And* perhaps real love was the force, which held everything together. Without knowing it, she had made her decision days ago when she had talked with Harry, and then that morning, alone on the beach. Now it was time to act.

"Sheila," she began quietly, "This is not love. We are hurting each other too much."

"Please, Natty. Please forgive me," she whimpered.

Thinking of Josef, she reached out for Sheila. Cupping her chin in her hands, she drew her close and said with a sad smile,

"Yes. I really do forgive you, Sheila. *And* I hope that will be some comfort to you." Natasha looked deep into her eyes to see Sheila's first glimmer of triumph. "I forgive you because you simply cannot understand me, yourself, or anything else that is important to me."

Because Natasha's words were so warmly spoken, Sheila missed their import. "Thank you, Natty. I promise. I'll never do anything like that again." Sheila got up, and with a bright smile, said, "So, let's forget about all this horrible stuff. Do you want to order in some dinner? My treat."

"I said I *do* forgive you," said Natasha quietly. "But, I will never forget."

Sheila turned back nervously. "What do you mean?"

"You've tried everything you could to make me someone I'm not—to make me choose. When I couldn't become the person you wanted, you betrayed me not once, but twice. You have no idea of love, Sheila. Fortunately you've made it easy to choose." She could see the tears begin to course down Sheila's cheeks.

"Please, Natty. Don't do this. I really do love you."

Natasha shook her head sadly. "I have already chosen."

Sheila rushed to her. "You can't just forget all the years we've been together. It *has* to mean something to you, darling!"

Natasha closed her eyes. "Please leave now. I'm feeling quite rotten."

Sheila knew enough not to press her further. "Sure, sweetie. Let's talk about this when you're feeling better. I'll call you in the morning."

In silence, Natasha held the door open for her and waited until the elevator came. "Please don't," was all she said as she closed the door softly. In her apartment, she sank to a chair and sat motionless, lost in thought.

There would not be *another* time. She thought of Josef's smile and remembered his words—*Compassion does not require you to betray your inner self.* It was true. Although she could understand and forgive, she could still choose what was best for her. She hoped she really had, in her heart, forgiven Sheila.

And so, in the darkening room, she looked ahead to Harry's return. Once she had feared that her need of both of them might have resulted in having neither. She had even wondered if, detached from desire, she could find quietude and peace in a solitary state.

Was nature destiny? It was a good question, but applied in the wrong way. The only important nature of a person was honor, truth, and love. *And* there were infinite shades of love and desire. Smiling, she knew she could love and trust Harry. The problem of choice, which had ensnared her, was either extremely complex or unbelievably simple. By its exercise, she had simply walked away from dreary destiny.

CHAPTER 35

▼

Harry landed in Toronto mid-afternoon. On his front step, he braced himself for the hollowness of his empty house. But once inside, he felt huge relief just to be on his own familiar turf. He sat down heavily on the couch in the den and dialed Natasha, getting her on the first ring.

"I'm back, at last," he said. "May I see you?"

She spoke warmly. "Yes, of course, Harry. When can you come?"

"I have to see a client first." He checked his watch. "I should be at your place around nine thirty tonight." Then he asked cautiously, "Natasha? Did you receive a fax from me?"

"No, I didn't, darling."

"Or send one to me?"

"No ...?"

"Wonderful!" he breathed. "I'll see you tonight."

Dorothy had left him a message. When he called, he arranged to visit her right away. First, Dorothy, and *then* a trip to Norma's!

An hour later, he sat on Dorothy's tiny patio in the slanting shadows. Although she looked delicate and tired, she exuded a peace he had not sensed before.

"Harry, I'm sorry to have brought you over, but we really must talk about Norma Dinnick."

"Are you sure, Dorothy? Remember, I'm her legal guardian."

"Please. Let me go on."

"What are the police doing?"

"Not much. They seem to have lost interest."

"What do *you* want to do?"

With the sun glinting on the windows of the garden shed, she spoke quietly. "At the beginning, I thought thirst for justice was my motive in finding Richard's killer. But it wasn't that at all. I wanted to find his murderer, because I loved him. Pure and simple! Love drove me."

Harry remained silent. He knew he had dismissed Crawford as a libertine. Now, his widow, the one most hurt, was willing to forgive and love.

Dorothy continued, "You see, Harry, if I still loved him after everything...." Her voice dropped as she twirled the wedding band on her finger. "Then I must have truly accepted all of him." She smiled sadly. "Even his constant unfaithfulness. It was just *him*."

Harry waited for her to continue.

"Miss Giveny loved him too, you know."

Harry nodded. "Yes, I know." He startled as a flock of crows burst noisily from the branches of a neighbor's tree. Then he asked quietly, "Is there anything you'd like me to do?"

"No," she said, "He didn't die in squalid circumstances at the hands of some angry husband or jealous woman. He died trying to set a wrong to right. He wanted to redress an imbalance, a fraud."

"I know, Dorothy." Harry reached for her hand. "He was a remarkable man." What else could he say? "How do you feel about Norma Dinnick now?"

"She poisoned Richard, and God knows what else," she sighed. "But what point is there? The police think she'd never stand trial. I suppose that's why they've lost interest."

"I will go to see her, Dorothy. Is there anything you'd like me to say?"

"It doesn't really matter. I got the very best answer from her."

"Which was?"

"That she killed Richard because he was insisting she expose a fraud. Harry, if there is a middle ground somewhere, I think I've found mine. Instead of fighting anymore, all I need is to accept the man as he was. That gives me enough to make the most of the time I have left."

Back in the car, Harry's mind churned. Indeed, if anyone deserved a middle ground, it was Dorothy.

The low hills of Rattlesnake Point were illuminated in the soft, dying sun of the evening. Harry had called the Mercer to tell Norma he was coming. Today, he was in no mood for surprises. Driving upward through jagged rock, he saw flocks of black crows circling the sky.

When he entered the Mercer, the screen door slapped behind him. Off to his right, he saw a thin and entirely bald man seated with Mrs. Burke.

The man glanced about nervously as her voice rose.

"Donald! I'm your mother. What have you done with my money?"

Good grief, wondered Harry, *is this really the infamous Donald Burke, or just another innocent passerby?*

"Mother," the man began in a loud voice in order to be heard. "You've got *all* your money. How do you think we pay for this place?"

Harry knew the strain of having to shout patiently.

"You've spent it all on those women hanging about on Church Street. Now, didn't I tell you they were up to no good?"

Color rose swiftly from Donald's collar. "Mother. I'm an accountant. I have a wife and family. Have you forgotten your grandchildren?" Then his patience evaporated. "This is ridiculous! Let's find your nurse. It *must* be time for your medication."

Definitely, thought Harry as he turned to the reception desk, *lucidity is a thin and delicate membrane, destined to rupture at any moment.*

A smiling nurse approached him.

"Where's Mrs. Dinnick, please?"

"Oh, Mr. Jenkins? She's waiting for you on the veranda."

Harry had not seen her. Today of all days, she must be up to her games. Grumbling, he went outside.

Impatiently, he scanned the rows of rocking chairs. Vacant faces, with unseeing eyes, stared out onto the lawn. Green hospital gowns stirred in the breeze. Hunting for Norma was like finding one particular blade of grass in a field. Almost tripping over feet in slippers, he made his way from one end of the veranda to the other. Cursing, he started back again. This time, a hand fluttered up in a coy wave. There she was, right in the very middle of the field.

He stood before her.

"Hello, Harry. I fooled you, didn't I?"

He saw her with new eyes. *She is the cunning and patient predator—like a spider waiting,* he reflected. He said, "Norma, let's walk. We've got a lot to discuss." What tale would she spin this time, he wondered?

Norma rose obediently and took his arm.

"You're not angry with me, Harry? It's only a silly game."

"Not about that. We need privacy. Let's go into the garden."

"Did you get the money?"

"Yes," said Harry, marching her past the rose bushes and settling her on a bench. For a moment, he gazed upon the field below where only a few residents stood, watching the crows. Their stupidity angered and saddened him.

"How much is there?" Norma asked.

"Fifty million, American funds." He continued to watch the circling crows.

"Oh, my!"

He turned on her. "I was nearly killed getting it!"

"Harry, I'm *so* sorry! If I'd known you'd be exposed to danger...."

With great clarity, he saw the trickster glimmering from within her eyes. That sly creature was right there—had always been there—and Harry was amazed at his blindness.

He cut her off. "Robert Hawke is dead."

"Really!" she said with satisfaction. "He was another jailbird, just like that George Pappas."

"We've come to the end of the line, Norma."

"Well, I'm glad of that! So the money is mine now?" She smiled sweetly at him.

"No!" Harry felt his anger building. "You've talked to Dorothy Crawford."

Norma looked doubtful, as if she could not recall the name.

"She says you confessed to murdering her husband, my partner, Richard."

Norma said too quickly, "Good Heavens, no! I would never harm that dear man."

Harry shook his head. "Dorothy says you admitted poisoning him because he wanted you to give back the shares."

Norma pursed her lips. "And you believe that, Mr. Jenkins?"

Harry stared at her for a moment. "Yes, I do."

Norma huffed. "Well, I never said anything of the kind." She clasped his hands in supplication. "You must believe me! You're my protector. The court says so." As an afterthought, she added, "If I did, I must have been mad. They give you the most awful drugs here. They tear holes in your mind."

Harry had no reserve of pity. "Answer me! Did you poison Richard?"

"Please, Harry. Take me back in. I'm feeling ill in the sun."

"Not until you tell me."

With a faraway look in her eyes, she began to rock back and forth gently. "Richard was a foolish man. I think he was in love with me. He used to call me his *queen*."

Harry breathed deeply to calm himself. "You're very lucky. The police have lost interest in prosecution because you'd never stand trial, given your convenient mental state." He paused to scrutinize her face. He saw sweetness swiftly mask her fury. "Also, Dorothy sees no point in pursuing it."

"So, you're saying I'm safe?"

Such obvious and ugly shrewdness sickened him. He owed Richard. At last, he would set the wrong to right. He said, "The ownership of the money will be determined in court. If the judge rules in our favor, I'll ask for an order that it be paid to charity."

"What?" Norma face crinkled in horror. "After all I've been through?"

Infuriated, Harry rose and stood before her. "After all *you've* been through?" He nearly trembled with rage. "I was almost killed!"

Norma began to mutter. "Oh, I know, Harry. Those men are very cruel and dangerous … lurking by the road … at every turn. Pappas … Archie, and that despicable Robert Hawke. He was the very worst of them all!" As her eyes grew flat, she began to rock back and forth again.

He took her arm. "Don't start that Norma. I'm sick to death of your mad act! *You* are going to agree that the money goes to charity."

"Harry, please, don't make me."

"Yes. You must! You're *very* lucky. I'm giving you the chance to do *something* right in your life. Richard tried to persuade you and paid with his life. If you refuse to agree, I can and will donate it."

"I'll fire you. I can do that, can't I?"

"No. Not without an extremely good reason." Suddenly, he exploded. "You've manipulated everyone, and if you couldn't, you killed them or had someone else do your dirty work. Me? I was just lucky. Because I pitied you and tried to help, I was safe and *very* useful to you. Thank God I didn't oppose you. You would have me finished off too." Harry was almost gasping with fury. "How could you have poisoned Richard? He was a loyal and true adviser. And because he *cared* about you—but stood up to you—he got a slow and painful death."

Her features stiffened with rage. She clenched her fists.

"You are a truly *wicked* woman, Norma," he said quietly.

Her eyes hardened into tiny black beads. She bared her teeth. Swiftly, she raised her cane, ready to strike him.

"Stop, Norma!" He grasped her arm and the cane clattered to the cobblestones.

Harry held her hands tightly and looked deeply into her eyes. Locked in their struggle, he felt waves of true venom emanating from her. Suddenly, with shrieks and a cackle, she tried to break from him, but he held her fast.

"It's over, Norma!" he panted. He could not believe her strength.

With her eyes gleaming, she tried to bite his wrist, but he forced her jaw away from him. He did not want to hurt her in restraining her mad fury.

But, at last, she began to tremble and sank to the bench. Her eyes emptied of expression, and then finally she shrugged. "Very well then. What charity?"

He loosened his grip. Irony crept into his tone. "The Queen Mary Hospital, for their research into mental diseases of the elderly. It will be an appropriate use of that cursed fund."

She looked up at him keenly. "Can I keep a little bit, say ten percent—a sort of finder's fee? Then I could pay your bill."

Despite his anger, Harry laughed. "Yes. But only if the court approves it."

Norma bowed her head. Harry resumed his seat beside her, and they sat in silence for some moments. Suddenly, a rattling, chortling sound came from her breast and her breath came in short gasps. She slumped back against the wall and seemed not to be breathing.

Good God! Is she dead? Harry jumped up and took her wrist to find her pulse was strong. When he touched her shoulder, she screeched like a startled bird. Norma was only asleep, but undoubtedly, she was back in Venice with Arthur. Quickly, he found a nurse and put Norma in her charge. He could not get away from the Mercer fast enough.

Harry headed back downtown. Inching forward in traffic, he tried to order all the competing thoughts within. His mind spun from Dorothy to Norma to Natasha and back again. Angelo surfaced next. Thank God, he would be all right.

He saw the boy's face frozen with pride, and heard his words. In anger, he had said—*You think I'm sick and you're normal!* But his proudest statement was, *You don't understand. I like being me!*

Again, shame at his own arrogance flooded Harry. Angelo was exactly the way he should be. There was nothing to fix— nothing to change. Confronting his own fleeting moments of desire, he knew he needn't fear them. For just a moment, he *had* wished for some middle ground. But Angelo had pushed him away. Genuine love had teased him with fragments of desire. But Angelo, knowing him better than he knew himself, had refused.

Awareness of a new, yet vague understanding sobered him. An odd sense prevailed. He felt the slipping, sliding and shattering of the old ways of thought and feeling. Then, he glimpsed the shadows of something new and solid growing within him. With that came the sense of possibilities he was driven to explore.

His thoughts marched on. Dorothy had found her own middle ground of acceptance. Richard had betrayed her time and again over forty years of marriage. But despite her pain and fury, she had loved him, and she still *did* love him. Her passion drove her to find his killer. He smiled, picturing the tiny woman peering over the steering wheel of her immense Ford LTD.

At last, he entered Natasha's parking lot. He rushed to the concierge's desk and was let through with a wave. At her door, Natasha drew him in. He held her for long moments, feeling her breathing and her beating heart. He nearly lost his balance in the delight enveloping him.

"I love you," he said when he caught his breath.

They did not wait. In the bedroom, she pulled the curtains. He undressed her slowly, knowing he would always experience that strange mixture of passion and awe. She reveled in his touch and drew him onto the bed. Again, he felt the delicious sensation of the past falling away to be replaced with the new, strong and solid. Afterwards, they did not move or speak, but simply lay quietly.

"Harry?" she said propping herself up on a pillow. "What's all this about faxes?"

"You won't believe what I've been through finding this money!"

"But you did find it?"

"Oh, yes!" he laughed, "but only after a huge battle with the evil forces of the *dark* side!"

"What on earth do you mean?"

"I was followed every step of the way. The hotel manager, Fantino, was a spy for the dark side."

"Such drama, Harry!" Natasha laughed. "Now I *know* you're joking!

He sobered. "He gave me a fax, ostensibly from you, saying you couldn't come—very cold and brutal."

"But why would he do that?"

Harry shrugged. "Who knows? Just another trick to knock me off my stride." He took her in his arms and looked deeply into her eyes. "And then, guess what I did? I sent a fax asking you to marry me," he whispered close by her ear.

She cupped his face in her hands. "Oh, Harry! Do you really mean that?"

He drew apart from her and sat up. "Yes, I do. With all my heart."

When she rose from the bed and drew back the drapes, his heart sank.

"Harry, we have to talk. You must understand me—the person I really am. The problem is with Sheila."

In a flash, Harry saw Angelo's face, when he had smiled and said shyly—*Because I love you. Love does not need a reason, Harry.*

Next, he realized all at once that Natasha was *his* middle ground where his entire life came together with meaning. "I do understand," he said quietly. "Better than you think."

At the window, he held her close as they watched a small plane, its lights twinkling, land on the runway with a tiny bounce, and then race across the tarmac. Over the broad, darkening expanse of lake, heavy clouds had gathered, so that sky, water, and land seemed to blend and fuse together. Then they heard the deep roll of summer thunder in the distance. The last of the light faded and the wind picked up making stiff whitecaps along the shore.

"Have you made a decision about Sheila?" he asked.

Her eyes were deep and thoughtful. *He understands and accepts.* She said, "Yes, I already have. And it is a lifetime decision, Harry."

The telephone rang. Natasha did not answer. Suddenly a sobbing voice broke into the room on the answering machine. "Natasha, baby! Please don't do this. I love you so much. Please!"

Harry knew such pain intimately.

Natasha sank to the bed, remembering Sheila's cry—*Because it hurts!*

Harry sat down beside her. "You can't let her suffer like that," he said quietly.

Natasha gazed at him. She knew he *was* the right person—a man of compassion.

"I know. I will call her back soon. There has to be a way to make this better."

They crept back under the covers and held each other close. Suddenly, a huge crash of thunder and streaks of lightning filled the room.

At last, Harry understood Natasha's sense of intimacy and reserve, which had always teased, tantalized, and frustrated him. Of course, it was part of her allure. He knew shadow would always cover a part of her, but he hoped that he would be allowed within. He touched her breast and kissed her deeply. He desired her beyond his understanding.

"I want to tell you about a young man, whom I met in Venice—named Angelo. He taught me so much, and just in time."

Holding his face in her hands, she said, "I love you, Harry. What did you learn from him?"

His cell phone rang. He answered.

"Mr. Jenkins? It's the Mercer Hospital calling."

"Yes?" The tone of the voice alerted Harry. He sat up on the side of the bed and switched on the light.

"I'm terribly sorry to inform you, Mr. Jenkins, but...."

In an instant, a thousand images flew through his mind—Allegrini, the bank manager handing him the receipt—Paulo's face twisted in fear—the opera singer carried on the barge strung with twinkling lights. *And*, once again, the heartbreaking strains of the violins came to him.

"Mrs. Dinnick passed away this evening at ten-fifteen."

Harry checked his watch. *Not ten minutes ago*, he thought. Thunder crashed again, nearly shaking the windows. Sheet lightning flashed in the room and then sharp cracks of light split the sky. At last, torrents of rain began.

"How did it happen?" he asked.

"Very peacefully, sir. The nurse was with her. She sighed, turned her head on the pillow and said something that sounded like *the money*. Then she was gone."

Harry sighed deeply. Over his shoulder, he looked about the room as if he thought her spirit might be present. It probably was—soaring off somewhere unknown. *Right up to the end!* That money had governed her every thought and deed since the early 1960s.

He spoke quietly into the phone. "All right, and thank you for calling. Have the doctor sign the death certificate, and I'll make the arrangements with the funeral home."

After he hung up, he sat very still, as if a vacuum had filled the room. Then suddenly, he smiled at Natasha. "Shall we make something to eat? I'm starving."

Pulling on her robe, she nodded. "Who was that, Harry?"

"The hospital. My client, Norma Dinnick, just passed away. She's the one who sent me to Venice."

From the kitchen window, they could see the rain was abating. Natasha made an omelet, and he got out lettuce, tomato, and cucumber for the salad. As he began setting the table, he thought that it could not have turned out better. That enormous sum of fifty million dollars was under his control. He would apply to the court for directions. If no other claimant came forward, so much the better! Norma had no living relatives. The judges, most of them in their seventies, would no doubt approve his proposal to bequeath the money to the

Queen Mary Hospital for geriatric research. His bill would be *substantial.* After all, ten-percent was five million dollars! The money had caused so much havoc and death, it was time to set matters right.

When they sat down to eat, Harry said, "Angelo, the boy in Venice, was a desk clerk at the Hotel Grand." Smiling thoughtfully, he continued. "I can see now that it was almost like destiny. He saved my life in more ways than one."

Natasha's eyebrows curved upward in amusement. "You're so mysterious, Harry. Tell me about him."

"Not until you answer *my* question. Will you marry me?"

Natasha looked at him thoughtfully for a long moment. Then she smiled brilliantly. "Yes, my darling, I will."

Harry glanced about her apartment. At last, the journey was over, he thought. "Angelo is only twenty," he said. "But he taught me so much."

As they lingered over wine, Harry began his story.

When he had finished, Natasha's mood was reflective. She knew she could trust Harry forever. "Angelo reminds me of Josef," she began quietly. "Such people come into our lives for a special purpose."

Harry nodded. At last, they understood each other. She *was* his middle ground and he was hers.

978-0-595-44571-4
0-595-44571-3

Printed in the United States
110039LV00004B/1-72/A